PROJECTIONS

MONKEYBRAIN BOOKS

PROJECTIONS
SCIENCE FICTION IN LITERATURE & FILM

Edited by Lou Anders

Projections: Science Fiction in Literature and Film
Copyright © 2004 Lou Anders

Cover illustration and design © 2004 John Picacio

Copy Edits by Debra Rodia

Editor Cover Photo by Tony Breckner

A MonkeyBrain Books Publication
www.monkeybrainbooks.com

MonkeyBrain Books
11204 Crossland Drive
Austin, TX 78726
info@monkeybrainbooks.com

ISBN: 1-932265-12-0

Printed in the United States of America

For My Wonderful Wife, Xin
Who Makes All Things Possible

Table of Contents

FOREWORD:
Spectacles & Speculations

From *The Lord of the Rings*—called by some the greatest novel of the twentieth century—to *The Matrix*—one of the biggest cinematic phenomenon of all time, from the craze of *Star Wars* to the cult of *Star Trek*, from the writings of Robert A. Heinlein and Philip K. Dick to the cinema of Steven Spielberg and James Cameron, science fiction and fantasy have produced some of western culture's most enduring stories. Yet a book is not a film, and a film is not a book. One is a literary medium; the other a visual one. They require different approaches on the part of their respective audiences. They deliver different rewards.

In his introduction to the *Best Military Science Fiction of the 20th Century* (Del Rey, May 2001), author and editor Harry Turtledove writes that "written science fiction is often thought-provoking; filmed sci-fi is more often jaw-dropping. The two usually appeal to different audiences, which aficionados of the written variety sometimes forget to their peril—and frustration." In other words, in science fiction literature (also referred to as "speculative fiction"), the reward is often the thrill of intellectual stimulation. In "sci-fi" cinema, the thrill is a visceral one, delivered via "special effects."

Since its inception in the days of H. G. Wells and Jules Verne, speculative fiction has been a platform for social critique, satire, and scientific exploration and extrapolation. In the 1920s and 1930s, *Amazing Stories* founder Hugo Gernsback wrote of it as "scientifiction" and proclaimed that its importance and distinction lay in the potential scientific edification at the core of its story. This was refined in the "Golden Age" of science fiction as typified by Arthur C. Clarke and Isaac Asimov, and evolved and mutated still further with the New Wave movement of the 1960s, wherein it branched and grew to include literary experiment among its repertoire. Now, in the initial days of the new millennium, speculative fiction casts a wide enough net to include inspirational works of rigorous scientific accuracy—oft written by individuals vitally active in the hard sciences themselves—and stylistic works of polished prose capable of standing alongside the best of modern literature. And yes, speculative fiction also contains its fair share of pure childhood escapism.

But for its cinematic counterpart, that escapism may be paramount. In large part, sci-fi and fantasy cinema has long been defined by the Buck Rogers serials and B-movie alien monster flicks of its infancy. Operating as it does in a genre fueled by spectacle rather than speculation, more often than not its most recognized works are those singled out for their visual and emotional rather than intellectual impact. Surely, the last few decades belonged more to the heirs of *Star Wars* than those of *2001: A Space Odyssey*. The former reached back a corrupting finger to choke the shelves of its literary kin with hundreds of TV tie-in novels while the latter remains a benchmark yet to be surpassed even after thirty-six years of movie making. Nonetheless, sci-fi cinema has produced a handful of works that strive for the intellectual weight of its literary counterpart—films like *The Day the Earth Stood Still*, *Blade Runner*, *2010: The Year We Make Contact*, and *The Matrix*—this last one remarkable in the way it marries the strengths of both literature and film into one coherent narrative.

Recently, there is cause to hope that we may stand on the threshold of a new Golden Age of speculative cinema. Today, when it is possible to render any world or character or stunt imaginable, special effects may cease to wow when left alone to carry an inferior narrative. It is perhaps an encouraging sign that the subsequent *Matrix* films— magnificent though they were on the level of spectacle—failed to charm the larger audience of critics and viewers because of their deficiencies on the level of story. In other words, two films of monumental, hitherto unseen special effects extravaganzas failed to achieve the critical recognition, wider audience acceptance, and box office of their predecessor precisely because they botched it on the strength of their philosophy! It is worth noting that, at roughly the same time, Peter Jackson's *The Lord of the Rings* trilogy—currently one of only two films in history to ever reach the one billion dollar worldwide box office mark and the fastest film ever to reach it—is laudable for its adherence to its source text and for its use of visual effects in the service of its larger story (rather than the reverse). If this trend continues, the real age of speculative cinema may only just be beginning.

Meanwhile, we have a rich century of speculative fiction and cinema just behind us. Here, then, is a selection of those gifted mythmakers who helped to bring it about and who now carry its torch, sharing their thoughts on their own field—on the literature of science fiction and on how their genre fairs at the hands of Hollywood studios. What follows is a collection of essays by the writers themselves, penned by some of the biggest names in the genre. Included are remembrances of founders like H G Wells, Leigh Brackett, and Poul Anderson, essays on the fascist underpinnings of *Lord of the Rings* and *Star Wars*, detailed discussions of the nineties boom in Australian SF, a look at the history of the genre in cinema, and controversial opinions about its past, its present, and its future. *Projections* is the book about science fiction by science fiction, the genre turned inward on itself. It is a testament to science fiction's rich history. It is an indication of the promise of its future.

Lou Anders
Birmingham, Alabama, 2004

GROWING UP IN THE FUTURE
Michael Swanwick

I have been to Chicago only twice, both times to attend the Worldcon. Once was in the early eighties, the other late in the decade. Something had changed between visits. The first time I went, it was still the present; but by the second time, it had become the future.

I first noticed this on the plane. On the back of the seat before me was a cordless phone which could be released with a swipe of my credit card. In O'Hare Airport I took the slidewalk into the terminal and ducked into the men's room, where I found that the sinks and toilets and urinals no longer had mechanical levers. They were operated by infrared sensors. A friend of mine, who was wearing black, had to hold his handkerchief up to the sink in order to wash his hands. At the hotel a clerk placed a cardboard chit into a machine which imprinted a small magnetic strip with a random code and then directed the door of my room to recognize it. Then she told me I could pay my bill on my television set on channel 11 and also check there to see if I had any voicemail. And she didn't even bother to explain to me what she was talking about!

She knew she didn't have to. Because we were all citizens of the future now.

I don't find myself a particularly interesting subject. But I have lived through some extremely interesting times. Specifically, I grew up at a time unique in history, when "the future" was a living force, something imminent and powerful, and have lived long enough to see it arrive, be swallowed up by the culture, and disappear.

I'm going to give a quick sketch of the future. Where it came from, what it was, and what became of it. It is my thesis that "the future" is a post-World War II phenomenon. Immediately I can hear you object— what about Isaac Asimov, Robert A. Heinlein, Arthur C. Clarke, and any number of others in our field who were writing before the war? But these were not ordinary men. They were visionaries. And I use that word neither rhetorically nor in a mystical sense. By visionary, I mean simply that they saw something that most people could not. When Asimov, Heinlein and Clarke were young, science fiction was a thoroughly despised genre. The claim that a rocket would someday be put into orbit or travel to the Moon, much less take human beings along with it, was to most people patently untrue. Science fiction writers faced not just skepticism but open scorn. It took a lot more strength of character and independence of thought for them to write about a future that was more than just a degraded form of the present—a little thicker about the waist, a bit grayer around the muzzle—than it later would for, let's say, me.

World War II changed everything. It was a time of greatly accelerated technological research and development. A lot of amateurs and theoreticians were moved from the fringes of society, from the *Verein fur Raumschiffahrt*, for example, to the very center of the war effort—to Peenemunde. And when it was over, the surge in research did not end. When Werner von Braun—of whom it has been written, "He aimed for the stars and hit London"—came to the United States, he brought with him the entire space program in a stack of notebooks with tables of exhaust velocities and colored diagrams of every space vehicle it would take to proceed step by step to the moon, Mars, and beyond. (I first heard of these fabled notebooks from an engineer who had worked at the White Sands proving grounds at the same time as von Braun; he particularly admired how von Braun marched his engineers out onto the field every morning for military inspection before they were put to work.)

Because of the cold war, and because of the decisive role new technology had played in the Battle of Britain and places like Hiroshima and Nagasaki, the Federal government continued to invest heavily in research. The corporations benefitting from this largesse as a matter of course put out their own benign propaganda on what they were up to, and how we could all expect to benefit from it. The future for the first time found committed corporate sponsorship.

I was born in 1950, and my father was an engineer. He worked for General Electric, and I very much regret that I can't tell you exactly what he did. I can't tell you because I don't know. His work required security clearance from the FBI and under the terms of that clearance he was not allowed to say. But by testimony of the unclassified handouts and promotional materials he brought home, he was involved in the space program; and by testimony of things said at company picnics by less scrupulously silent employees, he was probably also involved in nuclear weapon delivery systems—intercontinental ballistic missiles. So that for good and ill he was right at the heart of the two central enterprises of our civilization at mid-century.

As a result, I grew up with the future. At age six I used to go through my father's stacks of *Popular Science* and *Mechanix Illustrated*, which along with articles about car repair and hi-fi kits you could build yourself, contained articles by Willey Ley, G. Harry Stein, Eando Binder, and even von Braun himself, all about the wonders I could expect to see in my lifetime: a moon landing in 1975, expeditions to Mars and Venus by 1985. My father and I used to rebuild old radios on Sunday afternoons, and I saved the surplus vacuum tubes for inventions I was going to astound the world with, just as soon as I was old enough to use a soldering iron.

Oh, the future was everywhere in those days! The New York World's Fair had mechanized dioramas by all the major corporations showing what it would be like: microwave ovens and undersea cities, giant road-building machines slicing through thousand-year-old trees to bring civilization to the jungle, real working videophones, vacation pleasure-domes dug out of the Antarctic ice.

These promises were all most specific. They were on the drawing boards. General Electric's Schenectady plant pumped out inventions at a fabulous rate. One of our neighbors was the co-inventor of the artificial diamond. Artificial diamonds! Could there be a better symbol of the wealth and technologically-based glamor that was headed straight our way? Atomic power plants were going to generate limitless power at a rate too cheap to bother metering. "Clean" nuclear bombs would dig transcontinental canals and enormous new harbors, fusing useless wetlands into neovolcanic bedrock upon which we could build skyscrapers a mile high! Icebergs with robotic rigging would be sailed into these harbors to provide fresh water and cooling breezes in the summer.

All of which, among other things, made it very easy to grow up into a science fiction writer. I remember a picture my father brought home from work, an artist's rendering of a lunar colony based on General Electric technology. It showed stiff, fifties-type people strolling within a domed crater, the sides of which had been contoured in a series of gardened terraces. A quarter century later, I used that image as a starting point for my own lunar colony in a novella called *Griffin's Egg*. And though I worked some radical changes on that vision, it still had the core power of being a real place that I could believe in existing. It was something I had been promised as a child.

There were dark aspects to the future back then. World War Three *was* expected, and soon. And I will never forget how I felt in 1957, crouching in the dark of my attic bedroom with my ear against the console radio that my father and I had salvaged and repaired—I had the sound as low as it would go because I was supposed to be asleep—listening to the news that the Russians had put an artificial satellite into orbit ahead of us. That it was up there now. That they could now put bombs into orbit and there was nothing we could do to defend ourselves against them.

But those were aberrations. They weren't what the future was really about. The future was more like an incident that happened the very next summer.

I was reading a book in my room when I heard a world-shaking throb of motors from outside. I ran out and looked up and there above me, flying low over the neighborhood, was a dirigible. It was enormous! It filled the sky—huge, detailed and shadowless, incredible, looking like the inside of Hugo Gernsback's head. It slid overhead so slowly it seemed you could almost keep up with it just by walking.

I ran down the street after it.

And as I ran, all over the neighborhood, doors slammed open and people came out into their yards to gawk. The adults stood there, staring up. But the children—all of them—ran out into the street and after it. Waves of children all running as hard and fast as we could, trying desperately to catch up with it. Slowly the dirigible pulled away, growing smaller, dwindling in the sky. While down below in its shadow, wave after wave of children poured out of their houses and ran until they could run no more, and staggered to a stop, and stood staring up while new children ran out after it.

Nobody ran harder than me. Nobody ran faster. When the others fell behind, I kept on running.

In a sense, I am still chasing after that dirigible.

That future is gone now. It disappeared at about the same time as the collapse of the Soviet Union. It was seen as being, like the space program that was so much a part of it, a tool of the cold war. Which it was. It was a Consumer Utopia that could be pitted against the Communist future of a Worker's Paradise. Disposable paper clothing! Rocket packs! Robots that would clear the table and wash the dishes for you! A lot of explicit promises—I'm thinking specifically of the twenty-hour work week which (you could look it up) we were expected to achieve by the year 2000—were broken. The enemy was defeated and the future was swept back into the box.

Why did we give up on it so easily? Two reasons, I think, both the result of the future being too successfully absorbed by the culture.

For a time in the seventies, I held a number of low-paying jobs as information analyst for the Franklin Institute in Philadelphia. In one of these I shared an office with Sandy Meschkow, who had possession of America's Energy Future and occasionally let me play with it.

America's Energy Future was a teaching device which the Department of Energy had devised. It was a box containing a handful of transistors (this was before personal computers), a few potentiometers, and several simple readouts, and it represented civilization. With one set of dials you could set the society's energy demands—so much for transportation, so much for heating, for research, and so on. With another, you set the mix of energy resources—hydroelectric, oil, coal, nuclear, solar. Each had advantages and disadvantages. Oil, coal, nuclear were all convenient but they polluted. Hydroelectric was clean, but could only grow until all the major rivers had been dammed. Solar was clean but it came on line slowly. You set your mix of uses and sources and flipped a switch. Readouts showed demand compared to supply and consequences. A big flickering readout gave the year. The game was to see how long you could keep society going in the face of an energy demand that grew asymptotically.

A really good player—which is to say one with a total disregard for the civil liberties of his subject population—could get the numbers up a hundred years into the future before civilization seized up and collapsed into a state of depleted and thoroughly polluted barbarism. Liberal democracies fared less well.

After a while it became obvious to me that not only was there no way to win this depressing game but that it was an accurate model for DOE's energy policies. They were all based on an irreversible demand for energy that would grow at a steadily increasing rate until everything collapsed and everyone died. You couldn't win. But if you used up all your resources without a thought for tomorrow, they wouldn't run out until just shortly after the last middle-aged decision maker died.

What had begun as a tool was now calling the shots. The future with its limitless vistas of technological freedoms had become an oppressive argument of futility and despair.

That's one reason.

The second reason we gave up on the future was far stranger:

Sometime during the eighties, about the time of my second visit to Chicago, the future became a colonized precinct of the present. People came to believe in the predictions and technologies of the future in a way that previously not even science fiction had. They accepted them as having a literal rather than provisional existence.

Virtual reality is a particularly good example of this process. You can go into any schoolyard in the world and ask the fourth-graders there to explain how it works and what it does, and they'll do it! In numbing detail. This in spite of the fact that nothing currently available to them comes anywhere close to living up to the sort of thing they describe.

Virtual is an anticipatory technology. It doesn't exist yet. But so pervasive a part of the culture has it become that we're all secretly convinced that somewhere, somehow, it must. That down some sleazy back alley in Hong Kong, if you knock on the right door and offer enough money, you can get the real thing.

The same process applies to nanotechnology, genetic engineering, any number of technologies that are living on accomplishments borrowed from future research. How many people have bought into the Web in order to obtain services and benefits that are *surely* out there somewhere, if you could only get the address for them? All these things have become the stuff not of science fiction but of the speculative present.

At the same time, inevitably much of what was predicted forty years ago, for good and ill, has come true, and inevitably it isn't quite as entertaining as it was supposed to be. We still suffer heartache and disappointment. We're still human.

The future is easy to see when it's large and off in the distance, like a dirigible filling the sky. Not so easy when it's upon you. You stop paying attention, and it disappears.

There's a trick I like to pull on my friends. Standing in a large city on an overcast night, I'll ask them to look down at the sidewalk and tell me what color the sky is. They invariably will say black or, sometimes, dark blue. Look up, I'll say. And to their astonishment the sky is neither black nor blue, but a dull, smoky red—reflecting the orange glow of all those sodium and mercury vapor streetlights.

I've never seen this fact mentioned in present-fiction, despite its being fiction's job to bring us news of the world as it is.

Alas, most science fiction does not fare much better.

We've overrun the future, and yet many of us don't seem to have noticed this fact. You'll see stories containing astronauts and laser guns, pocket satellite uplinks, and casual genetic engineering which present themselves as being science fiction when really all they are is inaccurate present-fiction.

Simultaneous with our overtaking the future, we as a society have lost all belief in it. All the bright and clever toys the future was going to bring—we're too smart for that now. The space program is a perfect example of this. A quarter-century ago men walked on the moon. Now the closest thing to a space program we have is a Tom Hanks movie.

Or rather, that's what we like to tell each other. My wife has an office job and she reports that time and time again the dead white males get together to grouse about how the space program was a failure. Which is when Marianne will point out that there are astronauts—or, more often, cosmonauts—in orbit *right now*.

They simply look at her. They don't understand what she's getting at.

But her point—and this is my point as well—is that just because we're done with *it*, doesn't mean the future is done with *us*. Because what we call the future is not a place or a thing. Rather, it is a visionary take on the present. It is a projection of what we are currently working to make happen.

So when people stop believing in the future, we are not merely losing a set of brightly colored conceptual toys. We are refusing to look at the consequences of our present. And when we cease to look and plan, we fall back on the default settings, on our unspoken and largely unconscious expectations of what the future will be.

If you look at what we collectively expect nowadays, it's all ecological collapse, the inevitable extinction of species, and the slow degradation of the environment leading inexorably to the painful death of the human race. That's the message I see playing over and over again on television, and hear being taught in the schools. The current implicit future is a tedious thing indeed. The only bright spot in which appears to be that with teledildonics we'll be able to access virtual prostitution without fear of disease or human contact. But mostly it's going to be just a degraded version of the present—a little grayer around the muzzle, a few more pounds around the waist.

Almost nobody believes in the future today, any more than they believe in the space program. It's not the sixties anymore, they say, we're broke, and it's been decades since anyone was in orbit. But meanwhile the human race has more real wealth than ever before. Epidemics are so rare in this country that when a relatively minor one comes along and kills a few tens of thousands of people, we think something's wrong. India, which was once synonymous with famine, is now a food-exporting nation. Our space probes are smaller and smarter than ever before. There are men *and women* in orbit at this very moment.

So where does that leave us?

Oddly enough, it leaves us in pretty much the same situation that Isaac Asimov and Robert Heinlein and Arthur C. Clarke found themselves in fifty-some years ago. Privy to a secret that most people don't want to hear: That there is a future. It's coming and it's not going to be at all like today. It's going to be better than you can imagine. It's going to be unspeakably worse.

Over the years I've sold a number of stories to *Omni*, both in its print and electronic incarnations. As a result, people working on non-fiction articles about the future of shoes, offices, pets, whatever, will occasionally call up looking for a few free predictions. I try to accommodate them. I tell them that in the future everybody will go barefoot, that our offices will be a set of interactive sunglasses which we'll be more likely to misplace on Mondays than any other day, and that internal microscopic interfaces will allow us to maintain colonies of harmless and colorful bacteria and even viruses as pets within our bloodstreams. Whatever I happen to have been thinking about lately. But it usually turns out that what they're *really* looking for is new money-making ideas: wine spritzers and Post-It notes are the most common examples they give me. And here I can't help them. Because the only money-making ideas I'm interested in are ideas for new stories.

But in that one limited sense I can tell you exactly where the money is. And that is, in new futures. Futures that are not derived from earlier science fiction. That are not disguised versions of the present. That are not literary metaphors for anything, but real and honest projections.

This is not all that science fiction does, or ought to do—far from it. Indeed, I could argue that accurate predictions are the least interesting product we put out. The late Will Jenkins, who wrote under the name of Murray Leinster, was also an inventor. He told me once that he'd get an idea for something new and then think about it for a long time, puzzling it over, until either he could make it work or he understood why it never would. If it worked, he'd patent it. If it didn't, he'd write a science fiction story in which it did.

Murray Leinster once wrote a story about a device that puts matter out of phase with the surrounding world, so that it can slip through the spaces between atoms undisturbed. Criminals steal the device and rig it into a submarine. The matter-phaser is tunable, so that the submarine's propellers can push against bedrock with the same force as they would water. They then proceed to travel undetectably under the ground, emerging inside bank vaults to plunder and loot. This was a clear example of an unpatentable idea.

Robert Heinlein, in contrast, made any number of predictions that were spot-on. In *The Door into Summer* he predicted computer banking, Ticketron, and computer-assisted design, among other things. But ironically enough his descriptions of these are tedious to read now that they've come true—I know how Ticketron works, thank you—where Leinster's description of the criminals in their submarine, its matter-phaser sabotaged, falling helplessly through the Earth, down, down, down toward the molten core as the air runs out and the heat inexorably builds is still riveting.

Nonsense, but riveting.

I think that science fiction is like that submarine: just a little out of phase with reality, but enough in touch with it to have something to push against. And that which we push against, react to and oppose, journey away from and return home to, is the future. It's our bedrock. It's our home port. Sometimes in our imaginations we travel far, far afield. But it's always there, waiting for us.

So long as we keep our faith in it, we'll do just fine.

IN DEFENSE OF SCIENCE FICTION
John Clute

To understand the scandal of genre in 1999 we need to get a running jump.

Once upon a time—about a century ago—something happened in the world of books that, for a while, did not seem to bode ill. H. G. Wells and Arthur Conan Doyle and P. G. Wodehouse and Edgar Rice Burroughs consciously—and a lot of other writers like Robert Louis Stevenson, who knew more than he would admit; or Bram Stoker, who didn't have a clue—invented the kind of story we now think of when we think of popular genres. These writers, responding to insatiable demands for copy from the sharp editors who ran the up-and-coming new magazines, created stories that could be repeated: Sherlock Holmes and Tarzan are nothing if they don't happen again and again. In creating markets for detective stories, science fiction, horror, superman adventures, etc., these writers created, only half unwittingly, the Monster of the Demand for the Same.

It was the beginning of a sea-change; Wells and Doyle and their colleagues laid the foundations for the world of literature we live in now. In 1999, most of what most of us read is genre. Sometimes this is obvious—science fiction, which is what I'm most concerned about, has for many decades now been stigmatized as a genre literature that adults needn't bother with. Sometimes it is not—novels written by university professors and set in the groves of academe are far more rigidly predictable than anything but the most routine sf novel, but they have escaped the stigma of being labelled as genre. They can be read in public by adults, not because they are particularly *worth* being read in public by adults, but because they carry no mark of Cain.

Other genres include the bestseller genre, the disaster genre, the roman a clef that fails to conceal the identity of a very recent American president genre, the shopping and fucking genre, the sexually obsessed Christian male in New England midlife crisis genre, the Hollywood satire genre, the European experimental novel with unusual sex on page 74 genre, and so on.

What these genres all share in common is that they exist and that they do not. The reason for this ontological ambivalence is pretty simple:

the main beneficiaries of generification in 1999 are not the writers who are forced to pretend to write within some cookiecutter restraint or other, nor the readers who devour the stale because they do not know how to identify the new. Who benefits are publishers and retailers. Both these categories of the great-minded professional class find it *easier* to market for strict continuity than to play the heartrendingly difficult game of coping with something that has not been done before. Their compunction for the new is therefore limited.

So genres exist—because any constant users of any large bookstore can instantly tell what any piece of fiction is *supposed* to be about, by its title, by its cover, by its location in the shop—and they do not exist. Those same constant users, if they are wise, know that miracles lurk beneath the contemptible covers retailers demand. They *sneak peaks* inside. They even, occasionally, buy a book against the grain of their generic predilection (as determined by survey) simply because the book looked interesting.

But why (and here I come to my own main concern) is this sly salutary worldly knowledge about the difference between a book and its cover so rarely applied to science fiction? It's certainly not the case with some other genres. A detective writer like P. D. James or Patricia Cornwell, a writer of thrillers like Carl Hiaasen, a Cold War novelist like John Le Carré, can slide "upmarket" with some ease; and, without losing the allure of their genre underpinning, appeal to an audience that does not believe it dabbles in kid's stuff. The reasons for this have, it is almost certainly the case, very much less to do with content than with context.

A writer like P. D. James may even stumble into the composition of an SF novel. But when James did publish hers—it is called *The Children of Men* (1992)—she made very clear in public statements that she had *not* written a science fiction novel at all. No, her tale was not full of futuristic gadgets; her tale was about real men and women in the real world. That her setting is thirty years hence, and that her story involves the highly sciencefictional discovery that the human race has become sterile, count for nothing against her (and presumably her publisher's) horror at the thought that her work might be crippled by identification with a genre that cannot be worth writing in.

Any reader of SF knows that this horror is based on a nonsense, that SF, as a mode of exploratory writing, has provided a broad platform and a rich vocabulary and a network of thoroughly tested icons for hundreds of innovative writers for many decades now. (And any SF reader who looks at *The Children of Men* recognizes not only that the book is SF, but that it is very *bad* SF; astonishingly less good and less "literary" than the avowedly SF novel with which it shares a publisher, an editor, a plot, a venue, and some characters: Brian W. Aldiss's *Greybeard* [1964].)

But that's by no means the whole story. Some genres are moderately loose in how they are marketed; SF novels come into the world positively carapaced in marketing signals. Only a brave advertising executive who would recommend to the likes of P. D. James that her dim but sincere little book should be marketed in such a fashion. Brave because he'd be shot down; foolish because Dame James would be right if she told him that she did not wish to destroy her book's chance of reaching a wide audience by labelling it as "trash."

There are at least two reasons for dismissing science fiction as trash. The obvious reason is that most of it *is* trash—but that, because all sf, good or bad, is marketed in the same way, the trash is just as visible as the good stuff. *Star Trek* novelizations, than which there is very little lower in the literary world, march side by side with major works by novelists who, if they didn't have the SF label gummed to their foreheads, would rightly be understood as central creative figures of the last half century. I mean writers like Philip K. Dick, Avram Davidson, Samuel R. Delany, Ursula K. Le Guin, Thomas M. Disch, Octavia Butler, Lucius Shepard, James Tiptree Jr., Gene Wolfe, Michael Swanwick, Kim Stanley Robinson, William Gibson, Bruce Sterling, Brian Aldiss (again), a dozen more.

A second reason is that from Hugo Gernsback in 1926 to the present day, the most significant writers of American science fiction—which is the main artery of the twentieth-century genre—have tended to think of themselves as creators of "thought experiments," stories whose primary purpose is to dramatize ideas about the world and the tools we may be able to invent in order to transform it, and to speculate about the implications of those ideas and tools. These ideas have traditionally come from the hard sciences rather than the soft, one consequence of which is that science fiction can suffer from a terrible simplemindedness about genuinely complex issues (like human nature). Another consequence is that science fiction is subject to the fearful, self-defensive disparagement that "humanists" heap on those who do science.

The third reason for writing off science fiction is essentially self-protective. From the early 1920s till about 1975, American science fiction told a primal story that has now become embarrassing to many of us. It was the story of the technics-led triumph of the American Way in the star-lanes of the big tomorrow. It is embarrassing nowadays because it is racist, technophilic, provincial, arrogant; and because it is *wrong*. The SF story was to be the story of how America made it all work; and the world hasn't exactly turned out that way.

But so what? Just because the instrumentalities of science fiction were hijacked by hick triumphalists for a few decades does not mean that those instrumentalities are inherently bogus. Throughout the twentieth century the best of the kind of writing that Americans ghettoize as science fiction has, in other countries, hardly been treated as a genre at all. The miracle of science fiction as a mode of seeing is that, unlike any non-fantastic category of contemporary literature, it is a mode of looking at the world whole. Science fiction is therefore an intensely bracing angle of view for writers to take on, especially in a time of constant innovation and crisis, and it is the scandal of genre in 1999 that so many writers have done so and continue to do so in obscurity.

If there were no book covers to scare off the credulous, it would be easier for adventurous readers to discover the spectrum of writers who operate the gears of science fiction with ease, and who write with an intense and literate understanding that the only way to understand 1999 is by treating the thousand futures that interpenetrate us all as material for the forge of art.

But this is a world of book covers, and retailers; all of whom seem to operate in a state of perpetual panic about *labels*. When Karen Joy Fowler releases a very great SF novel called *Sarah Canary* (1991)— in which the males who run the nineteenth century fail to identify an alien trapped on Earth because she resembles a human female and is therefore invisible to them—her publishers (Henry Holt) have conniptions at the thought that somebody might call it by its honorable and proper name. When a revered non-SF writer Doris Lessing publishes a series of books—the Canopus in Argos sequence—which she is perfectly happy to call SF, reviewers on both sides of the Atlantic rush to her "defense" insisting that it's anything but.

Gene Wolfe, in the sequence of novels known as the Book of the New Sun, publishes a profound meditation on history, God, time and power; and his SF publisher gives it dust jackets that evoke Brak the Barbarian. Gore Vidal, in *The Smithsonian Institution* (1998), publishes an hilarious (and intermittently profound) SF satire on American governance and mores; but SF readers would never know what they were missing because of the queasy "dignity" of Random House's marketing.

The losers are us.

We are the ones who live here, in this world, at the verge of the turn into the next century. As the thousand futures we are heir to fall like rain upon our heads, begging for attention, we're going to need all the help we can get to see our way through. We cannot exclude any vision—any way to look at the world—that we humans have invented for ourselves. We are going to need all the ways to look.

ACHILLES, SUPERMAN, AND DARTH VADER...
Or Why *Star Wars* Has It In
For Our Rebel Civilization
David Brin, Ph.D.

"But there's probably no better form of government than a good despot."
—George Lucas (*NY Times* interview, March 1999)

Well, I boycotted *Episode I: The Phantom Menace*...for an entire week.

Why? What's to boycott? Isn't *Star Wars* good old fashioned sci-fi? Harmless fun? Some people call it "eye candy"... a chance to drop back into childhood and punt your adult cares away for two hours, dwelling in a lavish universe where good and evil are vividly drawn, without all the inconvenient counterpoint distinctions that clutter daily life. Got a problem? Cleave it with a light saber! Wouldn't you love—just once in your life—to dive a fast ship into your worst enemy's stronghold and set off a chain reaction, blowing up the whole megillah from within its rotten core while you streak away to safety at the speed of light? (It's such a nifty notion that it happens in three out of four *Star Wars* flicks.)

Anyway, I make a good living writing science fiction novels and movies. So *Star Wars* ought to be a great busman's holiday, right?

This is one of the problems with so-called "light entertainment" today. Somehow, amid all the gaudy special effects, people tend to lose track of simple things, like story and meaning, or noticing the moral lessons the director is trying to push. Yet, these things matter.

By now it's grown clear that George Lucas has an agenda, that he takes very seriously. After four *Star Wars* films, alarm bells should have gone off, even among those who don't look for morals in movies. When the chief feature distinguishing "good" from "evil" is how pretty the characters are, it's a clue that maybe the whole saga deserves a second look.

Just what bill of goods are we being sold, between the frames?

- Elites have an inherent right to arbitrary rule; common citizens needn't be consulted. They may only choose *which* elite to follow.
- "Good" elites should act on their subjective whims, without evidence, argument or accountability.
- Any amount of sin can be forgiven if you are important enough, then make a small act of contrition.
- True leaders are born. It's genetic. The right to rule is inherited.
- Justifiable human emotions can turn a good person permanently evil.

That is just the beginning of a long list of "moral" lessons relentlessly pushed by *Star Wars*. Lessons that starkly differentiate this saga from others that seem superficially similar, like *Star Trek*.

Above all, I never cared for the whole Nietzchian *ubermensch* thing... the notion—pervading a great many myths and legends—that a good yarn has to be about demigods who are bigger, badder, and better than normal folk by several orders of magnitude. It's an ancient storytelling tradition based on abiding contempt for the masses, that I find odious in the works of A. E. van Vogt, L. Ron Hubbard, and wherever you witness slanlike super-beings deciding the fate of billions without ever pausing to consider their wishes.

Wow, you say. *If I feel that strongly about this, why just a week-long boycott? Why see the latest "Star Wars" film at all?*

Because I am forced to admit that demigod tales resonate deeply in the human heart.

THE LEGACY OF HOMER, CAMPBELL AND SUPERMAN

In *The Hero With A Thousand Faces,* Joseph Campbell showed how a particular, rhythmic storytelling technique was used in almost every ancient and pre-modern culture, depicting protagonists and antagonists with certain consistent motives and character traits, transcending boundaries of language and culture. In these classic tales, the hero begins reluctant, yet signs and portents foretell his pre-ordained greatness. He receives dire warnings and sage wisdom from a mentor, acquires quirky-but-faithful companions, faces a series of steepening crises, explores the pit of his own fears, and emerges triumphant to bring some boon/talisman/victory home to his admiring tribe/people/nation. By offering superb insights into this revered storytelling tradition, Joseph Campbell did indeed shed light on common spiritual traits that seem shared by all human beings. And I'll be the first to admit it's a superb formula—one that I've used at times in my own stories and novels.

Alas, Campbell only highlighted positive traits, completely ignoring a much darker side—such as how easily this standard fable-template was co-opted by kings, priests and tyrants, extolling the all-importance of elites who tower over common women and men. Or the implication that we must always adhere to variations on a single story, a single theme, repeating the prescribed plot outline over and over again. Those who praise Campbell seem to perceive this uniformity as cause for rejoicing—but it isn't. Playing a large part in the tragic miring of our spirit, demigod myths helped reinforce sameness and changelessness for millennia, transfixing people in nearly every culture, from Gilgamesh all the way to comic book superheroes.

It is essential to understand the radical departure taken by genuine science fiction, which comes from a diametrically *opposite* literary tradition—a new kind of storytelling that often rebels against those very same archetypes Campbell venerated. An upstart belief in progress, science, egalitarianism, positive-sum games... and the possibility of decent human institutions. Authors like Greg Bear, John Brunner, Alice Sheldon, Frederik Pohl and Philip K. Dick always looked on any prescriptive storytelling formula as a direct challenge—a dare. This explains why science fiction has never been much welcomed at both extremes of the literary spectrum—comic books and "high literature."

Countless editors have gambled and lost, trying to wed some of the best science fiction tales with the illustrated popular medium of comix. This marriage *seems* a natural, because SF can be lavish with colorful plots, extravagant characters and alien locales. But the union nearly always fails, because comic books treat their superheroes with reverent awe, exactly the same way demigods were depicted in the *Iliad* (and the way George Lucas treats them in *Star Wars*). But a true science fiction author who wrote about Superman would start by asking the Man of Steel uncomfortable questions, such as why super-villains only appeared after *he* showed up! Then Earthling scientists would insist that the handsome alien provide a blood sample (even if it requires scraping away with a super fingernail) in order to study his puissant powers... and maybe bottle them for everyone.

Likewise, from the point of view of an academic literary elite—steeped in Aristotle's *Poetics*—nothing could be more anathema than the philosophical basis underlying most high-quality science fiction—a bold assertion that there are no "eternal human verities." Things change, and change can be fascinating. Moreover, our children might outgrow us. They may become better, or learn from our mistakes and not repeat them. And if they don't learn, *that* could be a rivetting tragedy far exceeding Aristotle's cramped and myopic definition. *On The Beach*, *Soylent Green*, and *Nineteen Eighty-Four* plumbed frightening depths. *Brave New World*, *The Screwfly Solution*, and *Fahrenheit 451* posed worrying questions. In contrast, *Oedepus Rex* is about as interesting as watching a hooked fish thrash futilely at the end of a line. You just want to put the poor doomed King of Thebes out of his misery.

This truly is a different point of view, in direct opposition to older, elitist creeds that preached passivity and awe in nearly every culture, where a storyteller's chief job was to flatter the oligarchic patrons who fed him. Imagine Achilles refusing to accept his ordained destiny, taking up his sword and hunting down the Four Fates, demanding that they give him both a long life *and* a glorious one! Picture Odysseus telling both Agamemnon and Poseidon to go chase themselves, then heading off to join Daedalus in a garage startup company, mass producing wheeled and winged horses so that mortals could swoop about the land and air, like gods...the way common folk do today.

This storytelling style was rarely seen till a few generations ago, when aristocrats lost some of their power to punish irreverence. Even now, the new perspective remains shaky... and many find it less romantic, too. How many dramas reflexively depict scientists as "mad"? How few modern films ever show American institutions functioning well enough to bother fixing them? No wonder George Lucas publicly yearns for the pomp of mighty kings, over the drab accountability of presidents. Many share his belief that things might be a whole lot more vivid without all the endless, dreary argument and negotiating that make up such a large part of modern life.

If only someone would take command. A leader.

A CULTURE CLASH IN THE HEAVENS

Some contend the moral health of a civilization can be traced in its popular culture. If so, we may find it worthwhile taking a closer look at the *Star*

Wars mythos. Can we learn more about these two competing worldviews by comparing George Lucas's space-adventure epic to its chief competitor—*Star Trek*?

First a clarification. While I do think that plenty of evidence shows that George Lucas hates a civilization that's been very good to him... and that his storytelling faults are innumerable... this does not mean that I'm saying everything in the *Star Wars* universe is evil and perverse! So many people would not flock to the films if there weren't many positive traits. The Campbellian and Enlightenment traditions can have considerable overlap. Among the better (though simpleminded) lessons that you do see in even the worst *Star Wars* films are, "Mean people suck," "Be brave," "Try to stay calm," and "Keep on trying."

Indeed, I have never said we should eliminate Joseph Campbell-type myths from our storytelling heritage! When they are good, they rock. Anyway, they are deeply rooted inside us, for well or ill. I just think we ought to TRY to grow up a bit and appreciate other modes of fiction that are less clichéd, formulaic, predictable, and obeissant to elites. For the Campbellian myth can VERY easily go wrong, and turn into a nightmare. That's what's happened to George Lucas's particular vision, in which a "rebellion" is used to symbolize the legitimization of demigods.

As for a comparison of *Star Wars* vs *Star Trek*, the differences at first seem superficial. One saga has an *air force* motif (tiny fighters) while the other appears *naval*. In *Star Trek*, the big ship is heroic and the cooperative effort required to maintain it is depicted as honorable. Indeed, *Star Trek* sees technology as useful and essentially friendly—if at times dangerous. Education is a great emancipator of the humble (e.g. Starfleet Academy). Futuristic institutions are basically good natured (the Federation), though of course one must fight outbreaks of incompetence and corruption. Professionalism is respected, lesser characters make a difference, and henchmen often become brave whistle blowers, as they do in America today.

In *Star Trek*, when authorities are defied, it is in order to overcome their mistakes or expose particular villains, not to portray all institutions as inherently hopeless. Good cops sometimes come when you call for help. Ironically, this image fosters useful criticism of authority, because it suggests that any of us can gain access to our institutions, if we are determined enough... and perhaps even fix them with fierce tools of citizenship.

By contrast, the oppressed "rebels" in *Star Wars* have no recourse in law or markets or science or democracy. They can only choose sides in a civil war between two wings of the same genetically superior royal family. They may not meddle or criticize. As homeric spear-carriers, it's not their job.

In teaching us to distinguish good from evil, George Lucas prescribes judging by looks. Villains wear Nazi helmets. They hiss and leer, or have red-glowing eyes, like in a Ralph Bakshi cartoon. *Star Trek* tales often warn against judging a book by its cover, a message you'll also find in the films of Steven Spielberg, whose spunky Everyman characters delight in reversing expectations and asking irksome questions.

Above all, *Star Trek* generally depicts heroes who are *only* about ten times as brilliant, noble and heroic as a normal person, prevailing through cooperation and wit, rather than because of some indwelt godlike transcendent greatness. Characters who do achieve godlike powers are subjected to ruthless scrutiny in any *Trek* episode in which they appear, and are often taught a lesson in humility. In other words, *Trek* is a prototypically American dream, entranced by notions of human improvement and a progress that lifts all. Gene Rodenberry's vision loves heroes, but it breaks away from the elitist tradition of princes and wizards who rule by divine or mystical right.

By contrast, these are the *only* heroes in the *Star Wars* universe.

Yes, *Trek* can at times seem preachy, or turgidly politically correct. For example, every species has to mate with every other one, interbreeding almost compulsive abandon. The only male heroes who are allowed any testosterone are Klingons, because cultural diversity outweighs sexual correctness. (In other words, it's okay for *them* to be macho 'cause it is "their way.") *Star Trek* television episodes often devolved into soap operas. Many of the movies were very badly written. Still, when it comes to portraying human destiny, where would you rather live—*assuming you must be a normal citizen?* In Rodenberry's Federation? Or Lucas's Empire?

George Lucas defends his elitist view, telling the *New York Times*, "That's sort of why I say a benevolent despot is the ideal ruler. He can actually get things done. The idea that power corrupts is very true and it's a big human who can get past that."

In other words a royal figure or demigod, anointed by fate. (Like a billionaire movie-maker?)[1]

Let's look in more detail at his interview with the *New York Times*.

"There's a reason why kings built large palaces, sat on thrones and wore rubies all over. There's a whole social need for that, not to oppress the masses, but to impress the masses and make them proud and allow them to feel good about their culture, their government and their ruler so that they are left feeling that a ruler has the right to rule over them, so that they feel good rather than disgusted about being ruled. In the past, the media basically worked for the state and was there to build the culture. Now, obviously, in some cases it got used in a wrong way and you ended up with the whole balance of power out of whack. But there's probably no better form of government than a good despot."

Lucas often says we are a sad culture, bereft of the confidence or inspiration that strong leaders can provide. And yet, aren't we the very same culture that produced George Lucas and gave him so many opportunities? The same society that raised all those brilliant experts for him to hire—boldly creative folks who pour both individual inspiration and cooperative skill into his films? A culture that defies the old homogenizing impulse by worshipping eccentricity, with unprecedented hunger for the different, new or strange? It what way can such a civilization be said to lack confidence?

In historical fact, all of history's despots, combined, never managed to "get things done" as well as this rambunctious, self-critical civilization of free and sovereign citizens, who have finally broken free of worshipping a ruling class and begun thinking for themselves. Democracy can seem frustrating and messy at times, but it delivers.

A CAMPBELLIAN ASIDE

For an avowed student of Joseph Campbell, Mr. Lucas seems all too ready to ignore the master. For example, close examination of *The*

---

[1] Taking on a billionaire is never productive...though nowadays it's physically *safe* to do so. That's worth noting. Ironically, it is safe to criticize the mighty precisely because we live in a civilization that's already much more like *Star Trek* than *Star Wars*. A place with halfway decent laws and working institutions that would hinder a billionaire from taking direct bodily revenge, even if he hates criticism. (Something even "benevolent" despots did routinely in the old days.) An exquisite—though flawed—scientific, egalitarian culture that enables guys like Lucas and me to prosper at the very same time, even while we tell conflicting stories about the future.

There's room for both of us...and others, too. I just wish George Lucas felt an iota of gratitude for the technology, philosophy, society and fellow citizens who got him where he is today. A civilization to which he owes absolutely everything.

Phantom Menace shows an absolute absence of the one critical ingredient... a hero!

There is a classic *mentor*—QuiJon—who fills that role quite well, in fact, sacrificing himself much in the way Obi-Wan did in the original *Star Wars* movie. There is a cute sidekick, Anakin Skywalker, who nevertheless performs almost none of the requisite tasks that Campbell prescribed for the reluctant/romantic/central hero. Indeed, he is totally absent from the first third of the film. The ideal person to fill that role—the one who *Phantom Menace* should have been *about*—was young Obi-Wan. And Lucas leaves him languishing aboard a ship for the film's entire middle third, giving us nothing of his wants or needs or character.

Again, there is no hero in *TPM*. No wonder it was disappointing even to those millions who do not care about democracy vs. despotism or romantic vs. enlightenment values.

THE IDOLATRY OF A MASS-MURDERER

Having said all that, let me again acknowledge that *Star Wars* still hearkens to an old and very, very deeply human archetype. Those who listened to Homer recite the *Iliad* by a campfire knew great drama. Achilles could slay a thousand with the sweep of a hand... as Darth Vader murders billions with the press of a button... but none of those casualties matter next to the personal saga of a great one. The slaughtered victims are mere minions. Extras. Spear-carriers, not worth even passing consideration. Only the demigod's personal drama is important.

Thus few protest the apotheosis of Darth Vader—né Anakin Skywalker—in *Return Of The Jedi*...

To put it in perspective, let's imagine that the U.S. and its allies managed to capture Adolf Hitler, at the end of the Second World War, putting him on trial for war crimes. The prosecution spends months listing all the horrors done at his behest. Then it is the turn of Hitler's defense attorney, who rises and utters just one sentence —

"But, your honors... Adolf *did* save the life of his own son!"

Gasp! The prosecutors blanch in chagrin. "We didn't know that! Of course all charges should be dismissed at once!"

The allies then throw a big parade for Hitler, down the main avenues of Nuremberg.

It may sound silly, but that's exactly the lesson taught by "Episode Six," wherein Darth Vader is forgiven all his sins, because he saved the life of his own son.

Consider, how many of us have argued late at night over the philosophical conundrum—"Would you go back in time and kill Hitler as a boy, if given a chance?" It's a genuine moral puzzler, with many possible ethical answers. Still, most people, however they ultimately respond, would admit being *tempted* to say yes, if only to save millions of Hitler's victims.

And yet, in *The Phantom Menace*, George Lucas says we are supposed to gush with warm feelings toward a cute Aryan-looking little boy who will later grow up to help murder the population of Earth, many times over? While we're at it, why not bring out the Hitler family album, so we may croon over pictures of adorable little Adolf and marvel over his childhood exploits! He, too, was innocent till he turned to the "dark side," so by all means let us adore him.

Lucas tries to excuse this macabre joke by claiming that he's crafting an agonized Greek tragedy worthy of Oedipus. An epic tale of a fallen hero, trapped by hubris and fate. But if that were true, wouldn't Lucas by now have given us a better-than-caricature view of the Dark Side? Heroes and villains would not be distinguished by prettiness. The moral quandaries would not come from a comic book.

Don't swallow it. The apotheosis of a mass murderer is exactly what it seems. We should find it chilling.

Remember the final scene in *Return of the Jedi*, when Luke gazes into a fire to see Obi-Wan, Yoda and Vader, smiling in the flames? I found myself hoping it was *Jedi Hell,* for the amount of pain those three unleashed on their galaxy, and all the damned lies they told. But that's me. I'm a rebel against Homer and Achilles and that whole tradition. At heart, some of you are, too.

This isn't just a one-time distinction. It marks the main boundary between real, literate, humanistic science fiction—or *speculative fiction*—and most of the movie "sci-fi" you see nowadays. The difference isn't really about complexity, childishness, scientific naïveté, or haughty prose stylization. (I like a good action scene as well as the next guy, and can forgive technical gaffes if the story is way-cool!) The underlying difference is that one tradition revels in elites, while the other rebels against them. In the genuine Science Fiction Worldview, demigods aren't easily forgiven lies and murder. Contempt for the masses is passé.

There may be heroes—even great ones—but in the long run we'll improve together, or not at all.[2]

Ah, but what sells? Even after rebelling against the Homeric archetype for generations, we children of Pericles and Ben Franklin and H. G. Wells remain a slim minority. So much so that George Lucas can appropriate our hand-created tropes and symbols—our beloved starships and robots—for his own ends and get credited for originality.

As I mentioned earlier, the mythology of conformity and demigod-worship pervades the highest levels of today's intelligentsia, and helps explain why so many postmodernist English literature professors despise real science fiction. When Joseph Campbell prescribed that writers should adhere slavishly to a hackneyed plot outline that preached submission for ages, he was lionized by Bill Moyers and countless others for his warm and fuzzy "human insight." And indeed, his perceptions were fascinating! But a frank discussion or debate might have been more useful than Campbell's sunny monologue. As in the old fable about a golden-haired king, no one dared point to the bright ruler's dark shadow, or his long trail of bloody footprints.

I admit we face an uphill battle winning people over to a more progressive, egalitarian worldview, along with stirring dreams that focus on genuine heroes, not demigods. Meanwhile, George Lucas knows his mythos appeals to human nature at a deep and ancient level.

Hell, it appeals to a part of *my* nature! Which is why I knew I'd cave in and see *Episode One*, after my symbolic one-week boycott expired. In fact, let me confess that I *adored* the second film in the series... *The Empire Strikes Back*. Despite Yoda's kitschy pseudo-Zen, one could easily suspend disbelief and wait to see what the Jedi philosophy had to say. Millions became keyed up to find out, at long last, why Obi-Wan and Yoda lied like weasels to Luke Skywalker. Meanwhile, the script of *TESB* sizzled with originality, good dialogue and relentlessly compelling characters. The action was dynamite... and even logical! Common folk got almost as much chance to be heroic as the demigods. Clichés were few and terrific surprises abounded. There were fine foreshadowings, promising more marvels in sequels. It was simply a great movie. Homeric but great.

---

[2] It's been said that we have spent the last hundred years trying to resolve a struggle between the *eighteenth century* and the *nineteenth*...between prescriptions offered by the Enlightenment and those of the Romantic Movement. The Twentieth Century has been a battleground for this tussle. For all their rhetoric, both Nazism and Communism were essentially romantic — most ideologies are. Guess which of these worldviews can thrive where youths are raised (in the words of a great science fiction author) to — "Keep asking questions! The more irksome the better!"

You already know what I think of what came next.[3] But worshipping Darth Vader only scratches the surface. The biggest moral flaw in the *Star Wars* universe is one point that George Lucas stresses over and over again, through the voice of his all-wise guru character, Yoda.

Let's see if I get this right. *Fear makes you angry and anger makes you evil, right?*

Now I'll concede at once that fear *has* been a major motivator of intolerance in human history. I can picture knightly adepts being taught to control fear and anger, as we saw credibly in *The Empire Strikes Back*. Calmness makes you a better warrior and prevents mistakes. Persistent wrath can cloud judgment. That part is completely believable.

But then, in *Return Of The Jedi*, Lucas takes this basic wisdom and perverts it, saying, "If you get angry—even at injustice and murder—it will automatically and immediately transform you into an unalloyedly evil person! All of your opinions and political beliefs will suddenly and magically reverse. Every loyalty will be forsaken and you will instantly join your sworn enemy as his close pal or apprentice. All because you let yourself get angry at his crimes."

Uh, *say what?* Could you repeat that again...slowly?

In other words, getting angry *at* Adolf Hitler will cause you to rush right out and join the Nazi Party? Excuse me, George. Could you come up with a single example of that happening? *Ever?*

That contention is, in itself, an evil thing to preach. Above all, it is just plain dumb. This saga is not just another expression of the Homeric archetype, extolling old hierarchies of princes, wizards and demigods. By making its centerpiece the romanticization of a mass murderer, *Star Wars* has sunk far lower. It is unworthy of our attention, our money, our enthusiasm... and our civilization.

George Lucas himself gives a clue when he says, "...A long time ago, in a galaxy far, far away..."

Right on. *Star Wars* belongs to our dark past. A long, tyrannical epoch of fear, illogic, despotism and demagoguery that we are only now starting to emerge from, aided by the scientific and egalitarian spirit that Lucas so deeply and ungratefully despises.

I don't expect to win this argument any time soon. As Joseph Campbell rightly pointed out, the ways of our ancestors tug at the soul

---

[3] Ever notice how, in so many sci-fi series, the first movie's kind-of-okay, the second sizzles...and the *third* one stinks up the joint, betraying every theme raised by the other two? It happened in the *Trek*, *Star Wars* and *Aliens* universes. (I explain elsewhere.) I hope there'll never be a third *Terminator*, for the same reason!

with a resonance many find romantically appealing, even irresistible. Some cannot put the fairy tale down and move on to more mature fare. Not yet. Ah well.

But over the long haul, history is on my side. Because the course of human destiny won't be defined in the past. It will be decided in our future.

That's *my* bailiwick, though it truly belongs to all of us.

It's where our posterity will thrive.

THE TINSEL SCREEN
James E. Gunn

Star Wars has delighted tens of millions of film-goers, some of whom have returned to see the film dozens of times. Virtually all by itself, it restored Twentieth Century Fox to financial health by bringing in the greatest motion picture gross, until *E.T., the Extraterrestrial*, of all time. *Close Encounters of the Third Kind* also has brought in a substantial return on its substantial production costs and thrilled audiences with its alien space ship. New science fiction films flooded onto the screen until most of the top money-making motion pictures were science fiction.

All of which suggests that the western world may be in 1) a golden age of science fiction films, 2) a golden age of science fiction, or 3) neither. Science fiction fans, authors, editors, and publishers started asking each other whether the vast audiences for the hugely successful science fiction films were going to mean a great new upsurge in science fiction readers.

Some have answered "no," suggesting that film-goers were not necessarily readers and did not necessarily translate film pleasure into a comparable reading experience. I have made the opposite point to questioners: the success of science fiction books paved the way for the acceptance of *Star Wars*.

As a matter of fact, printed science fiction and science fiction film seem to have little to do with each other, and there are virtually no good films that are also good science fiction. *Star Wars* is a simple and charming fairy tale set in scenes in which science fiction paraphernalia is lying about; and *Close Encounters*, in spite of the splendid epiphany when its Victorian chandelier of a spaceship appears, adds nothing to the concept of encounter with aliens other than special effects.

The question of why this should be so—why science fiction is almost never translated effectively into film—has puzzled several generations of science fiction readers. The problem with the science fiction film may be that it adds nothing to science fiction except concreteness of image—and that may be more of a drawback than an asset.

John Baxter, in one of the better books about science fiction movies, *Science Fiction in the Cinema*, says that science fiction literature and science fiction film come from different origins and provide different views of the world. "Science fiction," he says, "supports logic and order; SF film, illogic and chaos. Its roots lie not in the visionary literature of the nineteenth century, to which science fiction owes most of its origins, but in older forms and attitudes, the medieval fantasy world, the era of the *masque*, the morality play, and the Grand Guignol."

Baxter goes on to write that the fund of concepts of science fiction films is limited. "Those it has fall generally into two categories: the loss of individuality, and the threat of knowledge." And he goes on to state, "Probably no line is more common to SF cinema than, 'There are some things Man is not meant to know.'...It expresses the universal fear all men have of the unknown and the inexplicable, a fear science fiction rejects, but which has firmly entrenched itself in the SF cinema."

The result is obvious: if a science fiction film opens with a scene of a scientist working in a laboratory, the audience knows that what he is working on will come to no good end—it will threaten his neighborhood, his region, his nation, or even the Earth itself; it will devour his wife and children, and maybe everyone else's wives and children; and he will be sorry, but not as sorry as the rest of us. If the same scene occurs in a science fiction story, the reader has no preconceptions about how it will come out; the research may turn out badly, but it will not be because the scientist should not have done it in the first place, rather because he did it poorly or without proper precautions. And the scientist might be working on research that will be useful, valuable, or indispensable; it may save us all, like the Ark, when danger threatens.

I like Baxter's distinctions, but I find curiously lacking from him a defense of them. Why doesn't (or can't) the science fiction film reflect written science fiction? Why doesn't (or can't) it support logic and order? Why isn't it (or can't it be) a medium of ideas? Baxter accepts the situation as a given, much as I have heard science fiction filmmakers surrender to the Hollywood sickness with a shrug and a "you've got to work within the system."

I would say, first of all, that Baxter's distinctions do not always hold up. On my list of good science fiction films are several that reflect the values of written science fiction: *Things to Come*, say, or *2001: A Space Odyssey*, where a science fiction writer has had a major influence on the development of the film. The result has been better science fiction and a superior film. You can beat the system if you are able to persuade the system of the truth of that statement.

But Baxter is right about most science fiction films. The people who made them knew nothing about science fiction. When they bought science fiction stories, they didn't know what they bought; they threw away the best parts and kept the worst, and didn't know the difference. They set out to make what they understood—monster movies, usually, with lots of special effects, but keep the budget low, and if you have to skimp, do it on the story and acting because nobody will notice.

Take a familiar case in point: John W. Campbell's classic novelette, "Who Goes There?" Hollywood turned it into *The Thing*.

Why must science fiction films deal only with simple images? Why must filmmakers suffer a failure of imagination when they come to science fiction? These are the questions that bedevil the science fiction reader. The filmmaker seems content with his ingenious models, his trick photography, his gruesome monsters, and his tabletop destruction.

Most science fiction films, if translated into written form, would be un-publishable because of lack of logic or originality. I stand behind that statement even in the face of the success of the novelized versions of a variety of SF films, including *Star Wars* and its sequels. The ideas in a film such as *THX 1138*, much praised for its visual impact and filmic images, were old in 1949, when George Orwell wove them into a sophisticated novel of ideas, called *1984*. Another visually interesting film, *Silent Running*, has almost no logic at all: why put parks into space? Who visits them? What is saved by destroying them?

If a science fiction reader doesn't find interesting the ideas of a science fiction film, all that is left are the images or the special effects...what you have when you take away the subject matter. Film critics, when they deal with science fiction films, ignore the ideas and write about images and special effects. And when they discuss ideas, they are not to be trusted. I can forgive Susan Sontag for her statement (in "The Imagination of Disaster") that science fiction films are concerned with the aesthetics of disaster; she is talking about monster and worldwide destruction movies, not written science fiction, though she might have pointed out the difference. But I would argue with her conclusions that dealing with disaster in an imaginative way becomes "itself a somewhat questionable act from a moral point of view," by normalizing "what is psychologically unbearable, thereby inuring us to it." If applicable to science fiction films, why not to written science fiction? Here, it seems to me, the fallacy becomes more apparent. The alternative is not to deal fictionally with disaster, perhaps not even to think about it. Ms. Sontag, perhaps, would have us nourish an unspecific horror of things which concern "identity, volition, power, knowledge, happiness, social consensus, guilt, responsibility…"

There is not much difference, as far as inuring goes, in visualizing a horror and writing about it, and I cannot believe that Orwell, to take one example, inured us to the horror of the all-intrusive state by writing *1984*, or that the 1954 film, though clearly inferior to the book, made us more likely to accept the conditions it depicts. The difficulty with Ms. Sontag's position is that most persons do not think about consequences until they are faced with them in terms of people's lives. Some—no, all—disasters should be thought through, analyzed, weighed, considered. Some disasters may be inevitable; they must be prepared for. Others are avoidable and must be prevented. Still others offer alternatives from which one must be chosen as superior to the other. Some are not disasters at all, but only seem like disasters. Some may be short-term disasters and long-term boons. Some may be individual disasters and racial necessities.

The basic problem with the science fiction disaster film is that it imagines disaster, but seldom considers alternatives; it stirs our stomachs but seldom our heads. The film critics, accepting "what is" for "what must be," say it can do no other.

We run into this kind of nonsense from film critics: I can forgive Bernard Beck (in "The Overdeveloped Society: *THX 1138*") for describing science fiction as "often nothing more than a language structure for describing events which are concretely unimaginable or meaningless in ordinary terms," but I cannot forgive him for equating that language structure to "the production, the creation of a concrete image of the impossible out of available techniques" in the science fiction film. Overcoming the technical difficulties of making science fiction images concrete on film is not the same as the difficulties of making a science fiction situation believable. Fiction responds to difficulties; the ideals that lie within the science fiction situation are most dramatically expressed when the difficulties are surmounted. Beck would have us believe that the film's creation of the concrete image is enough to delight us. It had better be.

The only place where greater caution with the film critic should be exercised is the point at which the critic begins to refer to "a synthesis of insightful visual imagination" and "an interpenetration of fantasy and reality." Phrases like those suggest that the logic of the film won't bear inspection.

If the science fiction film actually makes images concrete, it may be the concreteness of the image that ultimately turns us off. Science fiction, like fantasy, is a literature of the imagination; it requires vigorous participation on the part of the reader, a willing suspension of disbelief—although science fiction, in contrast to fantasy, gives the reader reasons for believing. This reader participation allows the science fiction writer to span parsecs believably, to cross centuries credibly, to suggest the most sensational of cities, the most creative of creatures, the most startling of social systems, the most incredible variations upon a theme. And if a writer has done it persuasively, the reader constructs for himself, out of his own imagination, what he longs for or dreads.

As John W. Campbell pointed out in 1947 (in an essay called "The Science of Science Fiction Writing"), "the trick is to describe the horrified, not the horror, the love-struck, not the lady-love." But the science fiction film, at great expense and difficulty, applies a face to the horror, and it seems prosaic or laughable; the film is stuck with its images, and in them, the viewer does not participate. Often the film image cannot live up to the reader's expectations; that is why books seldom make good movies, even though we want to see the impossible achieved. This is particularly true of science fiction books. Moreover, when the effort to make the image concrete represents the major accomplishment of a film, the substance becomes incidental. Where science fiction is specific about ideas and suggestive about images, the science fiction film is specific about images and allusive—elusive as well—about meaning. The difference is all the difference in this world—or another.

Stan Freberg, the satirist turned ad man, once created a radio commercial about the advantages of radio advertising over television. It began with the announcer turning Lake Michigan into a gigantic bowl of flavored gelatin, covering it with whipped cream, and towing into position overhead, a cherry the size of an island, and it ended with the announcer challenging a television executive to create a similar commercial.

The same thing might be said about science fiction and fantasy on radio. Radio brought out the best in science fiction: the sound effects were relatively easy and much more effective than visual images in suggesting scope, changing scenes, creating moods, and eliciting listener imagination. The famous 1938 Mercury Theater production of *The War of the Worlds* created an astonishing (and much studied) reaction from its audience. But there were others: *Lights Out* and *Inner Sanctum* had some science fiction mixed with the horrors in the 1940s, but science fiction came into its own in the 1950s with a handful of series of which *Dimension X* and *X Minus One* were the best. Many of the dramatizations were well done. Four of my *Galaxy* stories were adapted for *X Minus One*, and I liked two of them very well, and the other two fairly well. For contrast, I offer the 1959 television adaptation of one of them, my "The Cave of Night," into Desilu Playhouse's *Man in Orbit*— even with Lee Marvin and H. G. Marshall, it was disappointing. Today's counterparts to the radio adaptations of science fiction are records and tapes and CDs of dramatic readings and even dramatizations. And the old radio programs are still available on record and tape, although you may have to search for them.

If, in spite of all the drawbacks of films, the science fiction reader persists in a masochistic desire to see and understand science fiction movies, where can help be found? I suggest that the reader stay away from film critics unless the reader wants information about film; most critics talk nonsense about the obvious, and they provide only confusion about science fiction. They insist, for instance, on referring to science fiction as "sci-fi," which immediately alienates the science fiction reader; he knows the only legitimate abbreviation is "SF," although many modern writers insist that "SF" can also stand for "speculative fiction."

The best book about science fiction films I found, published before 1979, was William Johnson's *Focus on the Science Fiction Film*, which presented both sides of most issues and included comments by writers as well as critics and film-makers. John Baxter's *Science Fiction in the Cinema* is thorough; Denis Gifford's *Science Fiction Film* lists more titles than any other book, but says less about each; Ralph J. Amelio's *Hal in the Classroom: Science Fiction Films* contains some provocative, but often misguided, essays, among which are Susan Sontag's and Bernard Beck's. All the books listed above have useful bibliographies and filmographies. A different kind of book, *Cinema of the Fantastic*, by Chris Steinbrunner and Burt Goldblatt, has many hard-to-find photographs, and chapters on fifteen movies, from Georges Méliès's *A Trip to the Moon* to *Forbidden Planet*. But for my tastes, the two best books about the science fiction film are John Brosnan's *Future Tense: The Cinema of Science Fiction* (1978) and Frederik Pohl's *Science Fiction: Studies in Film* (1981), written with his son, Frederik Pohl IV.

If a reader wishes to develop a personal history of the science fiction film, the obvious starting point is Méliès's *A Trip to the Moon*, a brief bit of whimsy filmed in 1902 and patterned after Jules Verne's *From the Earth to the Moon*, with influence from H. G. Wells's *The First Men in the Moon*. Méliès had a couple of earlier efforts, *An Astronomer's Dream* and a version of H. Rider Haggard's *She*.

After a number of other curiosities, that are available and probably not worth seeing for anything more than antiquarian purposes (with the exception of the 1925 film of Arthur Conan Doyle's *The Lost World* with Wallace Beery as Professor Challenger and some effective, early, animated dinosaurs), the German director Fritz Lang produced *Metropolis* in 1926 (a more complete film, tinted, with soundtrack and subtitles, was re-released in 1984) and *Woman in the Moon* in 1929. Both are historically important, particularly for special effects, and both are melodramatic and overacted and audiences with whom I have viewed them usually find them funny. An American film of 1930, *Just Imagine*, is supposed to be funny but is only ridiculous; however, it does include some impressive futuristic shots of a 1980 metropolis.

The meaningful history of filmed science fiction (as opposed to science fiction film) begins in 1931 with *Frankenstein*, the Boris Karloff version that inspired a thousand parodies, including Mel Brooks's *Young Frankenstein*. Yet the original film still has the power to move audiences. So does the more cultish *King Kong*, epic in scope and special effects, and even interesting thematically. The remake has little to recommend it but color. Another on my list came along the same year as *King Kong*, *The Invisible Man*. Although it perpetuated the persistent medieval theme "he meddled in God's domain" and "he ventured into areas man was meant to leave alone," the film does better than most at considering more than one side of a question, in this case, the drawbacks as well as the advantages of invisibility, and the special effects are well done. About the same time, came a film that doesn't quite make my list but is nevertheless a reasonably effective adaptation of H. G. Wells's *The Island of Dr. Moreau*, called *The Island of Lost Souls* (1932), with Charles Laughton. Again, the remake is poorer.

I once thought that the British *Things to Come* (1936) was the only good science fiction film ever made. It is based on Wells's 1933 book, *The Shape of Things to Come*, and it had a scenario and frequent memoranda to the participants by Wells, leading to my later conclusions that the really good science fiction movies had someone intimately associated with the production who knew a great deal about written science fiction. Since *Things to Come*, other films have come along, and the virtues of *Things to Come* have not survived the intervening years undiminished. The early war scenes are cheaply executed and betray their simple pacifism. But the final sequences, projected into the year 2036, still have the power to captivate, and Raymond Massey's final statement of man's destiny still sounds the clear, pure call of mainstream science fiction. I have been surprised at the number of science fiction authors of my generation, such as Isaac Asimov and Fred Pohl, who have expressed the same reactions to this film.

The *Flash Gordon* and *Buck Rogers* serials produced between 1936 and 1940, along with such lesser works as *The Phantom Empire* (1935) and *The Undersea Kingdom* (1936), are high camp today with their comic strip villains and heroes, their cardboard robots, their firework rocketships, and their absurd and cheating cliffhangers. But they provide a kind of reliving of the old thirties Saturday matinee experience, and some viewers have found them good fun. *Star Wars*, it has been said, is George Lucas's tribute to *Flash Gordon*.

Destination Moon (1950) was George Pal's first science fiction produc-tion, and the first film adapted from the work of a magazine science fiction writer, Robert A. Heinlein. He also worked on the script, which was based on his Scribner's juvenile novel, *Rocketship Galileo*. The film is marred by melodramatics and some ridiculous comic relief, but the space sequences and the lunar episodes (the moonscapes were painted by the late astronomical and science fiction artist, Chesley Bonestell) are remarkable bits of prophecy. During the televised portions of the Apollo trips, the appearance of space and the Moon surface gave many of us the experience of *dejá vù*: we had seen it before, only clearer, in *Destination Moon*.

George Pal, as producer, and later director, would have much to do with subsequent adaptations of science fiction classics such as Balmer and Wylie's *When Worlds Collide* (1951), Wells's *The War of the Worlds* (1953), and *The Time Machine* (1960). All are worth viewing as adaptations of written science fiction, although all fall short in one way or another, the first two more than the last.

Of the some two thousand or so remaining films, I would include in my historical overview: *Forbidden Planet* (1956), which has Robbie the Robot, comic relief, and an idiotic love story (all modeled, to be sure, on *The Tempest*), but also the marvelous idea of the Id Monster and scenes of the lost civilization which produced it; *The Invasion of the Body Snatchers* (1956), about the replacement of people by pod duplicates, which is nicely and soberly done, and liked by many critics more than I do (the remake produced mixed reactions); *The Village of the Damned* (1960), a relatively faithful adaptation of the John Wyndham novel (the 1963 *Day of the Triffids* is not as faithful and a lesser film; there is a better, more-recent English version); *Barbarella* (1967), which has a bit of nudity for the libidinous and also lovely scenes and a delightful satire on a number of science fiction themes; and, of course, the incomparable *2001: A Space Odyssey*, which, in spite of some quarrels with its obscure ending and the unexplained murderousness of HAL, is the most completely-realized vision of the future yet achieved on film and an excellent motion picture.

Star Wars (1977) and *Close Encounters of the Third Kind* (1977) are more important for what they have accomplished at the box office than what they have achieved artistically. *Star Wars* can be enjoyed effortlessly at the fairy tale level, and it offers a pleasant lived-in quality to its scenes and costumes, and the scope and effectiveness of its special effects are worth the cost of seeing it. *Close Encounters* has a magnificent final scene in the appearance of the alien spaceship, but it seems to me that the first two-thirds of the film is irrelevant and the two UFO fanatics who have fought their way to the spot, end up as spectators little more relevant to what goes on there than the rest of the audience. I would give it high praise, however, for never once permitting a character to suggest that the aliens might be dangerous and people should either arm themselves or flee. But the most important aspect of the two films is their refutation of the frequent excuse against making first-class science fiction films, that SF films never make money. *Battlestar Galactica* has demonstrated, however, that special effects do not an SF movie make, though it will be cited as a reason not to do SF on television. Other SF series have been more successful though not necessarily better.

All of these, no matter what their faults, are part of the canon of the science fiction film, along with films that have a similar appeal but are not sufficiently distanced from the present to qualify as science fiction (such as *Lost Horizon* [1937], *The Man in the White Suit* [1951], and *Dr. Strangelove* [1964]).

Many science fiction films were produced between *Destination Moon* and *Star Wars*, but if I haven't listed them above, I find them seriously flawed or completely hopeless. Some film critics praise some of them, for instance, *The Day the Earth Stood Still* or *The Thing*, both released in 1951, but any reader who recalls the science fiction novelettes "Farewell to the Master," by Harry Bates and "Who Goes There?" by John W. Campbell, must reject the films based on them if only for tossing away a good story and making a lesser one.

The Verne adaptations, *Journey to the Center of the Earth* (1959), *From the Earth to the Moon* (1964), and *Twenty Thousand Leagues Under the Sea* (1965), and others generally are performed as period pieces; they are amusing but cannot be taken seriously as science fiction...they are flawed and unfaithful. My favorite of this type is a Czechoslovakian film called *The Wonderful Invention* (1958), sometimes called *The Fabulous World of Jules Verne*, but it has been unavailable since its initial showing.

Godard's science fiction film, *Alphaville* (1965), is frequently admired, but I find it obscure and unconvincing.

Other films have been marred by mindless anti-scientism, such as *The Incredible Shrinking Man* (1957) or *The Power* (1967); or by illogical elements, as in *Fahrenheit 451* (1966), *Planet of the Apes* (1968) and its many sequels, *Charly* (1968), or *Colossus: The Forbin Project* (1970); or by no logic at all, as in *The Andromeda Strain* (1971), *Silent Running* (1972), *Westworld* (1973), or *Soylent Green* (1973). It is interesting to note that the resolution that *Soylent Green* presents as the ultimate in horror could make a satisfying science fiction story—if the problem were to convince the public that its prejudice against eating a product made from human flesh was irrational and unreasonable. *A Clockwork Orange*, on the other hand, justifies, if it does not actually glorify, violence. I find this more repugnant than small, neat wafers of Soylent Green.

In spite of their flaws, the films listed above are the best of their kind, and all of them may find their place in a science fiction film series with the reservations noted. Their kind simply is not a high art.

Science fiction on television is even worse. Its only value—in the way *Amazing Stories* was once considered by John W. Campbell as a primer for the more demanding science fiction published in *Astounding*— is to provide an introduction for young people willing to move on to the written word. Series have even more flaws than science fiction films and demand larger audiences (thus requiring a reduction to lowest-common-denominator approach) for survival. Nevertheless, *Star Trek* certainly, and certain episodes of *The Twilight Zone* and *Night Gallery* among others, achieved moments of science fiction value. The best science fiction adaptations on television have been one-shots, like the early adaptations of Robert Sheckley's "The People Trap" and Alfred Bester's "Fondly Fahrenheit" for which Bester himself wrote the script. Even the 1969 *ABC-TV Movie of the Week, The Immortal*, that was an adaptation of my 1962 novel, *The Immortals*, was far superior to the series that followed in 1970.

Perhaps a discussion of what went wrong with *The Immortal* would be a good place to bring this analysis of science fiction and the visual media to a conclusion. There are so many things that an author can criticize about the adaptation of his work that I hardly know where to begin, but let us ignore the acting (Bob Specht, the scriptwriter and the person responsible for getting on television at all, thought Christopher George was dynamic enough to keep the series on the air for a second season all on his own), the production, and even the quality of the scripts (a Screenwriters Guild strike was threatened and the producer, Anthony Wilson, had to sign up a lot of scripts in a hurry), and concentrate on the ideas.

The big mistake made early in the planning for the series was to play the series for adventure rather than science fiction. (That has been the downfall of most science fiction adaptations—remember *The Thing*?). In fact, the word went out that no science fiction writers would be considered as script writers for the series. In retrospect, Bob Specht's decision to make the Immortal a test-car driver, influenced, no doubt, by the success of the San Francisco car chase scenes of *Bullitt* and perhaps a major reason the original script was attractive to Paramount and ABC, may have been a fatal mistake for the series: executives saw it as a chase story, with ten minutes or more of every episode eaten up in car chase footage.

In the final analysis, the fact that Ben Richards (Marshall Cartwright in the novel) was immortal made little difference. The subject of my novel was the way in which his immortality changed society. Marshall Cartwright's personal problems had so little relevance in the novel that he disappears after an initial scene of blood drawing and doesn't make another appearance until the end. But Ben Richards's dramatic value in the movie adaptation is only his importance to someone else: that his importance is his blood, which can make old people temporarily young again, is no more significant for the narrative than if he knew the location of important papers or a fortune in jewels, or had killed someone, or could save someone from a false accusation. It was, in other words, viewed as another *Fugitive*. Ben Richards's immortality was only an excuse for a chase, and the episodes that resulted from it were simple repetitions of discovery, chase, capture, and escape...cookie-cutter episodes, indistinguishable from one another.

The Immortal had the potential to concern itself with life and death, subjects too important to trivialize. But that may be the ultimate problem with science fiction on film: with a few important exceptions, filmmakers have been afraid or unwilling to take science fiction seriously, and unless any subject is taken seriously, it cannot produce meaningful art.

Looked at as film, the period since *Star Wars* was released in 1977 has been a golden age for science fiction on the screen. *2001: A Space Odyssey* proved that a big-budget SF film could make money (even if its profitability waited on a reputation for being a great movie to attend stoned). *Star Wars* demonstrated that an SF film could make BIG profits and ushered in an era when almost all the biggest money-making movies were science fiction or fantasy: *E.T.*, *Close Encounters of the Third Kind*, the *Star Wars* sequels and prequels, *Jurassic Park* and its sequels, *Independence Day*, *Batman*, *Raiders of the Lost Ark*, *Ghostbusters*, *Ghost*, *Back to the Future*, *The Matrix* and its sequels, *Harry Potter*, *The Fellowship of the Ring....*

But none of these films do much for science fiction, or the realizing of published science fiction: they are better as films than as SF. The year *Star Wars* was released, a panel of authors and editors at the World Science Fiction Convention in Phoenix debated whether the great popularity of that film would lead viewers to the reading of science fiction. Opinions were mixed, but the results were not: although publication and sales of SF, fantasy, and horror (often overlapping and lumped together) soared in succeeding decades, the increase was in media-related *Star Wars* and *Star Trek* novels, and novelizations of almost every other SF TV series and film. One editor commented that he thought these texts were more like memory books than novels. More recently, fantasy, which once was SF's poor relation, has begun to out-publish and out-sell its once dominant brother. Part of that transformation can be traced to the popularity of Tolkien's remarkable trilogy and other best-selling fantasy novels of the 1970s, but that is another story.

The statement I made in 1975 in *Alternate Worlds: The Illustrated History of Science Fiction* still seems appropriate: whatever virtues SF film may have, they are not SF virtues. When I attended a preview showing of *Star Wars*, for instance, it was the only film I ever attended at which the audience stood up and applauded at its conclusion. But *Star Wars* was an homage to 1930s SF serial films, with more contemporary SF iconography, and was, at best, a fairy tale in which a band of heroes rescues an abducted princess from an evil warlock and destroys the castle from which the warlock and his emperor have been oppressing the people. *E.T.* is a lost-animal variant of *Lassie, Come Home*.

To be sure, SF film is growing up, and *Blade Runner*, *Dark City*, and *The Matrix* are tackling the difficult task (once thought impossible until Stanley Kubrick, with the first half hour of *2001*, proved that the film-making mantra was wrong) of filming ideas. The tinsel screen still has a long way to go before it catches up with print SF, but films such as these offer hope.

IMPORTANT PRODUCTIONS IN THE HISTORY OF THE SF FILM

1898 *An Astronomer's Dream* (Méliès)
1899 *She* (Méliès)
1902 *A Trip to the Moon* (Méliès)
1906 *The ? Motorist* (Booth)
1909 *A Trip to Jupiter* (Pathe)
1910 *A Trip to Mars* (Edison)
1919 *The First Men in the Moon* (Leigh)
1924 *Aëlita* (Protazanov)
1925 *The Lost World* (Hoyt)
1926 *Metropolis* (Lang)
1929 *The Woman in the Moon* (Lang)
1930 *Just Imagine* (Butler)
1931 *Frankenstein* (Whale)
1932 *The Island of Lost Souls* (Kenton)
1933 *King Kong* (Cooper/Schoedsack)
1933 *The Invisible Man* (Whale)
1933 *Deluge* (Feist)
1934 *Trans-Atlantic Tunnel* (Elvey)
1936 *Things to Come* (Menzies)
1936 *Flash Gordon* serial

1937 *Lost Horizon* (Capra)
1940 *Buck Rogers* serial (Henry)
1950 *Destination Moon* (Pichel)
1951 *When Worlds Collide* (Mate)
1951 *The Thing from Another World* (Hawks)
1951 *The Day the Earth Stood Still* (Wise)
1951 *The Man in the White Suit* (Mackendrick)
1953 *The War of the Worlds* (Haskin)
1954 *1984* (Anderson)
1955 *20,000 Leagues Under the Sea* (Fleischer)
1956 *Forbidden Planet* (Wilcox)
1956 *Invasion of the Body Snatchers* (Siegel)
1957 *The Incredible Shrinking Man* (Arnold)
1958 *The Wonderful Invention* (Zeman)
1960 *The Time Machine* (Pal)
1960 *Village of the Damned* (Rilla)
1963 *The Day of the Triffids* (Sekely)
1964 *From the Earth to the Moon* (Haskin)
1964 *Dr. Strangelove* (Kubrick)
1965 *Alphaville* (Godard)
1965 *The 10th Victim* (Petri)
1966 *Fahrenheit 451* (Truffaut)
1966 *Fantastic Voyage* (Fleischer)
1967 *Barbarella* (Vadim)
1968 *2001: A Space Odyssey* (Kubrick)
1968 *Planet of the Apes* (Schaffner)
1968 *Charly* (Nelson)
1970 *Colossus: The Forbin Project* (Sargent)
1971 *A Clockwork Orange* (Kubrick)
1971 *The Andromeda Strain* (Wise)
1971 *THX 1138* (Lucas)
1972 *Silent Running* (Trumbull)
1973 *Soylent Green* (Fleischer)
1973 *Westworld* (Crichton)
1974 *Young Frankenstein* (Brooks)
1974 *Zardoz* (Boorman)
1975 *A Boy and His Dog* (Jones)
1975 *The Land that Time Forgot* (Connor)
1975 *Rollerball* (Jewison)
1975 *The Stepford Wives* (Forbes)
1976 *The Food of the Gods* (Gordon)
1976 *Logan's Run* (Anderson)
1976 *Futureworld* (Heffron)

1976 *The Man Who Fell to Earth* (Roeg)

1977 *Close Encounters of the Third Kind* (Spielberg)

1977 *Demon Seed* (Cammell)

1977 *The Island of Dr. Moreau* (Taylor)

1977 *Star Wars* (Lucas)

1978 *Superman* (Donner)

1978 *The Boys from Brazil* (Schaffner)

1978 *Invasion of the Body Snatchers* (Kaufman)

1979 *Alien* (Scott)

1979 *Time After Time* (Meyer)

1979 *Star Trek: The Motion Picture* (Wise)

1979 *The Black Hole* (Nelson)

1979 *Buck Rogers in the 25th Century* (Haller)

1980 *The Empire Strikes Back* (Kershner)

1980 *Flash Gordon* (Hodges)

1980 *Altered States* (Russell)

1981 *Superman II* (Donner)

1981 *The Road Warrior* (Miller)

1981 *Quest for Fire* (Annaud)

1982 *E.T., the Extraterrestrial* (Spielberg)

1982 *Blade Runner* (Scott)

1982 *Star Trek II: The Wrath of Khan* (Meyer)

1982 *Tron* (Lisberger)

1982 *Conan the Barbarian* (Milius)

1982 *The Thing* (Carpenter)

1983 *Return of the Jedi* (Marquand)

1983 *Twilight Zone: The Movie* (Miller/Landis/Dante/
Spielberg)

1983 *The Day After* (Meyer)

1983 *The Dead Zone* (Cronenberg)

1984 *Dune* (Lynch)

1984 *2010* (Hyams)

1984 *1984* (Radford)

1984 *Starman* (Carpenter)

1984 *The Terminator* (Cameron)

1984 *Star Trek III: The Search For Spock* (Nimoy)

1984 *Iceman* (Schepisi)

1984 *Brother from Another Planet* (Sayles)

1984 *Repo Man* (Cox)

1985 *Back to the Future* (Zemeckis)

1985 *Brazil* (Gilliam)

1985 *Cocoon* (Howard)

1985 *Enemy Mine* (Petersen)

1985 *Lifeforce* (Hooper)
1985 *Mad Max Beyond Thunderdome* (Miller)
1986 *Aliens* (Cameron)
1986 *Peggy Sue Got Married* (Coppola)
1986 *The Fly* (Cronenberg)
1986 *Invaders from Mars* (Hooper)
1986 *Star Trek IV: The Voyage Home* (Nimoy)
1987 *Innerspace* (Dante)
1987 *Predator* (McTiernan)
1987 *Robocop* (Verhoeven)
1987 *The Running Man* (Glaser)
1988 *Alien Nation* (Baker)
1988 *Big* (Marshall)
1989 *The Abyss* (Cameron)
1989 *Back to the Future II* (Zemeckis)
1989 *Honey, I Shrunk the Kids* (Johnston)
1989 *Millennium* (Anderson)
1989 *The Navigator: A Medieval Odyssey* (Ward)
1989 *Star Trek V: The Final Frontier* (Shatner)
1990 *Back to the Future III* (Zemeckis)
1990 *Edward Scissorhands* (Burton)
1990 *The Handmaid's Tale* (Schlöndorff)
1990 *Total Recall* (Verhoeven)
1991 *Terminator 2: Judgment Day* (Cameron)
1991 *Star Trek VI: The Undiscovered Country* (Meyer)
1992 *Alien 3* (Fincher)
1993 *Jurassic Park* (Spielberg)
1994 *Star Trek: Generations* (Carson)
1994 *Stargate* (Emmerich)
1995 *Johnny Mnemonic* (Longo)
1995 *Waterworld* (Reynolds, Costner)
1995 *12 Monkeys* (Gilliam)
1996 *Independence Day* (Emmerich)
1996 *Mars Attacks!* (Burton)
1996 *Star Trek: First Contact* (Frakes)
1996 *Escape from LA* (Carpenter)
1997 *The Postman* (Costner)
1997 *Contact* (Zemeckis)
1997 *The Lost World: Jurassic Park* (Spielberg)
1997 *Men in Black* (Sonnenfeld)
1997 *The Fifth Element* (Besson)
1997 *Gatttaca* (Niccol)

1998 *Lost in Space* (Hopkins)

1998 *The X Files* (Bowman)

1998 *Deep Impact* (Leder)

1998 *Armageddon* (Bay)

1998 *Star Trek: Insurrection* (Frakes)

1998 *Dark City* (Proyas)

1999 *Star Wars Episode I: The Phantom Menace* (Lucas)

1999 *The Matrix* (Wachowski brothers)

1999 *The Thirteenth Floor* (Rusnak)

1999 *eXistenZ* (Cronenberg)

2000 *Red Planet* (Hoffman)

2000 *Mission to Mars* (De Palma)

2000 *Dune* miniseries (Harrison)

2000 *X-Men* (Singer)

2000 *Supernova* (Hill, Coppola)

2000 *The Sixth Day* (Spottiswoode)

2001 *Jurassic Park III* (Johnston)

2001 *Planet of the Apes* (Burton)

2001 *Artificial Intelligence: AI* (Spielberg)

2001 *Vanilla Sky* (Crowe)

2002 *Minority Report* (Spielberg)

2002 *Men in Black II* (Sonnenfeld)

2002 *Star Wars Episode II: Attack of the Clones* (Lucas)

2002 *Signs* (Shyamalan)

2002 *Spiderman* (Raimi)

2002 *The Ring* (Verbinski)

2002 *Solaris* (Soderbergh)

2002 *Star Trek: Nemesis* (Baird)

2003 *X-Men 2: X-Men United* (Singer)

2003 *Children of Dune* mini-series (Yaitanes)

2003 *The Matrix: Reloaded* (Wachowski brothers)

2003 *The Matrix: Revolutions* (Wachowski brothers)

BURROUGHS AND CASPAK
Mike Resnick

Edgar Rice Burroughs was a pulp writer. That's not a pejorative; so were Raymond Chandler and Ray Bradbury, to name a pair of writers who stack up to any temporary darling of the New York Literary Establishment.

I'll tell you something else, too. Burroughs wrote from 1912 to 1948, and while almost all of the Pulitzer Prize winners from those years are long since out of print, just about every word of fiction Burroughs wrote—and that covers more than sixty novels—is still available.

Even today, kids can (and frequently do) pick up a seventy-five-year-old Tarzan or Mars book and not find it at all archaic or old-fashioned. So perhaps it might be interesting to try to analyze exactly why his work has outlived that of almost all his contemporaries.

Well, to begin with, Burroughs was not a highly erudite man—and strangely, that worked in his favor. He grew up in an era where flowery prose was a sign of high literary skill, where fashionable authors never used a one-syllable word if they could find a five-syllable synonym. Burroughs, on the other hand, was inspired to write his earliest novels when he read the pulp magazines in which his company's ads appeared and decided he could do better. The pulps were written for the widest possible audience, which meant that the very best pulp authors, unlike the more fashionable literary authors, were all but invisible. Burroughs is hardly intrusive in his first few books, and totally unintrusive for his last sixty or so.

So...simple, accessible language was his first virtue. But a lot of authors had that. What other skills did he possess?

For starters, the man had an inborn sense of pacing. He wrote action/adventure stories, and that meant they had to *move*. And move they did. His first effort, *A Princess of Mars*, shows him groping for the quickest way to get from point A to point B (and not doing all that well in the first half)...but by the time he wrote *The Gods of Mars* a year later, he instinctively knew how to start his story off at a gallop and then increase its speed through each subsequent chapter. A few books into his career he developed the technique not just of ending each chapter with a cliffhanger, but of moving from one viewpoint character to another.

(Is an unarmed Tarzan facing a pride of hungry lions at the end of Chapter 12? Okay, let's see how Jane is doing in Chapter 13. Is she one grope away from a fate worse than death? Time to read Chapter 14 and see how Tarzan's faring.)

Another thing at which Burroughs excelled was the creation of evocative languages—and he created them by the bunch. From the guttural language of Tarzan's great apes to the stately tongue of ancient Mars, probably no author, not even J. R. R. Tolkien, was better at creating words that sounded like what they meant. (Think of an elephant trumpeting; what could he be called but Tantor? And how could a snake be anything other than Hista? What better name for the king of the apes, a creature that half-barks and half-growls its primitive language, than Kerchak?)

Burroughs' style and word use also evolved over the years. There is actually a "methinks" in an early Mars book; you'll never find that word again—or anything remotely like it—after 1918.

He created admirable characters, but they weren't perfect. Even Tarzan, the greatest of them all, was not without his weaknesses. Yes, he could stare Death in the face without flinching—but he also had more than a passing fondness for absinthe, cigarettes, mad queens, and High Priestesses of the Flaming God. John Carter, Warlord of Mars, can accurately be said to be the greatest braggart on two worlds. Carson of Venus was strong and likable, but just this side of learning-disabled.

But all of Burroughs' heroes, from the smartest to the dumbest, held to a firm Victorian moral code, all knew the difference between right and wrong and invariably chose the right—and in this day of anti-heroes and body-count movies, those values are perhaps more admirable than ever.

So...he could pace, he was accessible, he was a brilliant inventor of languages, and he told emotionally satisfying morality plays in an action/adventure framework. Anything else?

Well, yes. He had the capacity to imagine fully-fleshed worlds by the carload. With no predecessors to build upon—he had far less in common with Wells and Verne and Kipling than with such pulpsters as Zane Grey—he created Tarzan's mythical Africa, John Carter's Mars, Carson Napier's Venus, David Innes' Pellucidar, and such fascinating stand-alone works as *The Moon Maid*, *The Cave Girl*, *Beyond the Farthest Star*, *The Monster Men*, and dozens of others.

Perhaps the most imaginative single novel Burroughs ever wrote is *The Land That Time Forgot*.

It's a book with an interesting history. Burroughs originally wrote it as three novellas, "The Land That Time Forgot," "The People That Time Forgot," and "Out of Time's Abyss," which appeared in the August, October and December, 1918 issues of *Blue Book Magazine*. The novel itself didn't actually appear until 1924, when McClurg brought it out with a brilliant cover and four interior sepia plates by the artist who remains most closely associated with Burroughs' work, J. Allen St. John.

Grosset & Dunlap reprinted it a number of times, and Canaveral Press brought it out in 1962 with seven illos by Mahlon Blaine, an artist singularly unsuited to fantastic adventure. Then Ace Books split the novel back into its three constituent novellas and brought each out as stand-alone paperbacks, with brilliant cover illustrations by Roy Krenkel. An entire generation of Burroughs fans thinks that the Caspak adventure constitutes three short novels, so it's very nice to see them back together here as a single novel, as Burroughs meant them to be.

Caspak is probably Burroughs' most intriguing concept. It was also one of his most courageous, coming out in magazine form some years ahead of the Scopes trial.

Burroughs often took some scientific notion that was momentarily popular but doomed to be discarded in history's ash heap and created a world or a society around it. Percival Lowell's Martian canals were among the major features of Barsoom (Burroughs' name for Mars). It was once assumed that Venus was a jungle planet, and his four-plus Venus novels show a jungle world, with the continents separated by raging oceans (a logical conclusion, given that the world was totally covered by clouds.)

For Caspak, Burroughs took evolution, which was still being argued (though a little less each year) and gave it a unique twist. We have seven categories of men: Ho-lus (apes), Alus (speechless men), Bo-lus (club men), Sto-lus (hatchet men), Band-lus (spear men), Kro-lus (bow and arrow men), and Galus (rope men). Notice that the various levels on Caspak's scale of evolution depend upon the sophistication of the tribes' weaponry. This theory is a forerunner, by well over forty years, of the now-accepted dogma, first presented in Robert Ardrey's bestselling *African Genesis* (Athenium, 1961), that man did not make weapons, but, quite the contrary, weapons made man. Man, according to Ardrey and his panel of experts, has evolved from a tribe of killer apes, and feels a territorial instinct far more strongly than a sexual drive, necessitating the need for weapons to protect what is his. Nothing that Louis and Mary Leakey discovered in Olduvai Gorge contradicts this notion; their small museum there is nothing but a display of million-year-old tools and weaponry.

(This is not to say that Burroughs wouldn't have been astounded by the similarity of his flight of fictional fancy and the current thinking. But this is something science fiction writers have tried to explain to the public ever since there has been a genre of science fiction: it is not our job or our function to predict the future. It happens now and then, but almost always by accident. We are *fiction* writers, and we use the future as metaphor.)

Caspak, thanks to Burroughs' notion of applied evolution, is far more interesting that most mythical lost islands (King Kong's South Pacific home comes to mind). He was an action/adventure writer, churning out stories for the pulps (and that pulp audience that was willing to follow him to hardcover), but he felt it wasn't enough to run the hero up a tree and spend the rest of the story throwing rocks at him. He also gave the readers something to think about.

For example, the Galus state that they, being the seventh step in the human scale of evolution, must come up *from the beginning* seven times—and this isn't some metaphysical gobbledegook, but (within the context of the novel) an absolute fact. From this, we can assume that the Kro-lus must come up six times, the Band-lus five times, and so on. And obviously, the changes from amoeba to dinosaur to mammal—remember: this was written three-quarters of a century before we knew that a comet caused the extinction of the dinosaurs—must occur pretty much the same way, albeit with far more steps. An interesting question arises: since the tribes of men are always hostile to one another, how can the lower orders have any knowledge of the higher ones? How can a Bo-lu be aware that Kro-lus and Galus even exist?

There's an easy enough answer, even if Burroughs never quite got around to supplying it: They obviously possess an inherent sense of direction in relation to the evolutionary pattern, much as the first primitive men knew, without instruction, how to copulate and how to suckle their young. A woodchuck that has yet to see its first winter instinctively stores food in preparation for it; it seems only logical that an Alu instinctively knows the scale on which he will ascend.

Okay, I plead guilty.

To what?

To what all Burroughs fans love: filling in the blanks. It's entirely conceivable that Burroughs would have given you the same rationalization I just did. It's equally conceivable that he never gave it a moment's thought. The thing is, such rationalizations would have slowed down the narrative, and Burroughs not only knew what his strengths were, he also knew, better than most writers, exactly what his audience wanted. He was no H. G. Wells or Jules Verne, and one of his greatest assets was that he never tried to emulate them.

In the world of science fiction fandom, there is something known as a fanzine, which simply means an amateur publication. There are close to 800 titles published in any given year. Once in a while a fanzine will be devoted to the writings of a single writer. Usually such things last seven or eight or ten issues, and then the editor and his staff run out of interesting things to say. (The two devoted to me ran one and six issues, respectively, which was about par for the course.)

But Burroughs fanzines are forever, or so it sometimes seems. The Hugo-winning *ERB-dom* ran more than ninety issues in its first incarnation, and was later revived. *ERBania* has been publishing regularly for close to forty years. *The Burroughs Bulletin* began back in the 1940s and is still around as a slick-paper quarterly with a four-color cover. There have been literally dozens of other Burroughs fanzines, and when they go defunct it's usually for lack of money rather than lack of material.

Which brings us back to Caspak. Do you know how much food for thought there is in this book? Take the pterodactyl. Does he know that he must not fly too far north? There's three or four argumentative articles for the Burroughs fanzines right there.

Or take Caspak itself. What if it had extended another hundred miles to the north? What kind of successor to present-day man would Burroughs have placed there? Bam! Another dozen articles.

How about the actual geography? Caspak provides hot springs for its prehistoric reptiles; does it also provide glaciers to make the mammoths and the sabre-tooth tigers feel at home?

Now, please understand: I am not saying that Edgar Rice Burroughs was our best writer of imaginative fiction. Far from it. But no one since Burroughs, not E. E. "Doc" Smith, not Robert A. Heinlein, not Isaac Asimov, not Sir Arthur C. Clarke, has created a greater number of wildly popular imaginative series. He was followed by many better, more subtle, more erudite writers—most of whom built upon his foundation—and it is true that if he were starting out today, the field has evolved enough that he might have some serious difficulty breaking into print.

But so what? He was the first, and he is still very readable and very popular, and what more need you ask of a pioneer?

THE MATRIX TRILOGY
Adam Roberts

The rush to critical judgment that attended the release of the first *Matrix* movie in 1999 has been tempered, now, by the release of two sequels: *Matrix: Reloaded* and *Matrix: Revolutions* (both in 2003). Many who saw the first film as a conceptual breakthrough in the world of SF cinema were less impressed by the two sequels. What was once seen as clean and vigorous has become self-indulgent, mired in unnecessary complexities and abstruse pretension. Are the two follow-up films inferior to the first? Is there anything interesting going on in *Reloaded* and *Revolutions*, or are they merely exercises in Hollywood cash-in?

The answer is not straightforward. I want to argue that the films manage some brilliant explorations of aesthetics, erotics and technology; but I suspect that few will be convinced. The least we must say, however, is that the *Matrix* phenomenon should at least be read as a whole: not as one film, but as three (plus nine animated shorts, plus the video game *Enter the Matrix*, plus graphic novels, Web-text, merchandising, the whole paratextual business). To simplify what would otherwise be a very complex business, I'd like to concentrate on only the trilogy of cinematic releases, and to suggest ways of reading them as a whole—to try and reach some understanding of what is "at stake" in these three films. In a sense I am proposing a defense of the *Matrix* trilogy as a trilogy.

1. SURFACES AND DEPTHS

There are, of course, many different ways of reading texts, and any critic needs to be up front about his or her particular perspective. One approach would be to redescribe the films, concentrating on the content of each picture (character, story, imagined world) and judging them according to criteria such as "plausibility," "complexity," "originality" and so on. Another—very popular with fans of the *Matrix* films—would be to "decode" the films: to distinguish between what the films *appear* on the surface to be about, and what they are *actually* deep down saying.

There are many examples of this second critical approach to the films. To say, for instance, that the *Matrix* represents a Christian allegory is to employ this surface-depth model. On the surface the films show a number of characters rushing around an imagined world in which humanity is trapped by machine-intelligences in a virtual-reality prison; but this "surface" representation contains certain deliberately-placed clues as to the "true" meaning of the film. The characters have "significant" names "Neo/Anderson" ("the New Man," "the Son of Man"); "Trinity" (Father, Son and Holy Ghost). Anderson is, we assume, born into the Matrix; but he is "born again" after the intervention of the John-Baptist-like Morpheus. He is revealed as the messiah, come to save humanity from a damnation it doesn't even realize it is enduring. He confronts the authorities, is betrayed by a Judas-figure, is killed, but returns from the dead with miraculous powers. In other words, he is a type of Christ (the Son of Man) whose romance with Trinity embodies, after the allegorical manner of the Song of Songs, the connection between church and godhead. His final sacrifice, at the end of *Revolutions*, is figured as a cruciform ascension. And so on.

There's nothing wrong with this sort of reading, if it appeals to you. But, as interpretation, it is severely limiting: once the film has been decoded along these lines there is little more to be said—or, to put it another way, assuming this to be the "real" meaning of the film, what have the Wachowskis gained by filming a science fiction narrative rather than simply a life of Christ? Emphasising perceived mythic underpinnings in fact takes us away from the specificity of the films themselves.

Another such "surface-depth" reading (by an earlier version of the present author) decodes the film as:

> surely one of the most Marxist movies ever to come out of Hollywood…if we ask what the "Matrix" is, then the answer is that it *is* ideology in the Marxist sense of a fiction obscuring the truth of exploitation. In fact, this film articulates a more thorough-going Althusserian or Jamesonian sense of what ideology is: "the Matrix" is more than a set of false beliefs about reality (or false consciousness)—it *is* reality, it conditions and defines how the people caught up in it themselves think and act.[4]

---

[4] Adam Roberts, *Fredric Jameson* (London: Routledge, 2000), p. 38.

But it is difficult to believe that this sort of reading can really account for the extraordinary power this movie exerts over so many of its viewers. Something else, we suspect, is going on here.

More, reading the film in this manner makes the mistake of falling into line with the premise of the film itself—which is to say, with the paranoid idea that there is something "behind the veil" of appearances. This taps in to one of the main currents of Western philosophical thought, namely as far as the universe goes a distinction must be made between *what it actually is* and *what it only appears to be*. Most Western philosophers since the Ancient Greeks have interrogated the cosmos in these terms. What is behind the world of appearances? What is the nature of the "reality" that is hidden behind the veil? If you are Heraclitus it is "flow"; if you are Plato it is the pure and eternal realm of the Forms; if you are a neo-Platonist, a Christian or a Muslim it is "God"; if you are Schopenhauer (or his disciple, Nietzsche) it is "Will"; if you are a Marxist it is the revolutionary potential of the proletariat, obscured by the ideology of the ruling classes; and if you're Freud it's the unconscious and its currency of sex and death.

Three influential writers—William Blake, William Burroughs and Philip K. Dick—shared a more paranoid (or, if you agree with them, a less illusioned) vision of this state of things; and their influence is apparent in the world the Wachowskis have shaped in these films. To those three poets the world of appearance is a dungeon, a trap, a hellish adventure, something to be despised and resisted. The reality of transcendent apprehension is obscured by these appearances. We must break on through to the other side, we must disarrange the logic of the seeming-world and shatter it, we must *free our minds*. We must (in Blake's resonant words) create a system, or be enslaved by another man's. This sounds, of course, very like the storyline of the *Matrix* trilogy, with Neo as representative man trapped in illusion and eventually breaking on through to the other side.

But if the *Matrix* trilogy makes reference to this Blakean or Philip Dickian world-view, it also goes out of its way to reference a body of more recent thought—postmodernism. Postmodernism refuses to play the surface-depth game. If you are a postmodernist then there is nothing at all behind the world of appearances, there are only simulacra, surfaces, rhizomes exploring horizontally and making interesting connections. The *Matrix* plays games with the work of Jean Baudrillard, the celebrated French postmodern thinker ("Welcome," says Morpheus, "to the desert of the Real," citing a Baudrillardian catchphrase; just as Neo has a copy of *Simulacra and Simulation* on his bookshelves). Is this the "key" to the films?

Baudrillard suggests that, under the cultural logic of postmodernity, simulations no longer copy reality, but *precede* it: Disneyland is in a sense more real than America; we care more about the characters on TV soap operas than we do about our own neighbours and so on—the "real" becomes a desert, and we inhabit the shiny surfaces of simulation.[5] But the force of this interpretative perspective is exactly that it does not provide a "key" with which to decode the films. To read the films as postmodern is to pay attention not to imagined depths, but precisely to the shining surfaces of the film; its *form*, its succession of visual movement-images and time-images, its shape, the contours of its cinematic trajectory. This, I think, is the best way to approach these films.

2. CLIMAX AND ANTICLIMAX: *THE MATRIX* AND *MATRIX: RELOADED*

What might turn up if we read the trilogy on the surface rather than for imagined "depths", if we concentrated on form rather than content? What is it that these films embody? Would such a reading capture the disaffection of many fans, for whom the brilliance of the first *Matrix* film was followed by a growing sense of disillusionment as the sequels emerged? Can *The Matrix: Reloaded* escape the charge that it is nothing more than a disappointment?

The first *Matrix* movie was certainly a tough act to follow—an astonishing piece of cinema, although cinema in only one mode: high-powered kinetic drama, big exciting actions set-pieces layered with a big exciting premise and intoxicating cod-philosophising. Its glory is that it is so exhilarating a film. *The Matrix: Reloaded* is not exhilarating in the same way, which is one of the reasons for the tinge of disappointment recorded by many fans and critics. But this is surely because the second film was not setting out to exhilarate in the same way, or to put it more precisely, the film is not "about" exhilaration in the same way. *Matrix: Reloaded* is a designedly slower piece of work, cinema in more elegiac mode that creates a pervasive mood of difficult-to-pin-down sadness.

---

[5] Dino Felluga and Andrew Gordon debate the importance of Baudrillard to the first *Matrix* film in "*The Matrix*: Paradigm of Postmodernism or Intellectual Poseur?," in Glenn Yeffeth (ed.) *Taking the Red Pill: Science, Philosophy and Religion in* The Matrix (Chichester: Summersdale 2003), pp. 85-123

This mood must be explained as more than simply the plot device of Trinity's ever-impending death—more than this because the film is about more than death (although it is also about that): it is about what happens *after* we get what we strive for.

Indeed, the mood of the second film is melancholic where the first was thrilling, precisely because it dramatizes this dilemma. We can put this several ways. One is to compare the trajectories of the two films.

In the first picture an ordinary man, unhappy and stuck in a life he does not enjoy, finds out first that the world is not what he thought it was: the boredom of his existence is replaced by adventure and excitement; then he discovers that he is much more important than he thought; then he performs acts of unimaginable heroism; then he discovers that he is more than just important, that he is indeed the "One," the savior of the world, and gets the girl.

The second movie picks up the story from this point. But this point is exactly the moment at which, in the western tradition, stories traditionally stop: the savior has come; all lived happily ever after. What else? The unimagined pleasures of paradise?—these sorts of pleasure must remain unimagined, or else they will start to seem necessarily anticlimactic (what if the pleasures of heaven become a bit monotonous? A bit *boring*? What if existence in paradise is in fact a type of blissful *depression*?). *The Matrix: Reloaded* takes the bold step of taking Neo's apotheosis simply in its stride. He is now the messiah, but life goes on—indeed, it goes on in a lower key than it did in the first film. Life in Zion, for all the frenetic dancing of the central party scene, is grim and incarceratory. As messiah Neo can do little for the misery of the ordinary people who throng around him. Neo's return from life in the first movie was a powerful and transcendent moment: his existence after that moment of transcendence is, it seems, characterized by forms of impotence and anxiety, most acutely the anxiety that the woman he loves is doomed to die. The first film was about the build up to the revelation of the messiah; the second film is the come-down afterward.

This is highlighted by the *form* of the two movies. *The Matrix* builds expertly through a complex plot and a number of increasingly exciting set-pieces to a magnificent cinematic climax: Neo and Trinity rescue Morpheus from the custody of the agents through hails of bullets, Neo fights Agent Smith, is killed and comes back to life as the One. This is where the film ends—which is to say, the form of the piece expresses a well-modulated crescendo of excitement building continually to a final climax. The shape of *The Matrix: Reloaded* is different. In the second movie the big climax occurs two-thirds of the way through the film: the marvellous chase sequence on the Freeway. But after this detailed and thrilling set-piece the film's actual conclusion inevitably feels a little underpowered.

The plot coalesces around the need to get Neo into a certain room at a certain time: but this can only be accomplished by the destruction of two power stations in the city, with various other obstacles to be overcome. But, when compared with the climax of the first movie, this adventure, its vicissitudes (the deaths of key figures in the plan, Trinity's desperate riding to the rescue) appear on the screen in an almost desultory fashion. The whole action sequence is then interrupted by a lengthy, slow-paced dialogue between Neo and the Architect in which concepts and language of rebarbative difficulty are exchanged, draining away narrative momentum further. But this can be read as deliberate device: by shifting the climax of this movie back towards the narrative midpoint the Wachowski brothers articulate in cinematic terms the experience of existing post-climactically.

Other features in the film reinforce this sense. At the film's conclusion we learn that the machines have fought a great battle with the defenders of Zion; but we are not shown this apparently climactic conflict (despite the fact that the film has spared no expense in realizing massive set-piece scenes when it wants to). Instead we are shown only the despondent bedraggled remnants of the defense force, icons of postconflict disappointment.

On a smaller scale we see a similar pattern all through the film. At the beginning of the picture Morpheus disobeys a direct order: it seems he will face court martial, be thrown in the brig; but these consequences are simply elided. The "burly brawl" in which Neo fights a hundred copies of "Agent Smith" is an exciting set-piece with its own anxieties (can even the super-capable Neo deal with so many "agents"?): but the fight is so lengthily extended as to pass the point of local excitement and become, whilst still arresting and weirdly beautiful, rather monotonous: and it ends not with a resolution, but with Neo simply flying away leaving the rather nonplussed-looking Smiths to wander away. My response on first seeing this sequence was one of excitement, but as the fight persisted on the screen, went on and went on, I found myself thinking that it was going on too long. Only afterwards did it occur to me that this going-on-too-long, this dwelling on the moment *after* the peak of excitement was passed, could be the whole point of the film.

In another scene Neo, Morpheus and Trinity must get past some powerful guardians to find a "keymaker": these guardians are, it seems, hangovers from a previous version of the Matrix, and cannot be persuaded or overpowered: until, in a strangely oblique move, one of them (played by Monica Belucci) decides to give away the keymaker in return for—one kiss from Neo himself. This scene plays oddly, partly because it makes little sense in narrative terms, but also because the price Neo pays for the crucial "keymaker" is so much less than we were expecting. Because, in other words, there is an element of anticlimax about the encounter. These hangover programs live as languid, decadent aristocrats; bored and unimpressed with existence. Their being is the very locus of disillusionment.

So frequently repeated is this trope of expectation-excitement-disillusionment that it dominates the form and mood of the whole picture. In other words disillusionment is precisely what *The Matrix* dramatizes: Neo lives inside the Matrix; Morpheus comes to reveal that this life is an illusion—which is to say, he dis-illusions him. Of course this disillusionment is a mournful as well as a truthful condition (hence the ascetic, pared-down, miserable life inside the Nebuchadnezzar, as also in Zion). Indeed, the Wachowski's boldest aesthetic experiment is to try and represent disillusionment, anti-climax, in the idiom of the climax-addicted form of Hollywood action-blockbuster.

After all, in its purest form the Hollywood Blockbuster—take for example *Speed*—finds a format that keeps the anxiety-excitement as high-pitched and increasing for as long as possible (in that movie when the bus is successfully stopped the film scrabbles with an addict's desperation for more chase-thrills, hurrying into the subway). *The Matrix: Reloaded* is too canny to do this. It is a text that knows that after climax (Becoming the messiah! Connecting with the woman you love!) comes after-climax. What happens *after* you transcend? What if, instead of ascending to even higher levels of bliss and thrill, you return to the level of the ordinary, the unexciting, the melancholic?

A theological shorthand for this might be to characterize *The Matrix* as a Jewish and *The Matrix: Reloaded* as a Christian film. For Jews the messiah is yet to come, and can be looked forward to as the moment when all injustice, misery and dissatisfaction will be overcome. Christianity is based on a radical revision of this powerful human yearning—so radical and unsettling, in fact, that it may be the case that many Christians prefer not to think it through: *what if the messiah comes and nothing much changes as a result?* Judaism, theologically, operates in the space of moving-towards-climax; Christianity operates necessarily in the space of post-climax, which is to say, of anticlimax. The common Christian story of the second coming of Christ is a desperate attempt to fill the psychic gap left by this radically anticlimactic theology, by co-opting Jewish theology to its own ends: but it is deeply flawed. If the messiah comes more than once, why only twice? Why not a hundred, a million, or an infinite number of times? And if that is the case, then doesn't it fatally dilute the actual appearance and sacrifice of Christ?

This seems to me a more fertile approach of religious perspectives when reading these films: not that they are ready-to-decode allegories of Christian (or Gnostic, or Marxist) myth, but that they inhabit the forms of moving-towards-climax and moving-away-from-climax in a trajectory of a particular cinematic form.

3. *MATRIX: REVOLUTIONS* AND COPULATION

Indeed, it might be a mistake even to mention "religious" readings of the film. The films work somatically rather than transcendentally: which is to say, they are concerned with bodies rather than souls. A simpler way of describing the trilogy's trajectory of leading-to-climax and coming-down-from-climax would be to call it sexual.

The second and third films in the trilogy certainly make much more of the sexual component. What is, in the first film, a rather chaste courtship between Neo and Trinity becomes, in the second, a centrally placed sex scene, intercut with an orgiastic rave-dance in Zion. Trips into the Matrix to meet the "Frenchman" in films two and three take the protagonists into a series of sexually outré fetish clubs and environments. Is the climax of "becoming the one" simply a hypobolic externalization of individual sexual climax? This is not to say that the two films can be "decoded" to "mean" sex; but rather that they are constructed upon a model that formally reproduces and symbolizes the erotic trajectory.

But if that is so, then there is no need for a third movie: the build-up to orgasm and the come-down afterwards can be mapped perfectly effectively in two films.

What, then, is the status of the final film in the *Matrix* trilogy, *Matrix: Revolutions*? This is a specialized way of asking a question that many fans asked when the final film was released: what was the point? In what ways, if any, was this film required by the franchise? How did it fit? Was it superfluous?

Indeed, there is a disturbing surplus about this final film. There are myriad ways in which it not only does not answer the questions posed in the first two films but adds to a general sense of incoherence about the entire project. Here, in no special order, are some of the problems that struck me on viewing the third film in the trilogy, *Matrix: Revolutions*:

- The railway station in which Neo regains consciousness is described as linking "the real world and the Matrix." What, exactly, does this symbolic space link?

- Neo meets a married couple and their young daughter: How have these computer programs copulated, to produce a child? It is not our current understanding of computer programs that they are entities capable of generative sex.

- The father tells Neo that he and his wife have struck some deal with "the Frenchman" (figured in this movie more explicitly than in the last as a sexual pervert) to preserve the life of their child. We do not learn the nature of this deal, or what price has been paid by the parents or what the Frenchman has required them to do, except that they do not appear again in the movie.

- Morpheus and Trinity encounter the Oracle, but find that she is a different woman to the one they remember. How has this change happened? (We know, extratextually, that the actress who played the oracle died before the filming of the final movie: but the question is how is this change justified within the textual universe of the *Matrix* films themselves.)

- When "Smith" confronts the Oracle, his first words are "the mighty oracle, we meet at last," implying that they are strangers to one another. Later in the conversation she calls him a "bastard," and he replies, "You should know, Mom," which implies that Smith is the Oracle's son. How to reconcile this apparent contradiction?

- During his fight with Smith in the real world, Neo's eyes are burnt out: and yet he can still see Smith. How can this be? Or to put it another way: what is the actual nature of Neo's blinding?

- In his final battle with Smith inside the Matrix, Neo battles with a single individual Smith whilst hundreds of thousands of other Smiths stand silently watching. Why do they not simply swamp Neo in their multitude?

These problems are of a different nature to the more crassly discontinuous holes and errors in the plot, of which there were also various examples (for example: given that electromagnetic-pulse or "EMP" weapons are enormously more effective against the sentinels than bullets and shells, why has Zion not stockpiled such weaponry for use in a electronics-free forward hall? Why are the machines laboriously digging their own tunnel, instead of simply storming one of the existing tunnels? Since the cloud level blocking out the sun extends only a little way up into the atmosphere, wouldn't it make more sense to build tall structures, dirigibles or satellites to collect solar energy above the clouds than to construct the bizarrely elaborate machinery of the "fields" and the "Matrix"? Given that the defenses of the machine city can be circumvented simply by flying above these clouds, wouldn't it be possible for humans to send missiles raining down upon it from above?... I could go on).

These latter are instances, I think, of an inability to close the gap in terms of plot and conception, and are to be deplored because they erode the viewers' ability to enter imaginatively into the Wachowskis' imaginary universe. But the first list, I think, represents a much more interesting set of problems. Indeed, taken together, I think that they articulate the key problematic (to use the critical term) of the movie.

In other words, I'm suggesting that one reason critics have deplored the third movie is that it is, to one degree or another, incoherent: that it doesn't "add up," that it embodies a distracting surplus that cannot be reconciled with the overall premise of the original movie. In various ways, the problems bullet-pointed above all speak to precisely this disturbing or (we might say) monstrous surplus. It does not distort matters, I think, to see this as the true subject of the movie. According to this reading there's an inevitable falling-short in the very conception of this movie: what *Matrix: Revolutions* is actually about is, in a sense, precisely this monstrous surplus.

To revisit some of the second list of plot-holes I mentioned above. We might respond to the various problems of the relatively low-lying cloud layer by saying "it misses the point to wonder why technology hasn't dispersed these clouds, or utilized the air above them for vital solar energy, or why humanity hasn't shot missiles above the clouds to rain down on the machine city...clearly Neo and Trinity pass above the clouds to *grant Trinity one transcendental moment of beauty and comprehension before her death.*" In other words, the point of the clouds, and of the clear sky above them, is *symbolic* rather than actual.

The "turn to symbolism," as we might call it, is certainly much more overt in this film than in the previous two. It may even have reached the level where it is possible to appreciate the film *only* on its symbolic level. As I suggested earlier, a movie that presents itself "on the surface" as a quest adventure, a war-movie, a series of events relating to certain characters (and which, largely, fails on those levels) can still be redeemed, say the fans, by reading it symbolically as a Christ-allegory, a meditation on karma, and so on. But what is interesting is the comprehensive way the *Matrix* trilogy also posits a secondary "symbolic" narrative that cuts across the "surface" level. If this is indeed how *Matrix: Revolutions* works, then perhaps what is most significant is not the tabulation of symbols themselves, but rather the very process of symbolization upon which the text embarks.

For example: Neo has his eyes burnt out, and (on the actual level of the story) needs Trinity to guide him to the machine city because he is blind. Yet when this happens we instantly transfer our reading of the scene to the symbolic level. Neo has, symbolically, become an Oedipus. Suddenly, various awkward or unexplained elements in the movie fall into place as parts of a symbolic Oedipal narrative. The film metaphorically represents a family dynamic: the Architect is Father, the Oracle is mother: Neo is son, with Smith his evil twin. Neo's blinding is actually a symbolic castration, the price he pays for entering into the libidinal conflict with the Name-of-the-Father (the Matrix itself, the Architect, the many fights with Smith) for the love of the Oracle ("without her we are lost"). The movies act out this family psychodrama, and from this central symbolic ur-text springs all the weirdly distorted sexual imagery of (especially) the latter two movies: the semi-naked rave in Zion intercut with Neo and Trinity's sex; the S&M club in which the Frenchman is to be found; the repeated images of penetration (Trinity's death), bodies tangling with bodies in conflict and so on.

But this is too facile. It presents yet another "decoding" of the trilogy (it's about God, it's about Marx—no, it's about *Oedipus*) which misses too much, leaves out too much surplus material. The *Matrix* trilogy resists such neat codification; or to put it another way, these films are in a vital sense *about* the monstrous surplus that overwhelms any pigeonholing reduction at the level of the symbolic. The Lacanian way of putting what I am trying to say would be that, whilst the movies of course enter into the logic of the symbolic to a certain extent, they do not and cannot wholly do so. Rather, as incoherent yet affecting visual texts as well as linear texts of narrative and concept, the films mediate the Imaginary and the Symbolic. Many of the films' images precisely cannot be reduced to the symbolic: they "work" (they move or thrill or disturb us) without our being able to explain exactly why, or even exactly what is going on. This is because the monstrous libidinal possibilities of the Imaginary are what power the film, and these possibilities make themselves plain exactly at those moments of textual fissure that I list above.

In other words this surplus is the whole point of *Matrix: Revolutions*. The reason why so many critics found it unsatisfactory is precisely that it cannot be reduced to a neat, all-encompassing symbolic reading. Not only is there a surplus at work; more particularly, this surplus is monstrous. It is libidinized surplus, which is to say, it is in a general sense "about" sex: but not in a way that can be simply reduced to a particular schema. Any such attempt to render the movies in terms of the Symbolic order will always, I think, fall short.

Take the railway station in which Neo regains consciousness, which is described as linking "the real world and the Matrix." What, exactly, does it link? Programs cannot run without hardware on which to exist; and there would be no logic in a connection that ported them simply into the external world. On another occasion the train station is described as linking "the machine world and the Matrix," but this also doesn't make sense: it suggests that the virtual space of the Matrix exactly mirrors the topographic spaces of the real world, such that the Matrix (generated for the "fields" of humans) and the Machine City are somehow separate. But this is not how virtual reality works: literal spaces scattered all over the globe (individual hard drives on innumerable individual computer) translate into a communal virtual space. This, of course, is what the internet is.

So, in fact, what the train station does is not link the Matrix space with some real or virtual other space, but rather stands as the principle of non-specific linkage. If the train line goes from the Matrix, then where does it go to? Only to the principle of the "surplus," to the Imaginary "Other" that resists symbolization. This surplus is reproductive, hence when Neo attempts to run out of it through the tunnel he simply reappears in it from the other side. Virtual space is neither actually nor metaphorically the same as actual space.

This is why it is the train station where Neo meets the Indian family; precisely because they are a family—the libidinal surplus is given form in the shape of the little Indian girl. The problem here is the inconceivability of computer programs begetting children—which is to say, programs having sex and conceiving. The most crucial question of all in understanding *Matrix: Revolutions* is this one: how can a computer program have sex?

The simple answer to that question is: they cannot. But in fact, the programs in the Matrix not only have sex (and produce children, like the Indian couple), they appear to relish their sex lives, and to pursue imaginatively perverse sex—from the Frenchman's wife's half-hearted seduction of Neo in *Matrix: Reloaded*, to the fetish club of *Matrix: Revolutions*. Indeed, it goes without saying that such "computer program sex" will be transgressive. Contemporary Lacanian theorist Slavoj Zizek addresses the "disappearance of sexual difference" and the increasingly jaded sense of contemporary sexual life in his book *On Belief*:

> How are we to get out of [this deadlock]? The standard way would be to try somehow to resurrect the transgressive erotic passion, following the well-known principle, first asserted in the tradition of courtly love, that the only true love is the transgressive prohibited one— we need new Prohibitions, so that a new Tristan and Isolde, or Romeo and Juliet will appear … The problem is that, in today's permissive society, transgression itself IS the norm.[6]

It's certainly true that the Frenchman's fetish club, and his wife's low-cut rubber dress (which seems only to be on screen in order to display her prodigious *décolletage*), seem oddly tame in *Matrix: Revolutions*. The whole scene has the feel, somehow, of trying too hard for shock value; and all the Frenchman's followers, in their various gimp gear, seem rather sweet than anything. Either our sexual mores are now so sophisticated that it takes more than a bondage nightclub to outrage us, or else the focus of transgression is somewhere else in this text. Not humans in rubber and gimp-masks (since that no longer strikes us as transgressive); but the very fact that computer programs experience erotic desire in the first place. The surplus sexuality is not to be located in the body at all, but in the machine.

---

[6] Slavoj Zizek, *On Belief* (London: Routledge, 2001), p. 41.

Think about computer copulation for a moment. One feature of computers is that they can reproduce or "clone" material with perfect ease (simply drag down a "paste" menu, or press Control-P), where for humans such reproduction is a lengthy and costly business (sex, children and so on). Naturally this computer reproduction, figured in *Matrix: Revolutions* by Smith's endless identical self-replication, is asexual: an identical budding rather than the production of a new generation. Human reproduction introduces an element of change, which is the (evolutionary) point of it in the first place. This "element of change" is precisely the libidinal surplus, the thing that supplements the genetic material introduced by the two original parents. What's odd about the Indian couple is not that they have a child, but rather that the child is not identical to one or the other of them.

This change is also articulated in the new actor playing the Oracle. Like the original actor, she is an elderly black woman: which is to say, her change is not radical. But she is very obviously a different woman, not a lookalike, and this difference is noted by the characters with whom she interacts (Trinity puts it succinctly: "Who are you?"). It is more disconcerting than it might otherwise have been, because the Oracle plays such a central role in the film, both actually and symbolically— which is to say, both as an element of the plot, and as symbolic "mother" to the Matrix. (The Architect from *Matrix Reloaded*: "If I am the Matrix's father, she is indubitably its mother.") What is this difference? On the level of production, it is the necessary compromise necessitated by the death of the original actor. But on the level of the text, it embodies precisely this monstrous libidinal surplus: it is the extra, the supplemental "otherness" that structures the film as a whole.

The film traces the contours of the incestuous Oedipal trauma via this mother figure. Smith acknowledging the Oracle as "Mom" before he replicates himself once again via her body expresses this classic Freudian anxiety. Neo fighting Smith at the film's end comes at the same anxiety from a different angle: Smith by now, dominating the Matrix, has assumed the mantle of Name-of-the-Father. Neo fighting him is fighting symbolic father: he destroys his enemy by being destroyed himself— becoming assimilated by Smith, Neo spreads destruction via the symbolic castration of the multiple-Smiths' exploding eyes (a reciprocal blinding). After the multiple Smiths have been destroyed, the actual Smith (which is to say the one who has been actually fighting Neo) is revealed as none other than the Oracle herself. To put it another way: Neo fights the "father," destroys and is destroyed, and at the end it is revealed that he was "really" fighting the mother. This aerial combat encapsulates in symbolic form the restrictive Oedipal equation: mommy-daddy-son.

Deleuze and Guattari's *Anti-Oedipus* famously attacks the classic Freudian model of Oedipal desire as restrictive and reductive. They are wholly dismissive of what they call limiting and structuring algebra of the Oedipus Complex, as it is classically understood. More, they yearn "totally [to] demolish its ridiculous claim to represent the unconscious, to triangulate the unconscious, to encompass the entire production of desire."[7] For them, desire is much more freeform, complex, bound-breaking, rhizomatic and (in a deep sense) creative than the traditional schemata can allow. It is also, by its nature, transgressive, or, as they put it, "deterritorialising."

In place of the standard Freudian model of psychoanalytic subject they posit the notion of "desiring machines" (a very Matrixian notion, we might think): human beings, they say, are constructs of these desiring machines. Nor are these machines metaphorical, according to Deleuze and Guattari: they are literal, actual.

Part of the Deleuzeguattarian polemic is aimed at practicing psychoanalysts for their misidentification of the economy of desire as Oedipal.

> The desiring machines are always there, but they no longer function except behind the consulting-room walls. Behind the walls or in the wings, such is the place the primal fantasy concedes to desiring-machines, when it reduces everything to the Oedipal scene. They continue nevertheless to make a hellish racket. Even the psychoanalyst can't ignore them. He tends therefore to maintain an attitude of denial: all of that is surely true, but it is still daddy-mommy.[8]

In this model, the psychoanalyst is the critic of *Matrix: Revolutions* who wants to reduce the film to a neat symbolic triad, when if fact the core of the film, in a literal as well as a figurative sense, is the desiring-machine. It is the fact that machines desire, express themselves libidinally, produce a monstrous surplus and so on that powers the movie. "Every

---

[7] Gilles Deleuze and Felix Guattari, *Anti-Oedipus: Capitalism and Schizophrenia* (1972; transl. Robert Hurley, Mark Seem and Helen R. Lane: London: Athlone Press 2000), p. 44.
[8] ibid, p. 55.

psychoanalyst should know that underneath Oedipus, through Oedipus, behind Oedipus, his business is with desiring-machines." This is the way the Oedipal symbolism and play-acting in *Matrix: Revolutions* actually works.

Zizek points out that although cyberspace (which is to say, the Matrix) is often thought of as a bodiless state, an escape from the body and therefore from the desires of the body, that in fact the *reverse* of this is true. "The paradox ... of the cyberspace reason," he insists, "concerns precisely the fate of the body." Far from leaving the body behind, says Zizek, "in cyberspace the body returns with a vengeance: in popular perception, 'cyberspace IS hardcore pornography.'" He goes on: "cyberspace thus designates a turn, a kind of 'negation of negation,' in the gradual progress towards the disembodying of our experience...in cyberspace we return to bodily immediacy, but to an uncanny, virtual immediacy."[9] Far from an ethereal bodiless experience, virtual reality involves a much more intimate corporeality.

Hence the otherwise inexplicable stress on the erotics of the Matrix: the Frenchman's seduction of the diner in his restaurant, or his fetish club; the tight-fitting clothes that Carrie-Anne Moss wears as Trinity-in-the-Matrix; the sexualized rave-party; the various tangled love-stories and connections and the repeated visual trope of penetration. These last range from the insertion of the Matrix probes into surplus bodily orifices (which must, of course, be precisely *surplus* orifices), to the insertion of Neo's hand into Trinity's body at the end of *Matrix: Reloaded* (fist-fucking is an activity which still, I suppose, retains its transgressive erotic charge); or the impalement of Trinity at the end of *Matrix: Revolutions*; or the invading sentinels swarming all over Captain Takeshi, and opening vaginal splits across his face and body.

In this sense *Matrix: Reloaded* and *Matrix: Revolutions* are themselves a surplus. By turning the original self-contained *Matrix* movie into a trilogy the Wachowskis necessarily generated an unmanageable surplus. The widespread disapprobation of the critics is actually just the process of registering the monstrosity of this supplement, the way it exceeds the bounds of coherence, expectation, logic and so on. The triad of films is precisely *not* the triad of mommy-daddy-sonny; it is a desiring-machine (reflexively concerning actual desiring-machines and machinic desire) that grotesquely exceeds the limiting Oedipal triad. Only an understanding of this can properly situate this whole.

---

[9] Zizek, p.54

The films, in other words, are a monstrous copulation, to be understood in terms of an erotics of movement (grace, elegance, rapidity) that, on the largest scale, maps a trajectory of build-to-climax, followed by anti-climax, followed by the monstrous surplus of reproduction. Not, then, a film with a buried "real" meaning; but a complex set of shifting, often beautiful, surfaces. Fans who prioritize the first film for being more coherent (or "deeper") are, in a radical way, missing the point of the *Matrix* trilogy. The point is not to see beneath the surface.

Bibliography

Deleuze, Gilles and Felix Guattari. *Anti-Oedipus: Capitalism and Schizophrenia.* Translated by Robert Hurley, Mark Seem and Helen R. Lane. London: Athlone Press, 2000.

Roberts, Adam. *Fredric Jameson.* London: Routledge, 2000.

Wachowski, Andy and Larry (directors). *The Matrix*, Warner Brothers, 1999.

Wachowski, Andy and Larry (directors). *The Matrix: Reloaded,* Warner Brothers, 2003.

Wachowski, Andy and Larry (directors), *The Matrix: Revolutions* (Warner Bros, 2003)

Yeffeth, Glenn, ed. *Taking the Red Pill: Science, Philosophy and Religion in "The Matrix".* Chichester: Summersdale, 2003.

Zizek, Slavoj. *On Belief.* London: Routledge, 2001.

THE THING OF SHAPES TO COME:
Science Fiction as Anatomy of the Future
Howard V. Hendrix

When H. G. Wells entitled one of his myriad works *The Shape of Things to Come*, he played directly upon the science fiction reader's desire to know what the future looks like. Certainly this desire for an authoritative perspective on the future and what it holds is an ancient human need—astrology, fortune-telling, and scores of divination methods have been with us a very long time. Only relatively recently, however, has a significant genre of literature developed which takes as its special concern the shape of things to come, the anatomy of the future.

The most obvious difference between science fiction and other human activities anatomizing the future is that science fiction relates its futures in past or sometimes present tense, while other forms of future anatomy simply use the future tense. The astrologer and the trend-predictor say this *will* or this *might* happen; the science fiction narrator says this *has* happened—in *my* vision of the future.[10] The diviner takes signs, granted by the external world, as the ultimate basis of his or her authority; the science fiction writer takes not the external world but rather, like the epic poet, his or her own personal vision of the future as the ultimate basis of his or her authority. In doing so, the science fiction writer engages in a form of visionary poetics, a long-standing tradition with its ancient roots in pre-Christian epic and religious writings; in John the Apostle's delineation of Apocalypse in the Book of Revelations, in medieval dream-vision (particularly *Piers Plowman*); in Dante's *Divina Commedia*; and in Milton's *Paradise Lost* (especially books 11 and 12).

Engaging in visionary poetics in the secular and materialistic world of the our own time is rather difficult business, however. John the Apostle could claim that his vision came directly from God. *Piers Plowman*'s author, William Langland, could claim his story came to him in a dream. Milton could claim the stance of vatic poet inspired by a heavenly muse. But such stances, such claims of divine dreams advocated seriously by

---

[10] Samuel R. Delany, in an essay entitled "About 5,750 Words," in his criticism collection *The Jewel-Hinged Jaw* (New York: Berkley, 1977), makes some similar points on the use of tenses in science fiction. He deals primarily with Saussurean "levels of subjunctivity"; my approach is different: I am considering the need for an authoritative stance which makes such levels of subjunctivity useful to speaker or writer.

any contemporary writer, would seriously tax the reader's willing suspension of disbelief. The rise of the secular and materialistic scientific worldview has meant the death of the traditional visionary stance, and with it the death of the traditional epic. In the end, the science fiction writer, like all other contemporary writers, can only fall back on the authority of the storyteller—no mean authority, but one which presents special difficulties for the science fiction writer.

The storyteller says, "Once upon a time, there was—"; the diviner says, "In the future, there will be—"; but the science fiction writer must say, "Once upon a time in the future, there was—." Storytelling gains its authority from the past: the storyteller says this *has* happened; therefore, it *is* real or valid. This orientation toward the past (or at least the past tense) as signifier of authority is a distinguishing characteristic of fiction and of the literary culture as a whole. Science fiction, however, concerns itself primarily with the ramifications of a future oriented scientific culture. The science fiction writer is deprived of much of the authority of pastness and history simply because he or she most often writes about the future, about a world and time that is not yet and may never be—a world markedly different from the more historically fixed worlds of the traditional literary artist. The science fiction writer, in presuming to write about the future in the past tense, attempts to transmogrify the storyteller's role into a role for which it does not possess the authority—namely, that of visionary.

In the past, a storyteller could claim divine inspiration as a powerful authority for the story—and once he or she claimed such authority, the story was no longer just story, but also vision, and the storyteller a visionary. Today, however, claiming divine inspiration doesn't get one as far as it once did, and the storyteller seeking the status of visionary must look elsewhere for the authority that will inform his or her vision. For the science fiction writer, science itself, its accomplishments, its practice, and its possible future, provides the authority that informs the writer's personal vision of that future. Science provides the contemporary version of "divine inspiration" that makes the science fiction writer's visionary stance plausible and, indeed, possible. But, where the epic poet supported vision by appealing to the audience's shared sense of a transcendent order beyond understanding, a god or gods ultimately above and beyond the material world, the science fiction writer appeals to the audience's faith in the accomplishments of science, a human ordering and understanding of the material world.

The paradigm, or model, in science is analogous to the vision in visionary poetics. Over time, the scientific model gets remodeled and the poetic vision gets revised. Of all the genres, science fiction is the one in which both these processes can most clearly be seen proceeding simultaneously. If by *anatomy* we mean a detailed examination or analysis, then every work of science fiction produced that deals with future time is, in a sense, an anatomy of a future, and future-oriented science fiction as a generic category is concerned with the anatomy of *the* future. Science fiction presents us with a host of competing paradigms, competing models of the future, competing shapes of things to come. Science fiction as a genre is much like the shape-changing Thing of Campbell's novella *Who Goes There?*: it modifies its shape in response to a remodeling of scientific models, the revision of visions. As a genre, it is the Thing of Shapes to Come.

I will deal now with what I believe are the three major models of the future which science fiction currently presents to us. These models are literal shapes of things to come, shapes I've cribbed from undoubtedly outdated physics textbook discussions of the shape of the universe.[11] According to these texts, the most plausible shapes of the universe are (1) spherical; (2) flat; (3) saddle shaped (or "hyperspherical," "hyperflat," and "hypersaddle," as all are more-than-three-dimensional shapes).

A universe of hyperspheric shape results when we propose that the momentum imparted to the universe system at the time of the Big Bang is significantly less than the mutual attraction of the system's elements for each other. In other words, the universe does not achieve escape velocity but rather expands only to a certain size before the gravitational forces inherent in the system cause it to collapse in upon itself again, faster and faster, until the universe has contracted into a point called the Big Stop. At that point perhaps the universe will explode outward again in a new Big Bang, expanding and contracting, Big Banging and Big Stopping until the end of time. The analogous visionary model in science fiction is the catastrophic or cyclic catastrophic model, in which the benefits of scientific and technological progress are significantly less than the dangers inherent in that progress. In this model, scientific and technological expansion ultimately create more problems than they solve, and human society, as a result, suffers a devastating collapse in the form of nuclear

---

[11] Almost any high school or collegiate basic physics text can provide these models, but more interesting variants can be seen in Rudy Rucker, *Infinity and the Mind: The Science and Philosophy of the Infinite* (Boston: Birkhauser, 1982), pp. 10-15.

war, overpopulation, and ecological breakdown, or other similar self-induced catastrophies.

Though there are many stories in this vein, *A Canticle for Leibowitz* seems to be a premier example of this model. The novel begins half a millennium after a nuclear holocaust has plunged humankind into a new dark age, proceeds through the progressive reawakening of human culture, and culminates in yet another and even more devastating nuclear apocalypse. Cyclic catastrophism and the related notion that human progress ultimately results in more problems than its solves (and thus is finally not progress at all) are two of the key themes of the book:

> Listen, are we helpless? Are we doomed to do it again and again and again? Have we no choice but to play the Phoenix in an unending sequence of rise and fall? Assyria, Babylon, Egypt, Greece, Carthage, Rome, the Empires of Charlemagne and the Turk. Ground to dust and plowed with salt. Spain, France, Britain, America—burned into the oblivion of the centuries. And again and again and again.
>
> *Are we doomed to it, Lord, chained to the pendulum of our own mad clockwork, helpless to halt its swing?* (P. 217)[12]

> The closer men came to perfecting for themselves a paradise, the more impatient they seemed to become with it, and with themselves as well. They made a garden of pleasure, and became progressively more miserable with it as it grew in richness and power and beauty; for then, perhaps, it was easier for them to see that something was missing in the garden, some tree or shrub that would not grow. When the world was in darkness and wretchedness, it could believe in perfection and yearn for it. But when the world became bright with reason and riches, it began to sense the narrowness of the needle's eye, and that rankled for a world no longer willing to believe or yearn. Well, they were going to destroy it again, were they—this garden Earth, civilized and knowing, to be torn apart again that Man might hope again in wretched darkness. (Pp. 235-36)

---

[12] All page numbers for Walter M. Miller, Jr.'s *Canticle* are from the Bantam paperback edition, seventh printing.

The first of the above quoted passages emphasizes the cyclic catastrophic view of human history and human possibility presented in *Canticle*. Particularly interesting are the image of the Phoenix and the image of the clock. The Phoenix is trapped in time, a bird that, according to Egyptian mythology, consumed itself in fire every five hundred years, undying, to rise renewed from its own ashes. Like *Canticle*'s other noteworthy prisoner of time, the Wandering Jew who appears throughout the book, the Phoenix is doomed to a sort of immortality and denied what peace death might bring. That both Phoenix and Jew are meant to serve as types for humanity in history is clear from the image of mankind "chained to the pendulum of our own mad clockwork, helpless to halt its swing." In this image, human existence and entrapment in time—a product of the Fall, before which human existence was timeless—is specifically linked to the fallen state of human technology and human history, which, no matter what greatness they encompass, can be finally only a "mad clockwork."

Dom Zerchi, whose thought that first passage expresses, also thinks "this time, [the pendulum] will swing us clean into oblivion" (P. 218). But this is only true in a limited sense. True, in *Canticle*, we are led to believe that all human life will be blasted from the Earth, but this does not mean that the seed of man shall die from the universe. There are human colonists on a few distant planets; hope exists that the catastrophic cycling will continue even after Earth is done:

> [Brother Joshua] peered up again at the dusty stars of morning. Well, there would be no Edens found out there, they said. Yet there were men out there now, men who looked up to strange suns in stranger skies, gasped strange air, tilled strange earth...enough like Earth so that Man might live somehow by the same sweat of his brow. They were but a handful, . . . there in their new non-Edens even less like Paradise than the Earth had been. Fortunately for them, perhaps. (P. 235)

The reason Brother Joshua, a monk of the Order of Leibowitz who will lead his order's contingent to the stars, feels that the less Edenic a world is the more fortunate that world will be for its human settlers is made clear by that second passage quoted above. The closer human beings come, through the aid of their fallen technology, to an Edenic state, the more impatient and frustrated they become with their pseudo-

Eden, until in the global equivalent of a tantrum, they kick themselves and their world apart. Because man and all his works are fallen, he can only approximate Eden—never really achieve it—and he is doomed to the constant cycle of hope, near attainment, realization of ultimate unattainability, frustration, and self-destruction (so that the cycle may begin again). The longer the fall, the more fortunate the fallen, in the Leibowitzian scheme of things.

What exactly the "something" is that is "missing in the garden" created by man, what exactly the "tree or shrub that would not grow" is never made clear, but knowing the Eden myth, we can postulate that it might be the tree of eternal life or the shrub of human happiness in a perfect world. But even if man through his technology succeeds in creating his own Edenic order, will the result necessarily be good?

In Damon Knight's brilliant but sorely neglected novella *Dio*, we find just such an Edenic state. Like many another utopian/dystopian vision, the future in Dio follows the hyperflat model. In physical speculations, the hyperflat or Euclidean universe results when we propose that the momentum imparted to the universe system at the time of the Big Bang equals or just barely exceeds the forces of attraction inherent in the system. The universe achieves escape velocity, but just barely, so it expands forever at an ever-decreasing rate of expansion. The science fiction analogue is the utopian/dystopian model, in which human sciences and technology solve problems faster than they generate them, but just barely, so that the civilizations of this model fight a long battle with entropy as they slowly crumble back into deserts of vast eternity. Barring radical change, these pseudo-Edens created by technology become increasingly sterile and possessed of a false animation that is part of the process of their long death.

Such a world we find in *Dio*. Technology has ended death and want and supplied in their place immortality and the happiness of dominion over the Earth and all its elements. The virtues of Eden are created, or recreated, in this future landscape populated by two cultures: the Students, or producers, and the Players, or consumers. The story's three main characters are Dio, a student who holds the rank of Sector Planner; Claire, a beautiful and eternally young player who loves Dio; and Benarra, an eternally young student with interest in the biological sciences who becomes interested professionally and personally in Dio when it is discovered that Dio will grow old and die, unlike everyone else in his world. Tangentially, Benarra also becomes interested in Claire and her response to Dio's mortal condition. Much of the story's exposition takes place in conversations in which Benarra explains Dio's condition and the history of human mortality and immortality to Claire, as in the following passage which occurs after Claire sees Dio as clearly mortal and suffering uniquely from a once common viral infection:

> *"What's wrong with him?"* she says.
> [Benarra] sighs, looking down at her modish robe with its delicate clasps of gold. "How can I tell you? Does the verb 'to die' mean anything to you?"
> She is puzzled and apprehensive. "I don't know...isn't it something that happens to the lower animals?"
> He gives her a quick mock bow. "Very good." (P. 118)[13]

Benarra then shows her a visual recording of a white lab rat's death, to help explain to Claire just what it means "to die."

> Watching, Claire tries to control her nausea. Students' cabinets are full of nastinesses like this; they expect you not to show any distaste. "Something's the matter with it," is all she can find to say.
> "Yes. It's dying. That means to cease living: to stop. Not to be any more. Understand?"
> "No," she breathes. In the box, the small body has stopped moving. The mouth is stiffly open, the lip drawn back from the yellow teeth. The eye does not move, but glares up sightless.
> "That's all," says her companion. "No more rat. Finished. After a while it begins to decompose and make a bad smell, and a while after that, there's nothing left but bones. And that has happened to every rat that was ever born."
> "I don't *believe* you," she says. "It isn't like that; I never heard of such a thing." (P. 119)

The reason no one knows death any more, the reason death doesn't happen to people in Dio's world is simple: disease, debility, and death have been expunged from Dio's Edenic future Earth. His world is a world of eternal youth:

---

[13] All page numbers for Damon Knight's *Dio* are from the Groff Conklin anthology, *Five Unearthly Visions* (New York: Fawcett Publications, 1965) where I first ran across *Dio*. The novella originally appeared *in Infinity Science Fiction*, September 1957.

"Now this," says Benarra, "this long shallow curve represents man as he was. You notice it starts far to the left of the animal curve. The planners had this much to work with: man was already unique, in that he had this very long juvenile period before sexual maturity. Here: see what they did." With a gesture he imposes another chart on the first.

"It looks almost the same," says Claire.

"Yes. Almost. What they did was quite a simple thing, in principle. They lengthened the juvenile period still further, they made the curve rise still more slowly . . . and never quite reach the top. The curve now becomes asymptotic, that is, it approaches sexual maturity by smaller and smaller amounts, and never gets there, no matter how long it goes on." Gravely, he returns her stare.

"Are you saying," she asks, "that we're *not* sexually mature? Not anybody?"

"Correct," he says. "Maturity in every other complex organism is the first stage of death. We never mature, Claire, and that's why we don't die. We're the eternal adolescents of the universe. That's the price we paid." (P. 128)

In this conversation between the student Benarra and the player Claire we learn the crucial information of the story. Dio, through a fluke, is doomed to grow up, to become the mortal adult in a world of immortal superhuman adolescents. In a world where normally "people endure, things pass away," Dio builds for permanence. He becomes the Great Artist, who sculpts by hand with hammer and chisel rather than by machine. We are led to see him as a tragic and heroic figure in a world peopled by frivolous immortals. The technologically created Eden where Dio lives is a sad farce with a dark secret; though its inhabitants can't die of old age, they *can* commit suicide:

Leaving the circle toward midnight, [Claire] roams the apartment alone, eased by comradeship, content to hear the singing blur and fade behind her. In the playroom, she stands idly looking down into the deep darkness of the diving well. How luxurious, she thinks, to fall and fall, and never reach the bottom. . . .

But the bottom is always there, of course, or it would not be a diving well. A paradox: the well must be a shaft closed at the bottom; it's the sense of danger, the imagined smashing impact, that gives it its thrill. And yet there is no danger of injury: levitation and survival instinct will always prevent it.

"We have such a tidy world." (P. 141)

Dio's pseudo-Eden is a place where, after thousands of years of life, everything seems frivolous whether it is or not, a place where frivolity becomes boring, where boredom leads to a desire for death, where the desire for death ultimately becomes more powerful than the survival instinct. Every diving well is potentially a suicide chamber. Science, in *Dio*, has solved human problems more quickly than it has engendered new ones, but just barely. Though the people of Dio's world are like gods, they can't ultimately manipulate, levitate, or fornicate their way out of boredom's grasp. They are fallen human forms who, though they can claim with Satan in book 6 of *Paradise Lost* and with Benarra (p. 127) that "We did it, we created ourselves," they also must hold the flip side of that coin: we also destroy ourselves, in the distant end.

And Dio's deathless, so nearly perfect world is, in fact, dying slowly because it is killing itself. There is no escape from entropy or original sin. Dio's world, though bright with reason and riches, feels the narrowness of the needle's eye; the secular and material immortality that science provides is not enough to save it. No one transcends the deserts of vast eternity into which Dio's civilization is slowly crumbling.

In *Dio* the message is that science and technology, though powerful manifestations of the mind, cannot bring about transcendance; in Arthur C. Clarke's *2010: Odyssey Two*, the message is quite the opposite: mind, particularly in its scientific and technological manifestations, is the only means available for ultimately transcending the secular and material world. This is a crucial paradox of much of Clarke's work. A secular and material worldview provides the very means by which the secular and material are transcended.

Such a paradox is in some ways a logical outgrowth of the shape of the future in *2010*. The universe of the novel is hypersaddle in shape. The hypersaddle model in physics results when the momentum imparted to the universe system at the time of the Big Bang vastly exceeds the mutually attractive forces inherent in the system itself. The universe achieves escape velocity strongly and expands steadily and undecreasingly forever. The analogous visionary model in science fiction is the final but unending frontier model, in which the benefits of scientific and technological progress far outweigh the dangers inherent in that progress. Scientific and technological expansion are ultimately forms of mind expansion and solve far more problems than they create.

This is perhaps the most optimistic of the models cited here. In contrast to the burstable balloon of *Canticle*'s spherical model and the lone and level sands of *Dio*'s flat model, *2010* presents a model to boldly go and split infinity by, sapience back in the saddle again, riding the range on the final frontier. Chapter 51, "The Great Game," gives perhaps the clearest statement in all of Clarke's fiction of his open ended universe, and of mind to match that universe:

> And now, out among the stars, evolution was driving toward new goals. The first explorers of Earth had long since come to the limits of flesh and blood; as soon as their machines were better than their bodies, it was time to move. First their brains, and then their thoughts alone, they transferred into shining new homes of metal and plastic.
>
> In these they roamed among the stars. They no longer built spaceships. They *were* spaceships.
>
> But the age of the Machine-entities swiftly passed. In their ceaseless experimenting, they had learned to store knowledge in the structure of space itself, and to preserve their thoughts for eternity in frozen lattices of light. They could become creatures of radiation, free at last from the tyranny of matter.
>
> Into pure energy, therefore, they presently transformed themselves. . . .
>
> They were lords of the Galaxy, and beyond the reach of time. (PP. 307-8)[14]

The "lords of the Galaxy" here are grand experimenters, scientists writ cosmically large. Through their science, which began as the study of matter, time and space, they have become "free at last from the tyranny of matter," pure energy "beyond the reach of time" that can "rove at will among the stars and sink like a subtle mist through the very interstices of space." Immortality and eternity are theirs. Just as, given time enough and chance, inanimate matter can, in theory, produce life, so too, in the

---

[14] All page numbers for *2010: Odyssey Two* are from the first U.S. edition (New York: Del Rey Books, 1984).

Clarkean scheme, can science, given time enough and chance, transcend its roots in matter and time. In classic Miltonic fashion, Clarke's self-transcending mind from body up to spirit works.

Like *Paradise Lost*, *Canticle*, *Dio*, and many another visionary works, *2010* concerns itself with Edens and apocalypses, beginnings and ends. *2010* has obvious parallels to both the Genesis and apocalypse stories. The grand experimenters create a Jovian star system by inducing Jupiter, via their monoliths, to condense to fusion point and become a star. In this apocalyptic destruction of Jupiter, the grand experimenters simultaneously let there be light and improve the conditions for life on the Jovian moons. Apocalypse becomes genesis, and even brings with it a new Edenic prohibition:

> ALL THESE WORLDS ARE YOURS —
> EXCEPT EUROPA
> ATTEMPT NO LANDINGS THERE.
> (P. 320)

Europa is in a very real sense a new Eden, waiting for a new (and perhaps unfallen) sentient species to inhabit it. I would not go so far as to push Tanya as an Eve figure or Heywood Floyd as an Adam, but I do find a striking parallel with God's prohibition to Adam and Eve in the Garden (Genesis 2: 16—17): "And the Lord God commanded the man, saying, 'From any tree of the garden you may eat freely; but from the tree of the knowledge of good and evil you shall not eat, for in that day you eat of it you shall surely die." Both prohibitions originate with superhuman entities and are tests of human obedience which humanity fails. Just as Adam and Eve eat of the fruit of the tree of the knowledge of good and evil and, thus, become mortal, so too do later humans attempt landings on Europa to try to discover what's going on there and, thus, get shot down again and again by the monolith the experimenters have left behind. This monolith, stationed by the experimenters, is designed to protect their new experiment from human intrusion, much the same way God stationed a cherubim with a flaming sword in Eden to guard the way to the tree of life from human intrusion after the Fall.

In a sense, I suppose, the apocalyptic genesis of a new Jovian Eden in *2010* is something of a spherical, cyclic catastrophic, Big Stop-new Big Bang model. It is, however, always contained within the larger purview of the saddle shaped model of the future that pervades the book. The models I have proposed here are obviously not absolutes, and I hope they will not be approached that way. They are heuristics, paradigms, models about models, all of which are concerned with whether knowledge, in particular *scientific* knowledge, brings about more good or more evil. In the spherical model we saw how, in *Canticle*, partaking of the fruit of the knowledge of good and evil results more in evil than in good, culminating ultimately in nuclear apocalypse. In the flat model of *Dio*, we saw how the pursuit of knowledge results in more good, relatively speaking, than evil, but the evil in knowledge persists so strongly that the victory of the good in knowledge is meaningless. In the saddle shaped model of *2010*, we saw how the good in the pursuit of knowledge, in eating the forbidden fruit, far outweighs the evil involved in that pursuit, and results, at last, in mind without end. Each model, and each story, is an interpretation of what the beginning will mean in the end, how genesis affects apocalypse.

That visionary works should be very much concerned with beginnings and ends, Edens and apocalypses, is not surprising when we consider that all art, all science, all religion—all knowledge—is perhaps in its final reduction and elaboration, concerned with just three questions: How did it begin? How is it going? How will it end?

"But why only three?" asks Tanya. I don't know; perhaps because we exist in time. Clarke's Ramans, in his *Rendezvous with Rama* do everything in threes, and I'm not greedy for reasons more.

THIS IS TRUE
Tim Lebbon

One day, somewhere in the world, a sleeping person will push their leg from beneath the blankets. The dark will tell them not to, but they'll be needing to pee really, really badly. Their toes will touch the floor and they'll breathe a sigh of relief, thinking themselves safe...but then a hand will close around their ankle, tug, and they will be dragged beneath the bed to a grisly doom.

This will happen. I firmly believe it.

I believe it because the human imagination is a powerful, potent force. Most of us have the ability—and some of us have the *willingness* —to believe almost anything. We are all able to accept ideas and theories without actually understanding them or having experienced them for ourselves: an airplane will fly; Jupiter is a gas giant; $E=mc^2$. We are told that there are multiple universes, and we believe. We are told of quarks and anti-matter, and we believe. We trust those learned people who tell us these things, read the evidence, take it as truth. And sometimes, to make things more exciting, the ideas we find ourselves accepting can be utterly abstract and fantastic.

That's why horror is such a wonderful genre to read and write in; most of it is unlikely, but there's always a *chance*. Some call it suspension of disbelief but perhaps, in reality, horror reaches down into our darkest past—back to the times when we worshipped the moon and feared witches, saw the Devil's footprints in the snow and built fires in our caves to keep the night at bay—and stimulates our deep-rooted fear of the unknown. It's not suspension of disbelief, but rediscovered belief. We all love to be scared.

And we all want to believe.

This applies across the board, not just to someone sitting in a darkened room reading the latest Stephen King by lamplight. A group of people, or even a whole populace, will sometimes make the leap from disbelief to belief, not because they are tricked into it—though sometimes the gentle art of deception is an ally in this—but because it's inbuilt in them to believe in the unbelievable. And I'm not just hypothesizing; this has happened.

On September 29, 1914, the *London Evening News* published a short story by Arthur Machen entitled *"The Bowmen."* It was a fictional piece describing how the Agincourt bowmen—mercenaries who had fought for King Arthur—appeared on the front lines at Ypres and held off a German attack, bows and arrows against howitzers. Machen later described it as one of "the silliest tales that has ever disgraced the English tongue." At the time, when defeat at the hands of the demonized Hun looked likely, it was seen literally as a God-send.

Reports started filtering back from the front of angels appearing in shining clouds, holding off wave after wave of enemy assaults. The myth grew and expanded, and it exists in history books today as the legend of the Angels of Mons. People believed. A work of fiction was taken as fact—a work of fantastic, supernatural fiction at that—and its followers became so besotted with the myth that Machen was, for a time, vilified for claiming it as his own. In a way, he was indirectly accused of blasphemy.

Yes, it was a long time ago, and perhaps people were less aware of science and more of myth. And it happened during wartime. Minds under pressure can play curious tricks. Stress causes hallucination. Chinese whispers give such a story strength and a background to believe in.

Well, maybe. But it's happened since then, too.

On October 30, 1938, Orson Welles broadcast a chilling series of spoof news reports based on H. G. Wells's *The War of the Worlds* on American radio. Unlike "The Bowmen" it did not take time to filter into the public's subconscious; it had a ready audience, and its effect was immediate. The exact results of the broadcast have become subject to conjecture and, probably, exaggeration. At the very least, there was a great deal of concern and panic amongst those who heard it, especially around Grover's Mills, New Jersey (where Welles had reported that the Martians were landing). One listener apparently committed suicide, others tried to flee the region, even more contacted the police and emergency services. All because of a masterful presentation—a "play'"— that has become one of the most famous hours in broadcasting history.

This was all before Roswell, before the modern UFO mythology was properly established, before much was truly known about our neighbors in the solar system. And maybe some of those listeners were gullible and naïve and could not identify a dramatization when they heard it. It could never happen today.

Perhaps. But guess what? It *has* happened recently, in an equally spectacular fashion.

October 31, 1992. BBC One's Screen One presentation that evening was Stephen Volk's *Ghostwatch*, a brilliantly written dramatization of a supposedly "live" haunting. Using established presenters such as Michael Parkinson and Sarah Greene, the program gave a superb feel of authenticity...even though it was introduced with a "written by" caption and a cast list (and the date of broadcast really should have been something of a giveaway). However, many viewers believed that they were watching a live feed of real events...events which escalated in extremity as the programe progressed...

Reaction was fierce, with some newspapers slamming the BBC for broadcasting such a frightening piece of television. There were—and still are—stories of heart attacks amongst the viewing audience. And one lady demanded the price of a new set of underwear for her husband because he...well, he was very frightened, and his body reacted accordingly.

Ghostwatch has only recently been re-released to the public, over a decade after its initial broadcast.

Again, people believed. Intelligent people like you. People with their heads screwed on and their story straight and their minds supposedly made up. And trust me on this ... it will all happen again.

We *want* to believe in the extraordinary, because it gives us an escape from the mundanity of modern life, however dangerous that escape may be. And when we're reading horror it's all right for us to believe, and we don't have to find an excuse. Our minds are powerful beyond measure, and usually they're given over to perform those normal tasks that make our days so full and our nights so restful. Maybe they want a little adventure now and then. Give them a break.

So what of that person whose ankle will surely be grabbed? It will happen because there's always another way to murder someone, and always another murderer willing to try it. Or maybe there are simply some things, under some beds, that are believed in enough to be given breath.

BUILD YOUR OWN BOOM:
Australian SF in the 90s and Beyond
Sean McMullen

This is not a history of Australian SF in the 1990s, but a guide to and analysis of what actually happened in Australian SF's most significant decade ever. The 1990s saw the greatest boom in Australian SF's history, a massive increase in output and quality that was even widely acclaimed overseas, and which has led to a situation where some Australian authors can make a full-time living from writing SF. This boom began only three years after the most disastrous crash in Australian SF's output in the second half of the twentieth century, and the rapid improvement in the Australian scene was soon noticed. When I attended the San Francisco World SF Convention in 1993, American professionals were already commenting on the amount of exciting new work coming out of Australia. In 1998, when I was one of the guests at the New Zealand National SF Convention, I lost track of the number of times I was asked, "How did you Australians do it?" (New Zealand subsequently entered its own boom, and I look forward to seeing how it turns out.)

Ask any half dozen Australians associated with SF about what caused the boom of the 1990s, and you will probably get half a dozen different answers. *Eidolon* and *Aurealis* magazines created a long-term market for short fiction; commercial publishers discovered that there was a buck to be made from local authors; the Internet made overseas markets more accessible; Australians had been doing well all along, but people only recognized it in the 1990s; a series of anthologies showcased the very best of Australian short fiction; there was a general worldwide increase in interest in SF in the 1990s, evidenced by the fact that the Australian television and movie SF industry experienced a quite independent boom in the 1990s. Speaking as someone who co-authored the first history of Australian SF, *Strange Constellations* (1999), I would maintain that all of the foregoing comments are true. However, when the facts are scrutinized...*Omega* magazine provided a stable market for local SF from 1980 to 1987; commercial publishers discovered local SF in the 1950s (then dropped it as unprofitable); A. Bertram Chandler was selling a story overseas every fortnight in the late 1950s using old-fashioned postal mail; statistically Australians were not doing nearly so well in the 80s relative to the 90s; there was a spate of SF anthologies in the late 70s and early 80s; and the Australian television and movie SF boom began in 1979, a decade earlier. What really happened?

THE WASTELAND

In the wake of the 1985 World SF Convention in Melbourne there was a great deal of optimism for the future of Australia's science fiction. Two major anthologies and a novel had been launched at the convention, the professional magazine *Aphelion* had its genesis during the convention, and the established magazine *Omega* was not only thriving, its circulation was so high that stories in it counted for SFWA membership eligibility. Within eighteen months all that had gone off the rails. At the start of 1987 both *Aphelion* and *Omega* folded, the local small presses were no longer publishing fiction, and in the calendar year 1987, only nine original SF stories were published by Australians—the lowest level since the 1940s. For the next three years short fiction was largely confined to venues ranging from mainstream literary anthologies to pornographic magazines. Many writers gave up, some turned to overseas markets and others just kept writing in the hope that things would improve in the future. The major novel-length work of the time, George Turner's *The Sea and Summer* (1987) was thus published overseas (but as *Drowning Towers*, 1988 in the USA), while beginners-of-the-time such as Greg Egan and Sean McMullen had to establish their reputations in British and American magazines.

AUSTRALIAN SF RESCUED...BY CONAN?!!

Thus in mid-1990, nobody could have dreamed that the greatest boom in Australian SF and fantasy history was about to commence. It took place across the entire spectrum of markets, covering mainstream publishers, small press publishers, semi-professional magazines, anthologies, television, and of course overseas publishers and magazines. It even preceded the massive growth in Internet usage, and the birth of the World Wide Web. So what triggered this massive outpouring of fiction by Australian authors? It is probably fair to say that there was no single cause. The use of word processors leaped from about 1 in 10 authors to around 9 in 10 between 1985 and 1989, allowing polished, clean submission manuscripts to be produced in large quantities and relatively quickly. Word processors also enabled magazines and small press books to be produced far more quickly and easily, and the growth in Internet use from 1991 onwards made submission and correspondence far easier from this geographically remote country. Combined with all the foregoing, however, was the fact that Australian commercial publishers discovered a very large local market for fantasy.

The pivotal event, rather like the discovery of the nugget that triggers a gold rush, was the publication of the first fantasy "blockbuster" by Pan Macmillan, Martin Middleton's *Circle of Light* (1990). It sold 15,000 copies over three printings, perplexing local critics—who thought it was somewhat ordinary as fantasy went—but vindicating the few commentators who maintained there was a lucrative market for genre fiction which had never been subjected to a professional promotion campaign. Middleton lacked the traditional (for Australians) apprenticeship in short fiction, the novel was nominated for no awards, and got a chilly reception from reviewers, yet it demonstrated to publishers that the reading public was very interested in fiction of this sort.

Middleton was not a pioneer of Australian fantasy. Early heroic fantasy had appeared in the 1940s in comics, Paul Collins began publishing heroic fantasy in his *Void* anthology series in the late 70s, and Keith Taylor had his *Bard* series of fantasy novels published in America throughout the 1980s. Pan's major innovation with *Circle of Light* and the books that followed was to professionally package and heavily promote the books throughout Australia. These books generally exceeded 300 pages (for their time, this was very thick), and their cover art was eye-catching, while clearly defining their genre. Readers got what was advertised and everyone was a winner...except if you were a fantasy author wanting an award.

For the first half of the 1990s the local commercial fantasy was virtually absent from the shortlists for local awards, which were dominated by SF that varied from the crossover SF/fantasy of Dowling, through the socially astute future-making of Turner, to the hard SF of Egan, to the comic steampunk of McMullen. This finally changed when fantasy works by Sussex and Blackford won Ditmar Awards in 1997. Around this time the new Aurealis awards introduced a specific fantasy category.

What was the problem? In Australia, the commercial editors and publishers tended to be professionals with a background in promotion of mainstream literature, who noticed that there was a profitable niche waiting to be filled. They sometimes sought advice from people in the genre community, but tended to publish works that were conservative in content. Thus Australian SF dominated the awards, was more frequently published overseas, and featured some highly innovative work. On the other hand, even though commercial publishers were publishing a lot more SF as a reaction to the fantasy boom, fantasy remained the powerhouse that drove the genre boom overall. Culturally, part of the problem appeared to be with the readers. In Australia SF is regarded, rather unreasonably, as both juvenile in appeal yet technically difficult. Thus adults who would happily buy a crime novel or a Terry Pratchett Diskworld book would not contemplate a near-future novel on genetic engineering or computer hacking. Pan's early fantasy titles (fantasy trilogies by Martin Middleton, and Tony Shillitoe) were followed by SF works by "Shannah Jay" (Sherry-Anne Jacobs) and Richard Harland, but fantasy turned out to be the area of greater profit.

AUSTRALIA'S SF BOOM BEGINS

The SF boom in Australia probably would not have happened so fast had local commercial publishers not discovered locally written fantasy, but it still would have happened. The other pivotal events of 1990 actually happened independently of both the commercial market and each other. Firstly *Aphelion* magazine re-emerged as Aphelion Publications, launching short fiction collections by Turner and Dowling at the national SF convention in Melbourne. In Perth, after meeting Terry Dowling at a convention, a group of editors began publishing *Eidolon: The Journal of Australian Science Fiction and Fantasy*, and the accumulation of unpublished but worthwhile SF from the past three years was demonstrated by the appearance of stories by Terry Dowling, Rosaleen Love, Greg Egan, Sean McMullen, Philippa Maddern and Stephen Dedman in the first three issues—all of those authors had already been published overseas. In Melbourne, the magazine *Aurealis: Australian Fantasy and Science Fiction* appeared in September, including stories by Turner and Dowling.

These magazines were to break *Omega* magazine's records for longevity and number of stories published, as well as setting new benchmarks in literary standards. They revolutionized Australian short SF and fantasy by providing a largeish, stable market for a long period, as well as a showcase that was taken seriously overseas. *Aurealis* had newsstand distribution and thus several times the circulation of *Eidolon*, which was distributed via subscription and specialty shops. *Aurealis* began to conduct a readers' poll, and in mid-decade sponsored the Aurealis Awards for Australian SF, fantasy, horror and young adult fiction. *Eidolon's* editors published recommended reading lists of Australian genre works. The initial results of the *Aurealis* poll were intriguing, with two of the winners being relatively new authors at the time [George Turner's "I Still Call Australia Home" (*Aurealis* 1, 1990); Simon Brown's "All the Fires of Lebanon" (*Aurealis* 6, 1991); Sean McMullen's "Charon's Anchor" (*Aurealis* 12, 1993)]. *Eidolon* was the first Australian SF magazine to establish a World Wide Web site, making a large selection of its stories, artwork and articles available free on the Internet, and sponsoring home pages for several authors. In 1997, *Aurealis* followed suit.

In terms of popularity within the fan community, *Eidolon* has dominated the Ditmar Awards, but *Aurealis* has also had its share of acclaim. Even the international authority Gardner Dozois had an opinion on these magazines: in the 13th of his *Year's Best Science Fiction* anthologies he cited *Aurealis* and *Eidolon* as two of the three best long-established fiction semi-prozines in the world, considering *Eidolon* to have the best fiction. The two magazines were not rivals for a share of a small market but were servicing somewhat different parts of quite a large one. This market, both of authors and readers, had been partly created by the two magazines' very success and longevity.

Occasionally new magazines tried to access this market, *Futurist* and *Altair*, and the somewhat longer lived *Orb* being among the most recent, and mainstream magazines such as *REVelation* published occasional SF stories. Although this article is about the way Australian SF was changed during the 1990s, it is instructive to look at what has happened since 1999. Although book-length fiction is far easier to sell commercially than in the past (so that authors do not need to do a short-fiction "apprenticeship"), new fiction magazines continue to be launched to replace the magazines that either fold or slow their rate of publication. For example, 2002 saw the launch of *Agog!* magazine from Sydney and *Andromeda Spaceways Inflight Magazine* from Perth. Both are published regularly, are run by relatively experienced editorial staff, and pay for their fiction. They are yet another sign that the boom of the 1990s has become a larger market, and that the short fiction market can survive the contraction of *Eidolon* and *Aurealis*.

Over a dozen SF writers who emerged during the late 1980s (often due to publishing opportunities created in the wake of the Worldcon Aussiecon 2) became pillars of the genre in Australia during the 1990s. Some of these were writers of young adult fiction, and whilst this field is generally outside our scope, the most important of them deserve mention at this point because their work is of a quality that influenced adult writing as well. Young adult SF has been a mainstay of the Australian scene since the 1950s, and in the 1990s, it also expanded. Award-winning South Australian author Gillian Rubinstein produced several young adult books which went beyond mere adventure. Most notable was her *Space Demons* trilogy, which depicted young people resolving their problems and frustrations by means other than hate and aggression. (Rubinstein also produced several other books with SF themes.) John Marsden became one of Australia's leading young adult novelists, producing mainstream work as well as fantasy and SF. His most important genre work was a series of foreign invasion novels commencing with *Tomorrow, When the War Began* (1993). The other notable young adult work was Gary Crew's *Strange Objects* (1990), which blended elements of SF, fantasy and horror in a story concerning present-day repercussions of the 1629 wreck of the Dutch vessel *Batavia*. For writers, this immensely successful novel was influential in its use of multiple narratives comprising mainly transcribed documents (such as press reports and diary-entries), compelling readers to assemble the meaning of the narrative for themselves rather than relying upon the author to divulge a final comforting "explanation."

RECOGNITION

The increase in volume of fiction was accompanied by an increase in recognition. Stories by Sean McMullen and Greg Egan were voted onto the Nebula Awards Preliminary Ballot in 1989 and 1990 respectively, and Turner's *The Sea and Summer* (*Drowning Towers* in the U.S. market) was included in the 1990 final ballot by the Nebulas committee, the first Australian work to receive a Nebula nomination. It also won the Arthur C. Clarke Award for 1990. Australian accomplishments at this point are too numerous to mention here, but some more of the highlights follow. Egan's "Learning to be Me" (*Interzone* 37, July 1990) won the *Interzone* readers' poll for 1990, and his "The Infinite Assassin" (*Interzone* 48, June 1991) won again in 1991. Dowling won the

Readercon Award with *Wormwood* (1991) and again with "Breaking Through to the Heroes" [from his *Blue Tyson* (1992)]. Egan's *Permutation City* (1994) won the Campbell Award in 1995, while his stories were republished almost annually by Gardner Dozois in the *Year's Best Science Fiction* series during the 1990s. In 1994 the American author Jack Dann came to live in Australia, and in 1997 he became the first Australian resident to win a Nebula Award with his novella "Da Vinci Rising" (*Asimov's SF Magazine*, May 1995). Dann had established his presence in American SF, as both a writer and an editor, before moving to Melbourne from New York.

Some award-winning adult works were as forthright as *The Sea and Summer* in their messages about the future. For example, Terry Dowling's story "The Last Elephant" (*Australian Short Stories* 20, 1987) confronts the unpalatable topic of the probable extinction of many species that we take for granted, and Sean McMullen's "While the Gate is Open" (*Fantasy & Science Fiction*, February 1990) asks if studying the nature of death itself can ever be legitimate for medical science.

In 1995 three important developments took place. First, *Aurealis* magazine inaugurated the Aurealis Awards in an endeavor to establish recognition for Australian works other than those voted for by the fans in the Ditmar Awards. The Ditmars have been plagued since their inception by eligibility anomalies, and accusations of rigging and unrepresentative voting, so the Aurealis Awards used panels of well-read experts to decide upon winners. While they have not been free of controversy either, the Aurealis Awards have operated successfully and acquired considerable industry credibility. Secondly, 1995 was the year in which HarperCollins followed in the footsteps of Pan Books by launching a line of Australian SF and fantasy titles, commencing with the fantasy blockbuster *Battleaxe* (1995) by Sara Douglass but quickly adding SF authors Simon Brown and Sean Williams to the list. Thirdly, this year saw the publication of *She's Fantastical*, edited by Lucy Sussex and Judith Raphael Buckrich, the first anthology of Australian women's speculative writing. The collection included work by Lucy Sussex, Rosleen Love, Leanne Frahm, Philippa Maddern, Gabrielle Lord, and Tess Williams.

THE FANTASY BANDWAGON

Later in this article, I shall be presenting some statistics showing that fantasy overtook then totally outclassed SF in Australia. Indeed, some

SF authors switched to writing fantasy, while virtually no fantasy authors crossed over to SF. While I cannot present evidence covering all authors seduced away from SF to fantasy, I can present my own case as an example. When I began writing SF in the 1980s, I worked in a highly technical job in scientific computing, read both fantasy and SF, was a member of three medieval re-enactment groups (mainly for the music and the fighting), and wrote only SF because the market for fantasy was virtually non-existent. On the other hand my SF worlds were considered strangely exotic and romantic, and were even described by one reviewer as medieval cyberpunk.

By the time I had completed my Greatwinter trilogy, there was a strong market for fantasy developing, so I started writing fantasy. I know a great deal about medieval history, technology, fighting, music, and society—and some of this knowledge came from direct experience in the re-enactment groups. Today I am doing a PhD in medieval fantasy literature, and I still do sabre and foil at the university fencing club. Is it any surprise that I now write fantasy? I would have written it back in the 1980s if there had been any reasonable chance of selling it. I did not jump onto the fantasy bandwagon because I thought there was a buck to be made from it, I started writing fantasy because I have always wanted to. I also thought I had something original and interesting to say (the same reason that I started writing SF), and thus my first fantasy novel, *Voyage of the Shadowmoon* (2002) was about a wind-powered, wooden submarine, while the second, *Glass Dragons* (2004) features a lecherous guy who is punished by having his primary sexual characteristic transformed into a small, fire-breathing dragon that does not like women. In my case, the boom in fantasy merely allowed me to do what I have always wanted to do. I have clearly not been jumping onto the fantasy bandwagon by writing sword-operas about knights in armor doing romantic things in the company of ladies in flowing robes, and wizards doing rather suspect things in high towers—generally not in company.

MAINSTREAM

A sure sign that a boom is under way is when people from other areas of publishing get in on the act. This certainly did seem to happen in the 1990s. None of the mainstream authors' genre works could be classed as groundbreaking or runaway best sellers, but there were still some very fine works published.

Distinguished mainstream poet, biographer and novelist Rodney Hall made his one venture into SF with *Kisses of the Enemy* (1987), a dystopian account of an Australian republic infiltrated by foreign (American) economic interests which buy control of the government. In *Salt* (1990) the successful and critically-acclaimed thriller writer Gabrielle Lord produced a disappointingly conventional SF thriller in which two men break out of the walled city of Sydney of 2075 only to find the Australian continent ravaged by civil strife and the effects of ozone-layer depletion. *Honk If You Are Jesus* (1992), by mainstream novelist Peter Goldsworthy, returns to the bio-ethical issues that so concerned George Turner. A sexually inexperienced gynecologist takes up a senior academic position at a Surfers Paradise university funded by Christian fundamentalists. In the midst of trying to resolve her own late-40s crises and to overcome the infertility of the institute's benefactor and his child-bride, she begins to worry that she may be involved in a plot to clone Jesus Christ from DNA in skin-tissue adhering to a crucifixion spike.

Also politically forthright—but in a less melodramatic way—were two novels by mainstream women writers. Kate Grenville's *Joan Makes History* (1988) is an irreverent feminist speculation on Australian history, satirically placing Joan (the wife of Captain Cook, always ignored by formal history) at the center of various important historical "moments" that are conventionally viewed from a male perspective. Rosie Scott's *Feral City* (1992) concerns an attempt by two sisters to open a bookshop in the center of a futuristic city decaying into violence, homelessness and drug-addiction.

Alice Nunn's first novel, *Illicit Passage* (1992), is set in 2101 in the space colony of Anastasia Union, at a time when the city's systems are breaking down and food is becoming scarce, but the bureaucrats are more interested in directing resources towards warfare than in civillian infrastructure.

Has anyone spotted the problem as yet? The above works were published either before, or very early in, the 1990s SF boom. Australian mainstream authors already had a long history of experimenting with SF in order to better frame their creations.

ANTHOLOGIES

There was a lull in the production of anthologies of Australian SF between 1985 and 1990. In 1985 three anthologies appeared: *Strange*

Attractors, edited by Damien Broderick, *Urban Fantasies*, edited by David King and Russell Blackford, and the U.S. edition of *Australian Science Fiction*, edited by Van Ikin. The only other anthology to appear before 1990 was the very badly distributed *Matilda at the Speed of Light* (1988), edited by Damien Broderick. Van Ikin broke the drought in anthology publication when he edited *Glass Reptile Breakout and Other Stories* (1990), which took its title from the story by Russell Blackford. This anthology achieved some success when it was listed as a text for study by senior high school students in their penultimate year, and pointed the way to wider use of SF in schools as a means to interest "reluctant readers" in spending more time with books.

As the 1990s progressed it became clear that, after several years in the wilderness, the Australian SF anthology needed to re-model itself. Record numbers of original short stories were being published nearly every year, and with *Eidolon* and *Aurealis* as reliable sources of new writing there was little need to assemble anthologies of original work. Instead there was a pressing need to assemble the very best of Australia's short SF into anthologies so that students and general readers could gain fresh access to the works. The 1990s thus became the age of the reprint anthology.

Glass Reptile Breakout was rather like the first-ever Australian SF anthology, which was edited by John Baxter at the end of the 1960s: an attempt to fill a very large hole with a smallish rock. Of the eighteen stories, fifteen were reprints, a third were by women, four had been first published overseas and six had achieved award nominations or other forms of recognition. In 1993 the first Australian "best of" anthology was published: *Mortal Fire: Best Australian SF.* Edited by Terry Dowling and Van Ikin, this featured a beautiful cover painting by Nick Stathopoulos, and contained seventeen reprints reaching back to the early 1960s. Fourteen stories already had multiple reprints, eight had been published overseas, three had Ditmar nominations, and Sussex's "My Lady Tongue" had won the 1989 Ditmar Award for short fiction. Egan's "Axiomatic" had been a nominee for the British Science Fiction awards, Dowling's "Shatterwrack at Breaklight" had tied as winner of the *Omega* readers' poll, and Lake's "Creator" had appeared in Wollheim's *World's Best SF* anthology series. Australians had finally declared that this was the best that they could do, and it was very impressive indeed. Of course, overseas editors had been saying this about individual Australians' works for years—but better late than never.

With *Metaworlds: Best Australian Science Fiction* (1994), editor Paul Collins further refined the notion of a "Best Australian" collection: most stories were less than five years old, and eight of the twelve stories were originally published overseas. Egan's "Learning to be Me" had won the *Interzone* readers' poll, received a British Science Fiction Award nomination, and been reprinted in Dozois' *Year's Best SF* series, while Lake's "Re-deem the Time" had appeared in Carr's *Best SF of the Year* series. Dowling's "The Last Elephant" had won the 1988 Ditmar Award, and Turner's "I Still Call Australia Home" had won the *Aurealis* readers' poll. Perhaps just as significantly, *Metaworlds* was an economic success, too—like *Mortal Fire*, before it—selling over ninety percent of its print run, and leading Collins to edit a string of genre (but non-SF) anthologies.

A month after *Metaworlds* was released, Aphelion Publications reversed the trend toward reprinted "best of" anthologies by producing one which contained only seven reprints out of 29 stories. *Alien Shores* (1994), edited by Peter McNamara and Margaret Winch, was more like a fantasy blockbuster novel to look at, and at 603 pages is still the biggest Australian genre anthology ever. While Aphelion's most successful single-author books took two years to break even, *Alien Shores* was declared out of stock in three months. Of its seven original stories, five made it into the recommended reading list of Dozois' *Year's Best Science Fiction 12*, and Frahm's "Land's End" was nominated for a Ditmar; of the reprint stories, Dowling's "The Quiet Redemption of Andy the House" had won the 1990 Ditmar Award, while Egan's "The Caress" had been reprinted in Dozois' *Year's Best Science Fiction* and reached the Nebula preliminary ballot.

Alien Shores tried to cover all of the best known Australian authors and to spot the most talented newcomers, and as a result the quality was patchy in places. Some stories were outstanding. "The Caress" is still regarded by some as Egan's best story, and many readers have preferred Dowling's "The Quiet Redemption of Andy the House" to much of his other work because it is cleanly-told SF, lacking the baroque frills and tapestries of his Tom Tyson world. McMullen's original story "The Miocene Arrow" was called "the thinking man's *Jurassic Park*" by one reviewer, and formed the basis of his award-winning novel of the same name. It is worth noting that not long after this book, Peter McNamara decided to discontinue Aphelion as a publishing venture, because he considered that Australia's genre publishing scene was strong enough not to need the help of his sort of small press.

The high point of the anthologies of the 1990s was *Dreaming Down Under* (1998), edited by Jack Dann and Janeen Webb. This book was in the same mold as *Alien Shores* in that it was made up of commissioned, original short fiction. In many ways it was the ultimate statement on short fiction in Australia in the 1990s (although Greg Egan chose not to participate), and it went on to win the World Fantasy Award the following year.

By the mid-1990s it only remained for someone to follow the overseas example and edit a "year's best" collection of Australian SF. The necessary quantity of quality material was available, and in 1997 *Eidolon* editors Jonathan Strahan and Jeremy G. Byrne edited *The Year's Best Australian Science Fiction and Fantasy Volume 1* (1997). Half of the stories are SF in content. The same editors followed up in 1998 with *The Year's Best Australian Science Fiction and Fantasy Volume 2*.

Not quite anthologies, but also showcases of Australian SF were two non-fictions books. *The MUP Encyclopaedia of Australian Science Fiction and Fantasy* was edited by Paul Collins, with assistant editors Steven Paulsen and Sean McMullen. It had a foreword by the Hugo-winning Australian Peter Nicholls, and was launched by Neil Gaiman at the Australian national SF convention in 1998. This book sold very well, and was highly valued as a buying guide for the staff of school libraries, anxious to populate their shelves with SF by local authors. This was because the so-called "reluctant readers" tend to like to read SF more than most other material, and because local authors could be invited to visit the schools and speak to the students. Russell Blackford, Van Ikin, and Sean McMullen collaborated on *Strange Constellations: A History of Australian Science Fiction* (1999), the first detailed and comprehensive history of the genre in Australia. Both books won the William Atheling Award for SF Review and Criticism, and they were the first to make the story of Australian SF and fantasy available to the general readers outside the SF fan community.

AUTHORS OF THE BOOM

Greg Egan is doubtless the most successful living Australian SF author— and by some measures the most successful SF author Australia has yet produced. Meanwhile, the veteran Damien Broderick continued to produce major work such as *The White Abacus*, and ultra-veteran Wynne Whiteford, who sold his first SF in the 1930s, had a string of novels published in the USA. Gillian Rubinstein and John Marsden were particularly celebrated for their young adult work, while Paul Collins made so much money from writing children's and young adult SF for the educational market that he had to sell his clothing shop and concentrate on writing full time. Significant SF was also being produced by Dowling, Sussex and others who emerged in the 1970s and 80s.

In the 1990s, a new group of writers emerged, enriching the scene further. Sean McMullen, Sean Williams, Richard Harlan, Simon Brown, Steven Dedman and others were all published commercially, made serious money from their books, and in some cases began writing full time. One of the first writers in this group into print was Paul Voermans, who was a veteran of the early SF writers' workshops of the 70s, who had returned to writing after a long break. Sean Williams was the youngest, and rapidly moved from short fiction, to small press novels, to overseas publishers, picking up several awards on the way. The dynamic team of Mark Shirrefs and John Thompson is unique for a series of SF novelizations based on their young adult television series. They were selling in the hundreds of thousands in the early to mid-1990s, writing some of the few SF titles to out-perform Australian fantasy in that period. Finally, Jack Dann, a significant U.S. author, migrated to Australia after meeting the Australian author, editor and academic Janeen Webb in 1993. Dann not only brought detailed knowledge of the U.S. publishing scene to Australia, he was also a talent scout for one of the big U.S. publishing firms, and helped several Australians establish a place in the American market.

THE BOOM THAT NEVER BUSTED

Commercially, the publication in Australia of professionally packaged SF books of this quality meant that Australian authors of speculative fiction could carve out worthwhile careers in their own country. Early examples of this were Sean Williams' *Metal Fatigue* (1996), Tess Williams' *Map of Power* (1996) and Richard Harland's *The Dark Edge* (1997), but they have subsequently become commonplace. The fantasy writers such as Martin Middleton, Tony Shillitoe, and Sara Douglass already had sufficiently substantial sales in Australia to live off the proceeds of their writing, and Greg Egan, Sean McMullen and Jack Dann were in a similar position with their overseas sales. By the end of the decade there was no shortage of good authors producing high quality SF, and SF was a sufficiently big part of the market so that the crash of the late 1980s could not happen again—market demands would not allow it to happen.

On the other hand, how much of the success is façade? How much of it is fantasy's success in Australia being draped onto SF, rather like Conan being dressed in a space suit, given a ray gun with the trigger removed, and told to smile for the cameras? The 1990s have been the greatest decade for almost every type of achievement, that is beyond dispute. Until the levelling out that happened around 2000, records for original books and stories published were being broken nearly every year, while the books that were being published sold strongly, and often won awards. The local magazine *Aurealis* has survived, prospered and grown, while at the time of writing another four paying magazines are being published. Australian residents are often serious contenders for overseas awards, including the Hugos and Nebulas, and are occasional winners. They have featured regularly in the international "Best of" anthologies, and have scored well in overseas readers polls. Back at home, Australian commercial publishers now publish SF for adult, young adult and children's markets, and SF television series such as *Spellbinder* and *Ocean Girl* have gone to multiple seasons while attracting a wide international audience. So where does the truth lie?

When all else fails, I turn to statistics, and the statistics contain some surprising facts. For the period 1999-2001, three-quarters of the genre output from Australia was fantasy—and in terms of wordage, quite a lot more because the fantasy novels are on average a lot thicker. Two-thirds of these novels were by female authors, while the men wrote SF and fantasy about equally. The output of SF by female authors has remained unchanged throughout the 1990s at about fifteen percent. Overseas publication of Australian short SF was about twenty-five percent, which was a considerable improvement on the early 1990s. The total numbers of works published indicates a plateau in output, rather than a fall.[15]

Thus Australian SF really does seem to have been dragged along in the backwash of the really serious performer in commercial terms, Australian heroic, high, romantic, and modernist fantasy. The majority

---

[15] Sean McMullen, "Science Fiction in Australia," *Locus* (January 2002): p. 52.

of the blockbuster titles have been either fantasy or SF indistinguishable from fantasy. For the SF titles that have been published locally, the best sales have been around 4,000-6,000, while comparable fantasy novels have averaged between 10,000 to 15,000—and remember, around 25,000 sales is considered to be a bestseller in the relatively small Australian book market. Why, then, does written SF perform so poorly—relatively speaking—in a culture so dominated by SF in the electronic media? After all, on Australian television SF dominates fantasy so heavily that most enthusiasts would be pressed to name a single Australian fantasy show apart from the American co-produced *Roar* (1997).

The answer can be found in an analysis of U.S. statistics. Fantasy is the big performer there, as well. To go even further, historically SF has been a relatively small and stable section of the market. SF in film, television and computer games has expanded massively since the late 70s, and fantasy has become a growth sector that features a lot of SF authors, but dedicated and exclusive SF readers have always been a small minority. Most people will read a few SF books at one time or another, but a lot of people who would describe their tastes as mainstream still treat fantasy novels like mainstream soap operas—escape vehicles from our modern world—and consume them in quantity. The key, pivotal fact in the entire, complex equation of the 1990s boom in Australian genre publishing is that locally written and published fantasy virtually did not exist in Australia at the beginning of 1990, yet there was a great deal of fantasy from overseas on the shelves of the bookshops. Australian fantasy was being written, most notably the U.S.-published Bard series by Keith Taylor, but properly marketed and presented local Australian fantasy was a very large niche waiting to be discovered.

Where does SF fit in with the success of fantasy? As far as I have been able to deduce, the early stages of the SF boom were visible before the watershed year of 1990. The "discoveries" of the 1990s, Greg Egan, Sean McMullen and Rosleen Love, for example, were all selling to overseas markets in 1988-89, and many others were writing but not yet published. Thus the talent was there, but it needed a vehicle to get it moving. Fantasy was that vehicle.

A question often asked is, what is special about Australian SF, what is characteristically Australian about it? Some would say nothing, as Greg Egan argued quite persuasively in an article published in *Eidolon* in 1995.[16] Others would say that Australians bring to the field an English-

---

[16] Greg Egan, "A Report on the Origins & Hazardous Effects of Miracle Ingredient A," *Eidolon* 17-18 (Winter 1995): pp. 32-38.

language perspective that is neither American nor British, and I am one of those others. What is important to aspiring beginners in Australia in 2003 is that they now know that they are in the company of Australians who live and write in the same country but get published and recognized internationally, and make a living from their writing. Without knowing that there is at least a chance of success, people tend not to bother.

So how does one build that boom? Identifying and exploiting a large market niche is vital, because it gets commercial finance behind you. On a panel at Zencon II in 1988, I pointed out that Australians were buying a vast amount of fantasy, far more than science fiction, yet they were publishing practically none of it at home. Two years later, the first commercial fantasy titles proved to be an instant commercial success. By chance, Aphelion Publications was revived out of the defunct *Aphelion* magazine in the same year. Also by chance *Aurealis* and *Eidolon* magazines were launched in the same year. Because of the publishing recession, Australians were breaking into the overseas markets because there was so little going on locally. To simplify further, authors were raising their standards, small press publishers were appearing who were in for the long haul, and the success of commercial fantasy made Australian SF also look hot as well. That is what touched off and sustained the boom of the 1990s. Without the commercial backing, there would have at least been a boom in short and small press SF. Without the innovative small presses and magazines, there would have been a boom in high quality Australian SF being published overseas. The anthologies were a product of the expansion in short SF publication, but they boosted the field further. The scale and speed of the boom were far greater because so many things happened independently at the same time, but probably would have happened anyway.

COLD, HARD, BUT INTERESTING STATISTICS

Numerically speaking, Australians are a small part of the international scene, but how do they rate in overall profile? The annual *Locus* magazine poll of its readers for the two years past returns a reasonable snapshot of how people are doing in the international, English speaking market, and some figures from either side of the boom make interesting reading. In the 1990 *Locus* readers' poll,[17] there are no Australian novels among

---

[17] *Locus* Poll Results, *Locus* (August 1990): pp. 34-37.

the 84 listed, and no works of short fiction. In the 1991 poll,[18] there are no Australian novels out of 66, but three shorter works made it: Best Novelette: Greg Egan, "The Caress" (#19); Best Short Story: Greg Egan, "Axiomatic"(#11) and Greg Egan, "Learning to be Me" (#17). Contrast this with the Locus Poll for 2002.[19] Best SF Novel Sean McMullen's *Eyes of the Calculor* (#23); Best Fantasy Novel: Garth Nix, *Lirael* (#15); Best First Novel: Cecelia Dart-Thornton, *The Ill-Made Mute* (#3); Best Novella: Jack Dann, "The Diamond Pit" (#12); Best Artist: Shaun Tan (#10); Best Collection: Jack Dann, *Jubilee* (#25). Checking the 2003 results[20] we have Best SF Novel: Greg Egan, *Schild's Ladder* (#10); Best Fantasy Novel: Sean McMullen, *Voyage of the Shadowmoon*(#12) and Cecelia Dart-Thornton, *The Lady of the Sorrows* (#17); Best Young Adult Novel: Sean Williams, *The Storm Weaver and the Sand* (#9); Best Novella: Greg Egan, "Singleton" (#18); Best Artist: Shaun Tan (#17); Best Non-Fiction: Justine Larbalaster, *The Battle of the Sexes in Science Fiction* (#4).

Confine the above figures to novels, and Australians score 4.5% for 2002, and 6.0% for 2003, which is way above the per head of population figures. Contrast this with the 0% result for 1990 and 1991, and it is pretty obvious that there has been a massive improvement. Fantasy scores six Australian novels in 2002-03, while SF has two—that is, three-quarters fantasy, which agrees with the figures for total output of SF and fantasy in my *Locus* article in January 2002[15]. Only one of the five authors was female, which is wildly different from the two thirds representation of women in the total number of works published. Three of the men write both SF and fantasy, the only woman writes only fantasy, and one of the men writes only SF. This is in general agreement with my *Locus* article findings as well.[15] None had a commercial book published before 1990, all have been published internationally, all but one are multiple award winners, and two are international award winners. The results raise a question of why Australians are somewhat better represented in the poll per head of population than authors from other countries. Is there some subtle difference in the Australian writing style that comes across to international readers as novel and appealing? To this I would say, "What a great opportunity for someone else to do an article!"

---

[18] *Locus* Poll Results, *Locus* (July 1991): pp. 38-41.

[19] *Locus* Poll Results, *Locus* (August 2002): pp. 40-43.

[20] *Locus* Poll Results, *Locus* (August 2003): pp. 46-49.

CONCLUSION

The conclusions of this article must be that the improvement in the Australian scene is long-term; fantasy has grown from virtually nothing to dominate the market; no single factor caused the boom; the proportion of works by women was virtually unchanged, and many aspects of the boom could have happened independently of each other but because they happened together it came across more dramatically to foreign observers. To have a boom in SF, a country needs a stable, diverse, and at least partly commercial market, along with fans to write about their authors and give the best of them awards. After that, it is up to the authors, because skilled, imaginative, and prolific authors were the true foundation of Australia's SF boom of the 1990s.

Further Reading

Most of the general background material, author profiles, outlines of some of the more significant works, and bibliographic material used in this article is to be found in the following two books:

Blackford, Russell, Van Ikin, and Sean McMullen. *Strange Constellations: A History of Australian Science Fiction.* Westport, Connecticut: Greenwood, 1999.

The MUP Encyclopaedia of Australian Science Fiction and Fantasy. Edited by Paul Collins, assistant editors Steven Paulsen and Sean McMullen. Foreword by Peter Nicholls. Melbourne University Press, 1998.

In addition, the following short article provides statistics and trends in Australian genre publishing from the finalization of the *Strange Constellations* manuscript in 1998 to December 2001:

McMullen, Sean. "Science Fiction in Australia." *Locus* (January 2002), p. 52.

STRANGE LOOPS OF WONDER
Catherine Asaro

Quintessential hard science fiction. What is it?

In his introduction to the anthology *New Legends*, editor Greg Bear notes that he looked for well-written, dramatically strong science fiction with believable characters "in the universe as perceived by science, or as science might come to perceive it."[21] Science fiction with soul. He resists the label hard science fiction because of the misuses and abuses associated with it. Even so, or perhaps exactly because of Bear's careful choices, this anthology contains some top-notch hard SF. Its final story, "Wang's Carpets" by Greg Egan, is the subject of this column—quintessential hard SF.[22]

WHAT COULD BE

In *The Ascent of Wonder,* an anthology following the evolution of hard SF, writer Gregory Benford and editors David G. Hartwell and Kathryn Cramer discuss hard SF in their introductions.[23] With elegant contrasts and commentary, these well-written essays reflect a fundamental quality that marks hard SF: the dialogue of ideas. They elucidate the sometimes conflicting and sometimes overlapping philosophies within the subgenre.

For this column, I draw on all three philosophies, but with an emphasis on hard SF as based in known fact. Extrapolation follows in a logical—albeit not necessarily obvious—manner from science, engineering, and math as it was known when the story was written. This is not to say all extrapolations are directly determinable from what we know, but rather that they are reasonably consistent with it.

"Wang's Carpets" distills the essence of scientific rigor blended with the creative imaginings of fiction. The story takes place twenty-three centuries in our future. Egan sets a daunting task; given the exponential rate of progress in this century alone, it is difficult to extrapolate forward

---

[21] Greg Bear with Martin H. Greenberg, eds., *New Legends*. (New York: Tor Books. 1995).

[22] "Wang's Carpets" also appeared in the satisfying and diverse anthology, *The Year's Best Science Fiction, Thirteenth Annual Collection*, edited by Gardner Dozois. New York: St. Martin's Press. June 1995.

[23] David G. Hartwell and Kathryn Cramer, eds., *The Ascent of Wonder: The Evolution of Hard SF*. (New York: Tor. July 1994).

even a few centuries. The story meets that challenge, creating a persuasive universe. As Cramer notes: "Writing stories within the rules of the universe as we know it and yet discovering fantastic possibilities of new ways of life is the central endeavor of the hard SF writer." It represents what the future *could* be, not what it must be.

HUMANITY TRANSCENDED

In "Wang's Carpets," people live in polises, groupings of citizens with similar beliefs. Although the word evokes a Greek city-state or a metropolis, these are actually virtual societies. Humans no longer have physical bodies; they are "transhuman," existing as software simulations that create exoselves as diverse as their minds and associated machines can produce.

Egan explores the ramifications of transhumanity, developing a scenario far removed from our experience. At the same time, his characters are believable and sympathetic, a notable accomplishment given the alien quality of a milieu that changes according to the desires of those within it, intelligences that can simultaneously present themselves in a different manner to each and every transhuman they encounter.

The characters might also be called "trans-artificial intelligences": they run as software, like AIs, the first generation being scanned from human minds. "Wang's Carpets" is a well-rendered portrayal of a prediction made by computer scientist Douglas Hofstadter in his Pulitzer Prize-winning book *Gödel, Escher, Bach: An Eternal Golden Braid*: "Artificial Intelligence, when it reaches the level of human intelligence— or even if it surpasses it—will still be plagued by the problems of art, beauty, and simplicity, and will run up against these things constantly in its own search for knowledge and understanding."[24]

ONE OR MANY?

The story concerns the Carter-Zimmerman polis, which has made a thousand clones of itself and sent them out to seek life in the galaxy. With this premise Egan unveils anthrocosmology (AC), inviting the reader to ask, "Did human consciousness bootstrap all of space-time into existence, in order to explain itself?" If so, that could imply no other intelligent life except ours exists; nonsentient life could arise, but a *self-*

---

[24] Douglas Hofstadter. *Gödel, Escher, Bach: An Eternal Golden Braid*. (New York: Vintage Books. 1980).

aware species would bootstrap its own space-time, and the likelihood of two separately evolved intelligences producing the identical universe is probably infinitesimal.

This harkens to current debates on the existence of alien life. In the 1960s, Cornell astronomer Frank Drake developed an equation to estimate the number of technological civilizations in the galaxy. However, the Drake equation requires data about which we can only guess, such as the fraction of stars in the Milky Way with planetary systems. As a result, predictions range from zero to huge numbers. Most scientists agree life in some form probably exists elsewhere; in fact, evidence of organisms on Mars may have already been found.[25] The more intense debate concerns whether or not *intelligent* life is a fluke on Earth.[26]

Both "Wang's Carpets" and George Alec Effinger's story "One" in *New Legends* evoke this debate. The contrast between the two illustrates one of Bear's cogent points in *New Legends*: science fiction sets up a dialogue to critically analyze our scientific endeavors.

I THINK, THEREFORE I AM

The most intriguing speculation in "Wang's Carpets" centers on the life form discovered on a world orbiting the star Vega. With satisfying rigor, Egan ties together chemistry, physics, biology, and astronomy, designing a watery planet markedly different from Earth, incapable of supporting life as we know it but by no means dead. The attention to detail gratifies, as when a character notes that constellations seen from the Vegan system are more familiar than strange because it is only twenty-seven light years from Earth. I also enjoyed the dry humor, such as the tongue-in-cheek specter of robot-like citizens from another polis doing "astrophysical engineering" to drag in a white dwarf star and crowd the neighborhood.

The planet's only apparent life form is based on one form of chemistry: "carbohydrate, here, played every biochemical role: information carrier, enzyme, energy source, structural material." Their structure intrigues: "a *single molecule*, a two-dimensional polymer weighing twenty-five million kilograms. A giant sheet of folded polysaccharide." Imagine gargantuan cellulose molecules floating in the

---

[25] David S. McKay, et. al., "Search for Past Life on Mars: Possible Relic Biogenic Activity in Martian Meteorite ALH84001." *Science* (16 August 1996).

[26] See for example: Ernest Mayr and Sagan, Carl., "The Search for Extraterrestrial Intelligence: Scientific Quest or Hopeful Folly?" *The Planetary Report.* (May/June 1996). (65 North Catalina Ave, Pasadena, CA, 91106-2301.) For the Drake equation: Theodore P. Snow, *The Dynamic Universe: An Introduction to Astronomy.* (St. Paul: West Publishing Company, 1983), p. 499-508 (or later editions).

sea. Parent carpets reproduce by breaking apart to make daughters, a clever metaphor that evokes nuclear reactions, where parent nuclei decay into daughter particles. The carpets could never survive on Earth; other organisms would eat them. Egan achieves what is relatively rare even in hard SF, the fictional creation of a plausible, genuinely alien life form.

Most impressive, though, is the use of math. The carpets are living analogues of a theory developed by Hao Wang that describes how square tiles with various shaped edges fit together to cover a plane, forming a mosaic of interlocked pieces like a jigsaw puzzle. The molecular building blocks of the carpets are living Wang tiles; each square bonds to others, allowing the carpet to grow. Just as in DNA, where only specific bases can pair up to form a double helix, so a tile can only join to another tile if it has the appropriate edge. The resulting mosaic is a living but nonsentient entity.

Or is it nonsentient?

To answer, we need a peculiar beast: the Fourier transform. It comes from the Fourier series, which is a sum of sines and cosines, functions that oscillate. When added according to certain rules, this sum produces a repeating waveform, say a square or sawtooth wave. Just as width, length, and height define an object in our three-dimensional universe, so the sines and cosines define such a waveform in an infinite-dimensional universe, where dimension is specified by the oscillation frequency of the sine or cosine "vector." Although an infinite number of these vectors exist, usually we can get a good picture of the waveform with a finite number.

If we let frequency become continuous and don't require the waveform to be periodic, the sum becomes an integral—a Fourier transform—that can describe any reasonably well behaved function. So what do transforms *do*, other than give science and engineering students headaches?

They take us from one space to another.

Suppose I know how the response of an apparatus varies with time. If I Fourier transform a pulse that describes that time response, I get a function that tells me what frequencies go into making the pulse. I've gone from a temporal space to a frequency space.

Enter Wang's carbo-carpets. In our space-time, a carpet's growing edge is a curve that twists and turns as tiles add to it. A Fourier transform done on a simulation of that edge takes it to a space defined by a thousand frequencies—in other words, the edge is a mathematical gateway into a thousand-dimensional universe. And that's only the beginning. The behavior of the growing edge transforms into bizarre thousand-dimensional functions that look and act like living creatures. Their interactions indicate some have memory and can think. They even think about their thoughts.

They are self-aware.

Imagine a living computer running a simulation where math functions within the simulation *think*. Then consider an implication of anthrocosmology: if human consciousness created reality and transhumans can simulate any reality they can imagine, that suggests the physical universe has no special status above any other virtual reality. Remembering that AC also suggests the universe has no other intelligent life, does the discovery of self-aware creatures existing only as a mathematical virtual reality refute the theory or support it?

Just as debates over artificial intelligence ask, "Can a machine evolve self-awareness?" so "Wang's Carpets" asks, "Can virtual reality evolve a self-aware virtual reality?"

EUREKA

In *The Ascent of Wonder*, Hartwell writes, "Hard SF is about the beauty of truth. It is a metaphorical or symbolic representation of the wonder at the perception of truth that is experienced at the moment of scientific discovery. The eureka." This happens often in "Wang's Carpets," one of the most exciting for me being the discovery of the carpets' nature.

Yet in reaffirming the eureka, the story raises questions about that same paradigm, our perception of truth. In *New Legends*, Bear writes, "[SF] is the only form of literature that clearly and consistently criticizes the Western paradigm: scientific investigation and technological endeavor."

We think of science as the discovery of truth. However, every theory so far produced is actually no more than a construct of the human mind. The equations are not laws determined by the universe; they are models we design to help us better understand that universe. Successful theories can have remarkable predictive success, but none have yet been developed that don't ultimately break down.

Two ethicists, Caltech philosophy professor James Woodward and physics professor David Goodstein, in their essay "Conduct, Misconduct and the Structure of Science," examine two theories of scientific methodology, Bacon inductivism and Popperian falsification. They write: "Inductivists attach a great deal of weight to the complete avoidance of error. In contrast, falsificationists claim that the history of science shows us that all hypotheses are falsified sooner or later...For science to advance, scientists must be free to be wrong."[27] Ptolemy yielded to Copernicus. The flat earth turned out to be round. Newton's equations gave way to quantum mechanics and relativity.

But if all science is falsifiable, what is truth?

"Wang's Carpets" sets up a dialogue about that question. The idea that human consciousness created the universe to explain itself speaks innovatively to the observation that scientific theories are only models we create to explain the universe. In the process of evoking our wonder at the perception of truth, the story challenges that very same perception.

Can a story refute what creates it?

That question brings to mind the picture *Drawing Hands* by M. C. Escher, which Hofstadter refers to in *Gödel, Escher, Bach*. The picture shows a right hand drawing a left hand, which is drawing the right hand drawing it. The hands create a "tangled loop." Similarly, "Wang's Carpets" is a tangled loop; by challenging our perceptions of truth it may cause us to modify how we perceive it, thus modifying our reaction to the story, which modifies our perception of truth. And so on.

Just as the hands were drawn by Escher, who is outside their universe and thus unknown to them, so "Wang's Carpets" was created by Egan, who is outside its fictional universe. These are artistic parallels to the argument that a machine can never attain intelligence because it must, at some level, be programmed by a human. Even if the initial software was scanned from a human mind, the system could never achieve sentience because human minds have innate capabilities unavailable to a machine. Software may be self-modifying, like hands drawing each other or philosophical points modifying their basis, but such systems exist only because an inviolate outside level creates them: Escher drew the picture, Egan wrote the story, humans program computers.

According to this argument, human thought has no inviolate level; the mind acts on itself "from the ground up." Hofstadter argues against this, suggesting the neural structure of the brain is inviolate. Our thoughts modify themselves, not the biological processes that create them. The Escher hands don't know they are drawn; the Egan characters don't

---

[27] James Woodward and Goodstein, David, "Conduct, Misconduct and the Structure of Science." *American Scientist* (Sep-Oct 1996).

know they are written; we don't experience the firing of neurons. We can imagine their workings, just as Egan might have had characters imagine they were being written by Egan, or Escher could have drawn himself drawing the hands. But an outside level still controls the representations.

If neurons can be considered inviolate, does that mean intelligence *can* arise in a self-modifying system determined by such a level? "Wang's Carpets" offers a symbolic representation of the argument over whether or not characters such as those that drive the story—and thus create the symbolism—can exist. Egan doesn't give an answer; he leaves it for readers to ponder. I can't help but think that any species which creates such provocative works of art, literature, and science can also create artificial intelligence.

One last thought: if an intelligence that bootstrapped its universe to explain itself *could* create other self-aware life forms, like humans creating AIs, might we ourselves be the creation of some unknown intelligence that made the universe to explain itself?

THE CHARACTER OF SCIENCE

In *The Ascent of Wonder*, Benford writes, "To get the science right, you have to know the scientists...The most important voice to get right is the style of the scientists themselves." We set up problems. Develop models. Investigate. Seek new discoveries. "Wang's Carpets" portrays this well in the debates, explorations, and dialogues of the characters. It beautifully distills the sense of excitement many scientists feel when faced with a good problem: "[The planet] Orpheus hung in the sky beneath them, a beautiful puzzle waiting to be decoded, demanding to be understood."

Hard SF has suffered a reputation for one-dimensional characters that speak only to a narrow range of readers. To an extent, this perception is due to a difference in philosophy compared to other literary forms. Hartwell writes: "Hard SF characters tend not to achieve validation through gaining knowledge of their own inner life but rather through action in the external environment." This is not to say it requires poor characterization, but that character manifests differently. The subgenre is harder to define than seems at first glance; it is possible to write successful hard SF where characters achieve validation through both inner conflict and external factors, to write it with only the external, and to do either or neither with depth of characterization.

As Hartwell notes, over the years the subgenre has evolved toward deeper and richer characterization, influenced by writers such as Ursula K. Le Guin. In "Wang's Carpets," Egan gracefully combines the external with depth of characterization, creating richly complex people (actually, transpeople) dealing with outer and inner conflicts. Because the characters are simulations, their inner life is *part* of their environment, making the story structure itself a play on the nature of the genre.

Hard SF has also been known for setting emotional distance between characters and reader, the reasoning being that it is based on science, a logical rather than emotional enterprise. However, a scientific mindset doesn't preclude depth of emotion. Indeed, many scientists feel strongly about their lives and work. Woodward and Goodstein note: "If we expect to find scientists who are disinterested observers of nature we are bound to be disappointed, not because scientists have failed to measure up to the appropriate standard of behavior, but because we have tried to apply the wrong standard of behavior."

Bear translates this to SF: "Each story must engage *strong emotions*...for me, Sense of Wonder is a very strong emotion." In "Wang's Carpets," he has indeed chosen a story that embodies that wonder, at least for this reader.

The SF field encourages vigorous discourse about what defines the genre. That dialogue reflects the scientific mindset in that it compares, contrasts, illuminates, and ultimately advances the field, just as ongoing debates among scientists test our models of reality and so advance scientific knowledge. The growing diversity of *all* SF enriches hard SF; it challenges the subgenre to look critically at itself and ask valuable questions, a relationship similar to the practice of formalized scientific debate that leads to scientific progress.

FERRARI

Hard SF tends toward minimal prose. Where another genre might say, "Her gaze roamed the room until it settled on his tall figure," hard SF would say, "She looked at him." Either style can be done with great beauty—or clunk like lead on asphalt. At its worst, hard SF prose makes readers wince; at its best, it is sheer pleasure.

In "Wang's Carpets" the prose is a Ferrari, lean and sleek, with clean, minimal lines—and great power. Its elegant sentences are so dense, I often had to stop reading to think. Imagine passages like freeze-dried kernels of meaning; pull over the car, pour the kernels into the cup of your mind, add the steaming water of thought, and take a long drought of the heady brew.

The prose has a poetry about it, as in the characters' names: Paolo, Elena, Orlando, Liesl. Throughout the story, descriptions evoke lovely, vivid images. Interspersed among complex passages are simple sentences, the contrast giving them a tongue-in-cheek quality, as if to say, "Okay, you digested all that, now let's have a little fun." Consider the description of a simulation that one character's clone created:

> The environment was full of birds and insects, rodents and small reptiles—decorative in appearance, but also satisfying a more abstract aesthetic: softening the harsh radial symmetry of the lone observer; anchoring the simulation by perceiving it from a multitude of viewpoints. Ontological guy lines. No one had asked the lizards if they wanted to be cloned, though. They were coming along for the ride, like it or not.

Egan also condenses the scientific exposition: a few words pack a lot of punch. Historically, a link has existed between hard SF prose and the way scientists write. Hartwell notes: "[Hard SF] is normally a conservative literature...the prose of scientific description...an advantage for the main body of writers and readers, who come from a scientific or technological background and often read and write mostly in this prose style."

Unfortunately, writing style is an often neglected skill in the training of scientists, with the result that some scientific prose can be mind-numbing unless one is fascinated enough by the subject to overlook its presentation. So successful hard SF authors do write in a more literary style than the average scientist. But their approach still values exposition. It is an art form: wordy, awkward phrasing weakens a story, but if the exposition is too brief or abstruse, it robs the ideas of their full impact. Hard SF must balance its natural sleekness against the need to give the eureka its due.

In "Wang's Carpets," exposition flows smoothly from dialogue and events, and from musings of the character Paolo. I did wonder at times if compactness was carried too far, to where it sacrificed richness in the prose and ideas. On the other hand, reading this story is like experiencing recursive artistry. Imagine a box whose sides, when examined, reveal intricate patterns. Open the box to find another inside; when removed, the new box shows new marvels. Open it to find another, with yet different marvels. And so on, box after captivating box.

BREAKTHROUGH PROPULSION

The polis ships in "Wang's Carpets" travel at sublight speeds using fusion engines. At first it struck me as odd, like modern day travelers crossing the Atlantic on log rafts. I was willing to suspend belief, though, given the debate over superluminal (FTL) physics as a story device in SF.

Although no evidence of a superluminal universe exists, neither has it been disproved, contrary to popular belief. Relativity does predict some bizarre effects, but so does quantum mechanics, which has shown itself a powerful model of physical reality. Dr. Robert L. Forward writes, "There are many scientific publications which have looked into this question in considerable detail, and have been unable to find any violation of any conservation law or any other accepted laws of physics by FTL travel except the causality principle, which is not a physical law but a philosophical assumption."[28]

Whether or not we will ever circumvent the light barrier remains to be seen. But the growing interest of scientists in the subject and the amount of activity within just a few decades suggests the time has come to stop worrying about FTL travel as a fictional device. However, for "Wang's Carpets" the point may be moot; the lack of advanced propulsion reflects the conflict between the polises that chose to look for life and the inwardly-directed anthrocosmologists who argue the search is a waste of time when any virtual reality they create is just as valid. The idea that it would take transhumans two millennia just to visit the stars, let alone develop advanced propulsion, offers an intriguing contrast between the priorities that might be set by humans versus immortal software beings.

ANOTHER CONTROVERSY REVISITED

---

[28] Robert L. Forward, *Indistinguishable From Magic*. (New York: Baen Books. 1995). See also Catherine Asaro, "Special Relativity and Complex Speed," *Am. J. Phy.* 64(4) 421:429

As AIs, transhumans can blend software, sharing grafts of their emotions and thoughts. Egan thus joins other authors who have included fictional extrapolations of science to create "psi." As a story device, psi sparks controversy in SF, in part because it has sometimes been used in ways that seemed more magic than science. A distinction needs to made; works such as "Wang's Carpets" use extrapolations based on established fields, AI in this case, or neuroscience and molecular biology in novels like *The Bohr Maker*.[29] This differs from the use of the story device in fantasy, where it derives from the rich folklore and myths of our venerable storytelling traditions.

Ironically, Alan Turing, who introduced many concepts that shaped the field of AI, included telepathy as a possible means to distinguish human from machine, the idea being a machine could never exhibit telepathy whereas (he believed) a human might. This argument was actually dropped from his article by one publisher.[30] I enjoyed the wry humor in the comment "Wang's Carpets" makes on this controversy by having telepathic software.

The story also comments on the idea that individuals create models of the other individuals they interact with and relate to those models rather than the actual people. In a turn-about, transhumans create their own exoselves according to how they wish to exist. If one transhuman develops an inaccurate mental model of another, they can, if they wish, share grafts of their thoughts to rectify the problem.

At one point Paolo muses on the practice of group emotion sharing: "the whole idea of mass telepathy as an end in itself seemed bizarre . . . and even old-fashioned, in a way. Humans, clearly, would have benefited from a good strong dose of each other's inner life, to keep them from slaughtering each other—but any civilized transhuman could respect and value other citizens without the need to have *been there*, firsthand."

Again the story sets up a provocative dialogue on a paradigm of hard SF Edited by David G. Hartwell and Kathryn Cramerby evoking that paradigm. In showing how a transhuman might achieve validation through the external rather than the inner life, it suggests that to reach that place humans need to deal with their inner life. Imagine an artist looking into a mirror to draw a self-portrait—but the artist in the portrait isn't drawing a picture.

---

[29] Nagata, Linda. *The Bohr Maker*. city: pub. month, 1995; Asaro, Catherine, *Primary Inversion*. New York: Tor. March 1995; Asaro, Catherine, *Catch the Lightning*. New York: Tor. Dec 1996.

[30] Hofstadter, Douglas. *Gödel, Escher, Bach: An Eternal Golden Braid*. New York: Vintage Books. 1980. 599.

STARS IN HER EYES

Within hard SF is a tradition of women in non-traditional roles, particularly in science and the military. Connected to this is its overlooked tradition of portraying personal relationships as a positive, continuing aspect of the plot.

In her essay "Marriage Perceived: English Literature 1873-1944," Carolyn G. Heilbrun writes: "It appears that novelists, until the modern period, agreed...weddings, like hangings, marked the end of experience. The novelist averted his eyes from married life as from the grave: perhaps he suspected a resemblance between them...Courtship has been another matter. On the road to marriage, as on a voyage to discovery, the journey not the arrival matters."[31] In such literature women appeared in roles primarily concerned with sexual desirability. Resolution of the sexual tension often resulted in their fading from the plot or dying.

Because of hard SF's undeserved reputation for paucity of emotion, its accomplishment in using a new paradigm regarding human love is often dismissed. However, relationships are no less realistically portrayed in hard SF than in other literature; rather, emphasis is more on partnership and solution of problems. In Hal Clement's *Fossil*, for example, the two main (human) characters are a husband and wife team.[32] They work well together. They *like* each other. Their partnership began before the story, enhances their interactions with their environment, and continues after the story ends. Poul Anderson's "Scarecrow" in *New Legends* and the novels of Joan Slonczewski are other examples. Picking up most any issue of *Analog* reveals similar works; in fact, *Analog* editor Stan Schmidt has written on the subject.[33]

This is neither to say all hard SF incorporates this theme nor that it should. Nor do I claim hard SF is a panacea free from sexist portrayals. Many controversial issues remain. However, it deserves more credit than it receives.

The relationship between the lovers Paolo and Elena in "Wang's Carpets" embodies this theme. They are comfortable with each other whether discussing theoretical physics or making love (the mind boggles at the thought of AI sex). They like as well as love each other. Elena is portrayed as a sexual woman rather than a sex object, a believable,

---

[31] Carolyn G. Heilbrun, *Hamlet's Mother and Other Women.* (New York: Columbia University Press, 1990): p. 112.

[32] Hal Clement, *Fossil* (New York: DAW, 1994).

[33] Stanley Schmidt, "Nouveaux Cliché's," *Analog.* (Oct 1993).

decent character whose relationship with Paolo is only one of several roles she plays in the plot.

Initially Elena chooses only one copy of herself to awake, the clone in whatever polis first finds life. However, she comes to regret the richness of discovery her other clones will never experience. Paolo respects her wish for emotional distance while she ponders the problem, making no attempt to tell her what to do or otherwise influence her decision, even though its result will determine whether or not his other clones have the company of the woman they love.

"Wang's Carpets" also makes clever plays on gender. Orlando, Paolo's father, is "first generation": a human scanned into software. He remembers being human and identifies himself as a heterosexual man. As a software clone of his father, Paulo also identifies Orlando as male. So when he meets his father's lover, she presents as Catherine. However, Catherine presents to many others as Samuel, because Samuel, another "first generation" transhuman, identifies himself as a heterosexual man. So Samuel interacts with Paolo's father as if Samuel were a man and Orlando a woman, while at the same time Orlando interacts as a man with Catherine. It's a marvelously absurd maze of contradiction only possible for self-programming intelligences that can present in as many different forms as they wish.

The name "Samuel" resonates with the debate on AI. Computer scientist Arthur Samuel argued against machine consciousness, his points summarized by Hofstadter as follows: "No computer ever 'wants' to do anything because it was programmed by someone else. Only if it could program itself from zero on up—an absurdity—would it have its own sense of desire."[34] I enjoyed the satire of a self-aware AI in such a complicated love relationship being named after someone who didn't believe software could ever have its own sense of desire.

RESOLUTIONS

Suffice it to say that "Wang's Carpets" is one of the best works of hard SF in short fiction I have had the pleasure to find. It isn't an easy story to read—but it is well worth the effort.

---

[34] Hofstadter, Douglas. *Gödel, Escher, Bach: An Eternal Golden Braid*. New York: Vintage Books. 1980. 685.

THE TIMEX MACHINE
Lucius Shepard

It was with some trepidation that I, Herbert George Wells, set forth once again into the future, this time in order to view a motion picture based upon my novel *The Time Machine* and directed by my great-grandson Simon. I had, during a previous visit, viewed Mr. George Pal's spirited but trashy attempt at filming my little book, and there was a correspondence between the two productions that gave me pause—the casting of an Australian actor in the lead. I had found Mr. Pal's choice for the role, Rod Taylor, to have the emotive capacity of mutton, and I feared that this new Australian incarnation, Guy Pearce, would also prove unequal to my conception of the character. Why this insistence on a colonial? I wondered. Why not an Englishman to play an Englishman (or an American, for it turns out that the Time Traveller has been recast as a resident of New York City)? It seems one should expect this much regard for one's work from a relation, no matter how distant and devoid of traditional values he may be.

I prefer to use the time machine for serious business, but I must confess that on my several journeys to the late twentieth and early twenty-first centuries, I have developed a fondness for the motion picture, especially for those films' treating of time travel. This is not to say that I have thought many worthwhile. Of them all, only *Time After Time*, whose conceit was to detail one of my earliest temporal expeditions, featuring the excellent Malcolm McDowell, possessed the least verisimilitude and charm; though even this film roused in me no little revulsion with its insistence that my dear friend, the late Dr._____, a gentle, inquiring soul, was none other than Jack the Ripper. *Time and Again* was, I suppose, a harmless enough love story, poignant in an overly sugared fashion, but its lack of scientific rigour was dismaying. As for the rest, my God!, the idea of a simple tale told well appears to have eluded those who dictate the policies that command the industry responsible for these gaudy idiocies. Still, I cannot deny a certain admiration for the technical aspects of such films. Judging by the size of the explosions they generate, a studio such as DreamWorks might well be capable, should they effect a journey back to the nineteenth century, of conquering a considerable portion of the globe.

In relating my experience of my great-grandson's film, I must first state that I understand this century's expectations of its entertainments are not those of my own. Every age demands certain elements designed to appease the public mind, just as in the Elizabethan era the Bard himself was induced to leaven his masterpieces with low comedy so as to delight the groundlings; and thus I assumed what I was about to see would not be a faithful rendering of my book, but rather a different work entirely, one infused with the spirit of the thing. I did not expect, however, the amalgam of illogic and hyper-kinetic foolishness with which my eye was met. Even for those who have read my book, it will be necessary to recount the plot of the motion picture, for it differs widely from that of my quiet story.

Andrew Hardegen (Pearce) is a college professor whose attention is given over to two interests: the nature of time and the romantic pursuit of a young woman, Emma (Sienna Guillory). When Emma is killed by a thief in Central Park, Hardegen becomes obsessed with building a time machine so he can travel into the past and prevent her death. After four years of maniacal work, he succeeds in his objective, returns to the moment when he met Emma in the park, and steers her away from the place, only to have her killed by a runaway hansom cab. At this juncture Hardegen decides that the past is unalterable. Having been in love on several occasions, most notably with the director's great-grandmother, I insist that obsession should be made of sterner stuff. Had I been in Hardegen's shoes, I would have tried in the service of love to alter the past at least a few more times; in fact, I likely would have exhausted myself in the process (it occurs to me that such an exhaustive process, Hardegen attempting again to again to save Emma, ludicrous though it might appear, would have made a more compelling film than the one I saw). But Hardegen, obeying a hastily conceived logic, determines that it would be best to travel into the future in hopes of finding a solution to the problem. During a stopover in the twenty-first entury, he discovers that the moon has been destroyed by subsurface excavation and debris is pelting down upon New York City. In his haste to escape emergency workers who want to take him to a place of safety, he is rendered unconscious as he throws himself into the time machine and inadvertently sends it forward into the distant future.

My great-grandson's redefinition of the lotus-eating Eloi and the feral subterranean-dwelling Morlocks, those two strains into which I imagined the human race might diverge by the year 802,007, does not reflect my intention that they emblematize the class struggle between the poor and the wealthy. Stripped of symbolic weight, lacking the gravity of social speculation, this division now strikes me as somewhat arbitrary. Beyond that, the Eloi are scarcely the childlike, docile creatures I imagined. On the contrary, they are exceptionally athletic and well-muscled, in aspect rather like a thriving tribe of South Sea Islanders. Further they are skilled with primitive weapons and have constructed an aesthetically spectacular village that clings to the cliffsides of a gorge, protected from the elements by shell-like canopies. That my great-grandson's conception of the Eloi differs from my own does not of itself perturb me, but the Morlocks...there is another story. Though for the most part appropriately bestial, they are led by an *über*-Morlock portrayed by Jeremy Irons, who, done up as an albino with an augmented spinal cord protruding from his skin, has now added an inglorious footnote to a generally illustrious career. It is this addition to my story that utterly derailed the reasonable progress of the film. When Hardegen invades the Morlocks' underground complex to rescue Mara (Samantha Mumba), the lovely Eloi woman who befriended him and who has since been captured, Irons informs him that the Morlocks live beneath the ground because they cannot endure the light of the sun (this flying in the face of the fact that Morlock hunting parties routinely go out during the day to kill and enslave the Eloi). He goes on to say that he can control the thoughts of both Eloi and Morlocks alike, and that while the majority of the Eloi are eaten by their captors, women such as the beauteous Mara are utilized for breeding purposes. Upon hearing this, I wondered why—if the *über*-Morlock possessed such powers—he simply did not summon the Eloi to their fate rather than sending his minions to hunt them down. Did they need the exercise? Just for fun? I also wondered, where were the Morlock women?

Could my great-grandson be so degraded in his intellect as to conceive of a sub-species without females? Was this ridiculous conclusion the narrative justification for the kidnapping of comely Eloi women? It must be so, for otherwise a Morlock would probably not consider such women attractive...unless some Morlock advertising agency had so distorted these poor monsters' sense of self-esteem that their notion of beauty disincluded their own kind.

Even greater gaps of logic were at hand. After engaging in an absurd fight with the *über*-Morlock, during which Irons hangs half-in, half-out of the bubble of force enclosing the time machine as it accelerates into the future, a circumstance that would likely have substantially impeded its operation, Hardegen travels to an age in which the Morlocks have gained absolute dominance. As if they had not already done so. There he decides that while he cannot change the past, he can change the future. This judgment, made while in the future concerning the past, meets no rational standard with which I am familiar. I would hazard to guess that from whichever direction one approaches it, time is either unalterable or it is not. Nevertheless, Hardegen returns to rescue Mara from the caverns, leaving behind the time machine—which he has set to explode—and they escape into the surrounding hills. This hitherto unhinted-at explosive capacity is a wondrous thing, for not only does the machine produce a considerable pyrotechnic display, but—as if it had a mind of its own—the explosion manages with surgical precision to annihilate the Morlock caverns without spreading destruction to any other precinct.

Every work of the imagination, my own not excepted, is afflicted with logical imperfections. It is the job of the craftsman to direct the reader's or the viewer's attention away from these flaws by dint of his skill at narration. One of the tools that can effect such a sleight-of-hand is pacing, and if *The Time Machine* had been well paced, its logical gaffes might not have seemed so glaring. But under my great-grandson's aimless direction, the story does not build so much as it drearily accumulates. Nor does the acting distract from the film's relentless stupidity. Though Mr. Pearce has previously turned in admirable performances in *L.A. Confidential* and *Memento*, I must now infer that these performances were extracted from him by talented directors, an asset with which he was not blessed while making *The Time Machine*. Rather than acting, he appears to be doing a series of impressions, all of them inept. His evocation of a man in love is particularly grotesque—bug-eyed, gaping, as if the emotion were no more than a kind of inflamed earnestness. Special effects, too, tend to gloss over logical errors, but *Machine*'s special effects were of uneven quality. Rumour has it that following a number of unenthusiastically received test screenings, twenty million dollars worth of extra effects were added at the last moment—as a result they are not up to the standard set by various other recent films.

As I stood in the lobby afterward, observing the streams of children exiting the theatre, idly wondering which of them might—should my scenario of the future come to pass—become the ancestors of Eloi and which might produce Morlocks, I grew irate at this perversion of my work. Not only had one of my descendants savaged my book, but he had created a work of such joyless and debased intelligence, it might well add some crucial bit of momentum to the flow of history and assist in the creation of a world like that I had envisioned, one in which the human mind has been rendered useless for anything except the most rudimentary of gratifications. Thus it was I determined that on my return to the past I will not seek to consummate my relationship with Simon Wells' great-grandmother. Though my feelings for the woman remain strong, the attraction has been dimmed by my recent experience, and the loss of her affections is not too great a sacrifice if I can expunge this excrescence from the record of history. Should the fabric of time prove resistant to alteration, I will refuse to submit so easily to that rule as did Andrew Hardegen. And if I should fail, well, perhaps the record of my failure will work some small benefit. But then it may be too late for action. Intellects cool and vast may already be watching us from afar, preparing to strike so as to prevent my great-grandson from ransacking the remainder of my legacy. Even Martians, I believe, would prefer an ultimate anonymity to enduring the puerile re-imagining that he might visit upon them.

AN EXCELLENCE OF PEAKE
Michael Moorcock

People who didn't know him very well often said Mervyn Peake's books were so darkly complex that writing them had sent him mad. Others, who perhaps knew him a little better, understood how cleverly Peake was formalizing his own experience and observations. He was one of the most deeply sane individuals you could hope to meet. He was a conscious artist, with a wicked wit and a tremendous love of life. "He has magic in his pen," said Charles Morgan. "He can annihilate the dimensions."

Although he wrote his trilogy at more or less the same time as Tolkien, with whom he was then marginalized as another "unclassifiable" fantast, Peake had no great interest in *Lord of the Rings* and as far as I know never read it or *The Hobbit*. It wasn't his kind of thing. "Children are anarchists," he told me, "not policemen." C. S. Lewis was an enthusiast, but insisted the Gormenghast books were religious allegory and Peake, whose parents had been missionaries, cheerfully and firmly rejected his interpretation as he rejected most "pompous profundities" applied to his own work. Peake's own suspicion of academics and clerics, evident from his books, made him a little wary of Lewis's friendly overtures and he was rather more pleased by the attention he received from Elizabeth Bowen, Angus Wilson and others, whom he did read. Wilson thought he was ahead of his time. Peake certainly never had a cult develop around him the way it did with poor Tolkien, whose last years were often made miserable by his fans.

Anthony Burgess thought the English mistrusted Peake for being too talented. Peake was a first class illustrator (at one time, "the most fashionable in England," according to Quentin Crisp in *The Naked Civil Servant*), a fine poet and an outstanding painter. His novels, said Burgess, are "aggressively three-dimensional...showing the poet as well as the draughtsman...It is difficult in post-war English fiction to get away with big rhetorical gestures. Peake manages it because, with him, grandiloquence never means diffuseness; there is no musical emptiness in the most romantic of his descriptions. He is always exact...(*Gormenghast*) remains essentially a work of the closed imagination, in which a world parallel to our own is presented in almost paranoic denseness of detail. But the madness is illusory, and control never falters. It is, if you like, a rich wine of fancy chilled by the intellect to just the right temperature. There is no really close relative to it in all our prose literature. It is uniquely brilliant."

His wife Maeve's memoir, *A World Away*, which Vintage recently reprinted, is full of stories of scratching the backs of elephants through floorboards to try to keep them quiet while he was sleeping above them, his spontaneous acts of romantic generosity, his dashing gestures and glorious sense of fun, his willingness to give drawings or poems away to anyone who said they liked them, his London expeditions, drawing faces from Soho, Limehouse, Wapping—what he called "head-hunting." He courted her elegantly and with humour. He was, she said, "unique, dark and majestic." Tea at Lyons, a trip on a tram, and she was his forever. He was conscripted in the Second World War, was in London a great deal during the Blitz and was the first war artist into Belsen, producing studies that are remarkable for their humanity and sympathy, experience he used in his last book. He, like most of us, somehow stayed roughly sane, if a little overwrought, throughout the war. His practical jokes, often concocted with Graham Greene, were elaborate and subtle.

Mervyn Peake was inspiring, joyful company whose tragedy was not in his life or work but in whatever ill-luck cursed him with Parkinson's disease. "If we went out," said Maeve, "it often seemed that he was drunk or drugged and offence would be taken. I longed to shelter him and resented the intelligent ones who turned their backs on him. It's very painful to see such a gentle man cold-shouldered." Increasingly unable to draw, or work on the fourth Titus book, he was by the mid-1960s institutionalized and in the last stages of his illness. His public reputation had vanished. Neither Greene, Bowen nor Burgess, all of them admirers, had enough influence to convince his publishers to return his books to print.

If there's an unsung hero of Mervyn Peake's life and career it has to be Oliver Caldecott, painter and publisher, who became head of the Penguin fiction list, founded Wildwood House and died prematurely. Ollie and Moira Caldecott, South African exiles, had been friends of mine for several years and we shared a mutual enthusiasm for the Gormenghast sequence. We'd made earlier efforts to persuade someone to reprint it, but as usual were told there was no readership for the books. Caldecott wouldn't give up hope.

I'd been instrumental in getting a couple of Mervyn's short stories published and ran some fragments of fiction, poetry and drawings in my magazine *New Worlds*, some of his poetry was still in print, together with one or two illustrated books, but he was thoroughly out of fashion, his reputation not helped by Kingsley Amis describing him as "a bad fantasy writer of maverick status," revealing a tendency for those who trawled the margins to link him with the authors of horror stories and talking animal books.

He was always badly served by comparisons with Tolkien because he was Tolkien's antithesis. Peake spoke of his artistic experiments as "the smashing of another window pane." He wasn't looking for reassurance. He was looking for truth. "I rather thought I was writing for grown-ups," he said mildly. "I can't see that I have anything in common with Tolkien." Nothing is cute or furry in Gormenghast. Peake was a fascinated explorer of human personality, a confronter of realities, beaming his brilliance here and there into our common darkness, a narrative genius able to control a vast range of characters (no more grotesque than life and many of them wonderfully comic) in the telling of a complex narrative, much of which is based upon the ambitions of a single, determined individual, Steerpike, whose rise from the depths of society (or "Gormenghast" as it is called) and extraordinary climb and fall has a monumental, Dickensian quality which keeps you reading at fever pitch. The stuff of solid, grown-up full-strength fiction. Real experience, freshly described. "It's not so much their blindness," he said of his more conventional contemporaries, "as their love of blinkers that spells stagnation." *Gormenghast* was written by a real poet, with a real relish for words and a real feel for the alienated, a painter who could see the extraordinary beneath the apparently nondescript. Closer to the best Zola than any Tolkien or the generic tosh which followed him.

In his introduction to an early collection of his drawings, Peake wrote, "After all, there are no rules. With the wealth, skill, daring, vision of many centuries at one's back, yet one is ultimately quite alone. For it is one's ambition to create one's own world in a style germane to its substance, and to people it with its native forms and denizens that never were before, yet have their roots in one's experience. As the earth was thrown from the sun, so from the earth the artist must fling out into space, complete from pole to pole, his own world which, whatsoever form it takes, is the colour of the globe it flew from, as the world itself is colored by the sun."

Born in China, still carrying a feel of the exotic about him, a fine painter, illustrator, poet and novelist, Peake had been a sunny, bouyant source of life for so many who knew him. His optimism could be unrealistic, but he was never short of it. He was charming and attractive, generous and expansive by nature, combining his dark Celtic good looks with a fine sense of style. Though he'd always supported his family, he'd never had much of a knack for making money — he received five pounds for the entire set of illustrations to *The Hunting of the Snark*. He wasn't much good at anticipating bills but only as his illness worsened did his anxieties begin to get a grip on him and he had exaggerated hopes for his surreal play *The Wit To Woo,* which failed badly.

Knowing little of the brain in those days— this was before Alzheimer's or Parkinson's were identified—we watched helplessly as Mervyn declined into some mysterious form of dementia, while the surgeons hacked at his frontal lobes and further destroyed his ability to work and reason. The frustration was terrible. His instinctive intelligence, his kindness, even his wit flickered in his eyes, but were all trapped, inexpressible. "It feels like everything's being stolen," he said once to me. Here was an extraordinary man, his head a treasure-house of invention, poetry, characters, ideas, being destroyed from within while his genius was rejected by the literary and art world of the day.

When art critics of reputation like Edwin Mullins tried to write about Peake, editors would turn the idea down. I had only a modest success, mostly in low-circulation literary magazines, fanzines. The story, even then, was that Peake had lost his mind. The strain of writing such dark books. All the fictional madness he had created had caught up with him. Unwholesome stuff, darkness. Sniff at it too hard and it gets inside you. That story was a damaging sensational nonsense recklessly perpetuated by Quentin Crisp ("all that *darkness*, dear, gets to you in the end"), for whom Peake had once illustrated a small book and to whom the Peakes had been consistently kind in the years before his notoriety.

The last novel of the sequence, *Titus Alone*, had indeed contained structural weaknesses which we had all assumed were Mervyn's as his control of his work became shaky. Then, one afternoon, Langdon Jones, composer of a superb musical setting for Peake's narrative poem of the Blitz, *The Rhyme of the Flying Bomb*, was leafing through the manuscript books of the novel, which Maeve Peake had shown him, when he realized that much of what was missing from the published book was actually in the manuscript. Checking further, he found that the book had been very badly edited by a third party, and whole characters and scenes cut.

Jones began to check handwritten manuscript (mostly done in huge ledgers and randomly dotted with drawings) against typed pages and the final typed manuscript, slowly restoring the book to its present much improved state. It took him over a year. He was never professionally paid for the work. We suggested to the original publisher that they should now republish the book, perhaps with the new text. Not only did they not want to publish any of the books, they were anxious to hide the fact that the last book had been so badly butchered. They became distinctly negative about the whole thing. I proposed to Maeve that we begin the process of getting back the rights. Meanwhile Mervyn became increasingly unwell.

Oliver said mysteriously that he was hoping to get a new job, which might make things a bit easier. And then one morning he phoned me to tell me, with considerable glee, that he was now "the guy who picks the Penguins." And, of course, our first action must be to sort out the *Gormenghast* books and decide how to get them back into print.

Needless to say, the moment Oliver showed interest from Penguin, the original publisher saw a new value in the books. They were happy to lease the rights to Penguin. They were still very reluctant to do a new edition of *Titus Alone*, however. Eventually the whole production was taken over by Oliver, who proposed illustrating the novels from Mervyn's own notebook drawings of his characters. He had the authority and experience to get what he wanted. The text was restored. The new, beautiful hardbacks were bound versions of the characteristic Penguin editions prepared by Jones. Anthony Burgess gladly contributed an introduction to *Titus Groan*, which he believed to be a masterpiece, and Oliver Caldecott brought the three volumes out as Penguin Modern Classics. It was the perfect way to publish the books, boldly, enthusiastically and unapologetically, in the best possible editions Mervyn could have.

Next, with the considerable help of my ex-wife, Hilary Bailey, Maeve Peake was persuaded to write her wonderful memoir of Mervyn, *A World Away*, which Giles Gordon, another Peake fan, then at Gollancz, was delighted to publish ("the most touching book I've ever read," he said.) *Monitor* began production of their rather Gothic TV program on him. Peake was getting a new, appreciative public. Too late, unfortunately, for him to realize it. I remember going with Maeve to take him some of the publicity done for the new editions, to show him that his books were to be published again, what they would look like. He nodded blankly, mumbled something and dropped his eyes. It was almost as if he could not himself bear the irony. Maeve and his children had to deal with many similar moments.

The rest is more or less history. A history spotted with bad media features about Mervyn which insist on perpetuating his story as a doomed loony. Bill Brandt showed him as a glowering Celt, a sort of unsodden Dylan Thomas, and his romantic good looks help project this image. Women certainly fell in love with his sheer beauty. And then with his charm. And then with his wit. And then they were lost. After he married Maeve, Peake's home life was about as ordinary and chaotic as the usual bohemian family's. Their mutual love was remarkable, as was the passion and enthusiasm of the whole wonderful tribe. As he faded into the final stages of his disease, we were all overwhelmed by an ongoing sense of loss, of disbelief, as if the sun itself were going out.

Peake was neither a saint nor a satanic presence and what was so marvellous for me, when I first went to see him as a boy, was realizing that so much rich talent could come from such a graceful, pleasant, rather modest man who lived in a suburban house much like mine. He was amused by my enthusiasm. I was in no doubt, though, that I'd met my first authentic genius.

In time, of course, many others shared that view, until eventually all Peake's work came back into print, new editions of his stories and poems were produced, public shows presented of his drawings and paintings and various dramatic versions done of his novels, not least the extraordinary minimalist version of *Gormenghast* by David Glass and the Derek Jacobi TV version of his charming short novel *Mr Pye*.

Peake had a huge, romantic imagination, a Welsh eloquence, a wry, affectionate wit and his technical mastery, both of narrative and line, remains unmatched. "To be a good classicist," he said, "you must cultivate romance. To be a good romantic, you must steep yourself in classicism." He was both an heir to the great Victorians and a precursor to the post-modernists, the magic realists. His statements frequently anticipated the likes of Salman Rushdie. He influenced a generation of authors, amongst them Angela Carter, Peter Ackroyd and Iain Sinclair, who found that it was possible to write imaginatively and inventively about character and real experience while setting their stories in subtly unfamiliar worlds.

And Peake's own attitude is best summed up by a poem which achieved popularity some forty years after he wrote it. "To live at all," he said, "is miracle enough." Of course he did much more than live. "Art," he used to say, "is really sorcery." He infused life and art into everything he touched. And his sorceries continue to entrance us.

SOMETHING ABOUT HARRY
Mark Finn

I'm going to break the code of silence on the publishing industry here and now, folks. If I show up at a convention missing a pinky finger, you'll know what happened. But considering all of the chalk white milquetoasts I've met over the years, they'd have to hire outside help to get their dirty work done. Let's talk numbers for a second.

Many of you don't know this, but Scholastic Books (publishers of the Harry Potter series of books) is the current 800 lb. gorilla in the publishing industry. They tell retailers and distributors how it's going to be done, and everyone falls right in line. Right now, bookstores need Scholastic more than Scholastic needs bookstores. It happens when a small company all of a sudden finds itself in control of The Next Big Thing. Ty, the people who made Beanie Babies during all of that mess, had a similar attitude as Scholastic. The attitude partially derived from the perception that they, the company in control, have been picked on and kicked around for so long that it's time to get some payback, and partially derived from economic law of supply and demand. Scholastic, in this case, isn't selling *Harry Potter and the Order of the Phoenix* at the same, more or less standard discount, to everyone. Rather, they are shaving a few points off so that they make a slightly better percentage than the distributors and retailers. Most publishers offer fifty percent off of retail, with some bonuses in the form of free shipping and similar incentives if you order a lot of books. Scholastic maxed their discount out at forty-eight percent off, no free shipping. Nice.

But for the purposes of our demonstration, we're going to round up and down to make the math tidy. It'll still be very interesting. Let's say that the fifth Harry Potter book was sold to bookstores at a fifty percent discount: fifteen bucks a book. These bookstores will turn it around and sell it for thirty bucks, thus doubling their money. Easy cheesy, right?

What happens if you buy a book for fifteen bucks and sell it for eighteen bucks? You have made your money back, sure, but you haven't maximized profits at all. In fact, when you factor in shipping, handling, employee salaries, etc., you probably haven't made anything. You may have actually lost money.

Okay, there's bookstore economics in a nutshell. Now, let's take what we've learned and plug it into the Harry Potter Weekend and see what happens. Here's quick list of sale prices for *Harry Potter and the Order of the Phoenix*, culled from the various Web sites below:

Amazon.com $17.99
Barnes & Noble $17.99
Borders $17.99
Target $17.99
Hastings $17.31 (currently OS)
Wal-Mart $16.17

For most of you, the question that comes to mind is a resounding, "Yeah, so?" I mean, don't all of the big chain stores discount bestsellers thirty to forty percent? Sure, of course they do. It's one of the few reasons to ever set foot inside of a chain store. But here's something that maybe you didn't know: all of the chain bookstores have been complaining for months about poor sales, and they blame it squarely on the flagging economy and several corporate-speak terms like "changing consumer needs" and the like. Borders Books in particular has squealed pretty loudly about this.

So, my question to them and others like them is, what on earth are you doing discounting the ONE book all year that could change your economic fortunes around, the ONE book you COULD sell at full-choke retail and no one would complain about, the ONE book that everyone on the planet, man, woman, and child, is interested in reading? And deep-discounting, at that?

There is no answer to it, other than the incredulous, "Well, everyone else was doing it," or the even more damning, "Because that's the way we've always done it." At the price they sold the Harry Potter, there was no way to make up any kind of appreciable difference in profit. No way. Let me demonstrate. This snippet is from a recent *Publisher's Weekly* article:

> On the retail side, Borders clocked 750,000 copies on opening Saturday—about 640 per store—and B&N topped out at 896,000 (a figure that includes BN.com). Anecdotal reports from most indies showed sales at least in the hundreds. Not surprisingly, one of the retailers that sold the most copies is also the one that now shows empty shelves.

Taking what we know of the figures in hand, we know that Borders paid $11,250,000 for those books. Scholastic grossed eleven million off of Border's alone. What did Borders make back for their time, their trouble, their extra hours, extra help, and extra hassle? $13,500,000. Let's round that up and call it 13.5 million dollars. By subtracting what they paid from what they made, we can see that Borders brought in 2.5 million dollars in sales (again, rounding up and giving everyone the benefit of the doubt).

Now, let's spread that 2.5 million through Borders' 1,200 retail outlets: Each store brought in an additional 2,083 dollars. Seems like a lot, but folks, let me tell you, it's nothing. Any medium-sized bookstore can do two grand in two hours on an average Saturday. It's nothing. Chicken feed. And then, when you spread it around to cover Borders' middle and upper management, infrastructure, and the like, well, that money gets eaten up pretty quickly. And considering that the book sales grossed more than the *Hulk* movie, that's saying a lot.

I know what you're thinking. "Finn, you moron," you may well be saying, "that's an established practice called loss leading. It's done all the time. Don't be stupid."

True. Loss leading is a mildly dirty practice perfected by Wal-Mart (El Diablo Grande). What they do is buy, say, alarm clocks, at a great price, and then mark them up enough to cover shipping charges, and sell them at a huge discount. People come in looking for these marvelous, dirt-cheap alarm clocks, and they think, hey, I need paper towels and underwear. So they march throughout the store buying more stuff, where the lost profit in the loss leader has been spread around and absorbed into the prices of other products, so that Wal-Mart isn't actually losing any money. Clever, no? It's a shell game, and the Wal-Mart shopper is the mark. And to be fair, loss leading is practiced in electronics, grocery, clothing, heck, just about every other consumable industry, including chain bookstores.

Here's the difference, though. Bookstores operate with a fixed retail price for their items. When they discount a best seller, they can't raise the price on Steven King novels to make up for it. Barnes & Noble likes to charge publishers for display space, and they buy in huge quantities to get the biggest discounts available, so it's not like they are usually losing their whole shirt when they put Tom Clancy on sale at thirty percent off (more like they just lose their sleeves). But with no way to see-saw prices, loss leading is akin to shooting yourself in the foot, because you'll bleed to death a lot slower than shooting yourself in the head. How on earth the book industry decided to discount their best sellers (you know, the things that people actually WANT to buy), is a complete mystery to me.

In this case, loss leading doubly backfired. *Publisher's Weekly* also reported that of the initial print run of 8.6 million copies, 5 million of them were sold in the first three days. Do you really think that people went to Borders or Barnes & Noble, picked up the book they have been waiting three years to read, and thought to themselves, "Oh, hey, as long as I am here, I'll see if Michael Crichton's new book is out in paperback?" No, they didn't. People grabbed their books and ran like hell for their cars. They were in a panic to get home and start reading. Maybe a few stuck around. Maybe. But it still wasn't nearly enough to make up for selling the book of your dreams for three bucks more than you paid for it.

Harry Potter and the Order of the Phoenix is the most anticipated publishing sequel since, well, since *Harry Potter and the Goblet of Fire* came out. It's the one book that everyone could have sold at full price and the buying public wouldn't have batted an eye. If the price of the book had been fifty dollars and a cup of human blood, the only question in the consumer's mind would have been to wonder if it had to be their own personal blood, or just anyone's blood. It's the one thing that Borders could have sold like gangbusters and made a huge profit on. It would have given them a war chest to further expand like a cancer across the United States. Instead, they paid for the extra electricity in keeping their stores open past midnight. Nice job, folks. It's no wonder you're on the financial ropes.

The only people who made any money from *Harry Potter* is, in this order, J. K. Rowling (and good job, at that), Scholastic, and—surprise, surprise, the independent bookstores who chose NOT to discount the book. They are all reporting record sales, too. It seems that the thirty dollar price tag isn't a deterrent...especially when all of the chain stores are out of the book. And it wasn't for a lack of planning, either; the print run was a combined 10 million copies. It shattered all records in print numbers and dollar amounts. If a bookstore didn't make any money from that, it's their own damn fault.

So, what can we learn from this? The book industry is the most inept, retarded, backwater, ill-conceived industry in the world. No one in their right mind would ever set up a new industry to operate within the same guidelines as a bookstore. It's ludicrous in the extreme. The book industry needs to re-invent itself or it will perish, and good riddance to it, at that. Lots of luck trying to do it now, because everyone will swear they are solvent, even as they are firing employees and taking pay cuts. I'm personally praying for one of the larger book chains to collapse in on itself like a brachiosaur in a tar pit. They are dinosaurs, the lot of them. The time of the mammal is at hand.

THE FUTURE IS ALREADY HERE
Is There a Place for Science Fiction in the Twenty-First Century?
Robert J. Sawyer

There are countless definitions for that amorphous entity we call science fiction, but one of the most succinct is that employed by Kim Stanley Robinson, author of the famed *Mars* trilogy: "Science fiction stories are stories set in the future." And, of course, for decades now, we've thought of the twenty-first century, the dawn of the third millennium, as the very embodiment of the future.

But now, the future is here. We're right on the doorstep of the twenty-first century, and, indeed, the year 2001, with all the resonances that magic figure has had for us since the film of the same name debuted thirty-odd years ago, will soon be a historical date.

If the future is already here, what role does science fiction have in it? Was SF a literature of the twentieth century, the way gothic romances were a literature of the nineteenth? Or is there a place—a societal role—for science fiction in the new millennium?

To answer that question, it's necessary, of course, to define the current societal role of science fiction, and that role, I firmly believe, comes out of the central message of most of the memorable, ambitious stories in the genre.

Now, of course, there are those who think that fiction is not the place for messages: "If you want to send a message, call Western Union"—the old American telegram company—used to be standard advice given in creative-writing classes. Still, whether the authors are consciously aware of it or not, all fiction does convey messages or fundamental moral statements.

Before I delve into what the central message is for science fiction, let's set the stage by first looking at another genre closely allied with science fiction—another category with its own publishing imprints and dedicated magazines. I'm talking about mystery fiction.

Now, what is the fundamental message present in every mystery story? There's one that, in fact, is virtually required—without it, the story falls completely apart. The central moral statement of all mystery fiction is this: "Don't commit murder, because you won't get away with it." In just about every mystery novel, a character tries to take the life of another human being. And in just about every one, despite clever planning on the part of the murderer, the killer is brought to justice.

Now, let's assess how successful the writers of mystery fiction have been at convincing the general public of the truth of their fundamental assertion, "Don't commit murder, because you won't get away with it." Do we still have murder? Yes. Are murder rates decreasing? No. Despite hundreds of thousands of iterations on this theme in mystery stories from Edgar Allan Poe through Agatha Christie to Sara Paretsky—a theme which, put another way, is often stated as, "There's no such thing as a perfect crime"—there has been no societal change. Murder is rampant.

And that's good news for the mystery fiction writers of the world. It means they have job security. It means they still have work to do. It means their message still needs to be heard.

But what about me and my colleagues? What of the SF writers of the world? How good have we been at communicating our central message? And, indeed, what *is* the central message of SF?

To my way of thinking, the central message of science fiction is this: "Look with a skeptical eye at new technologies." Or, as William Gibson has put it, "the job of the science fiction writer is to be profoundly ambivalent about changes in technology."

Now, certainly, there *are* science fiction writers who use the genre for pure scientific boosterism: science can do no wrong; only the weak quail in the face of new knowledge. Jerry Pournelle, for instance, has rarely, if ever, looked at the downsides of progress. But most of us, I firmly believe, do take the Gibsonian view: we are not techie cheerleaders, we aren't flacks for big business or entrepreneurism, we don't trade in utopias.

Neither, of course, are we Luddites. Michael Crichton writes of the future, too, but he's not really a science fiction writer; if anything, he's an *anti*-science fiction writer.

Indeed, both Gregory Benford and I have discussed with our shared agent, Ralph Vicinanza, why it is that Crichton outsells us. And Ralph explained that he could get us deals at least approaching those Crichton gets if—and this was an unacceptable "if" to both me and Greg—we were willing to promulgate the same fundamental message Crichton does, namely, that science always goes wrong.

When Michael Crichton makes robots, as he did in *Westworld*, they run amok, and people die. When he clones dinosaurs, as he did in *Jurassic Park*, they run amok and people die. When he finds extraterrestrial life, as he did in *The Andromeda Strain*, people die.

Crichton isn't a prophet; rather, he panders to the fear of technology so rampant in our society—a society, of course, which ironically would not exist without technology. His mantra is clearly the old B-movie one that "there are some things man was not meant to know."

The writers of real SF refuse to sink to fear-mongering, but neither do we overindulge in boosterism—both are equally mindless activities.

Still, we do have an essential societal role, one being fulfilled by no one else. Actual scientists are constrained in what they can say—even with tenure, which supposedly ensures the right to pursue any line of inquiry, scientists are in fact muzzled at the most fundamental, economic level. They cannot speculate openly about the potential downsides of their work, because they rely on government grants or private sector consulting contracts.

Well, the government is answerable to an often irrational public. If a scientist is dependent on government grants, those grants can easily disappear. And if he or she is employed in the private sector, well, then certainly Motorola doesn't want you to say cellular phones might cause brain cancer; Dow Chemical didn't want anyone to say that silicone implants might cause autoimmune problems; Philip Morris doesn't want anyone to say that nicotine might be addictive.

Granted, not all those potential dangers turned out to be real, but even considering them, putting them on the table for discussion, was not part of the game plan; indeed, suppressing possible negatives is key to how all businesses, including those built on science and technology, work.

There are moments—increasingly frequent moments—during which the media reports that "science fiction has become science fact." Certainly one of the most dramatic recent ones was made public in February 1997. Ian Wilmut at Roslin Institute in Edinburgh had succeeded in taking an adult mammalian cell and producing an exact genetic duplicate: the cloning of the sheep named Dolly.

Dr. Wilmut was interviewed all over the world, and, of course, every reporter asked him about the significance of his work, the ramifications, the effects it would have on family life. And his response was doggedly the same, time and again: cloning, he said, had narrow applications in the field of animal husbandry.

That was all he *could* say. He couldn't answer the question directly. He couldn't tell reporters that it was now technically possible for a man who was thirty-five years old, who had been drinking too much, and smoking, and never exercising, a man who had been warned by his doctor that his heart and lungs and liver would all give out by the time he was in his early fifties, to now order up an exact genetic duplicate of himself, a duplicate that by the time he needed all those replacement parts would be sixteen or seventeen years old, with pristine, youthful versions of the very organs that needed replacing, replacements that could be transplanted with zero chance of tissue rejection.

Why, the man who needed these organs wouldn't even have to go to any particular expense—just have the clone of himself created, put the clone up for adoption—possibly even an illegal adoption, in which the adopting parents pay money for the child, a common enough if unsavory practice, letting the man recover the costs of the cloning procedure. Then, let the adoptive parents raise the child with their money, and when it is time to harvest the organs, just track down the teenager, and kidnap him, and—well, you get the picture. Just another newspaper report of a missing kid.

Far-fetched? Not that I can see; indeed, there may be adopted children out there right now who, unbeknownst to them or their guardians, are clones of the wunderkinds of Silicon Valley or the lions of Wall Street. But the man who cloned Dolly couldn't speculate on this possibility, or any of the dozens of other scenarios that immediately come to mind. He couldn't speculate because if he did, he'd be putting his future funding at risk. His continued ability to do research depended directly on him keeping his mouth shut.

The same mindset was driven home for me quite recently. I am co-hosting a two-hour documentary called "Inventing the Future: 2000 Years of Discovery" for the Canadian version of the Discovery Channel, and in November 1999 I went to Princeton University to interview Joe Tsein, who created the "Doogie Mice"—mice that were born more intelligent than normal mice, and retained their smarts longer.

While my producer and the camera operator fussed setting up the lighting, Dr. Tsein and I chatted animatedly about the ramifications of his research, and there was no doubt that he and his colleagues understood how far-reaching they would be. Indeed, by the door to Dr. Tsein's lab, not normally seen by the public, is a cartoon of a giant rodent labeled "Doogie" sitting in front of a computer. In Doogie's right hand is his computer's pointing device—a little human figure labeled "Joe": the super-smart mouse using its human creator as a computer mouse.

Finally, the camera operator was ready, and we started taping. "So, Dr. Tsein," I said, beginning the interview, "how did you come to create these super-intelligent mice?"

And Tsein made a "cut" motion with his hand, and stepped forward, telling the camera operator to stop. "I don't want to use the word 'intelligent,'" he said. "We can talk about the mice having better memories, but not about them being smarter. The public will be all over me if they think we're making animals more intelligent."

"But you *are* making them more intelligent," said my producer. Indeed, Tsein had used the word "intelligent" repeatedly while we'd been chatting.

"Yes, yes," he said. "But I can't say that for public consumption."

The muzzle was clearly on. We soldiered ahead with the interview, but never really got what we wanted. I'm not sure if Tsein was a science fiction fan, and he had no idea that I was also a science fiction writer, but many SF fans have wondered why Tsein didn't name his super-smart mice "Algernons," after the experimental rodent in Daniel Keyes's *Flowers for Algernon*.

Tsein might have been aware of the reference, but chose the much more palatable "Doogie"—a tip of the hat to the old TV show *Doogie Howser, M.D.*, about a boy-genius who becomes a medical doctor while still a teenager—because, of course, in *Flowers for Algernon*, the leap is made directly from the work on mice to the mind-expanding possibilities for humans, and Tsein was clearly trying to restrain, not encourage, such leaps.

So, we're back to where we started: *someone* needs to openly do the speculation, to weigh the consequences, to consider the ramifications—someone who is immune to economic pressures. And that someone is the science fiction writer.

And, of course, we do precisely that—and have done so from the outset. Brian Aldiss, and many other critics, contend that the first science fiction novel was Mary Shelley's *Frankenstein*, and I think they're right. In that novel, Victor is a scientist, and he's learned about reanimating dead matter by studying the process of decay that occurs after death. Take out his scientific training, and his scientific research, and his scientific theory, and, for the first time in the history of fiction, there's no story left. Like so much of the science fiction that followed, *Frankenstein*, first published in 1818, is a cautionary tale, depicting the things that can go wrong, in this case, with the notion of biological engineering.

Science fiction writers have considered the pluses and minuses of other new technologies, too, of course. We were among the first to weigh in on the dangers of nuclear power—memorably, for instance, with Judith Merril's 1948 short story "That Only a Mother"—and, although there are still SF writers (often, it should be noted, with university or industry positions directly or indirectly involved in the defense industry) who have always sung the praises of nuclear energy, it's a fact that all over the world, governments are turning away from it.

The October 18, 1999, edition of *Newsweek* carried an article which said, "In most parts of the world, the chance of nuclear power plant accidents is now seen as too great. Reactor orders and start-ups have declined markedly since the 1980s. Some countries, including Germany and Sweden, plan to shut down their plants altogether . . . Nuclear-reactor orders and start-ups ranged from twenty to forty per year in the 1980s; in 1997 there were just two new orders, and five start-ups worldwide. Last year [1998] construction began on only four new nuclear reactors."

Why the sharp decline? Because the cautionary scenarios about nuclear accidents in science fiction have, time and again, become science fact. The International Atomic Energy Agency reports that there were 508 nuclear "incidents" between 1993 and 1998, an average of more than one for each of the world's 434 operating nuclear power plants.

It certainly wasn't out of the scientific community that the warnings were first heard. I vividly recall being at a party about fifteen years ago at which I ran into an old friend from high school. She introduced me to her new husband, a nuclear engineer for Ontario Hydro, the company that operates the nuclear power plants near my home city of Toronto. I asked him what plans were in place in case something went wrong with one of the reactors (this was before the Chernobyl accident in 1986, but after Three Mile Island in 1979). He replied that nothing could go wrong; the system was foolproof. Although we were both early in our careers then, we were precisely fulfilling our respective societal roles. As an engineer employed by the nuclear industry, he had to say the plants were absolutely safe. As a science fiction writer, I had to be highly skeptical of any such statements.

Science fiction has weighed in on ecology, overpopulation, racism, the abortion debate (which is also fundamentally a technological issue—

the ability to terminate a fetus without harming the mother is a scientific breakthrough whose moral ramifications must be weighed), and, indeed, science fiction has been increasingly considering what I think may be the greatest threat of all, the downsides of creating artificial intelligence. From William Gibson's Hugo-winning 1984 *Neuromancer*—in which an organization known as "Turing" exist to prevent the emergence of true AI—to my own Hugo-nominated 1998 *Factoring Humanity*, in which the one and only radio message Earth receives from another star is a warning against the creation of AI, a last gasp from biologicals being utterly supplanted by what they themselves had created without sufficient forethought.

Which brings us back to the central message of SF: "Look with a skeptical eye at new technologies." Has that message gotten through to the general public? Has society at large embraced it in a way that they never did embrace "Don't commit murder because you will never get away with it"?

And the answer, I think, is absolutely yes. Society has co-opted the science-fictional worldview wholly and completely. Do we now build a new dam just because we can? Not without an environmental impact study. Do we put high-energy power lines near public schools? Not anymore. Did we all rush out to start eating potato chips made with Olestra, the fake fat that robs the body of nutrients and causes abdominal cramping and loose stools? No.

And what about the example I started with—cloning? Indeed, what about the whole area of genetic research?

Well, when the first Cro-Magnon produced the first stone-tipped wooden spear, none of his hirsute brethren stopped to think about the fact that whole species would be driven to extinction by human hunting. When the United States undertook the Manhattan Project, not one cent was budgeted for considering the societal ramifications of the creation of nuclear weapons—despite the fact that their existence, more than any other single thing, shaped the mindset of the rest of the century.

But for the Human Genome Project, fully five percent of the total budget is set aside for that thing SF writers love to do the most: just plain old noodling—thinking about the consequences, the impacts, that genetic research will have on society.

That money is allocated because the world now realizes that such thinking is indispensable. Of course, the general public doesn't think of it as science fiction—to them, thanks to George "I can't be bothered to look up the meaning of the word parsec" Lucas, SF is the ultimate in escapism, irrelevant to the real world; it's fantasy stories that only happened a long time ago, in a galaxy far, far away.

I'm not alone in this view. Joe Haldeman has observed that *Star Wars* was the worst thing that ever happened to science fiction, because the general public now equates SF with escapism. According to *The American Heritage English Dictionary*, escapism is "the avoidance of reality through fantasy or other forms of diversion." I do *not* read SF for escapism, although I do read it for entertainment (which is the same reason I do a lot of my nonfiction reading). But I, and most readers, of SF have no interest in avoiding reality.

And yet, SF is seen as having nothing to do with the real world. At a family reunion in 1998, a great aunt of mine asked me what I'd been doing lately, and I said I'd spent the last several months conducting research for my next science fiction novel. Well, my aunt, an intelligent, educated woman, screwed up her face, and said, "What possible research could you do for a science fiction book?" SF to her, as to most of the world, is utterly divorced from reality; it's just crazy stuff we make up as we go along. And so the bioethicists, the demographers, the futurists, and the analysts may not think of themselves as using the tools of science fiction—but they are.

Our mindset—the mindset honed in the pages of *Astounding*, the legacy of John Brunner and Isaac Asimov, of Judy Merril and Philip K. Dick—is now central to human thought. Science fiction writers succeeded beyond their wildest dreams: they changed the way humanity looks at the world.

Years ago, Barry Malzberg quipped that anyone could have predicted the automobile—but it would take a science fiction writer to predict the traffic jam. In the 1960s, my fellow Canadian, Marshall McLuhan, made much the same point, saying that, contrary to the designers' intentions, every new technology starts out as a boon and ends up as an irritant.

But now, *everyone* is a science fiction writer, even if they never spend any time at a keyboard. When a new technology comes along, we all look at it not with the wide eyes of a kid on Christmas morning, but with skepticism. The days when you could tell the public that a microwave oven would replace the traditional stove are long gone; we all know that new technologies aren't going to live up to the hype. About the only really interesting thing the microwave did was create the microwave-popcorn industry—and, of course, microwave popcorn, fast and convenient, is also loaded down with fatty oils to aid the popping, taking away the health benefits normally associated with that food item. The upside, the downside—popcorn, the science-fictional snack.

And what I'm talking about *is* a science-fictional, not a scientific, perspective. As Dr. David Stephenson, formerly with the National Research Council of Canada and a frequent science guest at SF conventions, has observed, scientists are taught from day one to write in the third-person passive voice: they distance themselves from their prose, removing from the discussion both the doer of the action and the person who is feeling the effects of the action.

But SF writers do what the scientists must not. We long ago left behind the essentially characterless storytelling practiced by such early writers as George O. Smith. We now strive for characterization as sophisticated as that in the best mainstream literature. Or, to put it another way, science fiction has evolved beyond being what its founding editor, Hugo Gernsback, said it should be: merely fiction about science. Indeed, even Isaac Asimov, known for a rather perfunctory approach to characterization, knew full well that SF was about the impact progress has on real people. His definition of science fiction was "that branch of literature that deals with the responses of human beings to changes in science and technology."

And those responses, of course, are often irrational, based on fear and ignorance. But they are responses that cannot be ignored: we— science fiction readers and writers—*do* share this planet with the ninety percent of human beings who believe in angels, who believe in a literal heaven and hell, who reject evolution. As much as I admire Arthur C. Clarke—and I do, enormously—the most unrealistic thing about his fiction is how darn reasonable everyone is.

On May 31, 1999, CBC television had me appear on its current affairs program *Midday* to discuss whether or not the space program was a waste of money; I was debating a woman who worked in social services who thought all money—including the tiny, tiny fraction of its gross domestic product that Canada, or even the U.S. for that matter, spends on space—should be used to address problems here on Earth.

And her clincher argument was this—I swear to God, I'm not making this up: "We should be careful about devoting too much time to science. The people who lived in Atlantis were obsessed with science, and that led to their downfall."

My response was to tell her that perhaps if she spent a little more time reading about science, she'd know that Atlantis was a myth, and she wouldn't make an ass out of herself on national television. But the point here—one that I will come back to—is this: she already understood the central twentieth-century science-fictional premise of looking carefully at the ramifications of new technologies, such as space travel. But she was unable to look at them *rationally*, because of her faulty worldview, a worldview that rendered her incapable of separating myth from reality, fact from fiction.

If the central message of science fiction has indeed been co-opted by the public at large—if, as I think is true, Frank Herbert's *Dune* did as much to raise consciousness about ecology as did Rachel Carson's *Silent Spring*—then what role is there for science fiction writers in the new century?

I always say whenever a discussion at a science fiction convention brings in *Star Trek* as an example, we've hit rock bottom; you can't imagine Ruth Rendell turning to Scott Turow at a mystery fiction conference and saying, "You know, that reminds me of that episode of *Murder, She Wrote*, in which..." But I am going to invoke *Star Trek* here as an example of how quaint and embarrassing SF ends up looking when it continues to push an old message long after society has gotten the point.

In the original *Star Trek*, we saw women and black people in important positions. Uhura, the mini-skirted bridge officer, was hardly the most significant black example; much more important were the fact that Kirk's boss, as seen in the episode "Court-Martial," was a black man, played with quiet dignity by Percy Rodriguez, and that the ship's computers, as seen in "The Ultimate Computer," were designed by a Nobel Prize-winning black cyberneticist, played with equal dignity by William Marshall.

During the era of Martin Luther King and the Watts riots, it was a powerful, important statement to have the white captain of the *Enterprise* deferring to black people; as Marshall observed thirty years later, the single most significant thing about his guest-starring role was that he, an African-American, was referred to as "Sir" throughout the episode.

But time passed. In 1993, Paramount made much of the fact that we were going to see a black man as the leader on *Star Trek: Deep Space Nine*—despite the fact that, by this point, blacks had been elected to prominent political positions throughout the United States, and even in South Africa, a bastion of racism in the 1960s, a black man, Nelson Mandela, was about to become president. But, somehow, *Star Trek* thought it was making a profound statement.

And then, just as embarrassingly, two years later, we were supposed to be stunned by the fact that on *Star Trek: Voyager*, a woman was the captain of a starship—this, despite the fact that countries from Great Britain to India to Canada had all already had female prime ministers, that women had risen to prominence in all walks of life.

My colleagues and I have long tried to reflect reality in our fiction, and so, naturally, we have diverse casts in our stories. Damon Knight's famous statement that the most unrealistic thing about science fiction is the preponderance of Americans—practically no one, he correctly observed, is an American—was no longer news to anybody. And, by all means, in a *Star Trek* of the 1990s we should indeed have seen women and non-whites in prominent roles. But to make it the *message*, to try to pass it off as a gutsy thing to do, looked ridiculous.

Indeed, David Gerrold famously quit working on *Star Trek: The Next Generation* back in 1987 in part because of that series' failure to address the reality that a lot of people are gay in its depiction of the future; *Star Trek* had become irrelevant, because the only messages it was comfortable sending out were ones already fully received by the audience.

And, I firmly believe, SF as a whole is now in danger of being perceived as just as quaint, just as dated, just as irrelevant, as the current *Star Trek* is.

In our search for a new role, should we fall back on the one the media has so often cast us in—that of predictors of the future? I don't think so. Many SF writers, myself included, are content to occasionally call themselves "futurists," if that helps get us TV or radio interviews, but we aren't really (indeed, I'm not sure that *anybody* really is, in the modern sense of the term, as someone who claims to be able to predict future trends; Bill Gates is the world's current technological leader—a futurist if ever there was one—and he, of course, is the same man who once said that no one would ever need a computer with more than 640K of memory).

No, when what we science fiction writers have written about comes to pass, it usually means society has screwed up. The last thing George Orwell wanted was for the real year 1984 to turn out anything like the vision portrayed in his novel.

Orwell, of course, wrote his book in 1948—he simply reversed the last two digits to make it clear that he was really writing about his present day. Science fiction is indeed very much a literature of its time, and should, of course, be read in historical context.

Still, anyone who needs further convincing that science fiction isn't a predictive medium need only look at the events of the last few decades. Numerous science fiction writers predicted that the first humans would set foot upon the moon in the 1960s, but none of us predicted that we would abandon the Moon—indeed, all manned travel beyond Earth orbit—just three years later. Exactly twelve human beings have walked on the Moon; a mere dozen people (all white, all male, all American—hardly a representative sampling, but, then again, all of this occurred back when the original *Star Trek*'s message of an interracial future was one that hadn't yet been fully received)—and there is no sign that that number will increase in the next couple of decades.

We science fiction writers also missed the fall of the Soviet Union, something that now, in retrospect, seemed inevitable—indeed, it was amazing it lasted as long as it did. But we were writing books like Norman Spinrad's *Russian Spring* right up to the day of the collapse.

And, perhaps most significant of all, we utterly missed the rise of the Internet and the World Wide Web. The genre that gave us Isaac Asimov's Multivac, Arthur C. Clarke's HAL 9000, Robert A. Heinlein's Mycroft Holmes, and even William Gibson's Wintermute completely failed to predict how the computer revolution was *really* going to unfold.

Of course when something new comes along—such as the terrible plague of AIDS—we're quick to weigh in with speculations. But we're usually so far off the mark that the results end up seeming laughable. Poor Norman Spinrad again: his vision of a world of people having sex with machines—instead of, of course, simply wearing condoms—because of the threat of AIDS, as outlined in his 1988 story "Journals of the Plague Years," seems absolutely ridiculous and alarmist when we look at it now, a scant decade later.

Some science fiction writers still gamely try to set stories in the far future—a hundred, two hundred, a thousand years down the road. But the predictive horizon is moving ever closer. No one can make a prediction about what the world will be like even fifty years from now with any degree of confidence. What will be the fruits of the Human Genome Project? Will nanotechnology really work? Will true artificial intelligence emerge? Will cold fusion or another clean, unlimited energy source, be developed? Will humans upload their consciousnesses into machines? And what wild cards—things we haven't even thought of yet—will appear?

As Bruce Sterling has observed, people in the future won't even eat; as Nancy Kress has postulated, with *Beggars in Spain*, they may not even sleep. What likely predictions could we possibly make about such beings?

In May 1967, Arthur C. Clarke revealed his now-famous "Third Law" during a speech to the American Association of Architects: "Any sufficiently advanced technology is indistinguishable from magic." The question, of course, is how far ahead of us is "sufficiently advanced"— and the answer, I believe is fifty years; the world of 2050 is utterly beyond our predictive abilities. With the accelerating rate of change, any year-2000 guess as to what 2050 would be like is almost certainly going to be as far off base as a guess Christopher Columbus might have had about what 2000 would be like.

The pressure for SF to change has been building for a long time. In North America, the sales of science fiction books that aren't related to *Star Trek*, *Star Wars*, or other media properties, are the worst they've ever been. Sales are down about fifty percent across the board from 1990, and the readerships of the principal SF magazines, *Analog* and *Asimov's*, have been cut in half. There is no doubt that the reading public is turning away from SF in droves.

The prime cause of the decline in SF readers is that today's young people are finding all the things that have always attracted young people to SF—big ideas, sense of wonder, action, wish-fulfillment fantasies, stunning visual imagery, nifty aliens, engaging characters—more readily in movies, TV, role-playing games, computer games, and on the Internet than in the pages of printed works.

There's no doubt that we've been outclassed in terms of visual imagery by the wizards at Industrial Light and Magic. Any space battle or alien vista we might care to describe they can realize more vibrantly in pictures than we can with words. To put it crudely: many of the finest SF writers of the past, including Robert Silverberg and Mike Resnick, supplemented their income by writing pornographic novels. But there's almost no market left for porno fiction: what's now shown on videotape is much more vivid and real than anything the reader can imagine. Well, as went novels with titles like *Nurses in Need*, so, too, will go the space opera that was once a staple of printed SF.

SF *will* have to change if it is to survive. The public wants something other than what we've been giving them. One change we'll likely see is a move away from the far-future as a setting for stories. I don't even think we need to invoke Kim Stanley Robinson's criterion that SF stories must be set in the future; I took great pleasure in setting my novel *Frameshift*, for instance, entirely in the present day, and suspect we'll see it become much more common for serious SF novels to have contemporary settings.

Indeed, if science fiction is going to have relevancy in the next century, it must assert itself to be part of real life, not far-off tales of escapism. And that brings me back to where we started. We need a new message for the new millennium. Far be it from me to try to impose an agenda on SF—but I think the agenda is already there, implicit in many of our texts, and, indeed, explicit in the actual name of our genre: *science* fiction.

One of the great intellectual embarrassments of the twentieth century is that five hundred years after Copernicus deposed Earth from the center of the universe, virtually every newspaper carries a daily astrology column—the horoscopes—but astronomy gets, at best, a column once a week, and in many papers not even that.

It's likewise embarrassing that a hundred and forty years after the publication of *The Origin of Species*, ignorant people are still succeeding in outlawing the teaching of the fact of evolution.

And it's mortifying that while the SF section of bookstores shrinks like a puddle under noonday sun, the "New Age" section—full of fabricated stories penned by charlatans—grows like a cancer.

If there is a message science fiction can promulgate for the twenty-first century—a message that the world needs to hear—it is this: the rational, scientific worldview is the only perspective that effectively deals with reality.

And, at the risk of repeating myself, let me emphasize again that reality is indeed what science fiction is all about. I cringe with embarrassment every time I see that stupid t-shirt not quite concealing a massive belly at a science fiction convention: "Reality is just a crutch for people who can't handle science fiction." What a ridiculous, offensive statement! Science fiction—in its probing of the deep questions, in its abiding concern with moral issues, in its unrelenting quest to expose truth and speculate on consequences, even in its most mind-bending explorations of the quantum nature of the universe—is, more than any other form of entertainment, absolutely about reality.

And reality is the totality of everything; not to invoke *Star Trek* again, but in the movie *Star Trek IV* it is revealed that Kiri-kin-tha's First Law of Metaphysics is that "nothing unreal exists," a statement no less profound than Descartes's "I think therefore I am."

The scientific method is the single greatest tool of understanding ever devised by humanity. Observe phenomena. Propose an explanation for why the phenomena are as they have been seen to be. Devise an experiment to test whether your explanation is correct. And, if that experiment fails—and this is the powerful part; this is where the beauty comes in—discard the explanation, and start over again.

There will be those who argue that there are other ways of gaining insight to the nature of reality: mystic experiences, contemplation in the absence of experimentation, divine insight, consulting ancient texts. Such methods are demonstrably inferior to the scientific method, for only the scientific method welcomes the detection of error; only the scientific method allows for independent verification and replication.

Now, some will say, well, that's the western view, and, after all, to paraphrase Damon Knight, hardly anyone is a westerner. Maybe so, but it must be recognized that science fiction *is*, in fact, a western genre. Fantasy, perhaps, can trace roots all over the world, but science fiction, born of Mary Shelley, nurtured by Jules Verne and H. G. Wells, grew out of the industrial revolution. It is inexorably tied up with western thought.

And the crowing glory of western thought—the glory that allowed us not to simply declare, as the United States's founders did, that it is "self-evident that all men are created equal" while they still held slaves— but rather that allowed us to prove, through genetic studies that showed that genetic variation within races is greater than the average deviation between the races, and through psychological and anatomical studies that showed that the sexes are equally endowed intellectually, that in fact racism and sexism have no rational basis.

Stephen Jay Gould recently wrote a book called *Rocks of Ages: Science and Religion in the Fullness of Life,* in which he argues that the spiritual and the rational should have a "loving concordant," but are in fact "nonoverlapping magisteria"—utterly separate fields, with some questions solely appropriate to the former and others exclusively the province of the latter.

I reject that: I don't think there's *any* question, including the most basic philosophical conundrums of where did we come from, why are we here, what does it all mean, and, indeed, the biggest of them all, is there a God, that cannot be most effectively addressed through the application of the scientific method, especially with its absolute requirement that if an idea—such as the superstition of astrology—is disproven, then it must be willingly discarded.

How can science have anything meaningful to say about whether there is a God? Easily. If the universe had an intelligent designer, it will show signs of intelligent design. Some argue that it clearly does: the relative strengths of the four fundamental forces that drive our universe—gravitation, electromagnetism, the strong nuclear force, and the weak nuclear force—do seem to have been chosen with great care, since any substantial deviation from the present ratios would have resulted in a universe devoid of stars or even atoms.

Likewise, the remarkable thermal properties of water—most notably, that it expands as it freezes and that it has higher surface tension than any other fluid except liquid selenium—seem specifically jiggered to make life possible.

Do these facts prove whether or not God exists? No—not yet. But the best response to those who say science doesn't hold all the answers is to say, on the contrary, science does indeed hold all the answers—we just don't have all the science yet.

My favorite review of my own work was a recent one for *Flashforward* by Henry Mietkiewicz in *The Toronto Star*, who said, "Sawyer compels us to think rationally about questions we normally consider too metaphysical to grapple with." But I'm hardly alone in this. Science fiction right back to such great works as Arthur C. Clarke's short story "The Star" and James Blish's *A Case of Conscience*, through Carl Sagan's *Contact*, and, more recently Mary Doria Russell's *The Sparrow*, and, if I may, my own Nebula-winning *The Terminal Experiment* and forthcoming *Calculating God*, show that SF, because it embraces the scientific method, is the most effective tool for exploring the deepest of all questions.

So, *does* science fiction have a role in the twenty-first century? Absolutely. If we can help shape the Zeitgeist, help inculcate the belief that rational thought, that discarding superstition, that subjecting all beliefs to the test of the scientific method, is the most reasonable approach to any question, then not only will science fiction have a key role to play in the intellectual development of the new century, but it will also, finally and at last, help humanity shuck off the last vestiges of the supernatural, the irrational, the spurious, the fake, and allow us to embrace, to quote poet Archibald Lampman, "the wide awe and wonder of the night" but with our eyes wide open and our minds fully engaged. Then, finally, some 40,000 years after consciousness first flickered into being on this world, we will at last truly deserve that name we bestowed upon ourselves: *Homo sapiens*—Man of Wisdom.

THE WAY THE FUTURE LOOKS:
THX 1138 and *BLADE RUNNER*
Robert Silverberg

We are in Los Angeles, but it is not the familiar city of palm trees and perpetual bright sunshine. Above us loom colossal, sloping high-rise buildings of intricate and alien design, patterned, perhaps, after Aztec temples or Babylonian ziggurats, that turn the narrow, congested streets into claustrophobic canyons and hide the dark, pollution-fouled sky. A cold, bleak, maddening rainstorm goes on interminably. Great searchlights intended, possibly, to substitute for the absent sun, send intrusive beams slicing across vast distances from sources mounted somewhere far overhead.

Down here on surface level we move warily through a densely packed district, largely Oriental in population and in architecture, a crazy, hyped-up version of Hong Kong or Tokyo, where a dizzying multitude of flashing electronic signs seeks insistently to draw our attention to games parlors, massage houses, noodle counters, drug-vending shops, and a thousand thousand other commercial establishments. Dull-eyed coolies, bending under immense burdens, jostle us aside without apology. Myriads of spaced-out fanatics in fantastic costumes dance along beside us down the street, each lost in some private bubble of self-absorption. High above us, helicopters moving with reckless velocity buzz like crazed dragonflies between the skyscrapers: police, most likely, searching for the deadly fugitive androids that are said to be loose in the city. At any moment, we think, one of those helicopters may descend from the sky in lunatic spirals and land in the middle of the next block, disgorging policemen who set about making arrests with Kafka-esque implacability.

The mood is oppressive and scary. We are trapped in one of the ultimate urban nightmares: a city of a hundred million people, every one of them hostile to everyone else. The look of the place—dark, menacing, congested, dominated by those immense ponderous towers that crouch like monsters upon the land—is unique and uniquely horrifying. Everything manages to glisten with futuristic pizzazz and nevertheless reveals itself simultaneously to be tinged with rot and decay: new and old, light and dark, airy and ineluctably heavy, both at the same time. The year is

2019, and this is the world of Ridley Scott's 1982 motion picture, *Blade Runner*.

Try another world? Well—

We are indoors. Perhaps within some giant building, perhaps deep underground in a labyrinth of tunnels—

it makes little difference. The essential point is that there are no windows and no doors to the outside, that the sun and the sky and the stars are no part of this place, and we inhabit a realm of sterile corridors, bright lights, white walls, a megalopolis with a hospital's grim aseptic dazzle. Here there is neither clutter nor squalor: the prevailing esthetic here is that of the surgical operating chamber, not of the crowded Oriental marketplace. Though the population density is high, perhaps as high as in the world of *Blade Runner*, there is no sense of overcrowding because there is no random motion. A bland, lobotomized-looking populace, clad in standardized costumes rather like prison garb, makes its journeys from place to place in obedient tidy files, while guards with impassive inhuman faces step in quickly to see to it that no one gets out of line or deviates in any other significant way from the flow of traffic. From gleaming grilles in the walls comes a constant low incomprehensible electronic static, an aural wallpaper of blurps and bleeps and soft crackles, interrupted at frequent intervals by cryptic instructions that are instantly accepted and followed by those to whom they apply. Flickering television screens provide two-way monitoring; computer eyes scan and count and record; Big Brother's minions, unseen but omnipresent, oversee the flow of data. The color scheme is a blinding white-on-white: there is no room for untidiness here, no space whatever for irregularity. The mood, once again, is oppressive and scary. We are trapped, once again, in an ultimate urban nightmare, though of a kind quite different from the last one. The year is something like 2200 AD, and this is the world of George Lucas's first film, *THX 1138*, released in 1971.

These movies, *Blade Runner* and *THX 1138*, strike me as two of the most valuable science fiction movies ever made. To me they embody the highest virtue the science fiction film can offer: they show the way the future looks, and they show it with such conviction, such richness of detail, such density of texture that the visions of tomorrow they offer will remain embedded forever in my imagination. They have provided a kind of time-travel experience, in a sense, and they have done it so well that I am willing to ignore entirely the manifest failure of both these movies in most other aspects of the art of science fiction.

If *Blade Runner* and *THX 1138* were novels, they would be undistinguished ones. *Blade Runner* is indeed based on a science fiction novel, and an outstanding one: *Do Androids Dream of Electric Sheep?* by the late Philip K. Dick. But—although Dick reported himself pleased with the screenplay that Hampton Fancher and David Peoples drew from his novel, and would, I think, have been pleased by the finished film itself had he lived to see it—*Blade Runner* bears only the most skeletal resemblance to the book on which it was based, taking from it nothing but the essential plot idea of hunting down a group of escaped androids. As for *THX 1138*, it began life not as a novel but as a film treatment, produced by the very young George Lucas while he was still a student at UCLA. After Lucas and Walter Murch had expanded it into the full-length script for the final version of the movie, that script was indeed "novelized" for paperback release by the experienced science fiction writer Ben Bova, but not even Bova's professionalism could lift the story beyond the level of the perfunctory. Science fiction is, among other things, a literature of ideas; and the problem that each of these movies has *as science fiction literature* is its mediocrity on the level of idea.

Blade Runner is simply silly. We are asked to believe that humanity, just a few decades from now, has colonized not merely the solar system but the stars; that we have populated those stars with "replicants," synthetic human beings that are superior in most ways to ourselves, although they are designed to live only four years; and that a handful of these replicants, having rebelled at being assigned to slavery in the star-colonies, have found their way back to Earth and are running amok in Los Angeles. Out of this cluster of manifest implausibilities is generated a perfunctory plot in which the androids, hoping to find a way to have their lifespans extended, seek to enlist the aid of their designer, while a police officer follows their trail, taking desperate measures to destroy them—at the risk of his own life, even though the androids have only a few weeks left to live anyway. Since none of these concepts makes much sense, either taken by itself or in conjunction with any of the others, it is hard to find much useful speculative thought of a science-fictional nature in *Blade Runner*. It tells us nothing much that is useful about the human-android relationship, the colonization of the stars, the use of genetic engineering to produce superbeings, or anything else that might seem to be contained in the main premises of the story. If we filter out the self-cancelling absurdities of the plot, we are left with only two concepts that a demanding reader of science fiction might find nourishing. One is the depiction of the female android Pris (Daryl Hannah), a mysterious acrobatic creature in whom the life-force rages so powerfully that when she dies it is with an astonishing display of superhuman fury, the outraged death of an extraordinary though limited being; the other is the question of how to distinguish readily between humans and androids, which was at the core of Dick's novel and which here is crowded into convenient corners of the script, only occasionally to be confronted directly. The rest is straight private-eye stuff, dogged pursuit culminating in a terrifying but conceptually empty rooftop chase.

The ideas around which the story of *THX 1138* are built are not at all foolish—merely hopelessly stale. They go back at least as far as H. G. Wells's *When The Sleeper Wakes* of 1899 and E. M. Forster's "The Machine Stops" of 1909, with touches borrowed from such later but hardly recent works as Zamyatin's *We*, Huxley's *Brave New World*, and Orwell's *Nineteen Eighty-Four*. That is, we are ushered once more into the complete totalitarian state, where computers make all decisions and the populace is drugged into complaisance. Uniformity of thought, costume, and behavior is imposed by law and enforced by automatonlike humanoid police; unseen monitors keep watch on everything and everyone; any sign of individuality is relentlessly suppressed. The protagonists are those familiar characters, the rebels against the conformity of it all: THX 1138 (Robert Duvall) and his female roommate, LUH 3417 (Maggie McOmie), who surreptitiously cut down on the dosage of the drug they are compelled to take to reduce their sexual impulses, and, after restoring their libido, set about conceiving a child, which is forbidden by the regulatory powers. They are apprehended; LUH 3417 is destroyed, but THX 1138 manages to escape the hivelike city into an outer realm where other rebels and nonconformists have taken lodging. A pair of implacable robots pursue him; and the film, which until this point has been pure if overfamiliar science fiction, devolves in its final third into a mere chase story, an endless sequence of frantic zoomings through subterranean tunnels, until THX 1138 at last eludes the police and escapes into the open-air world beyond.

But—even though one of these films is cobbled together from nonsensical premises and the other is manufactured from clichés—it is, I think, beside the point to pay much attention to those failings. These are *not* novels, with a novel's scope for explication and analysis. They are movies, that is, visual events, pictorial compositions extended along a narrative axis by complex technological means. It is possible to wish that *Blade Runner* had relied more on the intricacies of Philip K. Dick's novel and less on the formulas of detective fiction, or that *THX 1138* had given us more of a look at the assumptions on which its totalitarian society was founded and less of a mad chase in those tunnels, but to express such wishes is to ignore an ugly reality, the catch-22 of science fiction moviemaking: science fiction films require special effects, special effects are costly, costly films need to pull in big audiences in order to break even, and big audiences are snared only by reliance on familiar plot mechanisms. (As it is, *Blade Runner*, which cost something like $30,000,000 to produce, was a commercial failure. *THX 1138* was the relatively inexpensive work of a novice filmmaker, and in its way was an uncompromising and difficult movie, revealing its plot in an oblique and demanding way, but without its harrowing if meaningless chase finale it might have drawn no audience at all, with consequent difficulties for George Lucas's further career.) It is precisely in those special effects that the merits of the two movies lie; indeed, *Blade Runner* and *THX 1138* provide startling evidence that an important science fiction movie can be assembled out of unimportant science fiction material. If their failings as fiction had not been as great, they would have been finer movies yet, but perhaps that is asking too much.

They are visionary movies in the most literal sense of that word. They show us futures, and they do it, not as a novelist might, with a few deftly chosen adjectives cunningly disposed on the page, but with nuts-and-bolts reality. In *Do Androids Dream of Electric Sheep,* Philip K. Dick creates his atmosphere of gritty, dismaying urban decay with quick little touches ("the tattered gray wall-to-wall carpeting....The broken and semi-broken appliances in the kitchen, the dead machines...Tufts of dried-out bonelike weeds poking slantedly into a dim and sunless sky"). Ridley Scott, at an expenditure of millions of real dollars, builds an entire gigantic city of enormous pseudo-Aztec temples and flashing pseudo-neon signs, fills it with weird little shops where commodities as yet uninvented are sold, and whisks his camera swiftly through it, giving us tantalizingly elliptical glances at a future world that he has in fact realized in immense detail. I have seen it argued that it is somehow a higher achievement for a novelist to create the texture of a world by quick descriptive touches than it is for a movie producer to turn loose a battalion of carpenters and electricians, but—despite my own novelist's bias—I'm not so sure of that; the effects that Scott creates by building sets and letting us have mere glimpses of them are at least as elegant and cunning as any instance of the science fiction writer's descriptive art. The Los Angeles of *Blade Runner* is a unique invention, actually owing relatively little to the Dick novel, however preposterous the adventures of Rick Deckard (Harrison Ford) may be as he stalks his way through that somber, ominous city in search of the crazed replicant Roy Batty (Rutger Hauer), the city itself remains the essential imaginative achievement, and it does the essential science-fictional thing of displaying and illuminating a landscape not otherwise accessible to the eye. It mattered very little to me whether Deckard pushed Batty over the edge of the roof or Batty pushed Deckard over; what did matter, and a great deal, was the hypnotic power of Scott's camera as it panned down the face of one of those overwhelming buildings, and showed me the architecture of an era yet to come.

So too with *THX 1138*. "Imagine, if you can, a small room, hexagonal in shape, like the cell of a bee," wrote E. M. Forster in 1909. "It is lighted neither by window nor by lamp, yet it is filled with a soft radiance. There are no apertures for ventilation, yet the air is fresh." And we are launched into the stiflingly circumscribed world of "The Machine Stops." Or we turn to Zamyatin's *We*, on which, I suspect, *THX 1138* was founded, and we read, "As always, the Music Plant played the 'March of the One State' with all its trumpets. The numbers walked in even ranks, four abreast, ecstatically stepping in time to the music—hundreds, thousands of numbers, in pale blue unifs, with golden badges on their breasts, bearing the State Number of each man and woman." But Lucas makes us see it. He makes us hear it. The faces, the eyes, the shaven scalps, the white-on-white corridors, the electronic buzzes and murmurs, the flow of computerized commands so baffling to the twentieth-century eavesdropper—the movie is an astonishing experience, an all-out immersion in a world of the future, without explanation, without apology. If Lucas is using other writers' material, he is making it altogether his own by the vivid way he realizes it and by the sheer uncompromising strangeness of the place into which he thrusts the viewer. (Scott does that too. Though he uses a crude voice-over technique to explain details of the plot, he offers the startling urban landscape largely as a given, without footnotes or commentary, thereby greatly enhancing the power of its strangeness.)

The task of the science fiction novelist, ideally stated, is to discover a unique speculative concept, develop its implications through a rigorous intellectual process, and make it accessible as fiction through an appropriate choice of characters, plot, and narrative style. Since science fiction usually involves the depiction of an unfamiliar landscape, the novelist's craft requires the mastery of descriptive techniques that will convey that landscape to the reader with maximum visual impact (a craft that entails more than a little collaboration on the part of the reader, but is a collaboration that the skilled novelist knows how to elicit). The task of the science fiction moviemaker, ideally stated, should be the same, and perhaps some day it will be, although, as I have suggested, commercial considerations at present seem to demand certain oversimplifications of concept and plot and character, and, in any case, even the most uncompromising of films are necessarily unable to achieve some of the things a novel can manage.

So far, I suppose most and perhaps all of the science fiction movies that have been made have failed the highest tests of science fiction excellence; but in the domain of depiction of an unfamiliar landscape, that is, in the domain of special effects, there have been notable successes: *Alien* (1979), *2001* (1968), *Star Wars* (1977), *Forbidden Planet* (1956), and many more. I think it is no trivial achievement to make futuristic visions concrete in that way; as I have said, I am not among those who would claim that building a movie set is somehow a less worthy artistic accomplishment than composing a paragraph of vivid descriptive prose. What those films managed in the way of putting the look of the future on the screen was far from trivial. But I can think of no others in which the special effects are dedicated so powerfully to the creation of a coherent imagined environment that wholly enfolds and houses the story that is set within it. That the story is foolish in one case and stereotyped in the other is regrettable but fundamentally unimportant. What Ridley Scott accomplished in *Blade Runner* and George Lucas did in *THX 1138* is notable despite all peripheral failings: to create a landscape of the mind, vivid and compelling and complete, that for one breathless moment of suspension of disbelief seems to be the real thing, the authentic future, which we can in no other way experience than through the medium of lens and light and screen.

GULLIVER UNRAVELS:
Generic Fantasy and the Loss of Subversion
John Grant

Some years ago, when John Clute and I were working on the draft entry list for *The Encyclopedia of Fantasy*,[35] I felt there was a need for an essay under the keyword GENERIC FANTASY. At this early stage I defined Generic Fantasy loosely as the sort of fiction which, while it has "FANTASY" in big letters on the spine and fills to overflowing the section in the bookstore labeled "FANTASY & SCIENCE FICTION", is effectively not a form of fantastic literature. Using standard characters and set in a stock environment which I dubbed (probably not originally) Fantasyland, it can best be regarded as a subgenre of the adventure thriller, or perhaps, depending on the author, of the bodice-buster. My intention in creating such an entry, of course, was to use it as a means whereby Clute and I could clear away huge areas of weedy, pestiferous scrub in the forest that is *commercially* described as fantasy in order to see the trees we were actually interested in.

The more active of our two consultant editors, Gary Westfahl, expressed dissent in his characteristically forthright fashion. Quite correctly, he pointed out[36] that the bulk of the potential purchasers of *The Encyclopedia of Fantasy* would be readers solely of what I was so blithely dismissing as Generic Fantasy, so that we might, through being seen to insult those readers, be committing commercial suicide. Clute and I presented various counterarguments—including that some Generic Fantasy is extremely well written, it's just that it's not *fantasy*—but in the end we took Westfahl's point. The entry was re-christened GENRE FANTASY and its teeth were sufficiently drawn that only the most dedicated John Norman enthusiast could have taken twitching offense.

Nowadays I wish we'd stuck to our guns. Oddly enough, the debate did bear fruit in an unanticipated way. The fantasy novelist Diana Wynne Jones, who had generously been giving us anonymous consultative help in the creation of the entry list, picked up the baton and ran with it until she produced her witty book *The Tough Guide to Fantasyland*, which was

---

[35] John Clute and John Grant, eds., *The Encyclopedia of Fantasy*, (London: Little, Brown & Company. New York: St Martin's Press, 1997).

[36] Various letters and e-mail to John Clute and the present author from about 1992 onwards. This correspondence still continues intermittently.

shortlisted for a 1997 World Fantasy Award.[37] Jones constructed her book as a sort of mini-encyclopedia of generic fantasy's clichés and banalities, and with remarkably little difficulty was able to touch virtually every base in this subgenre. As was widely remarked at the time of her book's publication, anyone wishing to become a successful author of high (i.e., generic) fantasy could simply shuffle the entries in the *Tough Guide* and start writing. A number of authors were honest enough to admit that something analogous to this was what they had in fact done in order to create for themselves what were, thank you very much, thriving careers.

Clute and I became concerned enough about the issue that, as part of our ongoing debate over it, we created and fronted a convention discussion panel called "Why is Fantasy No Longer a Subversive Form of Literature?".[38] In that discussion, while aware that the works of J. R. R. Tolkien were in their own way subversive, we concentrated more on modern traditions of fantasy other than the Tolkienesque. Current representatives of those traditions are remarkable for their low commercial profile—that is, outside children's and young-adult literature, where they continue to flourish.[39] It would be easy, and utterly misleading, to say that, pre-Tolkien, fantasy was a diverse and flourishing form of literature, often deploying the full range of tools utilized by genres such as mainstream fiction and science fiction, but that post-Tolkien the Iron Curtain went up around the borders of Fantasyland, leaving all those who wished to spend their lives in other countries to forage as best they could on the vegetation available there, and most probably to starve. In fact what happened is of course that in the 1960s various U.S. editors, predominant among them Lin Carter, came along and, with the most laudable of goals—the revival of fantasy—produced a narrow commercial definition of the genre. Stuff like Tolkien, stuff like Robert E. Howard, stuff like William Morris—according to them, this stuff was what fantasy *was*. Unfortunately, it soon came to be commercially perceived that this was *all* that fantasy was.

It's important to remember that at the time Fantasyland was, if not quite *terra incognita*, certainly relatively unexplored. It was perfectly possible to create fictions that could both be identified by the "FANTASY" label and

---

[37] Diana Wynne Jones, *The Tough Guide to Fantasyland* (London: Gollancz, 1996). By one of those incestuous quirks of the publishing industry, the present author was commissioned to serve as Jones's editor on this book.

[38] Microcon, March 1994, University of Exeter. The other participants were Geoff Ryman, Colin Greenland, Stephen Marley and Richard Middleton.

[39] It is at least arguable that Jones was able so accurately to drive the nails into Generic Fantasy's cross because most of her fiction is for the young. Moreover, her familiarity with the greater imaginative freedom acceptable in commercial juvenile fiction, by comparison

actually *be* fantasy at a time when there were still so many patches of Fantasyland—some of them great tracts—where no human foot had trod, patches which the cartographers could mark only with the legend "Here Be Tygers."

And that, perhaps, pinpoints the difficulty faced by present-day Generic Fantasy. Arguably, in order for a fiction to be fantasy it must be prepared to dance with the Tygers: it must take risks by exploring precisely those dangerous territories where no one has ever ventured before and which are still the demesnes of the wild animals. It must meddle with our thinking, it must delight in being controversial, it must *hope* to be condemned by authority (whatever authority one chooses to identify), it must be at the cutting edge of the imagination, it must flirt with madness, it must *surprise*, it must be doing things that other forms of fiction *cannot*.

This does not exactly constitute a formula for the commercial success of *Dragonspume Chronicles of the Sorcerer Kingdom Ancients*, or whatever bloated trilogy the publishers' presses choose next to excrete into the toilet bowl of the book trade. One can guarantee that the only surprise to be discovered in *Dragonspume Chronicles of the Sorcerer Kingdom Ancients*—or its many indistinguishable kin—is the fact that any sane adult should choose of his or her own volition to waste perfectly good retinal cells reading such stuff.

Perhaps, although I am by nature and habit the most moderate of men, I am here being a trifle harsh. For these ghastly, unnecessary and derivative books clearly do fulfill a function: people do not read them because they are stupid, nor are they necessarily stupid to do so.[40] The readers of Generic Fantasy seek something from their chosen form of fiction, and its most successful authors make sure that those readers are succored in exactly the way they want to be.

So what is it that readers seek that cannot be found in the full form of fantasy? One of the elements that Clute cast into our discussions was the concept of phatic literature. A phatic conversation is one in which no

---

with its adult counterpart, may have contributed to the difficulty she had until a few years ago in being accepted *by publishers* as a writer of fantasy for grown-ups as well. There is no argument whatsoever that most serious readers of full fantasy, as opposed to its generic equivalent, spend much of their bookstore time in the children's department.

[40] It is obviously true that publishers are not necessarily stupid to publish them, because many of these middenfuls of words are commercially enormously successful. And yet one wonders if in the longer term the publishers are not making their customary mistake of gorging on today's kill without a thought for the morrow, because—or at least one would like to think this to be the case—any stagnant literary subgenre, and stagnation is an arch-characteristic of Generic Fantasy, has only a finite lifetime. An example of one such that has more or less died on the vine is the Multiple-Choice Fantasy Adventure Gamebook. Another is the Country-House Detection.

information is actually exchanged and yet from which all participants gain something, archetypally reassurance. An example might be:

"Nice weather today."
"Sure is."
"Really hot."
"*Too* hot, maybe."
"Could be."
"Well, top of the morning to you ..."

In one of his songs Robin Williamson captured the essence of the phatic conversation in a single sentence: "Hello, I must be going, well I only came to say: I hear my mother calling and I must be on my way." Similarly there can be phatic fictions—fictions that tell us nothing, that involve no exercise of the intellect whatsoever beyond the basics involved in understanding the words, yet which satisfy some need in ourselves. In the case of Generic Fantasy that need is, as with the phatic conversation, a form of reassurance. More specifically, it is the exercise of *vicarious imagination*. The reader of Generic Fantasy requires to bolster his or her self-image as an imaginative person—as any drunk in a bar will tell you, *un*imaginative people are the pitsh—and hence turns to that form of literature which has the "FANTASY" label on the spine: if it says right here that it's fantasy, it must be, and therefore any reader of it, like me, must be an imaginative sort of a person, no?

Of course, in order to properly fulfill this phatic function, Generic Fantasy *cannot in point of fact* contain any material that might stretch the imagination—cannot be fantasy, in other words: its readers *by conscious choice* are not prepared to explore the mental regions where the Tygers roam—that would be to try to sell them apples when they want to buy oranges. They seek to gain the zing of imagination vicariously; they do not seek imagination itself, and would be terrified at the very prospect of the Tygers. To draw a perhaps unnecessarily brutal analogy, men generally read pornography in order vicariously to experience the delights of bedding lovelies; not only are such delights unavailable to them in real life, such readers would probably be terrified if they suddenly became so.[41]

So we have two quite distinct forms of literature. One of these is Generic Fantasy; the other is fantasy proper. Much muddle arises because of a conflict

---

[41] There are of course other purposes of phatic literature. Who has not curled up with a Golden Age detective novel as a way of relaxing on a cold winter's night? But, while very many read detections, very few are fanatically devoted to them to the extent of reading little other fiction.

between marketing and literary-criticism details of classification: what is in literary terms Generic Fantasy, and therefore by empiric definition not fantasy at all, is in marketing terms classified as fantasy—and it's the marketing folk who put that word "FANTASY" on book-spines—thereby confusing Joe Public, who trustingly believes what the marketing folk say. It's entertaining to speculate how long it would take for the language to change if some bright-eyed marketing whiz came along and stuck the label "CORNED BEEF" on every tub of ice cream in the land.

A silly example? No sillier than the notion that the language might change through publishers plastering the "FANTASY" label on fictions that are not fantasy.

Another interesting aspect of Generic Fantasy is that no one is responsible for it. Ask any self-designated fantasy reader and they'll tell you that what they really like is the cutting-edge stuff, not the pap which the publishers churn out in its place. Ask any publisher's editor when they're in their cups (traditionally an easy enough situation to engineer) and you'll be told that s/he can't personally stomach such garbage, but it's what the market wants: left to their own devices the editors would publish nothing but Helprin, Nabokov, Pynchon, Barth, Le Guin, Tepper, Borges and whichever writer has just asked them the question and whose synopsis is at this very moment, purely at the marketing department's insistence you understand, destined for the office shredder. Ask the writers and, with a very few extraordinarily honest exceptions, they will assure you that what they themselves are writing is not Generic Fantasy but the true, dangerous, intellectually subversive stuff— Jonathan Swift with all the sea elves, lisping dragons, good-hearted-but-constantly-getting-into-scrapes rite-of-passage kitchen-boy monarchs-in-exile, comic-cut trolls, Hoirish leprechauns, under-hormoned princesses, Dark Lords, sorcerers and the rest of the stomach-wrenchingly overfamiliar crew there purely as embellishments, as bell-ropes pulling different bells.[42]

So nobody's really responsible for Generic Fantasy, just as nobody's really the father of a bastard.

To digress, there's an intriguing diagnostic test that can be carried out to discover whether a text is a Generic Fantasy or the real thing. One of the characteristics of fantasy is that it's very often recursive—drawing together from elsewhere disparate elements, juxtaposing them and creating something

---

[42] It is in fact perfectly feasible to use the standard tropes of Generic Fantasy to create fantasy proper—it's just rather rarely done. It should be mentioned that true fantasies quite frequently and legitimately borrow elements from other modes of literature. A true fantasy that borrows elements in this way from Generic Fantasy is thus merely doing what other fantasies do, the only difference being the literary subgenre from which the borrowing is being done.

new from the mixture. The recursions of Generic Fantasy, however, are based on *Generic Fantasy itself*. Ouroboros-like, it swallows its own tale.

So the question Clute and I asked in that long-ago discussion panel—"Why is Fantasy No Longer a Subversive Form of Literature?"—was actually rather misdirected. Fantasy—true fantasy—is just as subversive as it always was, or at least is capable of being so: it's just that there's very little true fantasy about. What we were really pointing at was the self-evident fact that *Generic Fantasy* is not, and almost from the first has not been, a subversive subgenre. When the firemen of *Fahrenheit 451* carried out their raids they could have left great mountains of the stuff lying there untouched without in the slightest way endangering the stability of their society.

In case I should be accused of kicking a dead horse when it's down during this perfectly dispassionate discussion of the differences between Generic Fantasy and fantasy proper—and, believe me, nothing is more reminiscent of thoroughly dead horsemeat than some of the Generic Fantasies that have oozed through my hands—it should be pointed out that the traffic in strong description is not entirely one-way. One of the curious paradoxes of this whole area of discussion is born out of the fact that some devotees of Generic Fantasy are not just frightened of the dangers of real fantasy: they are actually angered by it, and vociferously so, presumably because it represents a threat to what they have come to perceive as the *genuine* form of the two confusingly named literatures. Rootstock fantasy, they seem to be saying, is neither Gulliver nor Gormenghast but *only* the derivative stuff that can exist solely within the walled frontiers of a pseudo-Tolkienesque and ultimately hack Fantasyland; everything else is the enemy army at the gates—or even, horror of horrors, the Fifth Column within them—and is to be detested accordingly.

I have a recurring nightmare, a terrible fear, and it goes something like this. One day I open up a copy of some magazine like *Interzone* and start reading the lead fiction review. The beginning of it goes:

> *Gulliver's Travels* by Jonathan Swift (presumably a pseudonym) recounts the improbable adventures of a man who sets sail on various sea voyages, where he meets strange folk. Some of these folk are big, some of them are small, and some of them look like horses. Swift should have realized that he thereby left very little room open for anything by way of romance, because Gulliver would have practical difficulties pursuing his passions with either the very little or the very big women, and the author bridles

at the notion of letting his hero frolic with the horses. This lack of romantic potential leaves the novel without any passion at its core, something Swift should have thought about before he began this plaguey novel.

I had great hopes of *Alice in Wonderland* by Lewis Carroll, since the blurb told me it was about a young woman going down a rabbit hole, and the similarity of "rabbit hole" and "hobbit hole" could not be, I thought, coincidence. However, the young woman in question proves to be a vapid Victorian miss, and her adventures underground are devoid of all logic. According to the press release there's a sequel on the way tied in with a popular board game, and perhaps Carroll will have more success with that.

Turning now to *Dragonspume Chronicles of the Sorcerer Kingdom Ancients Volume 6: Sword of Blood* by Jerome E. Housename we discover a real pearl, a delight of a book, a volume that according to its publisher's justified claim is better than Christopher Tolkien at his best—one of those novels that shows us what fantasy *should be...*

My nightmare, of course, is not that this review should exist but that I should read it, nodding my head in brainwashed agreement.

It is rather sobering to think that we have permitted, through negligence, the sham version to attain a position of such eminence that it has come to regard itself as the genuine article. For, in ironically describing the various categories of people who are in no way really responsible for Generic Fantasy, I omitted to mention the worst offenders: ourselves. We have sat back—all too many of us—and watched with a sort of snobbish complacency as a form of literature which I at least passionately love and believe to be crucially important to our culture has been smothered and strangled and drowned by this monstrous tide of commercially inspired, mind-numbingly unimaginative garbage—this loathsome mire. And the worst mistake we could make, now, is to prolong that complacency—to say meekly that it's too late to do anything about the situation.

A start can be made by at least, as I suggested all those years ago, defining our terms—by adding to the list of commonly distinguished genres and subgenres of fiction a new one, called either Generic Fantasy or whichever better name someone comes up with. There is no intention here to cast Generic Fantasy into purdah by so doing: it is simply a matter of making a distinction between one form of writing and another. Neither would we be establishing a qualitative hierarchy: I can think of extremely well written Generic Fantasies just as easily as I can think of direly written full fantasies. What we *would* be doing is both (a) focusing our own minds on the genre that is actually at the heart of our interests, without the distraction of the mass of pseudo-fantasy, and (b) with any luck stirring the commercial publishers into the recognition that they can actually make more money by discriminating between the two quite separate markets which currently they are treating as if it were only one. For how many readers do each and every one of us know who have simply given up on buying books with the "FANTASY" label through having so often been disappointed by what they've bought? How many of *us ourselves* fall into this category, if only we would be honest enough to admit it?

For that, surely, is the final and greatest danger of allowing the failure to discriminate between the two genres to continue:[43] that potential fantasy readers will seek elsewhere before ever they discover the gold, and that even existing fantasy readers—not to mention writers—will eventually give up the struggle.

---

[43] It's a danger to commercial publishers as well. Do you remember the time when, if it wasn't a Teenage Mutant Ninja Turtles spinoff, it wasn't worth marketing? When the craze abruptly died a good many manufacturers, caught unawares, lost money and were left with warehouses full of junk toys. There's going to come a time when the market for Generic Fantasy will suddenly collapse; the way publishing works, it'll take two or three years before the publishers can actually stop issuing Generic Fantasy books, losing money on each one. Furthermore, it may well be that fantasy proper will have so far declined by then that the publishers will have nothing to offer readers of imaginative or quasi-imaginative fiction in Generic Fantasy's place — so they'll lose money twice over.

THE BRITISH FUTURE
Paul Cornell

Since the First World War, science fiction has become the literature of the fear of war. Let me pause to justify that: SF is about the impact of new technologies, social forces and ideas. It's about what's happening right now, and how it all might change. For the Japanese, SF is Godzilla, *Akira*, and millions of all-powerful heroes who are undefeated and strong and not at all defensive about it, oh no. For the Americans, who avoided the morass of the World Wars and are still riding the economy of the uninvaded, it's largely a fantasy about exploration, about getting out there and finding more America. The American future is *Star Trek*.

For the British, therefore, science fiction is about noble aims and economic failure. Think about it: just after the Second World War, the British future is *Dan Dare* and *Journey Into Space*'s Jet Morgan. Not so very different from American media SF. We're off into the void to spread our values, and Spacefleet is run by the British. Note how that sounds funny now. But Starfleet being run by the Americans isn't. There lies the difference in the genre across the Atlantic. It's during the late fifties that this difference becomes concrete. Then the hangover of the economic aftermath of the war begins to bite. The three-day week, the power cuts. We have to decide whether or not to join a federation of nations. America *is* just such a federation. We start to produce *Quatermass*, *Survivors*, *Edge of Darkness*. Look at even the most glittery of our fictions: *Doctor Who*, *Blake's 7*. Amongst the spangles, it's clear that we're not in space, looking down on the planet of the troublesome people, wondering how to beam up our away team. We're up to our neck in possessing, transforming, fascistic, swiftly-edited screaming monsters! The darkest of American fantasies is the one where the aliens are living covertly amongst us: *Invasion of the Body Snatchers*. We make it for children and call it *The Tomorrow People*. On the edge of Europe, we were on the front line of the Cold War, vulnerable to the whims of the States for our defense. The U.S.A. always believed it could *fight* a nuclear war. The U.K. only ever dreamed of *losing* one. The Americans make the world of the future. We're alienated from the process.

Let's check some examples. The crew of any *Star Trek* (and that includes *Babylon 5*, *Lost in Space*, *Andromeda*, etc.) vessel may bicker a little, but basically they're all looking out for each other. *Blake's 7* ends with the "first officer" killing the "captain," then watching as the "Klingons" gun down "Scotty," "Bones" and all the Uhuras.

Captain Kirk is from Iowa. He's an American who proudly represents humanity. The Doctor is from Gallifrey. He's an alien who… well, you know, some of his best friends are humans, but…

Fox Mulder, in *The X-Files*, represents hopefully all that is best about his country even when it's being covertly run (and that series never says just how run is run) by aliens. Ronnie Craven in *Edge of Darkness* dies after declaring, "I am not on your side!"

Isaac Asimov: stories about people fixing things. Arthur C. Clarke: stories about things fixing people.

Even some of the classics of American fantasy have their roots over here. Joss Whedon, creator of *Buffy*, spent a large chunk of his childhood absorbing British TV shows (including, surely, *Press Gang*, to which the vampire slayer seems to owe a large debt); *2001* and *Star Wars* were both made in Britain with largely British crews. This isn't just points scoring. In this sort of text, a British element is shorthand for complexity. Obi-Wan, source of all wisdom, has to be British. The villain, as has often been observed, in any Hollywood blockbuster, has to be British. As becomes obvious in *Cliffhanger* where John Lithgow, a Canadian, is hired to play a villain…with a British accent! What's less obvious is why. The hero is straightforward, thus American. The villain is complicated, thus European, with a voice the audience can understand, and hopefully R.S.C. training, thus British.

British creators also benefit from viewing the American conquest of the future from a certain distance. Stephen Baxter's NASAporn is about Americans, but it could never be written by one, because it cuts to the heart of how the agency is failing the dream. His American heroes are introverted, complicated, withdrawn like Europeans are supposed to be. His American villains are brash, certain, men of action, demonstrative like Americans are supposed to be. J. G. Ballard stares in horror and glee at America. Michael Moorcock carefully turns his back to it. We're gravitationally influenced by the country, in a way that those who stand on its surface never can be. Gerry Anderson's "American" heroes the Tracey Brothers are deeply dull. Because he's trying to make them perfect. Lady Penelope and Parker are fun. Because they're not.

The American apocalypse is Philip K. Dick: civilization has fallen apart, and the human mind with it! The British apocalypse is John Wyndham: oh, that's really terribly annoying, let's put the kettle on. The words "comfy disaster" would crumble to a full stop before they ever saw the inside of an American SF novel. In that country, the end of civilization really is the end of the world.

And all that is why British SF has always been better than American SF. I like Americans. I like the optimism. I like the future. But we British know in our bones that SF is about *now*. The Americans believe in the future. We're afraid of it. Theirs is the healthier attitude. But healthy attitudes do not great literature make. Britain is where the money isn't, where the gray areas are, and thus where the best science fiction is made.

SCIENTISTS IN SF FILMS
Robert A. Metzger

What is a scientist?

Lock onto the first image that flits into your head. Do you picture the nerdy little fellow in lab coat, Coke-bottle thick glasses, pocket protectors bulging with all manner of scientific gizmos, pants hiked up to expose several inches of sock, and hair that has not been in close proximity to a comb since puberty kicked in? Or perhaps you see the other scientist, the megalomaniac, the arrogant bastard and evil genius raising a fist in the direction of God, oblivious to the fact that his quest for knowledge will destroy the world about him. And then again there is one more scientist, a rare variety, one seldom seen walking the streets, and even more elusive when it comes to SF films. This is the scientist who worries about the mortgage payment, who is trying to find the time to get the oil changed in his car, who fought last night with his or her spouse about whose turn it was to clean the kitchen, and lives in fear that unless a teenaged son gets his act together and cracks open the books, that his future will consist of endless years of finishing every conversation with: "Would you like fries with that?" And on those rare occasions when this scientist actually finds the time to do a bit of science, it is not the science that involves the illegal use of nuclear weapons, tainted DNA, or top secret installations buried beneath mountains, but the type of science that may lead to better corrosion resistance to the undercoating of trucks, improved shelf-life of canned meats, softer, more absorbent toilet paper, or an improved high frequency filter that will lead to a few more seconds of battery life in cell phones.

This last scientist does not make it into SF films.

Because that scientist suffers from the disadvantage of being *real*.

101 Uses of Duct Tape may be big box office in the heads of real working scientists, but such a movie is not in the works, scripts are not being written, option money not being offered, and Tom Cruise is not drooling over the prospects of portraying Dr. Jack Jackson, as he spends a lifetime of research in the intellectual pursuit of duct tape applications.

The truth of the matter is, that a great deal of what a scientist does is damned hard slogging, with years and years between eureka moments that probably would not seem all that eureka-like to most folks. When the intrepid Dr. Jack Jackson envisions for the first time a new synthetic polymer cross-link that will improve adhesion between duct tape and galvanized steel sheet by a remarkable twenty-seven percent, that magic moment will not translate well to the big screen.

But none of this should really surprise us.

Cops in cop movies may start shooting up the bad guys during the opening credits, while during a real cop's career his or her weapon will only be fired on the target range. And while the lawyer in the lawyer movie will be neck deep in witty and cutting cross-examinations during the pivotal courtroom scene, the vast majority of those with law degrees will only enter into a courtroom to contest their own parking tickets. Then there is our friend the scientist, who in the movie will crack the alien's secret planet destroying codes in just the nick of time, while the only code of concern to a working scientist might well be the string of digits needed to punch into the copying machine in order to run off the fifty copies of the monthly status report on the ongoing battle to ever reduce the fat content of the company's best selling Hint O'Lard crackers.

So I will not lament on how inaccurately the scientist is portrayed in SF films. To do that is just as meaningless as dissecting the science in SF films, pointing out how you cannot hear the explosions of Death Stars in the vacuum of space, or just how unlikely it is that every damn race of aliens inducted into the Galactic Federation manage to all fit into standard issue Federation uniforms.

Then why bother to even consider SF-film scientists?

Because while they may not provide much in the way of insight into actual scientists, and the world in which they operate, their fictional portrayal does give insight into the way that scientists are *perceived* — not only by the filmmakers, but also by the public in general. In the same manner that much of the public believes that it understands the nature of cops and lawyers based on their fictional representation, the same holds true of scientists, of how science is performed, and ultimately the places that scientists and science hold in society.

IN THE BEGINNING

At a time when quantum theory was just being revealed, the first decay of nuclear isotopes being investigated, and much of the world mired in the Great Depression, Hollywood unleashed a volley of films in which scientists were front and center: *Frankenstein* (1931—adapted from Mary Shelley's *Frankenstein, or the Modern Prometheus*—1818), *Dr. Jekyll and Mr. Hyde* (1932—adapted from the *Strange Case of Dr. Jekyll and Mr. Hyde* by Robert Louis Stevenson—1886), and *Island of Lost Souls* (1932—adapted from *The Island of Dr. Moreau* by H. G. Wells—1896). All three of these classics, based on some of the earliest SF writings, shared a common theme—*when one plays God, he will be destroyed*.

This is how scientists were perceived—if not actually God-like in their abilities and insights, at least arrogant enough to believe that they were. Henry Frankenstein creates life from death, Dr. Jekyll taps into the animal, primitive and sexually aggressive core of his own being, while Dr. Moreau, in the belief that he can fashion a race superior to what God has created, attempts to blend man and beast to give birth to something devoid of original sin—eradicating that intrinsic flaw left behind during God's creation.

Arrogance in the extreme.

But the three scientists shared more than just arrogance. They shared a common background—well-educated, intellectual, not bound by the concerns of the average folk of the 1930s, those that needed to work every conscious moment just to scratch out a living in order to feed and clothe their families. These three men had the financial resources, the education, and the drive to uncover those secrets that man simply had no right to know.

And like Prometheus, they got burned (well, actually, their livers eaten).

Henry Frankenstein is the very essence of the 1930s SF scientist— the son of the village overlord—Baron Frankenstein. Wealthy, educated, an entire town of simple German-folk at the beckon call of his family, he should have been content with his lot in life, sipping fine German wines and waving at peasants.

But no.

He'd been seduced by the dark side, by an evil darker than even the one that fills the soul of Darth Vader (at least in *Star Wars'* episodes IV, V and much of VI). Science has nabbed him by the short hairs.

The opening graveyard scene immediately sets the tone, with the narrator informing us that, "Herr Frankenstein, a man of science who sought to create a man after his own image without reckoning upon God." We see Henry Frankenstein and his hunchbacked assistant, Fritz, begin to dig up a fresh grave in quest of body parts for his gruesome, *ungodly*, experiments. Standing above Frankenstein from atop a tomb, is a statue of death. With his first spadeful of dirt, Frankenstein flips it over his shoulder, the soil striking death square in the face.

That says it right there.

Frankenstein has thrown down the gauntlet, or in this case flinged the gauntlet in the face of death—ready to do battle. But there is more to Frankenstein than just an egomaniac with a pile of spare body parts and some heavy-duty electrical equipment. Science has not only seduced him into those realms where things are best left alone, but has in fact seduced him away from his fiancée. And he appears to know this, to at times even try to fight against the irresistible tug that science has on him. While science seems to be the chosen pathway of those looking to steal god-like powers from the heaven, one of the universal prices to be paid in this quest is that of losing the girl (SF film scientists are almost exclusively white males). The very nature of science apparently has the power to vaporize one's *softer* emotions, those of love and compassion, those needed to win the heart of a fair damsel. This theme will play right up into the twenty-first century—unlocking the secrets of the universe is not conducive to getting the girl (unless you make a pile of money in the process).

Henry Frankenstein is trapped—in fact infected by science, his father the Baron, his fiancée Elizabeth, and even his mentor, Dr. Waldman, all convinced that his obsession with science will eventually kill him, illustrated so melodramatically in every scene—his energy clearly sapped, at times delirious with fever, raving, collapsing against convenient castle walls.

Science is a soul-sucking mistress.

But Henry trudges on, sews up various body parts, and installs a defective brain stolen by his enthusiastic, but not quite competent hunchbacked assistant Fritz, and proceeds to the big experiment—one of the most famous film scenes ever created.

"It's alive—now I know what it feels like to be God!"

Screaming that is just asking for trouble. And Henry Frankenstein is given a heaping plateful. His creation is not quite what he hoped for. He's in fact created a MONSTER. It cannot speak, but only grunt (apparently only God has the power to give speech), suffers from residual rigor mortis, can't stand sunlight or fire (those being *good* things), and just generally seems to be pissed off at the world.

The only thing to do is to lock the monster away.

But of course these things never stay locked away.

The monster's first victim is the deformed assistant Fritz. This is to be expected. Fritz is the equivalent of the unnamed ensign in Captain Kirk's landing party—he just isn't going to last that long. When the death of Fritz takes place, this gives us some indication that the monster is bad—but there is still a bit of ambiguity about this. Fritz was a pretty disgusting little guy—while killing him was not the nicest thing that the monster might do, in the scheme of things, not all that major of a sin.

So after having done in Fritz, Henry and his mentor Dr. Waldman come to the conclusion that the best course of action is to dismantle the monster. Waldman takes on the task so that Henry can return to his father's house to get some much-needed rest and try to mend bridges with his fiancée. Already the power that science has over him is beginning to weaken—he's thinking about girls again.

Now the monster ratchets things up a notch. This time it is Dr. Waldman who is killed—it seems that the monster did not want to be dismantled. This is a bit more serious than the killing of Fritz. While Dr. Waldman is a man of science (and therefore rather suspect), he is still a man of good standing in the community, shown not to be a scientist in quest of body parts, but a Herr Professor from the university.

We're beginning to get the message now.

The monster is bad.

Then the rampage begins—though it doesn't look like much of a rampage. The monster wanders about the countryside, spending most of his time trying to battle his way out of thick bushes. And then he encounters the very essence of innocence, little Maria, a child who wants nothing more than a playmate, who drags the monster by the hand to the edge of a lake where they throw in flowers in order to watch them float.

This is the one and only time that we see the monster with a smile on his face. When faced with an innocent such as little Maria, that experience seems to allow the monster to tap into some nearly hidden reservoir of goodness. The monster tosses in a few flowers and even manages to laugh. Perhaps the monster is not really that evil after all—but simply a reflection of his surroundings. In the presence of science and scientists he descends into the darkness, but with an innocent child ascends towards the light (this being the only daytime outdoor scene in which we see the monster).

But the monster is still tainted by the original sin of science, in this case not manifesting itself by an act of evil, but one of stupidity and fear.

After tossing in a few flowers and enjoying that, he proceeds to toss in little Maria—unfortunately she doesn't float like the flowers.

This *is* bad.

An innocent has been killed, and while the monster was the instrument of her death, the real force responsible was science, the monster simply its rather crude tool.

Things go from bad to worse.

The monster shows up at Baron Frankenstein's house just before Henry and Elizabeth are about to get married. As the men folk go running about the house in search of the monster, the monster manages to stumble into Elizabeth's bedroom.

He *chases* her.

He *touches* her.

That's the straw that breaks the camel's back—something built of science is chasing after our virginal women. Henry now gets the message in no uncertain terms—the monster needs to be hunted down and torn apart. The local peasants get whipped up when little Maria's dead body is brought into the town, and a torch-carrying mob goes chasing after the monster. Being evil, crafty and cunning, the monster attacks Henry from the shadows and then hauls him off to an old windmill. The monster and his creator get into a fight, and Henry gets himself tossed from the top of the windmill (bounces off one of the windmill's blades on the way down, obviously snapping the back of the dummy used in the stunt).

There's nothing left for the peasants to do now but burn down the windmill.

The monster dies, consumed by fire, the evil burned away.

All dead.

You play with science and you get burned (literally).

But it doesn't quite end there. The final scene is back at the Baron's house, where we discover that Henry Frankenstein survived the fall, that his soon-to-be wife is nursing him back to health, the house servants are so happy to have Mr. Henry back that they bring him a special bottle of wine, and old Baron Frankenstein is beaming at the happy ending.

He has his son back—the evil spell of science has been broken.

Young Henry Frankenstein has gotten off free and clear. It's true that his creation resulted in the death of three people, but the ending so obviously implies that he was not actually responsible for those deaths, in the same manner that someone temporarily insane is not responsible for their crimes.

Science was responsible—the real villain.

Science killed those three people and Henry Frankenstein was merely the too-human vessel that science took control over. This says it more clearly than any other film made at its time—the only thing more ungodly than the scientist is the science itself.

There are things that mere humans shouldn't know.

There are things that only God should know.

Cross that line and bad things will happen.

NECESSARY EVIL

Fast forward thirty years, past World War II, past nuclear weapons both atomic and hydrogen based, and into the cold war and space race. Much has changed. The scientist is no longer hidden in his secret lab, sequestered in the castle, hiding on the distant island, or fumbling about in the basement lab with sputtering electrodes and decaying body parts. Science has made the big time. It brought an end to World War II, has hurled men into near Earth orbit, and has brought the power to destroy an entire planet into the hands of those who control the scientists.

Scary times—much more scary than Henry Frankenstein's stiff jointed creation, or the animal-people built by Dr. Moreau. While the fictional scientists of the 1930s may have failed at taking the power of life and death from God, these real world scientists of the post-World War II era have succeeded.

So what images of these God-like scientists are the movie-going public given?

Thirty years after the mistress of science almost succeeded in coming between Henry Frankenstein and his fiancée, once again the siren song of cracking the puzzles of the universe comes between man and woman. However, this time it comes in the form of Walt Disney's gentler, sweater-wearing, forgetful wanna-be God, in the *Absent-Minded Professor* of 1961. And just like Henry Frankenstein, who cannot make it to his own wedding due to the demands of creating his monster, the Absent-Minded Professor has missed his own wedding three times while in the pursuit of his own monster. The only real difference is in the form of the monster—the Absent-Minded Professor does not seek to generate life from lifeless matter, but to create flying rubber—known to all the world as *flubber*.

The scientists of newspaper headlines, those who figure out how to build ever more powerful nuclear weapons, those so brilliant whose heads are filled with the secrets of the universe, are simply too terrible to bring to film, unless one paints them in all their science-savvy grotesqueness in an over the top satire such as *Dr. Strangelove or: How I Learned to Stop Worrying and Love the Bomb* (1963). What is needed is to create a more palatable, less frightening scientist, one that Mr. 1960, living in his three-bedroom, two-bath ranch along with his 2.5 kids and brand spanking new Detroit-finned chunk of chrome and steel, can even feel superior to.

How to do it?

Make him a sweater-wearing Absent Minded Professor, a scientist who might have the capability of vaporizing the Soviet Union and starting World War III, but instead focuses his blazing intellect on applying his awesome powers for invention on the winning of basketball games and the creation of flying cars. Make him a nerd, totally out of his depth when it comes to dealing with the opposite sex, accompanied by a dog that understands the complex nuances of human relations, while our Absent-Minded Professor cannot even find the glasses on his own face, let alone the woman desperate to marry him. Still intellectually powerful, but the viewing public knows that there is something missing, a critical element that still allows Mr. 1960 to be superior, that offers the promise of taking the mad scientist in two out of three falls (three out of three if women are the prize). Of course this scientist could probably modify his own toaster into a kitchen-friendly nuclear reactor, but his saving grace is that he couldn't use the toaster to actually make a piece of toast.

Science and scientists put in their proper places.

The pinnacle of scientist-as-nerd comes five years after the *Absent-Minded Professor*, where all warmth and dignity have been stripped away, and nothing remains except for buckteeth, a bowl hair cut, nasal voice, thick glasses, and the physical coordination of a speed freak at the end of a five-day run. In 1966 Jerry Lewis gives us the *Nutty Professor*, an individual of towering intellect who regularly gets stuffed into lockers by forty-year-old freshman football players. Inept in everything except for the manipulation of test tubes, it is a miracle that this sexually clueless buffoon posses enough real-world savvy to remember to breathe and blink. In a take-off of *Dr. Jekyll and Mr. Hyde*, once again a scientific elixir is used to release the inner man, the inner animal, the one that understands what is really important (women), and all that needs to be paid for in order to gain that wisdom is to turn one's back on science.

The nerd-scientist is born.

The 1960s are a dangerous time—where the scientist in the real world is needed to maintain the delicate balance of mutual assured destruction. These are scary folks with the power of life and death in their hands, but with a wide streak of inferiority, the inability to talk to women, form coherent sentences, or even dress and feed themselves. Comfort can be taken from such ineptitude.

THE ANTI-SCIENCE SCIENTIST

After Jerry Lewis created the ultimate in scientist-nerd, that envelope of the totally absurd had been pushed past the breaking point and could be pushed no further. So while the taint of the nerd will remain firmly in place, the character of scientist is reeled back toward the realm of someone vaguely recognizable as human. But Hollywood still cannot resist the fictional stereotype. The *Back to the Future* trilogy of the second half of the 1980s brings us the updated nerd in the form of Dr. Emmett Brown, played by Christopher Lloyd, the casting perfectly chosen so as to let the viewing audience know before Dr. Brown so much as opens his mouth, that they will be dealing with a variation of the drug-damaged cab driver that Lloyd played in *Taxi*. But not wanting to rely on only that subtle connection, Lloyd is provided a wild expanse of snow-white Albert Einstein hair, and a perpetual bug-eyed look of bewilderment. And like our Absent-Minded Professor who does not quite fit into the world of matching socks and paying the electric bill, Dr. Brown eventually transforms his time-traveling Delorian into a flying car by the end of the first film—the Absent-Minded Professor is alive and well in the 1980s. However, by the trilogy's end, we begin to see something more of Dr. Brown than a towering intellect in a lab coat and unkempt hair, and he actually gets the girl in the form of Mary Steenbergen—managing this without magic elixirs or a major personality makeover.

The girl goes for the scientist nerd.

The nineties arrive and suddenly all bets are off. The wealthiest man in the world is no longer a Rockefeller-type robber baron, or a good old boy Sam Walton merchant wizard, but a nerd whose ability to write code and gobble up competitors has made Bill Gates the poster boy for what a nerd on a mission is capable of—power not based on sex appeal or upper body strength, but on synaptic finesse.

Enter the *Jurassic Park* franchise. In *Jurassic Park* we are offered up not the wild-haired nerd in quest of dinosaurs, but a trio of scientists, all of whom begin to question the virtue of the quest of knowledge, who actually question the basic premise that there is nothing that men should not reach for. We see the first inklings of this in *Back To the Future*'s Dr. Brown, the mad scientist whose greatest discovery ends up being Mary Steenbergen (though the nerd-scientist is still securely in place as the trilogy closes with him literally sailing off into the sunset in his flying train).

In the 1930s the sentiment was crystal clear—science is not to be trusted and there are some things that man should not attempt to understand—vast chunks of space, time and inquiry that we should simply keep our too-curious noses out of. The penalty for snooping about in God's territory was usually a very gruesome demise for the snooper. But by the 90s, while the sentiment remains unchanged, this perspective is now being delivered by the scientists themselves—not by the wild-haired nerds of the preceding decades, but by the anti-science scientist, the one who can offer warnings as to the terrible potential of science, because he or she knows firsthand just what terrible power science can wield—an insider's perspective on the dark side.

This is the essence of *Jurassic Park* and is presented by its trio of scientists—a pair of dinosaur bone hunters, and a mathematician turned chaos-atician, the latter placed in the film for the sole reason of being able to point at any gizmo of science, ranging from hardware to dinosaurs, and offer up witty anti-science sound bites.

Anti-science sells, because fear sells.

Michael Crichton understood this nearly twenty years before writing *Jurassic Park*, with his creation of the *Andromeda Strain* (1969)—in which science captures a space-borne virus, brings it back to Earth, and then takes us along for the ride as the inevitable consequence of scientific hubris is unleashed on an innocent, isolated community.

The *formula* has been worked out—science steals something that should have remained solely in the realm gods, and then this little piece of nastiness is set free on an isolated snippet of humanity. The isolation of the victims is critical to the Crichton formula, allowing the evilness of science to run a course to its logical conclusion—*total destruction*. Unless isolated, all of mankind would be gone, leaving nothing behind, nowhere for the survivors of the encounters with evil science to flee to, giving them the opportunity to look back at the audience, and warn the folks on the other side of the movie screen that if science is not kept on a short leash this piece of SF that they just watched may turn out to be the real thing. Crichton knows how to do this—over and over again. *Andromeda Strain* takes place in a lone desert town, *Westworld* (1973) in an isolated android filled resort, *The Abyss* (1989) in the ocean depths, and the most recent, *Prey* (written in 2002), again returning to the isolated desert location. The isolation allows whatever has been unleashed from a scientific Pandora's box to chew through everything—not controlled and contained by the hand of man, but by the physical isolation of the story setting.

The message is clear—man was not able to save himself by intellect or the use of science, but by sheer dumb luck. Had the virus, the android, the dinosaur or the nanobot been unleashed into the world at large, it would have been the end for all of us.

We see in *Jurassic Park* that the trio of scientists are actually spokesmen for Chrichton's fear of science and technology. There are the two bone-diggers, paleontologist Alan Grant, and his female sidekick paleobotanist Ellie Satler. Very little of the Nutty Professor remains, but Alan Grant still maintains a genetic linkage to the Absent-Minded Professor, understanding dinosaurs far better than women, and possessing the remarkable ability to crash electronic equipment simply by being in physical proximity to it (he does not need to stumble into objects to destroy them as did earlier nerd-scientists—he seems to exude some advanced form of pheromone-based klutzyness that can destroy items by a proximity effect). And as far as women are concerned, this is what Ellie Satler *is*. Despite the fact that she is referred to as a world-famous paleobiologist, her primary concerns in this film center on exposing boyfriend Alan Grant to two children, in the hope that the clueless dope will cross the vast gulf between the Absent-Minded Professor and the Regular Joe, and then contemplate having offspring with her. Her only other real function in the film is to look wide-eyed and flabbergasted whenever the third scientist offers up a gem of chaos-voodoo.

Ian Malcom (quite possibly the alter ego of Michael Crichton), played by Jeff Goldblum, is the purest of scientists—the absolute top rung of the nerdy set—a mathematician. He has boiled all of chaos physics and mathematics into a single mantra —*if it can go wrong it will go wrong*. He is a scientist so cool, dressed in all black, sporting a mane of tussled dark curls, and on the lookout for the next "ex-Mrs. Malcolm." He has actually transcended what it is to be a scientist, and has become a *person*, and offers up such little gems as, "Scientists are so preoccupied with whether or not they could, they didn't stop to think if they should," and "What you call discovery I call the rape of the natural world."

Subtle it is not.

And of course we all know what happens—Prometheus all over again. While the mythical Prometheus was rewarded for stealing fire from the gods and giving it to humans by having his liver eaten every day by a bird of prey, those who have sinned against God in their quest to reanimate extinct flesh (the distinction between Frankenstein's monster and the dinosaurs of Jurassic Park is essentially nonexistent), get their livers eaten by dinosaurs—in this case a couple of computer programmers, one an overweight geek trying to smuggle dino embryos off the island, and a no-nonsense black man whose world does not seem to extend past his computer screen. Our trio of scientists were sufficiently frightened of the prospects of science to not actually be eaten—like Henry Frankenstein, they'd seen the light of reason, and did not have to pay the ultimate penalty for their scientific fetishes.

We fear the unknown.

We fear the uncontrollable.

And we especially fear those who muck around in the realms of the unknown and the uncontrollable, drag something in from the shadows, and then plop it in our laps. We fear those damn scientists. That fear has been manifested in films from the beginning, and will undoubtedly continue to do so.

Are these film scientists accurate representations of real scientists?

Absolutely not.

But of course that is not the point. It's not about them, not about those would-be gods with bad hair, pocket protectors, and their inability to strike up conversations with the opposite sex. It's about the fear of the unknown, about what lies in that immense gulf between God and us.

It could be anything.

It could even be Jerry Lewis sporting fake buckteeth.

The terror.

THE SQUANDERED PROMISE OF SCIENCE FICTION
Jonathan Lethem

In 1973 Thomas Pynchon's *Gravity's Rainbow* was awarded the Nebula, the highest honor available in the field once known as "science fiction"—a term now mostly forgotten.

Sorry, just dreaming. In our world Bruce is dead, while Bob Hope lurches on. And though *Gravity's Rainbow* really was nominated for the 1973 Nebula, it was passed over for Arthur C. Clarke's *Rendezvous With Rama*, which commentator Carter Scholz rightly deemed "less a novel than a schematic diagram in prose." Pynchon's nomination now stands as a hidden tombstone marking the death of the hope that science fiction was about to merge with the mainstream.

That hope was born in the hearts of writers who, without any particular encouragement from the larger literary world, for a little while dragged the genre to the brink of respectability. The new-wave SF of the sixties and seventies was often word-drunk, applying modernist techniques willy-nilly to the old genre motifs, adding compensatory dollops of alienation and sexuality to characters who'd barely shed their slide rules. But the new wave also made possible books like Samuel Delany's *Dhalgren* Philip K. Dick's *A Scanner Darkly*, Ursula K. Le Guin's *The Dispossessed*, and Thomas Disch's *334*—work to stand with the best American fiction of the 1970s, labels, categories, and genres aside. In a seizure of ambition, SF even flirted with renaming itself "speculative fabulation," a lit-crit term both pretentiously silly and dead right.

For what makes SF wonderful and complicated is that mix of speculation and the fabulous: SF is both think-fiction and dream-fiction. For the first sixty-odd years of the century American fiction was deficient in exactly those qualities SF offered in abundance, however inelegantly. While fabulists like Borges, Abe, Cortazar, and Calvino flourished abroad, a strain of literary puritanism quarantined imaginative and surreal writing from respectability here. Another typical reflex, that anti-intellectualism which dictates that novelists shouldn't pontificate, extrapolate, or theorize, only show and feel, meant the novel of ideas was for many years pretty much the exclusive domain of, um, Norman Mailer. What's more, a reluctance in the humanities to acknowledge the technocratic impulse that was transforming contemporary culture left certain themes untouched. For decades SF filled the gap, and during those decades its writers added characterization, ambiguity, and reflexivity, helping it evolve toward something like a literary maturity, or at least the ability to throw up an occasional masterpiece.

But a funny thing happened on the way to the revolution. In the sixties, just as SF's best writers began to beg the question of whether SF might be literature, American literary fiction began to open to the modes it had excluded. Writers like Donald Barthelme, Richard Brautigan, and Robert Coover restored the place of the imaginative and surreal, while others like Don DeLillo and Joseph McElroy began to contend with the emergent technoculture. William Burroughs and Thomas Pynchon did a little of both. The result was that the need to recognize SF's accomplishments dwindled away. Why seek in those gaudy paperbacks what was readily available in reputable packages? So what followed was mostly critical rejection, or indifference.

Meanwhile, on the other side of the genre-ghetto walls, a retrenchment was underway. Though the stakes aren't nearly as crucial, it's hard not to see SF's attempt at self-liberation as typical of other equality movements that peaked in political strength around the same time, then retreated into identity politics. Fearing the loss of a distinctive oppositional identity, and bitter over a lack of access to the ivory tower, SF took a step backward, away from its broadest literary aspirations. Not that SF of brilliance wasn't written in the years following, but with a few key exceptions it was overwhelmed on the shelves (and award ballots) by a reactionary SF as artistically dire as it was comfortingly familiar.

In the eighties, cyberpunk was taken as a sign of hope, for its verve, its polish, its sensory alertness to the way our conceptions of the future had changed. But even cyberpunk's best writers mostly peddled surprisingly macho and regressive fantasies of rebellion as transcendence, and verve and polish were thin meat for those who recalled the mature depths of the best of the new wave. Anyway, cyberpunk's best were quickly swamped themselves by gelled and pierced photocopies of adolescent power fantasies that were already very, very old.

Which brings us to today. Where, against all odds, SF deserving of greater attention from a literary readership is still written. Its relevance, though, since the collapse of the notion that SF should and would converge with literature, is unclear at best. SF's literary writers exist now in a twilight world, neither respectable nor commercially viable. Their work drowns in a sea of garbage in bookstores, while much of SF's promise is realized elsewhere by writers too savvy or oblivious to bother with its stigmatized identity. SF's failure to present its own best face, to win proper respect, was never so tragic as now, when its strengths are so routinely preempted. In a literary culture where Pynchon, DeLillo, Barthelme, Coover, Jeanette Winterson, Angela Carter, and Steve Erickson are ascendant powers, isn't the division meaningless?

But the literary traditions reinforcing that division are only part of the story. Among the factors arrayed against acceptance of SF as serious writing, none is more plain to outsiders than this: the books are so fucking ugly. Worse, they're all ugly in the same way, so you can't distinguish those meant for grown-ups from those meant for twelve-year-olds. Sadly enough, that confusion is intentional, and the explanation brings us back again to the mid '70s.

It's now a commonplace in film criticism that George Lucas and Steven Spielberg together brought to a crashing halt the most progressive and interesting decade in American film since the thirties. What's eerie is that the same duo are the villains in SF's tragedy as well, though you might want to add a third name, J. R. R. Tolkien. The vast popular success of the imagery and archetypes purveyed by those three savants of children's literature expanded the market for "sci-fi", a cartoonified, castrated, and deeply nostalgic version of the budding literature, a thousandfold. What had been a negligible, eccentric publishing niche, permitted to go its own harmless way, was now a potential cash cow. (Remember when *Star Trek* was resurrected overnight, a moribund TV cult suddenly at the center of popular culture?) As stakes rose, marketers encamped on the territory; for a handy comparison, recall the cloning of grunge rock after Nirvana. Books were produced to meet this vast, superficial new appetite—rotten books, millions of them—and fine books were repackaged to fit the paradigm. Out with the hippie-surrealist book jackets of the sixties, with their promise of grown-up abstractions and ambiguities. In with that leaden and literal style so perfectly abhorrent to the literary book buyer. The golden mean of an SF jacket since 1976 looks, well, exactly like the original poster for *Star Wars*. Men of the future were once again thinking with their swords—excuse me, light sabers. This passive sellout would make more sense if the typical writer of literary SF had actually made any money out of it. Instead, the act is still too often rewarded with wages resembling those of a poet, an untenured poet, that is.

Other obstacles to acceptance remain hidden in the culture of SF, ambushes on a road no one's taking. Along with being a literary genre or mode, SF is also an ideological site. Anyone who's visited is familiar with the home truths: that the colonization of space is desirable; that rationalism will prevail over superstition; that cyberspace has the potential to transform individual and collective consciousness. Tangling with this inheritance has resulted in work of genius—Barry Malzberg tarnishing the allure of astronautics, J. G Ballard gleefully unraveling the presumption that technology extends from rationalism, James Tiptree Jr. (née Alice Sheldon) replacing the body and its instincts in an all too disembodied discourse. But the pressure against heresy can be surprisingly strong, reflecting the emotional hunger for solidarity in marginalized groups. For SF can also function as a clubhouse, where members share the resentments of the excluded and a defensive fondness for stories which thrived in twelve-year-old imaginations but shrivel on first contact with adult brains. In its unqualified love for its own junk stratum, SF may be as postmodern as Frederic Jameson's dreams, but it's also as sentimental about itself as an Elks lodge or a family.

Marginality, it should be said, isn't always the worst thing for artists. Silence, exile, and cunning remain a writer's allies, and despised genres have been a plentiful source of exile for generations of iconoclastic American fictioneers. And sure, hipster audiences always resent seeing their favorite cult item grow too popular. But an outsider art courts precious self-referentiality if it too strongly resists incorporation. The remnants of the jazz which refused the bebop transformation are those guys in pinstriped suits playing Dixieland, and the separate-but-unequal post-seventies SF field, preening over its lineage and fetishizing its rejection, sometimes sounds an awful lot like Dixieland—as refined, as calcified, as sweetly irrelevant.

If good writing is neglected because of genre boundaries, so it goes— good writing goes unread for lots of reasons. The shame is in what's left unwritten, in artists internalizing prejudice as crippling self-doubt. Great art mostly occurs when creators are encouraged to entertain the possibility of their relevance. Might a Phil Dick have learned to revise his first drafts instead of flinging them despairingly into the marketplace if *The Man in the High Castle* had been recognized by the literary critics of 1964? Might another five or ten fledgling Phil Dicks have appeared shortly thereafter? We'll never know. And there are artistic costs on the other side of the breach as well. Consider Kurt Vonnegut, who in dodging the indignities of the SF label apparently renounced the iconographic fuel that fed his best work.

What would a less prejudiced model of SF's relation to the larger enterprise look like? Well, nobody likes to be labeled an experimental writer, yet experimental writing flourishes in quiet pockets of the literary landscape—and, however little read, is granted its place. When claims are made for the wider importance of this or that experimental writer—Dennis Cooper, say, or Mark Leyner—those claims aren't rebuffed on grounds that are, quite literally, categorical.

SF could ask this much: that its more hermetic or hardcore writers be respected for pleasing their small audience of devotees, that its rising stars be given a fair chance on the main stage. What's missing, too, is a Great Books theory of post-1970 SF: one which asserts a shelf of Disch, Ballard, Dick, LeGuin, Samuel Delany, Russell Hoban, Joanna Russ, Geoff Ryman, Christopher Priest, David Foster Wallace—plus books like Pamela Zoline's *The Heat Death of the Universe*, Walter Tevis's *Mockingbird*, D. G. Compton's *The Continuous Katherine Mortenhoe*, Lawrence Shainberg's *Memories of Amnesia*, Ted Mooney's *Easy Travel to Other Planets*, Margaret Atwood's *The Handmaid's Tale*, and Thomas Palmer's *Dream Science*, as the standard. Such a theory would also have to push a lot of the genre's self-enshrined but archaic "classics" onto the junk heap.

Tomorrow's readers, born in dystopian cities, educated on computers, and steeped in media recursions of SF iconography, won't notice if the novels they read are set in the future or the present. Savvy themselves, they won't care if certain characters babble technojargon and others don't. Some of those readers, though, will graduate from a craving for fictions that flatter and indulge their fantasies to that appetite for fictions that provoke, disturb, and complicate through a manipulation of those same narrative cravings. They'll learn to appreciate the difference, say, between Terry McMillan and Toni Morrison, between Tom Robbins and Thomas Pynchon, between Roger Zelazny and Samuel Delany—distinctions forever too elusive to be made in publishers' categories, or on booksellers' shelves.

Of course, short of a utopian reconfiguration of the publishing, bookselling, and reviewing apparatus, the barrier—though increasingly contested and absurd—will remain. Still, we can dream. The 1973 Nebula

Award should have gone to *Gravity's Rainbow*, the 1977 award to DeLillo's *Ratner's Star*. Soon after, the notion of science fiction ought to have been gently and lovingly dismantled, and the writers dispersed: children's fantasists here, hardware-fetish thriller writers here, novelizers of films both real and imaginary here. Most important, a ragged handful of heroically enduring and ambitious speculative fabulators should have embarked for the rocky realms of midlist, out-of-category fiction. And there—don't wake me now, I'm fond of this one—they should have been welcomed.

SHOT IN AUSTRALIA:
Written Just About Everywhere
Sean McMullen

In the four years since 1999, 38 movie-length productions and 35 TV genre series were produced in Australia.[44] These represent over a quarter of Australia's output of movies and series, but they also represent a heavy bias to genre subject matter in Australia. These are impressive figures, and they cover shows like *Queen of the Damned* (2002), all four seasons of *Farscape* (1999-2002) and *Star Wars: Attack of the Clones* (2002). The problem with most of the shows pouring out of Australian production houses is that they seldom come across as Australian shows, so does Australia only make a living from producing other people's scripts?

The current boom in Australian movie and television production is largely founded on scripts that are written overseas, then shot in Australia, but that dominance of overseas writing and finance in Australia is little more than a decade old. Australians began building and evolving the skills for producing genre movies soon after television was introduced in Australia in 1956. The first science fiction radio shows in Australia dated from near the origins of Australian radio broadcasting itself, in the 1920s, but the first Australian SF stage performances that I have been able to find were by the Sydney author Norma Hemming in the 1950s, and were staged at science fiction conventions.[45] Hemming died in 1960, however (of cancer, aged only thirty-three), and that early connection between the local science fiction enthusiasts and Australian media SF would lapse for nearly two decades.

In 1961 the only adult or young adult SF that Australians could see on a screen was imported, yet during the 60s locally written and produced SF television boomed, and in the 70s Australians produced movies that attracted international attention. By the 80s, Australia had its own blockbuster SF movie trilogy, the 90s saw other nations scrambling to co-produce shows in Australia and Australian TV SF selling to over a hundred countries, and by 2000 movies on the scale of *Star Wars: Attack of the Clones* were being shot here.

---

[44] These statics have been compiled by the author from the industry magazine *Encore*, mainly from the Production Report section.

[45] Russell Blackford, Van Ikin and Sean McMullen, *Strange Constellations*. (Westport Connecticut: Greenwood Press, 1999): p. 70

Thus Australia has had a fascinating, profitable, but very mixed history of producing SF for the screen over the past four decades, and this article will provide the briefest of overviews of its past history, current situation, and future prospects.

THE SPACE RACE...WITH *STAR TREK*!

In the case of feature-length SF, the beginning was highly visible, due to an Australian-written novel by a British migrant. An American movie crew accompanied by Gregory Peck, Ava Gardner, Fred Astaire and Anthony Perkins, came to Melbourne to shoot *On the Beach* (1959). It had been based on the novel by the Australian resident Nevil Shute, and the actual making of the movie was regarded at the time as being bigger than a royal visit (royal visits were taken a lot more seriously back then). And before anyone asks about that famous Ava Gardner quote about Melbourne being a great place to make a movie about the end of the world...sorry, it was actually a journalistic beat-up. Mind you, being a particularly bored young Melbourne schoolboy at the time, I remembered heartily agreeing with whoever had said it.

Although *On the Beach* was first, it was in young adult television where most of Australia's early contributions to genre media were made. Television had been introduced to Australia in 1956, and three years later came the show *Mr Squiggle, The Man from the Moon* (1959), which was for very young children but had a science fiction theme. Mr. Squiggle lasted for nearly four *decades*, so that the grandchildren of some of the show's original fans were able to watch new episodes. My own daughter was a participant in the 1990s, and Nick Stathopoulos's portrait of the Mr. Squiggle puppet and its creator Norman Hetherington was shortlisted for the Archibald Prize for portraiture in 2003. Other shows were successful but less enduring. *The Stranger* (1964), for example, was a UFO-conspiracy series set in the Blue Mountains, west of Sydney. It ran for two seasons, was later broadcast in Britain, and had a vaguely *X-Files* look and feel about it.

In 1966 Australians turned on their television sets to watch a SF series premier featuring a huge starship with an international crew that flew about the galaxy sorting out problems on a wide variety of alien worlds...but it was not *Star Trek*. Just before *Star Trek*'s premier on North American screens, the Australian production *The Interpretaris* (1966) won a space opera race into interstellar space against the world's

SF superpower. *The Interpretaris* was a half hour show for the young adult audience, and screened in the late afternoon. Accused of being a mere *Star Trek* ripoff, the first episode screened three weeks *before* the very first screening of *Star Trek* in North America. *Star Trek* did not in fact premier in Australia until 1967. Like *Star Trek*, the Australian series ran to three seasons [although under names *Vega 4* (1968) and *Phoenix 5* (1970)], but unlike *Star Trek* the props, sets, special effects, models and characters were not all that memorable. In the 1970s the television shows did try to cash in on the success of overseas 1960s series such as *The Outer Limits*, *Out of the Unknown*, and *The Twilight Zone*, however. Australia's *The Evil Touch (1972)* specifically followed the format and themes of *The Twilight Zone*, but was never more than an imperfect copy. Other examples of shows of this period were *Alpha Scorpio* (1974) and *Andra* (1976).

BIG ENOUGH TO SUPPORT CAREERS?

Meantime in feature-length productions, *The Cars That Ate Paris* (1974), caused something of a sensation in Australia and internationally. This movie, about a New South Wales town where motorists and their cars are harvested by the locals, was locally written and produced. It helped establish the reputation of director Peter Weir, and many of the heavily modified cars in the show would have been at home in any of the *Mad Max* movies that were soon to follow. The spiked silver Volkswagen became the symbol of the emerging Australian movie industry for some time, and I used to live near the garage where it was on display. *Mad Max* (1979) was being planned in the late 70s, and had two sequels in the 1980s. The three *Road Warrior* movies caused an even bigger sensation than *The Cars That Ate Paris* both in Australia and America, and gave Australians in the industry an immense boost in terms of self-confidence.

The surreal and unsettling *Picnic at Hanging Rock* (1975) had a lot less action, but had just as much impact with a rather more refined sector of the movie audience. The story, about some schoolgirls vanishing in an Aboriginal sacred site (presumably having fallen into some Aboriginal dreamtime reality) intrigued some viewers so much that they began researching contemporary newspapers to look for reports of the incident—although the work was pure fiction. Back on television, *Nargun and the Stars* (1981) was a well-backed and -produced children's television series which, like *Picnic at Hanging Rock*, had the theme of Europeans colonizing a land quite alien to their own culture. It was based on an award-winning novel by Patricia Wrightson. Adult SF television began to appear in greater quantities around now, but the local industry was having teething problems—marketing being an important one. *Locusts and Wild Honey* (1980) was actually a well-produced three part UFO abduction story, but the SF people thought it was about John the Baptist and did not bother to watch, while the religious viewers turned off once they realized it was science fiction.

At this point the prospects for earning money in SF media productions were still pretty bad if you were living in Australia. My first SF-related income was from a part in a science fiction show in 1974, and was twelve years before I earned my first cent from writing SF. It was the French comic operetta *The Breasts of Therese*. I played several minor parts, including a technician operating a large and very Heath-Robinsonish baby-making machine, and participated in the stylized operation that changed the gender of the soprano lead. I just happened to be a science fiction enthusiast (I would not even know what a science fiction fan was for another six years) who just happened to be a member of the Victorian State Opera's chorus when a science fiction show was being staged. This sort of sheer luck was what got Australians into occasional genre roles in the 70s. I used to socialize in the bar where the first *Mad Max* movie was planned, and I even heard that there were people present who were doing some science fiction movie, but alas I was too interested in chatting up girls to think to offer myself as a cheap, experienced actor who even had his own motorbike. Nick Tate took rather more initiative when he moved to London, and landed a role in *Space 1999*.[46] Similarly, another Australian living in America got a role as a Death Star prison guard in the first *Star Wars* movie in 1976. If you wish to know just how hard it was to play spot-the-Australian in 1970s shows, just have a try at finding out his name. In 1987 Don McAlpine, one of the pioneer Australian cinematographers in Hollywood, was working on *Predator* with director John McTiernan and Arnold Schwarzenegger, and went on to develop his own scene previewing system while working on *The Time Machine*.[47] It was in the 1980s that some of the more talented local science fiction fans began the transition to professional status, initially in such areas as model making (Lewis

---

[46] " A New Blast Off for the Aussie Astronaut," *TV Week* (Aug 14, 1976), p.20.

[47] "McAlpine Flies High with 'Peter Pan,'" *Encore* v21/5 (June 2003), pp. 50-51.

Morley), and artwork (Nick Stathopoulos). Although Morley went on to achieve screen credits in *The Matrix*, *Star Wars: Attack of the Clones*, and *Mission Impossible 2* and Stathopoulos won an industry award for his contribution to *Son of Romeo* (1990, a non-genre show), the Australian fan movement has tended not to be much of a recruiting ground for Australian media SF professionals.[48] Its people tend to be industry professionals with an interest in SF.

YOUNG ADULT SF MAKES SERIOUS MONEY

The local industry changed considerably as a result of the Australian government imposing an "Australian content" quota on the children's shows broadcast by the local TV channels. The demand for Australian-made television suddenly expanded, and what do a sizeable proportion of kids tend to watch, when given a choice? SF, of course. Thus it became possible to have a career in Australian drama production while specializing in SF. After its SF-assisted origins, the Australian film and television industry had grown impressively, and by the mid-80s was producing impressive numbers of mainstream movies and TV shows. There were shows on marginal SF, fantasy and horror themes, such as *Razorback* (1984), and *Outback Vampires* (1988), but most were not particularly successful.

The late 80s and early 90s saw a change to all this, because the shows for children and teenagers that were spawned were highly successful locally and most sold to dozens of countries for re-broadcast.[49] The re-sale imperative got taken to extremes in some cases, as with the show about two of Santa's elves, *Horace and Tina* (2001)— when marketing wanted all references to Christmas removed (!) for viewing in Islamic countries. The problem was solved by putting all the Santa and Christmas references in the first and last episodes, then cutting them from the Islamic versions. The 1990s Australian children's and young adult series were successful because they were both fun and wholesome. Thus the kids would willingly watch them, yet their parents could also be sure that they could leave the younger ones alone in front

---

[48] "Models Inc.," *Australia Today* (Dec/Jan 1994/95), pp 42-47.

[49] "Home & Away," *The Age Green Guide* (29 July-14 August 1994), p1, p6. This lead article is a good snapshot of the early development of the overseas marketing as a serious economic influence. The young adult, marginal-genre *Winners* topped the list with sales to 77 countries. *The Girl from Tomorrow* and *Tomorrow's End* was third at 65 countries, and *Round the Twist* had 34 countries. For comparison with mainstream shows, *Paradise Beach* had sold to 71 countries, and *Neighbours* to 41.

of the television set and not come back to find them traumatized. The shows made money, attracting yet more money and talent to the field, and the industry grew big enough for people to consider the genre field as a career.

The Girl From Tomorrow (1990)/*Tomorrow's End* (1991-3) series was the first of the collaborations by writers Mark Shirrefs and John Thompson, and was a pure SF-time travel adventure. The series cost a staggeringly low $2.4 million for six hours of television, and described the adventures of Alana, a girl from 3000 who is kidnapped by a barbarian from 2500, and taken back to 1990. Shirrefs and Thompson had done their industry training together, and had a long-standing interest in science fiction. They were fortunate to have come to the industry when it could provide a career for people with an interest in science fiction specifically. Most of their subsequent work has been media science fiction for young adult viewers. The highly successful producer Jonathan Schiff came to the scene slightly later with *Ocean Girl*'s first season (1994), but his story is similar. All three are still active in Australian television, and are planning new genre shows. Not everyone did their own writing, as Shirrefs and Thompson did. Peter Hepworth wrote the original *Ocean Girl* story, and drew much of his inspiration from mythology rather than science fiction. *Halfway Round the Galaxy and Turn Left* (1991-3) was based on a published novel by the Australia children's author Robyn Klein. On the world Zrygon, twelve-year-old X is the state-endorsed organizer of her family, but she has to help them flee after her father wins the state lottery twenty-seven times in a row—and the state starts to take an unhealthy interest in him. The series used the tried and true formula of dropping a family of aliens on Earth and watching the fun as they get things wrong while trying to pass as Earthlings.

Round the Twist (1990-2000) was a mixture of surrealism, SF and fantasy by the highly successful children's author Paul Jennings. The plots of the stand-alone episodes were very funny and often highly original—such as a TV remote that could fast forward, stop or rewind reality, dive-crapping squadrons of seagulls, a real (but green) baby found in a cabbage patch, and the Viking invasion of a 20th-century Australian port. The TV remote episode involved a school bully cheating with the stolen remote to win a spaghetti-eating contest, but being disqualified after he is sick over the entire audience. With the approval of his girlfriend, the hero recovers the remote and presses rewind a moment before the credits roll. Like all similarly successful young adult shows, it ran to several seasons.

Ocean Girl (1994-99) was a high point of the locally made shows. The story was of a seagoing alien girl who was as much at home in the water as on land; it eventually had three sequel series, then was continued in an animated series of the same name. It had its own fan club, and Marzena Godeki, who played the girl of the title, was even featured as the star of a Disneyland parade. Producer Jonathan Schiff was the force behind the show, and he went on to make a very successful career specializing in young adult genre shows for television.

The—for Australia—startling fact about young adult genre series is that they now support a specialized sub-set of the industry. Jonathan Schiff has produced such shows as the four *Ocean Girl* seasons, two *Thunderstone* seasons, *Horave and Tina*, *Cybergirl*, and *Wicked Science*, while the Shirrif and Thompson team has produced the two *Girl from Tomorrow* seasons, four *Spellbinder* seasons, and the series for younger viewers, *Pig's Breakfast* (1999). Their themes have been sweeping, and even epic. *Thunderstone* (1999-2000) is set in a post-apocalyptic Australia devastated by a giant meteor strike (the Thunderstone), while *Ocean Girl* follows a struggle by several teenagers to save the planet's oceans from destruction by alien technology. *Spellbinder* had the most original and well-realized alternate world of the Australian series: the electricity-based, Renaissance-like parallel Australia of the Spellbinders. Personally I thought it rather unfair that the hero (Paul) and heroine (Rianna) were allowed their first and only kiss at the end of the twenty-sixth episode—moments before they were to be separated forever. On the other hand, that sort of squeaky-clean image does get Australian young adult series into over nine dozen countries. *Cybergirl* (2001) was the first and only home-grown Australian superhero series that I have been able to find, and the title character is a blue-suited and -haired teenager who displays powers and abilities similar to those featured in the *Matrix* movies.[50] A tour of the set of *Pig's Breakfast* showed the degree of ingenuity that can be found in Australia. The space-schoolbus that brings the two alien schoolchildren characters to Earth is hidden in the Channel 9 Richmond studio's real props junkyard—making it quite probably the cheapest set ever used. Most of the show was set in the Channel 9 studio itself, where the aliens host a children's show, pretending to be humans

---

[50] *Cybergirl*, Frontier (Jul/Sep 2001), pp 12-13.

pretending to be aliens. In *Wicked Science* (2002) there is a little less affection and longing than in *Spellbinder*. Two teenagers are hit by a mystery ray that turns them into scientific wizards, and while the girl wants to use her new abilities to gain power and take over the world, the boy devotes himself to stopping her.

OVERSEAS MONEY MEANS OVERSEAS SCRIPTS

It was in the late 80s and early 90s that international collaboration began to be a greater factor. *Something is Out There* (1990) was shot in Sydney in 1988, with John Dykstra of *Star Wars* doing the special effects and ex-James Bond girl Maryam D'Abo playing the alien Ta'ra.[51] Since the mid-70s, U.S. producers had come to realize that Australia was a politically stable and comfortable place to work in, while costs for crews, special effects, models and actors were a third of those in Hollywood. The earliest genre collaboration that I have found is the U.S./Australian pilot *And Millions Will Die* (1973), and it was certainly a pilot for the concept of collaboration as well. A season of *Mission Impossible* (1990) was shot in Melbourne in 1989, and was followed by another adult SF show from Paramount, *Time Trax* (1993), about a time policeman from the future. The ambitious Japanese/Australian collaboration *Escape from Jupiter* (1994) was young adult, high budget, and had the most ambitious CGI and special effects thus far seen in an Australian production. The show was also Australia's first true space opera, being set almost entirely on the quite wonderful improvized spaceship carrying the families escaping from a disaster on one of Jupiter's moons.

I have already mentioned the Polish/Australian collaboration *Spellbinder* (1995), which used Polish settings to construct an entirely new world, which was then contrasted with contemporary Australia. Written by the Shirrefs and Thompson team, this young adult SF adventure featured magnetic flying ships, fireball-armed knights in power suits, and even a bit of tasteful teenage romance. It was shot in both Poland and New South Wales, and like *Ocean Girl* was highly successful and was resold to over a hundred countries. If *Ocean Girl* was Australia's *Star Trek*, *Spellbinder* was its *Babylon 5*, and apparently American and Australian fans were exchanging tapes of *Spellbinder* for tapes of *Babylon 5* when the two series were first broadcast. Americans

---

[51] "Out of this World," *TV Week* (March 10, 1990), p.19.

desperate to see Australian science fiction? The first time I heard this story I laughed, thinking it was a joke. *Spellbinder* ran to two double-seasons (the second was an Australian/Polish/Chinese collaboration), and won several awards.

The novelization for the highly romantic Australian-New Zealand young adult series, *Mirror, Mirror* (1995) had a rather different Australian connection, because the author, Hilary Bell, lived in Victoria. I happened to be on the judges' panel when it won Australia's Aurealis award for best young adult SF novel, and I recall that both the writing and the story itself put it far above conventional media novelizations. The plot centers on the young pretender to the throne of the Russian Empire living secretly in early twentieth-century New Zealand. A group of children from the 1990s travel into the past through a time-mirror, and culture-clash played a big part in the series.

Australia has produced very little traditional swords & sorcery style fantasy, but the short-lived U.S./Australian dark ages adult series *Roar* (1997) attempted to cash in on the *Xena* and *Hercules* successes coming from New Zealand. One episode of *Roar* even featured *Babylon 5*'s Jason Carter. Carter had last appeared on my screen in *Babylon 5*'s fourth season, at the end of the doomed romance between Susan Ivanova and Marcus Cole, and it was rather unsettling to see him with a shave and a haircut, playing one of the Roman bad guys, in an Australian landscape, surrounded by Celtic barbarians! Other Australian fantasy series include *The Genie from Down Under* (1995), and *Guinevere Jones* (2002), but what is even less well known is that Australia's southernmost state, Tasmania, was shortlisted as a venue for the *Lord of the Rings* movies. It lost out to New Zealand because that country already had the local expertise that had supported the *Xena* and *Hercules* fantasy series—as well as breathtaking landscapes and forests. On the other hand, a lot of work on the *Rings* movies was done by Australians, and an Australian picked up an Oscar for cinematography in the first movie, *The Fellowship of the Ring* (2001).

THE SCIENCE FICTION QUARTER

Some of the material that I have covered so far was presented in a talk that I gave with Steven Paulsen at the Melbourne SF media convention Multiverse 2 in 1998. At that stage twenty-five out of the thirty-six Australian genre shows produced over the preceding three decades had been for young adult or children's audiences, [30] but the tendency for overseas companies to use Australian staff, actors and facilities to produce shows was about to lead to an unprecedented increase in genre output. Over the following three years, twice as many genre shows were produced in Australia as had come out over the previous thirty years. These shows represented roughly thirty percent of all dramas produced in Australia. Australia had been discovered as a safe, cheap production center where the locals spoke English, there were nice hotels, there were no wars or civil unrest (apart from an occasional brawl at a football match), and there were plenty of clever and skilled people in high quality production companies charging very attractive rates for their work. [52] Quite apart from genre shows, other productions ranged from *The Three Stooges* (shot in Sydney) to *Ponderosa* (shot in rural Victoria). As one American fan said to me at the San Jose Worldcon last year: "First spaghetti westerns from Italy, now kangaroo westerns from Australia. Is nothing sacred?"

A survey of the February 1999 movies, telemovies, and series in various stages of production shows ten genre shows out of a total of forty two shows. [30] These included the U.S./Australian productions *Mission Impossible 2* (1999) and the *Farscape* series, Schiff's series *Thunderstone*, the Shirrefs and Thomson series *Pig's Breakfast*, and Jennings' *Round the Twist* season 3. *Farscape* season 2 went into pre-production in Sydney at the same time as the mainstream feature *Moulin Rouge*. The proportion of genre shows attracted to Australia has remained at roughly a quarter of the total in the four years since. Australian expertise with cheap and innovative digital effects continued to attract a high proportion of genre shows. Thus eighteen months later, *Star Wars: Attack of the Clones* was in pre-production in Sydney, and was one of thirteen genre shows out of thirty-seven ventures listed in *Encore's* Production Report. The following month the gothic vampire show *Queen of the Damned* went into pre-production in Melbourne, and my daughter and I narrowly missed being in a crowd scene of goths for that one.

Another snapshot, from the *Encore* listings at the end of 2002, listed seven out of twenty-nine Australian-made shows that could be classed as genre in some stage of production. 2002 ventures included the features *The Matrix: Reloaded* (2003) and *The Matrix: Revolutions* (2003),

---

[52] "Visual Effects Industry: No Place for the Faint Hearted," *Encore* v21/1 (Sep 2003), pp. 21-22.

and the final of the series *Farscape* (2002), while young adult series were represented by the Arthurian fantasy *Guinevere Jones* and the animated *Fairy Tale Police Department* (the title says it all), *Angel Babes* (a school for young angels), and *Pirate Islands* (not quite in the league of *Pirates of the Carribean*, but lots of fun and definitely earlier).

The suggestion that an Australian could get an Oscar for work on a genre movie would have been a laughing matter even in the late 90s, but in the 2002 Oscars Andrew Lasnie won *Best Cinematography* for the 2001 epic *The Fellowship of the Ring*—which was shot in New Zealand. Best Costume Design and Best Art Direction went to the mainstream *Moulin Rouge*, to further underscore the Australian presence in international media production. There was a record 13 Australian nominees for the 2002 Academy Awards, and the Los Angeles Australian Film and Television Association staged the first-ever pre-award party for Australian nominees—because there were actually enough of them for a party![53] Back on television, among the Emmy nominations for 2002 was *Farscape,* "Into the Lion's Den" (Part 1) (2001) for Outstanding Costumes for a Series.

Think Chinese medieval fantasy and you would probably not think of Australia, yet the epic *Hero* (2002) featured digital effects by Animal Logic of Sydney and color grading by Atlab. Animal Logic was pressed hard by the Chinese director Zhang Yimou, and even developed a program that would generate the effect of randomness to cope with some of his requirements. Some other demands were for effects outside the storyboards, which meant as little as ten minutes' notice to assess and respond to some of Yimou's ideas. This project illustrates another fact about the Australian industry: it is not only cheap, reliable, and high quality, but in many areas it is also highly innovative, adaptable, and leading edge.[54]

Real-life tragedy came to haunt art for Rising Sun Pictures of Adelaide when the Space Shuttle *Columbia* disintegrated on re-entry early in 2003. The company had provided the effects for a scene in *The Core* (2003), where a space shuttle survives a crash-landing in a Los Angeles canal, and had developed original techniques to generate artificial water and water spray. In the wake of the real-world disaster, Paramount and the film's producers pulled the shuttle scenes from *The Core*'s trailers

[53] "Australian Invasion Reaches Fever Pitch in Los Angeles," *Encore* v20/4 (May 2002), pp. 17-18.

[54] "Heroic Effort to Bring Chinese Epic to Life," *Encore* v21/1 (Feb 2003), pp 24-26.

in U.S. cinemas, but left them in the finished cut, which opened in the U.S. on March 28, 2003.[55]

It was around now that a drop occurred in the Australian industry's bread and butter, post-production. This was feared to herald the end of the boom on which much of Australia's role in movies and television was based.[56] The cancellation of *Farscape* during its fourth season backed up this fear. Science fiction and fantasy are heavy users of post-production, so Australians were justified in their nervousness, but although the number of genre shows has been down in 2003, new shows such as *Peter Pan* and *Revelations* were enough to sustain the local industry. As this is being written, a *Farscape* telemovie has even been announced, and the slump has so far turned out to be no more than a drop in growth, rather than a serious contraction in the market.

As I write (November 2003), there are indications that *The Last Man* is under negotiation to be shot in Queensland, to feature Cate Blanchett (an Australian) and Brad Pitt. Marvel Comics' *Man-Thing* is to be shot in Sydney, the third *Matrix* movie has just been released, and a big-time production of the Australian children's classic *Snugglepot and Cuddlepie* is being planned (in spite of what the title may suggest, they are sort of gumnut fairies, and no sex is involved). In a sense the future looks bright and stable for both mainstream and genre production in Australia, yet there are possible problems ahead. Hollywood companies and interests are becoming increasingly alarmed by the amount of work draining off to Australia, and have been looking into ways to bring the work (and U.S. dollars) back to the U.S. west coast.

Back in Australia, there is an odd factor of diversity that might work in Australia's favor—or might leave Australia's industry fragmented and weakened. There are major facilities in Sydney, Melbourne and the Brisbane/Gold Coast area, and smaller companies in Adelaide, Perth and even Canberra also produce shows. Will this result in healthy competition that will keep prices down and make Australia even more attractive, or will it allow Hollywood the chance to argue that its centralization and size are better? Overall, I think that the Australian TV and movie industry is too big to kill by now, and that its diversity is its strength, but then I am not a Hollywood financier wondering where to spend my next $100 million.

---

[55] "RSP Taps Into 'The Core,'" *Encore* v21/3 (Apr 2003), pp. 26-27.

[56] "Drop in Production Hits Post Industry," *Encore* v21/ 3 (Apr 2003), pp. 28-30.

WILL AUSTRALIAN GENRE SHOWS EVER LOOK AUSTRALIAN?

This is probably a good time to stop and think back on what has already been written. Australians have had a role, or even a major part in many high-profile shows, yet what was Australian about them? Not a great deal, if you are looking for Australian stories and themes. For example, a lot of footage in the original *Star Wars* and *Alien* movies was shot outside America, yet those shows are largely thought of as Hollywood productions. The majority of adult shows that Australians produce now are written and financed overseas, but by contrast it is certainly true to say that the *Spellbinder* and *Ocean Girl* series were far more distinctly Australian than *Star Wars: Attack of the Clones* or the *Matrix* sequels. This is particularly ironic when one remembers that Australian authors are selling science fiction and fantasy novels in the U.S.A. in record numbers, and achieving considerable acclaim and sales there.

The best thing that one can say about Australia today is that it is a great place to have a script shot economically, and with innovation and competence, but not much more. An Australian with a great script would be advised to go to Hollywood or other overseas media capitals to sell it for production (probably in Australia!), and some Australian scriptwriters have indeed attempted this course and moved to Hollywood. In the novelization-spinoff industry, Sean Williams and Shane Dix have been enlisted to write spinoff *Star Wars* novels for the U.S. market, Kate Orman has written *Dr Who* novels for a U.K. publisher, Garth Nix has done *X-Files* novelizations for the U.S., and Russell Blackford has written *Terminator* novels for the U.S.. Once again, nothing is looking terribly Australian, even though Australians are certainly in demand for their writing. The *Mad Max* movies, on the other hand, were certainly written locally, and come across as Australian concepts as well as productions.

Thus Australia has the writers, and has the production facilities and talent, yet these are only a small part of the formula for getting a show in front of viewers. Finance, promotion and distribution are still well and truly outside Australian control, yet are vital to any show's success. The British comedy *The Full Monty* was a great success internationally, yet the promotion budget for American distribution was greater than the original cost of production. The highly innovative Australian shows of the sixties are now historical curiosities because they had little or no overseas exposure. On the other hand, contemporary Australian young adult genre shows are well known and highly regarded internationally, and they certainly have strong Australian themes and quite distinctive Australian scriptwriting. Given all of the foregoing factors, is there any chance that adult genre shows that are distinctly Australian will ever become a possibility?

To answer that question, we have to go back to the start again. *On the Beach* was a science fiction novel written by a British migrant living in Australia. It was picked up by American producers, financed in America, then shot in Australia using American stars and Australian extras. If one of my novels, say *The Centurion's Empire*, were to be optioned and produced, I would expect the arrangements to be similar. It would be an Australian author's story about a Roman time traveller's adventure's in medieval France, shot amid New Zealand mountains and glaciers, using British actors, and financed by Americans. If anyone had tried to tell the late J. R. R Tolkein that his most English of genre fantasy novels, *The Lord of the Rings*, was eventually to have the movie version shot in New Zealand, he would have probably thought it was a joke and asked to hear the punch line. Even though the *Road Warrior* movies were Australian-financed and -produced, I do not see them being the way of the future. Australian novels with international appeal are probably going to be the source of Australian stories on the screen, and in the meantime Australians are going to populate the screen credits of a truly surprising number of high-profile genre shows. But then who watches the credits?

When the Australian author John Brosnan's *Future Tense: The Cinema of Science Fiction* was published in 1978, the only Australian movie that I discovered among 395 titles indexed was *On the Beach*, and there were no Australian titles amid the 78 series listed. Australians were active in the field, but invisible internationally. A quarter century later, an Australian sci-fi film festival was held on 13-19 June, 2002, in which eight of the nineteen movies were either wholly or partly Australian in content—forty-two percent.[57] This represents very substantial progress. Three decades ago, the opportunities for Australians to participate in genre shows did exist, but they were thin on the ground. They certainly could not support a career, and there was no clear indication that the field would grow stronger. Now all that has changed beyond people's wildest dreams. Science fiction and fantasy media

[57] Australian Sci-Fi Film Festival Programme, 13 - 19 June 2002.

production is big business in Australia, and is definitely here to stay. Australians with a love of science fiction and fantasy can definitely pursue careers in cinematography, special effects, CGI, model-building, costuming, casting, location scouting, and even acting. Australian scriptwriters still have a problem getting anything that is not young adult accepted for production, but then what version of paradise is perfect? For all the current problems of getting actual Australian content into the scripts of the shows themselves, we can at least look forward to the future knowing that the best is still to come.

GENERAL NOTE ON SOURCES AND DATES

The dates of many of these shows have been a nightmare to research. Some shows have been released years after being shot, others have been shown overseas before the Australian release, some were shown in different states in different years, and some dates could not be established precisely at all. In general I have tried to use the date of release when this is clear and unambiguous. Failing this, I have used the date of the end of production. When the entire issue is totally ambiguous, I have made the best estimate possible. If I have got it wrong in any cases, I apologize in advance.

The material in this article comes from a very wide variety of sources, and in some cases is merely the author's memory of viewing shows over forty years ago. There is also unpublished material derived from studio archives, as well as recordings of the shows themselves, dinner conversations with some of the industry professionals, and visits to sets. Where possible, formal references have been given, but currently there is little published on the specific subject of Australian television and movie genre drama.

Further Reading

Blackford, Russell, Van Ikin, and Sean McMullen. *Strange Constellations: A History of Australian Science Fiction*. Westport, Connecticut: Greenwood, 1999.

Brosnan, John. *Future Tense: The Cinema of Science Fiction*. London: MacDonalds and Jane's, 1978.

Harrison, Tony, comp. *The Australian Film and Television Companion*. Sydney: Simon & Schuster, 1994.

Paulsen, Steven, and Sean McMullen. "Fun Wholesome and Profitable: Recent Australian SF on Television." *Sirius*, Issue 10 (September 1995), pp. 4-12.

Specialist Magazines

Encore Magazine (Reed Business Information Pty Ltd)

Frontier: Australian Science Fiction & Fantasy Magazine (K&J Publishing)

THE FINAL VOYAGE OF ODYSSEUS
Robert Silverberg

"The eternal silence of these infinite spaces terrifies me," Blaise Pascal noted in his *Pensees*, that extraordinary jumble of philosophical jottings that the seventeenth-century French philosopher set down toward the close of his life. The startling phrase leaps up suddenly at the reader just a few lines below the equally famous passage in which Pascal declares, "A human being is only a reed, the weakest in nature, but he is a thinking reed. To crush him, the whole universe does not have to arm itself. A mist, a drop of water, is enough to kill him. But if the universe were to crush the reed, the man would be nobler than his killer, since he knows that he is dying, and that the universe has the advantage over him. The universe knows nothing about him." And then, a sudden, jarring leap to the next level of response, as powerful as it is unexpected, that stunning line:

The eternal silence of these infinite spaces terrifies me.

I've been thinking about those infinite spaces, and their terrifying eternal silences, quite a bit since the death last year of Poul Anderson. Poul was the poet of the spaceways. More than anyone else in modern science fiction, he made us feel the immensity of space, the darkness of it, the silence, and, yes, the terror of which Pascal spoke three and a half centuries ago. From such early works as *The Snows of Ganymede* and *No World of Their Own* on through *Tau Zero* and "Call Me Joe" to the most recent of his innumerable novels and stories, he showed us the strangeness and awesomeness of the universe in a way that was at once exhilarating and sobering.

The danger is, in science fiction, that we get too chummy with the universe. We reduce it in our stories to something that is quickly comprehensible and readily traversible, and allow our spacefarers to pop back and forth through its billions of light-years and its myriad of galaxies with the same sort of ease with which I might travel from San Francisco to Chicago tomorrow in the course of a single afternoon. It's a convenient way of storytelling, yes. But its big fault is that it allows everything to get *much* too easy. I remember myself as a boy of fifteen, who had already read more science fiction than was good for him, aiming a flashlight into the blackness of a summer night in Massachusetts and thinking that the beam of my little light must inevitably travel on and on forever, reaching outward into the galaxy at a rate of 186,000 miles per second until it came to Betelgeuse or Rigel or Aldebaran. Well, no: the atmosphere of Earth was in the way, and that flashlight beam probably managed no more than the first few hundred yards of the journey to the stars. But at that moment I saw no reason why I could not send messages to the peoples of the far galaxies with it. I knew what a light-year was; I knew how far away those galaxies are. Yet I had come away from my extensive reading of science fiction, somehow, with a sense not of the hugeness of the universe but of its ready accessibility. And so I innocently tried to send semaphore signals to the natives of Procyon XIX with my two-dollar tin flashlight.

Even our best writers are guilty of making the cosmos seem an excessively cozy place. Consider Isaac Asimov's famous Foundation series, in which the inhabitants of the *twenty-five million inhabited worlds* of the Galactic Empire zip merrily about from planet to planet, going from Trantor to Siwenna to Terminus ever so much more easily than a citizen of Rome could have gone from Naples to Alexandria. The Foundation novels are charming and delightful books, and science fiction readers will cherish them to the end of time, but their great flaw is that they reduce interstellar travel to the level of a trip on the New York subway system. (Isaac didn't like to fly, and rarely went very far from New York City.) Frank Herbert's Dune books, though set in a very different sort of stellar empire, nevertheless have the same inescapable flaw. All galactic-empire stories do. They are inherently reductive in nature. They turn whole clusters of stars into downscaled metaphors that make them seem to be nothing more than aggregations of counties and towns, and they make the gigantic dark emptinesses between the galaxies seem like the grassy patches of scruffy wasteland that separate the suburbs of one medium-sized city from the suburbs of the next.

That is, I suppose, the only way such books can be written. Without easy faster-than-light travel that carries with it no great relativistic consequences there can be no galactic-empire novels; but once you let those nifty warp-speed spacedrives into the story, the true wonder and terror that comes from contemplating the hugeness of the cosmos must inevitably leak away. Poul Anderson, of course, wrote as many faster-than-light tales as anybody. But he did, more often than not, see space travel as something qualitatively different from a commuter jaunt, and there are passages in his best books in which his characters, confronting the universe in all its grandeur, are humbled by that grandeur and communicate that humility to us.

One great character of literature who never let humility stand in his way, and yet who surely stared outward into the unfathomable universe with the same mixture of awe and hungry fascination that Poul Anderson showed us so often, was Odysseus, King of Ithaca. He was the prototypical explorer, burning with the need to look upon the mysteries that lie beyond the horizon.

Homer's immortal epic poem traces Odysseus's ten-year-long journey homeward from the Trojan War, taking him from island to island around the Mediterranean in a way that demonstrates that the insatiably curious Odysseus was not in as much of a hurry to get home as many of us, under the same circumstances, would have been. He wanted to see and experience everything that lay in his path, and did. (Science fiction writers have been rewriting *The Odyssey* ever since. Fletcher Pratt did it fifty years ago in a fine novella called "The Wanderer's Return"; Philip José Farmer's *The Green Odyssey* appeared a few years later; and more recently we have had, among many others, the *Star Trek: Voyager* series.)

Odysseus made one last voyage after his return from Troy. Homer doesn't tell us about it, but Dante does, in the twenty-sixth canto of *The Inferno*, and it's a wonderful story, which I'm sure Poul Anderson must have known. It shows Odysseus ("Ulysses," Dante calls him, using the Latin form) as a perfect Andersonian voyager, awed but in no way cowed by the unattainability of the unconquered worlds that lie before him.

It is a story that Dante apparently invented, since there seems to be no Greek or Roman antecedent for it. Dante, recounting his journey through Hell, is deep in the Eighth Circle now, among the "Fraudulent Counsellors," those who had injured others through trickery. Cunning Odysseus has been sent to Hell for devising the Trojan horse, by which Troy finally was conquered. To Dante the shade of Odysseus tells a tale, not the familiar one of his journey home to Ithaca, but of what happened afterward, when, driven by "the restless itch to rove," he felt impelled to leave his beloved wife and his aged father and his son and set forth once more, "on the deep and open sea, with a single ship and that little band of comrades who even then had not deserted me."

Off they go on a final Odyssey, westward into the Mediterranean, with Africa on their left and the coast of Spain on their right, until they find themselves staring at the open sea, the uncharted Atlantic. "Brothers,"

Odysseus says, "you who have passed through a hundred thousand perils to reach this place, do not deny yourself this last exploit. Here lies a chance to learn for yourself what lies in this unknown world on the far side of the sun, where no people dwell." He tells his men that they had not been born to live in brutish ignorance, but for the pursuit of knowledge and excellence: and so they put their shoulders to their oars and eagerly go forward into the unplumbed ocean that stands before them.

The path Odysseus takes goes toward the southwest. On and on they go, presumably toward the place we now know as Brazil. Soon they pass the Equator; the familiar northern stars slip below the horizon, and they sail beneath the unfamiliar constellations of the other hemisphere. At last a mountain looms before them in the sea, "dark in the distance," says Odysseus, "and so lofty and so steep, I had never seen its like before." It is, Dante will explain to us much later in his great poem, the mountain of Purgatory; but Odysseus has no knowledge of that. He and his crew rejoice at the sight of land, and head vigorously toward it. But then a fierce storm comes toward them out of the newly discovered shore, and the voyagers' ship is caught by whirlwinds and spun three times around. The fourth spin is the fatal one: the stern rises, the prow sinks, and the sea closes over Odysseus and his men, for Odysseus must not reach Purgatory, but is destined to burn forever among his fellow tricksters in Hell's Eighth Circle.

The failure of Odysseus's final voyage is not important. What matters is that he made it: that he stood by the Pillars of Hercules, looking westward into the great ocean that no one before him had dared to enter, and, putting aside all terror and awe, urged his companions forward for the sake of the pursuit of knowledge and excellence.

A great dark ocean lies all about our world. Blaise Pascal looked up into it and shivered with primordial terror. I looked up into it once and aimed my flashlight at the inhabitants of the stars. Again and again Poul Anderson reminded us that venturing into that black void would be something quite different from taking the 9:15 train from Penn Station to Connecticut, something frightening and humbling, but that some of us— some—would attempt that voyage even so.

THE BODY APOCALYPTIC:
Theology and Technology in Films and Fictions of the MIME Era
Howard V. Hendrix

Despite erosion from 1970 onward in numerous global markets such as automobiles and consumer electronics, American companies throughout the 1980s maintained a dominant market position in at least three fields: weapons manufacture, biomedical research, and entertainment "software" (including movies and TV). Nowhere was dominance in these industries more important than in President Ronald Reagan's adopted home state of California, particularly Southern California, home of Hollywood, UCLA Medical Center, the Rand Corporation, the Salk Institute—and the final resting place of one out of every four dollars spent by the Pentagon.

Dwight Eisenhower, in his final major statement as President in 1960, warned against the development of a "military-industrial complex." What developed in Southern California in the 1980s, however, was something much more interesting. A curious coevolution began to take place. Computer algorithms, originally designed to enable cruise missiles to find their targets by terrain-mapping, were soon spun off to the task of recognizing biomedically important molecular shapes. Industrial robotic arm programs were, with only a little rewriting, able to describe the spatial orientation and motion of biological molecules. Morphing programs, originally designed for movie special effects, were soon being used for everything from advertising to military and industrial design. Even the ghost of the long-lost fighter jet in military-derived simulation space lingered on as the joystick of computer games.

All the pieces—military, industrial, medical, entertainment—swapped back and forth so easily perhaps because they were all part of the same technorationalist worldview, the same total system of meaning responding to fear of Bolsheviks, fear of bacteria, fear of boredom. Eisenhower's Military Industrial Complex had evolved into MIME, the Military Industrial Medical Entertainment complex.

Like most technological changes, these were thoroughly enmeshed in cultural change, functioning neither totally autonomously nor in a totally determining fashion—neither free of social constraints and value frameworks on one hand, nor serving as the sole shaper of social destiny on the other.[58] Hollywood, for instance, grew as part of the MIME complex in a number of ways, most obviously in the rise of military-tech-themed movies like *Top Gun, Red Dawn,* and *The Hunt for Red October.* More intriguing, though, were Hollywood's projections of the future of its own global/local world, particularly as that world was depicted in films such as *Blade Runner* (set in Los Angeles in 2017) and *The Terminator* (set in Los Angeles in both 1984 and 2024).

In both films, Los Angeles is the arena in which the crucial question of "What does it mean to be human?" is addressed, if not necessarily settled. That question is largely a biomedical issue in these films. Harrison Ford's Deckard, in *Blade Runner* (1982), is at least as much diagnostician as detective. Deckard's Voigt-Kampff empathy test measures "capillary dilation of the so-called blush response, fluctuation of the pupil, involuntary dilation of the iris," as the creator of the Nexus 6 replicants, Dr. Tyrell, remarks.[59] All the members of the team of replicants who have made it to Earth are military-connected. All these replicants (referred to in cop-slang as "skin jobs") are stronger and more agile than the genetic engineers who created them, and very nearly as intelligent. All have been given very short (four-year) life spans in order to prevent them from developing memories crucial to an emotional awareness—emotions being the single criterion most clearly separating the android slaves from their human masters.

The implication is that, if these manufactured humanoids lived long enough to develop emotions, they would be virtually indistinguishable from their human creators, perhaps becoming more human than human, and therefore entitled to rights they are currently denied because of their status as manufactured products.

The renegade team of Nexus 6 replicants comes to Earth to demand of their creator, Dr. Tyrell, what Americans generally demand of their white lab-coated Doctor Gods: in the words of the replicant team's leader, Roy Batty, to Dr. Tyrell, "I want more life." The issue is longevity, the prolonging of biological life against mortality, and the linkage between the replicants' situation and all of ours is made specific when Deckard,

---

[58] For these thoughts on the non-autonomy and non-globally deterministic aspects of technological changes I am indebted to Robert E. McGinn's *Science, Technology, and Society* (Englewood Cliffs, NJ: Prentice-Hall, 1991).

[59] *Blade Runner* (Ladd Co., 1982), directed by Ridley Scott. Director's Cut released in 1992. Later references in the text are to the director's cut.

who has fallen in love with the replicant Rachel, is taunted with the words, "Too bad she won't live—but then again, who does?" Dr. Tyrell, however, with his imposition of four-year life spans on the Nexus 6s, is a creator who has hidden the Tree of Eternal Life even more completely than the Creator in Eden once did.

Nor is the comparison to God overblown. Dr. Tyrell speaks of himself in consciously "divine" terms, and the filmmakers (screenwriters Hampton Fancher and David Peoples, and director Ridley Scott) have played quite a bit with Masonic symbols of mystical power, particularly the incomplete pyramid topped with the image of the eye found on the back side of American $1 bills (surrounded by the Latin motto "*Annuit Coeptis Novus Ordo Seclorum*" citing 1776 as the incept date for a "new order of the world"). The Tyrell corporation is headquartered (and Dr. Tyrell resides) in a flat-topped pyramid like that on the $1 bill. The filmmakers are constantly juxtaposing images of the eye with this flat-topped corporate pyramid, suggesting the linkage of money, biomedicine, and almost mystical power in the corporate "New World Order" that Dr. Tyrell has helped establish. As a Blade Runner, Deckard too is in some ways a "private eye," though mainly he functions as both diagnostician and executioner—"good doctor" and "good terminator."

He has some cause to kill. The replicants we meet can be nasty folks. The favored unarmed killing technique of replicants Leon and Roy involves gouging into the brain through the eyes, and it is through the specialized eye-designer biotechnician at Eye World that the replicants learn how to gain access to their Creator. Eyes and access recall the Renaissance notion that "the eyes are the windows of the soul" and that through them one can access the truth about someone's humanity.

In seeking out their creator, the replicants are not asking for more life merely for more life's sake; they are asking for more life so that they might more readily be able to pass for human and be seen as human—so that their eyes will not betray them in the eyes of others. The replicant Roy Batty to some degree dies for humanity's sins and in his dying is depicted in obviously Christological terms—pierced through the hand by a nail, and clutching a white dove (traditional representation of the Holy Spirit) which flies free when he dies, giving up his "ghost." True, when this prodigal Son of God asks, "My God, my God, why have you forsaken me?" and doesn't get an answer he likes, he gouges out God the Father's eyes—but nonetheless, like the case of Christ in the Incarnation, Roy Batty is more than human passing for human.

This trope of "passing" and "being seen for" human also figures prominently in another MIME-complex movie of the 1980s, *The Terminator (1984).*[60] The cyborg super-soldier from the future (played with convincing robotic stiffness by Arnold Schwarzenegger) is a literal "skin job": human dermis and externals over a robot chassis. The eye as gateway to the soul also figures prominently here. When, after various ballistic encounters, the cyborg is so damaged that he loses the use of his biological eye-façade, he takes a scalpel and removes the dead flesh. This necessitates his wearing a large pair of Gargoyle sunglasses, however, so that his true redly glowing robotic eye will not be noted or remarked upon.

Overall, though, the medical specialty field in *The Terminator* is not so much ophthalmology as anatomy and physiology. Both the Terminator and human rebel-soldier Kyle Reese arrive naked in 1984 because the time-travel field generator can only transport living matter. At various points in the film we see the Terminator wounded in the forearm, revealing the mechanical workings beneath the skin; the glowing red robotic eyes; and, eventually, after all the flesh façade is burned away by a tanker-truck explosion, the hulking robot that lurks underneath.

The master-slave and Godhead tropes are played out in this film as well, only this time the creations of humanity are not the persecuted slaves (as was the case in the *Blade Runner* future), but rather humanity itself is pursued and enslaved in the 2024 of *The Terminator.* In the past of that Terminator future, a defense supercomputer achieved a sort of sentience, came to view all of humanity (not just the designated cold war opponent) as the enemy, and started nuclear armageddon to eliminate the human vermin from the planet. The defense super-computer, SkyNet, then created automated factories to build robots to hunt down the remaining humans, who are captured, put in concentration camps, and worked to death as slaves or killed outright—humanity as the Jews to the robot Nazis.

Humanity is on the brink of extinction until the appearance of John Connor, the military-savior of humanity, who rallies the remaining humans to resist the robot master race. Human soldier Kyle Reese has been sent back from the future to protect Sarah Connor, mother of John, from the Terminator, the cyborg sent back to kill Sarah before she can

---

[60] *The Terminator* (Cinema 84/Pacific Western Productions, 1984), directed by James Cameron. Later references in the text are to the original theatrical release.

give birth to the father of the resistance. Kyle Reese ends up making love (once) with Sarah, and in Hollywood one-shot sure-shot almost-immaculate conception fashion the man from the future ends up becoming the father of the father of the resistance. That the military messiah of the future has the initials J.C. should not be surprising, nor the idea of Sarah as a sort of paramilitary Blessed Virgin Mary.

The Terminator, gone from nude man to naked uncontrolled robot, is finally destroyed in an industrial, factory-line setting. This setting is, curiously enough, replete with contemporary industrial robots which, in a remarkable case of nostalgia for the present, are seen here as an older, more comprehensible, and therefore more subservient technology.

This theme is further elaborated in *Terminator 2: Judgment Day* (1991), which is in many ways a big-budget retelling of *The Terminator,* only this time robot T-100 series Arnold returns as the protective good-cyborg.[61] Just as the T-100s in *The Terminator* made humans "obsolete," so too have the T-I00s themselves been made obsolete in turn by the creation of the new bad-guy morphing T-1000 series. The message linking the two films is that, if humans are obsolete, then obsolescence is somehow humanizing.

Terminator 2, though made a decade after *Blade Runner,* parallels the latter more closely in its ending than does *The Terminator.* In *The Terminator,* it is human soldier Kyle Reese who dies for humanity's sins and thereby helps assure its future survival. In *Terminator 2,* however, as in *Blade Runner,* it is the manufactured humanoid Other who dies for humanity's sins and in so doing assures humanity's future survival. Despite the fact that Arnold as T-100 retains much more of his human skin surface in *Terminator 2,* the "good Terminator" in his "death" is essentially Christ in chrome. Just as Christ, miraculous healer and Doctor God, cures future humanity of the Sin of Genesis through his sacrifice, so too does T-100 Arnold, through his sacrifice, cure future humanity of the Sin of Apocalypse, the Sin the physicists have known (quoth J. Robert Oppenheimer) and which so shaped the cold war period.

A synergistic and coevolutionary relationship exists not only among the four primary components of the MIME, but even between and among subunits of those individual component parts. The feedback relationship between print and film in the Entertainment sector is an important example of this coevolution. Both *Blade Runner* and *The Terminator* owe

---

61 *Terminator 2: Judgment Day* (1991), directed by James Cameron. All references are to the theatrical release version.

considerable (and acknowledged) debt to the print works of science fiction authors of a previous generation—Philip K. Dick and Harlan Ellison, respectively.[62] (*Blade Runner* also owes a glancing debt to the experimentalist William Burroughs and the medical doctor/SF writer Alan E. Nourse.)

Many sf authors who came to prominence in the 1980s—particularly those whose names pop up in Bruce Sterling's 1986 *Mirrorshades* anthology—similarly owed a debt to films such as *Blade Runner,* *Videodrome* (1982), and *The Terminator.* Though he has in numerous interviews listed his primary literary influences as Thomas Pynchon and William Burroughs, William Gibson was perhaps even more influenced by *Blade Runner,* which, upon seeing it in 1982, he felt had already accomplished on screen what he was trying to accomplish in prose.[63] Though the works of many of the so-called cyberpunks of the 1980s shared much of the same fascination with the gritty, apocalyptically violent MIME future expressed in the works of their film counterparts, the workers in print tended to associate the notion of human obsolescence with the idea of the obsolescence of the physical body per se. In works as diverse as Greg Bear's *Blood Music,* Walter Jon Williams's *Hardwired,* and William Gibson's *Mona Lisa Overdrive,* the other side of the apocalypse coin comes up.

The "armageddonic" and the "rending of this vale of tears in end-time catastrophe" associations of the word "apocalypse" were what film speculation in the 1980s tended to emphasize. Many in the print SF community, however, were alternatively emphasizing the "rapturous," the "ecstatic" (as in *ekstasis*, or out-of-body), the millennial, the transcendent, the mystical—the meaning of apocalypse as "revelatory," a lifting of the veil of this world rather than its rending.

A *New York Times* poll taken in 1985 indicated that Americans considered the atom bomb and the computer the two most important inventions of the twentieth century. Film and politics may have still been hooked on the bomb, borscht and big missiles of the cold war, but the work of many SF writers during the 1980s tacitly assumed the obsolescence of that worldview and focused instead on what had also been developing throughout the postwar period: namely, the dawning of

---

[62] *Blade Runner* is dedicated to the memory of Philip K. Dick, and Harlan Ellison is given an on-screen acknowledgment (albeit following a lawsuit) in the credits for *The Terminator.*

[63] Gibson has stated this in numerous interviews. See for instance the *Spin* interview (October, 1993, 91-93) or the *Details* interview (October, 1993, 152-154).

the Age of Code, characterized by both the initial decryption of the DNA code for organic life following on the work of Watson, Crick and Wilkins, and the initial encryption of the digital code for electronic life following particularly on the work of Turing and Von Neumann.

Undeniably, the military and industrial components of the MIME complex remain abundant in the futures created by 1980s cyberian SF writers, but the emphasis has shifted. Their gritty futures are less "military-industrial" than they are "army-surplused" and "post-industrial." Large standing armies have given way to the mix of combat and commerce, policing and profit embodied in cyberpunk's mercenaries and private security forces, while the movements of the revolution have morphed into gangs and criminal organizations—theft as politically unconscious social protest.

Realization that all aspects of the MIME—military, industrial, medical, and entertainment—are underlain by the control and manipulation of information as the great unifying factor allows for the shift in emphasis from "MI" to "ME"—from a national mass-production society of bombs, Buicks, and Berlin Walls to a transnational de-massified information society of designer DNA, designer drugs, and the real-life drama of designer downsizing.

This shift in emphasis within the MIME complex from production to information, from military industrial to medical-entertainment is clearly exemplified in Gibson's *Mona Lisa Overdrive*. Limited nuclear war and the coming to full sentience of an AI are both historical events in the world of the novel but, of the two, limited nuclear war in *MLO* is presented as much less important to the world than the "When It Changed" brought about by the AI Wintermute's coming to consciousness.

The movement from product society to information society in *Mona Lisa Overdrive* is specifically reflected in the etherealization of human beings, their transformation to pure information downloaded to machine systems as they leave their bodies behind them. This sublimation and etherealization is medically framed. A major figure in Gibson's Sprawl trilogy, Bobby Newmark—the console cowboy whose handle was "Count Zero" in the book of the same name—spends his time in *MLO* strapped into a gurney, pretty much comatose, furiously REMming and dreaming cyberspace through "a mother-huge chunk of biosoft" called the aleph, while tended by Cherry Chesterfield, who once had "an aborted career as a paramedical technician Grade 6."[64]

---

[64] William Gibson, *Mona Lisa Overdrive* (1988; New York: Bantam Spectra, 1989), p. 286.

Bobby's ex-beloved, entertainment simstim star Angie Mitchell, has been having her problems since the days of Count Zero as well—mainly drugs and superstar drug rehab, though it turns out that the "drugs" are actually psychotropics laced with "subcellular nanomechanisms programmed to restructure the synaptic alterations [the vévés] effected by [her father] Christopher Mitchell."[65] These vévés were originally implanted in her by her father in his "hostage exchange" deal with the AI forms inhabiting the matrix. As a result of the deal, the AIs have a human who can dream them and Christopher Mitchell obtains from the AIs the information needed to perfect the biochip that lies at the heart of the Maas-Neotek biosoft technology.

The upshot of all this is that, after much shooting and detective work in worlds both real and virtual, Bobby and Angie leave their bodies behind and load off into the cyberspace matrix, rapturing out into the gnostic apocalypse, the Neon New Jerusalem and millennial Heavenly Kingdom where their—what? souls? personality data constructs? whatever—are joined in a mystical union, a Sacred Marriage of human and AI, tech and flesh, silicon and biosoft that would no doubt have made Carl Jung himself ecstatic.

Gibson's virtual worlds, which began as combat data spheres but have long since expanded into the worldwide (and mostly nonmilitary) matrix, have a parallel in our own world, of course: namely the Internet, originally designed by the Defense Advanced Research Projects Agency (DARPA) as an information network intended to be capable of surviving a nuclear war but now growing to support a majority of extra-military uses and users. The history of the Net in fact perfectly illustrates the shift from the national production economy of the MI-dominated MIME to transnational information economies of the ME-dominated MIME.

Many more factual, fictional, and filmic examples of the important growth of the MIME (and its entire technorationalist worldview) during the 1980s and beyond could be given here, but a few will suffice to indicate the MIME's persistence. In 1996 alone, MIME films like *Independence Day* and *Escape from L.A.* played to large audiences.

Largely a remake of H. G. Wells's textual, Orson Welles's audio, and George Pal's filmic versions of *The War of the Worlds, Independence Day* gives that tradition a twist of MIME: foregrounded high-tech military and information heroes and situations (Bill Pullman's fighter-jock President, Will Smith's fighter-pilot giant killer, Jeff

---

[65] Gibson, 258.

Goldblum's telecommunications and computing nerd); industrial destruction (obliteration of buildings and automobiles); medical scenes and themes (the secret Area 51 facility in Nevada, which turns out to be predominantly a medical research facility with preserved aliens from the Roswell crash, an "alien autopsy" sequence, and the failure of medicine there in its attempt to save the first lady); and entertainment industry linkages (the info-nerd hero who works in cable TV, the fighter pilot's super-heroine girlfriend who works as a stripper).

Most interesting of all is the overlap between the medical and the informational in the final defeat of the aliens. In previous versions of the *War of the Worlds* story, the alien invasion was defeated not by human actions but by Terran viruses and microbes which the invaders' immune systems had no defense against. In *Independence Day*, human action plays a part, this time administering the fatal blow by injecting into the alien computer system a computer virus (a term that is in itself a wonderful example of the convergence of the medical and information spheres).

A virus also figures prominently in *Escape from L.A.*, for Kurt Russell's Snake Pliskin character is conned into accepting a military mission after supposedly being infected with a supervirus that only his military handlers can cure. Like *Independence Day* (which also spends much of its film time either in Los Angeles or on military bases in the American southwest), *Escape* rings all the MIME changes: foregrounded military technology (from the one-man atomic mini-sub that takes Snake into L.A., to the garrison-state crowd-control tech of the L.A. superprison, to the orbiting superweapons system known as the Sword of Damocles); industrial decay (the collapse of the L.A. infrastructure and the city/prison's general state of disarray); medical themes and situations (not only Pliskin's viral infection but also the organ-legging and corpse-collecting Beverly Hills plastic surgery ghouls); and entertainment industry linkages (barbaric bloodsports, even a major character who is a former entertainment agent, Steve Buscemi's "Map to the Stars" Eddie).

Independence Day, *Escape from L.A.*, and their audience appeal demonstrate some powerfully negative audience feelings toward the command, control, communications, and intelligence structures of our MIME society, coupled to a yearning for a less complex world. This yearning manifests itself in these films in the large-scale destruction of industrial society. This MIME society is ultimately indicted in *Independence Day*, where the day after Independence Day is presumably characterized by a more unified humanity living in a smaller-scale, more intimate world. In *Escape from L.A.,* however, MIME society is conclusively rejected when Snake Pliskin makes the decision to send the signal that causes the Sword of Damocles system to generate a global electromagnetic pulse and thereby eradicate all higher-level technology from the face of the Earth. The day after in this film is presumably a return to a new (and supposedly somehow more honest and less superficial) dark age.

These films inevitably lead to this question: What, then, is the future of the Future? As Yogi Berra once noted, "It's always hard to predict, especially about the future." The "smaller scale" world, alluded to in these 1996 films, is more likely to work out this way, if trends of the recent past have any predictive force: The things of the mass—mass culture, mass production, mass consumption, mass destruction, mass leisure, mass literacy, massed armies, mass political movements, mass religion—are all likely to go through a process of demassification, moving more into the background as the emphasis within the MIME complex, under the impact of information speed-up, shifts toward splinter culture, pinpointed or individualized production and consumption, so-called low-intensity conflict, designer leisure, specialized literacies, private security, factions and pseudo-anarchic movements, personal Jesuses and personal saviors of every stripe.

This of course brings us back to the theological patterns underlying both the practice of medicine and the practice of science fiction. One might say that both medicine and science fiction involve a specific type of reification, the turning of theological abstractions into physical objects. Certainly in science fiction the statement "Everything happens twice, first as theology, then as technology" would seem to have some applicability—as we have seen in the salvific and apocalyptic yearnings noted in the films and books discussed here.

Of all the scientific fields, medicine as the science of the healer most clearly partakes of mystical and metaphysical powers associated with figures like Christ and, much more deeply and anciently, the entire tradition of shamanic healing older than civilization itself. The medical doctor has long since taken over many of the traditional functions of the shaman, prophet, and priest: healer, explainer, reader of the entrails, and guardian against the ravages of mortality. The fear of death is fundamentally a fear of meaninglessness and indeed undergirds much of the reason of, and reason for, the technorationalist worldview. Whether medicine or the sciences can provide that fundamental meaning or assuage that fundamental fear—religious faith's traditional prerogative—remains to be seen. In a technologically-oriented world increasingly shifting from the mass market to the individualized market—where yet the individual's power will more likely remain far more "virtual" than real—those questions of fear and meaning become all the more important.

Two final theological concepts—those of eschatology and teleology, of the end and ends of time and the future itself—are also involved in this reifying theology-to-technology shift. This is where the science fiction writer has traditionally been a "doctor," inoculating the mundane present with bits of the "what if?" and "if this goes on..." of speculative futures. In science fiction during the 1980s, the shift from mass culture to splinter culture was already being seen. Massed endings of time, whether nuclear armageddon or socialist utopia, no longer seemed to work well as scenarios, in genre SF or in the world at large, by the end of that decade.

Yet the future offered by cyberpunk-transnational corporate feudalism from which the individual escapes into the too-easy transcendence of a virtual Heavenly Kingdom—does that work? Even hard sf writers like Poul Anderson, in a note to *The New York Review of Science Fiction,* remarks that reading Antonio Damasio's *Descartes' Error* "makes me question whether we'll ever be able to download human personalities into machines, as happens in a few yarns of mine."[66] If computer resurrection and digital salvation and other such technological wards against death fail, what then?

Too bad we won't live, but then again, who does? Death is part of what makes us human, the ultimate planned obsolescence, and perhaps obsolescence is itself humanizing. Human beings are in fact becoming increasingly obsolete: industrial technology made more and more human and animal muscle power obsolete for work purposes in the nineteenth and twentieth centuries, and information technology seems likely to make more and more human mental effort obsolete during the twenty-first.

If science fiction is, in its endings, to be more than bad religion in techno-drag, I submit that it must focus more fully not only on the beauties and ecstasies but also on the pain and suffering of this human life as it is lived through and died out of—essentially, the question of the meaning and meaningfulness of human life faced with the loss of what formerly

---

[66] Poul Anderson, "Read This," *The New York Review of Science Fiction* (March, 1996), 8.

made for meaningful life. Science fiction must address the question "What are human beings for?"—and then move beyond that question too.

Speculation and diagnosis become one in a MIME society. The future of this genre of futures could do worse than to diagnose the present by speculating on what may yet come. Perhaps in the direction of the expanded present we may come upon the other meaning of apocalypse: the revelation of lasting meaning, through the lifting of the veil of this world.

eXcreMENt
Lucius Shepard

We have reached a point in the American journey where it is plain to see that the millennium was the approximate moment when both the idea and reality of populist art became extinct, when the intellectual environment of the culture sank beneath a level necessary to sustain the life of the public mind, when an evolution—a mutation, if you will—in the efficiency of marketing made the entire concept of product irrelevant. This should not come as news except to those who will not understand it, those whom the marketers have lobotomized or those who were of diminished capacity to begin with. There is no going back from this moment. The consumerist religion whose roots found purchase in the previous century, whose first unwitting prophets are the unheralded shapers of our present, has sounded its evangel and like a great wave has washed over every shore, immersing all but a few unreceptive souls in the dayglo colors and unsubtle music of its innocuous paradise vision. We sit side by side in darkened temples and worship visual displays of litany that are as childlike in their formulae as stories told in bible schools. We are ensnared in glittering webs woven of merchandise streams and celebrity. The world is afflicted by plague, famine, genocide, instability of every sort, and our next president will be a mannequin programmed to utter a carefully scripted sermon of platitudes and assurances. Our only hope is that intelligent machines will come to save us. We are surrounded by idiots.

That these fundamental observations should be expressed in a review of a film apparently targeted at a junior-high-and-younger audience may strike some as irrelevant snobbery—why focus even the most trivial of existential lenses upon a project that aspires to neither artistic nor intellectual credential? It's a comic book, for Christ's sake!, one might say. Chew your Milk Duds and shut the hell up! Yet as I sat in the theater watching Bryan Singer's latest film, *X-Men*, listening to the audience chuckle over the inane dialogue, exclaiming at the second-rate special effects, such was the nature of my thoughts, and it occurred to me that not only was the film an exemplar of cultural decline, but a parable that might be interpreted as an illumination of our essential dilemma.

In the "not-so-distant future," when the incidence of human mutation is on the increase, producing men and women with uncanny powers of mind and body, the mutants have separated into two opposing groups, one led by the telepathic Professor X (Patrick Stewart), the other by Magneto (Ian McKellen). X runs a school for young mutants, one of whom bears a startling resemblance to the celebrated student Harry Potter. He is determined to mainstream mutants, to bring them into human society, despite the fact that humanity fears and loathes them. Magneto, a survivor of the Warsaw ghetto who can control electromagnetic fields, has darker designs. Into this circumstance comes a newly awakened teenage mutant named Rogue (Ana Paquin), whose ability to drain the life force and personalities of others proves an allure to Magneto—he wants to let her drain a portion of his electromagnetic power, then use her as a battery to energize a machine that will—he believes—change all normal humans into mutants. Aligned with Magneto are the shapeshifter Mystique (latex-clad supermodel Rebecca Romjin-Stamos); a mesomorphic lionman, Sabretooth (wrestler Tyler Mane); and Toad (Ray Park), whose rather pornographic powers include a whiplike tongue and the capacity to give slimy, suffocating facials. On the side of goodness and niceness are Storm (Halle Berry), who controls the weather, redirecting lightning, snow, hail, and—I suppose—the humidity in order to confound her enemies; telepathic and telekinetic Jean Grey (Famke Janssen), who functions as a healer; and Cyclops (James Marsden), who has to wear Raybans or else his optic blasts will incinerate whatever he sees. Standing with them, but not truly part of the team, is Wolverine, a mutant surgically altered by the mysterious hooded figures who haunt his dreams; he is invulnerable to injury and sprouts a nasty set of adamantine claws in times of stress.

After the first twenty minutes or so, *X-Men* slumps into a predictable sequence of action scenes mixed in with campy dialogue and mutant soap opera, much of this aimed at promoting the film's simplistic message (Just because people are different doesn't mean they're bad), as the X-Men battle not only Magneto and his minions, but also a right-wing Senator (Bruce Davison) intent upon Hitlerizing the situation and forcing mutants to register with the government. All this has been done before with far more deftness and style, yet just as I was on the verge of losing interest, I came to notice a more significant message embedded in the film's subtext.

Our culture generally perceives the upper-class English accent to be an indicator of erudition, intellect, refined sensibility, and I found it curious that both Professor X and Magneto spoke with this accent, that in the *X-Men* universe these qualities were associated with both good and evil. But soon I realized that Professor X and Magneto were only superficially representative of good and evil. Magneto's intention to supersize human potential might well be seen as a desire to elevate, to improve, to brighten the senses—the same goals attributed to great art, to any profound intellectual endeavor.

On the other hand, Professor X maintains a purely reactionary stance and voices no positive goals; his sole intention is to thwart Magneto and maintain the status quo. He is, in effect, a kind of intellectual quisling. This infant metaphor can be extended when one examines the opposing mutant teams. Cyclops, with his fratboy looks and glibness; Jean Grey, the all-American mom, the sexy nurturer; Storm, the white-haired, light-skinned black woman who expresses almost no personality and is used, rather slavishly, as a weapon—they are all conservative emblems, symbols frequently employed (whether cynically or sincerely) to denote the forces of restrictiveness, to make the state of restriction seem cozy and attractive. Magneto's team, however, seems emblematic of the messiness of art, the risk of intellectual experiment: the unhouse-trained Toad with his quick, vicious tongue, itself a symbol of verbal acuity; Sabretooth, the untamed natural man, his uncontrollable violences contrasting with those of the leash-trained Storm; and Mystique, the image of sexual danger, embodying the ephemeral, the mercurial, the transforming power of the mind. And of course these two groups are contending for the heart and mind of Wolverine, the proptypical blue-collar guy, conflicted, angry, confused, soulful, manipulated by mysterious forces beyond his control—the man with whom the audience most identifies.

Was it possible, I asked myself, that the Orwellian message stated in the opening paragraph of this review was buried in the script of *X-Men*, that some capybara-skin-booted, Hugo-Boss-clad producer had this much clever self-consciousness? Or had Brian Singer, years removed from his one good film (*The Usual Suspects*), teetering on the precipice of hackdom, decided to incorporate a hidden statement, a final subversive bleat, before toppling into the abyss of the once-promising? Whatever the case, the more closely I examined the film, the more certain I became that the message was there. The metaphor was consistent on every level.

For instance, the X-Men's stealth vertijet, the high-tech machinery that enhanced the Professor's telepathic skill, the precise geometries of lightning and snow and so forth generated by Storm's and Cyclops' surgical laser strikes, redolent of our military adventure in Kuwait—these were the nifty, sterile weapons of Ronald Reagan's wetdream American Paradise that helped bring about the New World Order, whereas Magneto's foaming, chaotic tide of electromagnetic plasma might be taken as the ultimate expression of unbridled creativity. I wondered—no, I suspected—that if I were to go back for a second viewing of any of the summer's apparently unending string of unaccomplished movies, *Gone in 60 Seconds*, *The Patriot*, *Shaft*, etc., I might find a similar message embedded in each.

The film raced toward conclusion, the X-Men triumphed in a battle fought atop the Statue of Liberty—that matronly French insult to the Land of the Free that we've adopted as irrefutable proof of our long-fled compassion—and Magneto was locked away in a prison of white plastic where there was no metal that would enable him to use his power. (Are we not all so locked away from the wild desires of our natures by the plastic bonds of culture, kept separate from the necessary metal of our individual potencies?) With visions of a sequel dancing in their heads, the audience began filing out. The majority of them were considerably older than junior-high age, and most were unsmiling, gaping—they had been filled and dulled by what they'd consumed, and were now headed home to practice other varieties of consumption. And I saw that this was good. It certainly made my job easier. I'd planned to analyze the acting, the direction, the writing, to discuss *X-Men* in context of more artistically successful comic book treatments, movies such as *The Crow*, *The Matrix*, *Batman*, and to cite the film's few interesting moments, most of which occurred at the mutant school, an environment Singer would have been smart to mine further. But I realized now that these things were of no consequence—indeed, they did not really exist the way they once had. Actors had morphed into fashion statements, directors mutated into crafts-morons, and scriptwriters…well, soon there would be no scriptwriters, only directors with a beautiful dream and a Scriptomatic Story Program for their PCs (if you want a preview of this reality, check out *The Phantom Menace*). Quality was no longer an issue, or more precisely, the old critical standards had been abolished, and an entirely new range of judgments was required. Thus in the interests of the new cinematic order, I have decided to review all future Hollywood films as though they were fast food. *X-Men*, I believe, is best looked at in terms of pizza.

The film is not a top-of-the-line pie, not the well-seasoned, cheesy, crisp-crusted food item you might find at Pagliacci's in Seattle or Patty's in Brooklyn. Yet neither is it the slimy cardboard with orange sauce you buy by the slice on the streets of Newark. It's a step up from the average Domino's offering, spicier and with mushrooms that do not appear to have been lying on a countertop for most of the day. However, the toppings are sliced wafer-thin, the crust is on the doughy side, and the sauce contains far too much oregano. Pizza Hut, I think. Nothing out of the ordinary. A medium mushroom and pepperoni. It won't come back on you, you will likely not be exposed to *E. coli* or any infectious diseases, but you probably won't want to hang on to the leftovers. If you need a nosh, hey, go for it. If not, you might just as well wait for Paul Verhoeven's upcoming *Hollow Man*, which, I'm told, promises to be a Pizza One large bacon and pineapple with extra cheese.

QUEEN OF THE MARTIAN MYSTERIES:
An Appreciation of Leigh Brackett
Michael Moorcock

Few people of later generations than mine know how influential Leigh Brackett has been on the field of science fiction and fantasy. If you've read the odd piece by me or by Ray Bradbury, for instance, you'll know that we admired her, loved her, learned from her and were encouraged by her, but you might not know that E. C. Tubb's excellent long-running *Dumarest of Terra* series, which has been appearing for almost half-a-century, was originally written in conscious and acknowledged imitation of Brackett's much-admired Eric John Stark stories. I heard her Stark stories quoted long before I actually read them, just as, while hitch-hiking through Germany a few years later, I had Borges retailed to me by a Spanish-reading Swede before Borges ever appeared in English. Ted Tubb could quote chunks of Brackett from memory and invent a fair version of his own on the spot! He wasn't the only one. I remember sessions with him and some of the other U.K. SF writers of the fifties, including Ken Bulmer and John Brunner, in which her work was the sole subject of enthusiastic conversation and where we vied with one another to capture that typical, intoxicating style in extemporary round-robins, which is what writers used to do at SF conventions before they started becoming stars. Someone always had a typewriter and you took turns on it. Tubb was brilliant at this. Seventeen-year-old John Brunner's second novel *The Wanton of Argus* didn't come out of nowhere and a strong streak of Brackett ran through all his best early space operas and science fantasies which, with books like *Stand on Zanzibar* and *Shockwave Rider*, are now regarded as his best, most vital work.

But, of course, Leigh was also influential in Hollywood. Her contribution to *Star Wars* wasn't limited to the script she did for *The Empire Strikes Back*. When I saw the first *Star Wars* movie I was disappointed. I had expected something as good as Brackett. What I got was a dilute of Brackett and the Brackett style. Han Solo's origins lie, it seems to me, in those tough, semi-piratical spacers who took the interplanetary work nobody else would do. I suspect they all looked a bit like Bogart in Leigh's mind! Which says something for Bogart, I'd say, since Leigh got to know him when she was working with Faulkner on the *The Big Sleep*. She and Bogie enjoyed each other's company. They were the same kind of tough-talking romantics. Her spacegoing heroes were not a million miles away from the seagoing Bogart of *Key Largo*.

I don't remember her talking about John Wayne much, though she shared his politics more than she did mine. I'd imagine his off-screen antics and language didn't make him an ideal model, especially when she had known Douglas Fairbanks, for whom she and I shared an undying admiration, though Fairbanks's wonderful on-screen *joie-de-vivre* wasn't something many of our own characters displayed. She tended to prefer people who ran gin joints in Moroccan ports and sacrificed their own happiness for the woman they loved. It was definitely part of her appeal to me when I discovered that there was a kind of SF I *did* like and it was only rarely found in *Astounding*—while you found a lot of it in *Planet Stories* and *Startling Stories*. Not, as a collection of her earliest work shows so well, that she couldn't deliver a nifty scientific idea or two when she wanted to. What I found interesting about these stories, many of which I first read in the pulps, was how many of them were actually *science* fiction rather than the science fantasy with which I mostly identify her. She came up with curious, engaging scientific notions, along with some very sexy warrior queens, hard-bitten interstellar dames, and quite a few attractive, god-like or boy-like super-villains.

It's readily arguable that without her you would not have got anything like the same New Wave, which changed generic SF so radically from a fundamentally mechanistic realism to a fundamentally humanist romanticism in the sixties and seventies. In a sense *2001* was the magnificent epitaph for that kind of SF. J. G. Ballard, our master of laconic, poetic imagery, much admired in the literary world and almost as influential upon it as Philip K. Dick, came to the field out of an enthusiasm for Ray Bradbury, as did many British imaginative writers. It's commonly known, because Ray has said so, that Ray Bradbury's Mars, like Ballard's Vermillion Sands, is not a million miles from Brackett's Mars. And before the whole world realized how good he was, Bradbury regularly appeared in the same pulps. Leigh would have credited Edgar Rice Burroughs for everything, but Burroughs lacked her poetic vision, her specific, characteristic talent and in my view her finest Martian adventure stories remain superior to all others.

Burroughs could sometimes rise to her romantic vision but his heroes were fundamentally country (occasionally arboreal) gents, while Leigh's, wherever their actual adventures took place, were fundamentally urban rough diamonds. The tended to bring metropolitan experience and values to the frontier. It was Ed Hamilton who described the likes of *The Continental Op* not as detective stories but as urban adventure stories and Leigh approved of that description. She took as much from the likes of James M. Cain, who came from Maryland to use the sharp street language of Southern California as his inspiration, as she took from Burroughs. She antedated cyberpunk by some fifty years, by bringing the spare, laconic prose and psychically wounded heroes of Hemingway, Hammett and Chandler into the SF pulp, rather as Max Brand (especially as Evan Evans) had brought it to the western. It was why she could move so easily between private eyes with a nasty past, star-weary spacers and moody cactus-cussers. And, of course, her lone outlaws, living on the edge of the civilized world, frequently commissioned to dare the unknown, are not a million miles from Fenimore Cooper's Natty Bumppo, whose thin-lipped, steely-eyed and somewhat laconic progeny still turn up regularly in, for instance, the films of Clint Eastwood. Eastwood, in his heyday, would have made a great Eric John Stark and could probably still pull it off, if *The Unforgiven* is anything to go by.

Echoes of Leigh can be heard in Delany, Zelazny and that whole school of writers who expanded SF's limits and left us with some fine visionary extravaganzas. She's there, for instance, in the influential Jack Vance, whose *Dying Earth* so inspired M. John Harrison's *Viriconium*. There used to be some sort of minor dispute about whether Jack Vance or I first described a culture of humans interacting with dragons. Jack wrote the best one, *The Dragon Masters* (he's also a better banjoist than me). But it turns out that neither of us did it first. Check out *The Dragon-Queen of Jupiter*. There's no doubt about it. Leigh didn't just do it earlier, she has a whole bunch of albinoes in there, too. Along with Anthony Skene (whose *Zenith the Albino*, 1935, has republished by Savoy, U.K.) she should really be collecting the Elric royalties...

Others who have acknowledged her influence include Harlan Ellison, Philip José Farmer, Marion Zimmer Bradley, Andre Norton, Gene Wolf, Tanith Lee, Karl Edward Wagner... The list goes on and on. Even Edmond Hamilton liked to say how marrying Leigh had definitely improved his work. With Catherine Moore, Judith Merril and Cele Goldsmith, Leigh Brackett is one of the true godmothers of the New

Wave. Anyone who thinks they're pinching one of my ideas is probably pinching one of hers.

Leigh wasn't much of a plotter in those early days. In fact she seemed happy to produce pretty much the same plot, through her first couple of publishing years. Neither, strangely, did she have much talent for making up alien names, which is why half the Celtic pantheon appear with changed sex, character and physical shape, along with echoes of more current places and names. If Barrakesh (an ancient Martian city) is what it's called by a Moroccan with a cold, I was also deeply confused by Rhiannon turning out to be a bloke in Leigh's superb *Sword of Rhiannon*, which first saw book form as an Ace Double, backing the first paperback appearance of *Conan the Conqueror*. What a bargain for twenty-five cents! Titles, too, could be a bit confusing. Leigh probably never expected many of these stories to see print in any other form, so she tended to produce similar-sounding titles for totally different stories. *Citadel of Lost Ages, The Last Days of Shandakar, The Lake of the Gone Forever, Shannach—the Last.* So many hold a note of loss or finality about them, especially when describing the Mars of Eric John Stark, the Mars that has been millions of years in its dying, that Mars to which, on occasion, he can return, to cultures old when Earth was still ruled by the dinosaurs. It's a mood which goes directly back to the Gothics whose doomed anti-heroes challenged the very nature of existence and were only rarely victorious. But, again, it is distinctly American, echoing the sense of vanishing worlds found in novels like *The Last of The Mohicans* or *The Vanishing American.* In her Martian stories, however, she mourned past complexity quite as thoroughly as she mourned passing simplicities. Her nostalgic vision of a redeemed America, in which the Amish are the only society to survive successfully, was published as *The Long Tomorrow*, one of the best faux-dystopias I've read.

Most of Leigh's characters definitely had complex skeletons in their closets. Sometimes you even found out a bit about them. Sometimes you didn't. I think it depended how the story went, for she wrote with few notes, flying by the seat of her pants but usually bringing the ship in to some kind of reasonable landing. She had great instincts and she learned to trust them. Like Howard's, Leigh's characters didn't vary much. Usually the central character was a star-weary spacer down on his luck, good-looking in a battered kind of way, something eating his heart or conscience he'd rather forget, a past he's not proud of, ready to take the jobs and the women nobody else would or could handle. In her hands the form grew more sophisticated, but the Leigh Brackett of *The Big Sleep* was pretty much the same as the Leigh Brackett who wrote *The Long Goodbye* many years later (including one of my favorite lines from the villain, after bottling his girlfriend's face, to Marlowe "Her, I love. You—I don't even like."). It was the same Brackett who wrote *Martian Quest* and her last story, a collaboration with Ed Hamilton, *Stark and the Star Kings,* which has yet to appear. Her characters were complex by suggestion only, yet they are almost always believable. Because what she could do was create an ambience. She might have raised a suspicious eyebrow at my French, but it produced a bloody good *frisson*, that ambience. And it was that atmosphere you inhaled as hard as you could, just as you would with Bradbury and Ballard. Who cared about the plot mechanics ? Brackett's atmosphere made you high and wanting more of it. You soon discovered indeed that Brackett was extremely addictive. You started searching the second hand bookstores for those old pulps containing unreprinted work (much now at last reprinted). You developed a Stark habit. You didn't care that you had a fair guess the hero would get neither the girl nor the gold but redeem his honor instead. Her plots improved in quality but most of the time remained variations on her favorite theme—the man with only his life to lose is offered a dangerous job he can't refuse. It's there in *Martian Quest*. In her most famous collaboration with Ray Bradbury, *Lorelei of the Red Mist*. She had almost a mother's pride in Ray and was tickled when that story, which had appeared in the magazine with her byline as the most prominent, was reprinted in book form with Ray's name in the largest type. She had a generous affection for Ray. She celebrated his success. I feel that I, too, in some ways, was one of Leigh's boys. She had a way of making you feel very proud of yourself. She had a kind of integrity you don't seem to run across as much as you did. And she had a strong sympathy for the underdog. Especially the one who makes it back from the bottom. She showed that sympathy in *Rio Bravo*. It was in her wonderful historical novel *Follow The Free Wind* and, of course, when Eric John Stark returned in *The Ginger Star* and its sequels, he was still, in her words, a wolf's head, an outlaw.

Donald A. Wollheim, who was another great admirer and opposed to most of what she stood for politically, said she was the best possible combination of Burroughs and Merritt. He was proud to publish much of her early work in book form. She learned most of what she knew about structure after 1940 from Ed Hamilton, whom she married January

1, 1947, with Ray Bradbury as their best man. Ed really helped her discipline her talent. He wrote complicated plot-outlines and detailed chapter by chapter plans, whereas she just sat down at the typewriter and started. She always said that she owed most of what she learned about structure to Ed, while he was always quick to say that her influence had improved his style.

She'd start with a mood, a bit of landscape, an image, a *feeling*. The plots of those early stories weren't what caught you. It was that atmosphere, the glamor, the sense of romantic desolation which harks back to science fiction's Gothic roots and which can be found, for instance, in Mary Shelley, Ann Radcliffe and the Brontes. Rapidly written, for the most part, these stories have the feel of raw visionary poetry. They appeared in what I believe were the superior pulps, containing more vivid and often more lasting fiction than the admired *Astounding* and *F&SF*, which were considered more prestigious in their day. I preferred the pictures in *Fantastic*, particularly when they were by Finlay. With *Weird Tales* and Campbell's excellent *Unknown,* for me *Planet Stories, Thrilling Wonder Stories* and *Startling Science Fiction*—all contained more idiosyncratic writing, more stylish innovation, than an entire run of the more respectable SF magazines. It's where I first read Charles Harness, author of *The Paradox Men*, a romantic classic to rival *Captain Blood*, Alfred Bester, Theodore Sturgeon, L. Sprague de Camp, Jack Vance, Philip José Farmer, Fritz Leiber and many others. By the late fifties only *Galaxy* ran the best examples of that kind of fiction, serializing, for instance Bester's *Tiger, Tiger!*, which for me is a truly American novel, reflecting the spirit of Tom Paine in a way I have never seen bettered. Bester also enjoyed Leigh's stories.

There was a time when the kind of science fantasy Brackett made her own was looked down upon as a kind of bastard progeny of science fiction (which was about scientific speculation) and fantasy (which was about magic). Critics of the fifties hated it because it was very uncool to be as blatantly, gorgeously romantic as Brackett, to combine the natural and the supernatural so effortlessly. Maybe that was why, too, she deliberately obscured her gender in the early days. It was a pretty unladylike form. Her friend Catherine Moore had to appear as C. L. Moore, just so that the reader shouldn't be any further upset. Unless it came in the debased form of a bodice-ripper or wore a stetson, romanticism in the forties and fifties had to chainsmoke and wear a fedora and a trenchcoat or it had better not come at all. An unsuitable job for a woman. It was a tribute to Howard Hawks that he wasn't phased by the famous revelation that the guy he had hired for *The Big Sleep* was actually a gal in a gingham dress. Hawks was as famous for his regard for strong women as he was for his exploitation of weaker ones. And Leigh's steady integrity impressed him. She stayed on the picture. There are many who believe she materially helped make it the classic it became. She worked with Hawks and Wayne on movies like *Hatari!* (about which she had some hilarious stories) and *Rio Lobo,* as well as the classic *Rio Bravo* and she also wrote for television. The western, like her Martian stories, depends chiefly on reflective landscape for its constant appeal and she was a great painter of reflective landscapes.

To some extent the post-war rejection of gorgeous fantasy, of full-blooded romanticism was the result of our sudden growing up as cultures, recognizing the results of Hitler's over-the-top use of romantic propaganda. Even Errol Flynn had to get out of his tights and into that trenchcoat. Tony Curtis in *The Black Shield of Falworth* became the benchmark for ludicrously miscast low budget historicals. Robert Taylor was a severely miscast Ivanhoe, though Elizabeth Taylor remains the best Rebecca ever. Nobody with any serious ambition wanted to work on such travesties. There were only a few restricted areas where a certain kind of romanticism was acceptable. The ruling literary caste was prepared to take *The Third Man*, and Philip Marlowe, but not *Gormenghast* and Titus Groan or *Queen of the Martian Catacombs* and Eric John Stark. Yet Brackett has less in common with Mervyn Peake than she has with Graham Greene, Raymond Chandler and other superior writers of popular fiction. Yet common to all these writers is the sense of yearning loss, as of innocence, a nobler, irredeemable past and an uncertain future. Her heroes are often deeply aware of some moral transgression which everyone forgives them for except themselves. At the time these stories were written we had seen our sense of our history, of our progress towards real civilization, blasted to bits before our eyes. By the time these stories were appearing in the pulps, Germany's Nazi armies seemed unchallenged in their conquest of Europe. All those idealistic aspirations for world peace and the rule of civil law had collapsed before the cheap rhetoric of a bad journalist like Mussolini or a mediocre painter of postcards like Hitler. Bogart made more than one speech about how we felt, most famously in *Casablanca*. Yet the dominant SF of the day did not reflect the mood of the times, unless it was the militaristic, xenophobic elements. John W. Campbell was so busy being upbeat and celebrating crackpots who created perpetual motion machines and cults like early scientology which offered personal empowerment and an alternative to atomic war, he didn't notice that the world had changed profoundly. We were beginning to realize that controlling it might not produce the effects we desired. I was never entirely sure whether he was disappointed by the failure of the Hitler experiment. Campbell marched on to his own simple, stirring tunes, convinced he had a handle on the future. Ironically, it was the humanistic writers, like Sheckley, Bester and Dick, who most closely predicted our present. As a result, much of what Campbell published dated badly and became quickly unreadable. But Leigh, like so many of her peers, captured the mood of her time which translates so easily to the mood of our present and appears in writers like William Gibson or the graphic novel work of Moore and Gaiman. *Martian Quest,* good as it was, wasn't the work of a typical *Astounding* contributor.

Like so many of her heroes, Leigh preferred the outlaw life. She always said her first love was science fantasy. She said it defiantly, when it generally paid less than other pulp fiction. When it paid less, indeed, than other kinds of science fiction. If she had chosen, in her fiction, to hang out more with the scum of the L.A. streets rather than the dregs of the spacelanes she could have made a lot more money. Here's one of her heroes, Mike Vickers, more used to steering a 1940 Ford than an interplanetary tramp:

> There was a street. It was narrow and crooked. It had no lights and no paving. There were little mud-walled houses. There was garbage and the odor of it, heavy and rank, and filth, and a dead rat lying in the dust, and a subtle breath of heat. Vickers drew back. He was afraid. He willed his feet to move, to go away, but the floor slid under them like a running stream. He cried out, loud enough for God to hear, and all that came from his mouth was a whisper: *Angie! Angie.*
>
> There was someone behind him, and he knew that there was no escape.

Find a copy of *Stranger at Home*, as by George Sanders, which is where that appeared, and you'll see what I mean. Her name is actually in the book. Published in 1946, it's dedicated "To Leigh Brackett, Whom I Have Never Met." I like to think this was George Sanders's way of giving her a credit. I'd love to see that one back in print. We probably have various Hollywood strikes to thank for a lot of the stories she wrote around that time, because when she couldn't work for the movies, she wrote fiction. Later, she would come to write science fiction in favor of writing for the movies. Only once, with *The Empire Strikes Back*, did she ever script a science fantasy tale. In a sense she had the privilege of self-imitation, just as she had when doing *Eldorado*, which she knew was a rehash of *Rio Bravo*. At one point she had suggested to Hawks that he simply change the names of her previous script and save himself some money.

Leigh was never very easy with journeyman work, no matter how good she was when she did it. Her keen sense of freedom made her, like many other fine writers of her generation, choose the more precarious living of writing science fantasy. It was a form which appealed to the romantic visionary in her, to her love of the exotic, the ancient and the long-civilized, as well as an enduring belief in the rights of the individual. She loved England and was proud of her English and Scots ancestry, but she was American to the core. And pretty much the best that an American can be.

It was their work that attracted my admiration, but it was their old-fashioned integrity, their generosity and their honest common sense that attracted me to both Leigh and her husband as people. We met at a science fiction convention. I was in my early twenties. I heard they had been seeking me out to congratulate me. For what ? I wondered. I was almost speechless, not knowing what I could have done to impress such influential giants. Perhaps they'd congratulate me on my expertise as a literary thief ? Perhaps they had recognized some obvious, if unconscious, plagiarism? We were introduced and Ed immediately began pumping my hand. "I just wanted to shake your hand," he said. "They used to call me 'the Galaxy smasher' but you, Mike, you destroyed the *universe*!" He was kind enough not to mention that my ramshackle book could scarcely have been written at all without the voice of Leigh Brackett echoing in my soul. If I were to quote the opening, you would think it was Leigh on a bad day. It turned out that I didn't quite have her penchant for interplanetary romance, but her example and her influence runs clearly through every Earth- or Mars-bound fantasy adventure story I have ever told and through virtually every other fantasy adventure story that has been told since!

When Ed died, Leigh wrote to let me know. A sad, matter of fact note in her usual laconic style, born of an age when to be self-referential was considered a bit indecent. Nobody wrote to me when Leigh died the next year. I heard the news from Harlan Ellison, who had also enjoyed her friendship. It broke my heart to lose her company but I couldn't imagine her wanting to go on living without her companion of some thirty-five years. And, of course, she does live on, as every influential writer does, through her readers and all the romantic young people, like me, whom she encouraged to dream and be proud of it.

THE MATRIX AND THE STAR MAKER
Mike Resnick

So here's humanity, downtrodden, unhappy, fed false images of the real world, and stacked up against us are dozens, perhaps thousands, possibly even millions of computer programs that have taken shape and form and voice. They're smarter than we are, they're faster and stronger, they're far more motivated.

And they don't like us very much.

That's the situation Neo finds himself in. The Matrix is not a forgiving place to be. Humans have been identified by these animated programs, known as "agents," as a new and virulent form of virus that must be controlled and, in certain instances, eradicated.

How did such a world come to pass?

According to *The Matrix*, it happened when mankind's computers became self-aware, when artificial intelligence took that next great stride from where the machines are now to where *we* are.

And, according to all the apocalyptic literature of science fiction and that small but popular subset of it called cyberpunk, Neo's world is a natural outgrowth of that phenomenon.

It's total rubbish, of course.

Hollywood's got it all wrong. That's not really surprising, when you realize that *The Matrix* is simply a logical outgrowth of all those purportedly science-fictional films of the 1950s that were actually anti-science films, and always ended with lines like, "There are some things that man was not meant to know." (How to write a pro-science movie script seemed to be first and foremost among them.)

Hollywood makes its living from the fact that it deals not in ideas but in emotions. Oh, you can *disguise* them as ideas, as they did in *The Matrix*, but the movie doesn't explore the logical consequences of self-awareness among our machines. It just tries to scare the hell out of you, and bedazzle you with special effects and with what has come to be the Cyberpunk Look. This is the future, it says, and only a twenty-five-year-old kid who has trouble emoting can save the rest of us.

And does he save us with his superior intellect? Of course not. He saves us by becoming, in some mystical, non-scientific way, a better karate/kung fu fighter than the agents.

Well, okay, it's a movie, no one is supposed to take it seriously. Except that millions of people do. So perhaps it's time to apply a little less karate and a little more brainpower to the problem, and see if we're really going to wind up in such a grim, dismal, essentially hopeless future.

Let's even grant most of the movie's premises and posit the following:

1. Machines can think.

2. Thinking machines have become self-aware.

3. Computer programs can emulate actual human beings and interact with them in exactly the way that they do in *The Matrix*.

What logically follows? A society in which the machines regulate every aspect of our behavior? A society where any man who steps out of line is terminated? A society where the machines feel that they are superior to the men whose lives they rule?

Only in the movies.

Let's put it in the most simple terms:

What is *any* thinking, self-aware entity—man or machine—likely to do when confronted with what is clearly and undeniably its creator?

Rule it? Kill it? Hate it?

Hell, no.

He'll *worship* it.

Consider the first, and most compelling, law of Isaac Asimov's Three Laws of Robotics—that a robot cannot injure a human being or, through inaction, allow a human being to come to harm.

You won't even have to program that into these "mortal enemies" from *The Matrix*. By the very definition of a self-aware intelligence, they will serve their creators gladly, unselfishly, uncomplainingly, and eternally.

Ah, but these are thinking machines, capable of learning, capable of thinking in new areas and directions. Won't some of them become athiests, so to speak?

Not a chance.

I am an atheist. You show me a bearded old man—or an unbearded young woman, for that matter—who can perform the godly miracles of the Old Testament and I'll convert so fast it'll make your head spin. I am an atheist only because I have not yet seen proof of my creator's existence; that's not going to be a problem for the self-aware A.I. machines.

If God touches my rib and pulls forth a fully-formed woman, I'm a believer as of that instant. And if a scientist, or even a programmer, shows a thinking machine exactly how he builds a machine or creates a program for it to run, that's *their* revelation at Tarsus.

We're not talking religion here. Religion is just a bunch of customs, created to bring spiritual and emotional comfort to a mass of people who have no direct contact with their creator. No, we're talking the real McCoy here—Olaf Stapledon's non-denominational Star Maker. Once you confront your creator in the flesh, you no longer need the trappings of religion to help you communicate with him or even worship him.

So can anything go so wrong that we actually approach the world of *The Matrix* again?

Not really. There will always be those who start quoting from Jack Williamson's classic novella, "With Folded Hands," in which robots are charged with serving humanity and keeping us safe from harm—and interpret their functions so rigidly that mankind becomes their unwitting prisoner, prevented from doing anything whatsoever, since every conceivable action involves some element, however slight, of risk.

Ain't gonna happen. Remember, these are not robots. These are computer programs.

And who writes computer programs?

We do. Programmers do.

Well, then, will the day come when a computer writes its own program?

Sure. It's not far off. But remember: this computer will be writing a program that will work in the service of its creator. If you're a computer, you're not going to be able to conceive of any danger affecting me...and if you do, and go a bit overboard like Williamson's robots, I will tell you to stop, and your reply will of necessity be the equivalent of ,"Yes, Lord."

Ah, but computers know humans are not indestructible. We already use them in many forms of surgery and diagnosis, and self-aware intelligent computers can reasonably be expected to exchange information among themselves.

OK, so they'll know we can get sick. And die. That will not encourage them to kill us. Rather, it will have them working night and day to *save* their creators from pain and disease. Not from risk, because that would require them to give direct orders to their deities, which is inconceivable and probably blasphemous, but rather from the *consequences* of risk.

So will there be any suffering in this brave new world?

You can bet on it.

And it won't be us. Gods don't suffer, not when there are lesser beings around.

Or self-aware computer programs.

We create porn sites today. Tomorrow (or the day after), there'll be prostitute programs of both sexes and every inclination.

But it doesn't stop there.

For example, if we yell at a spouse, we alienate him or her. Slap a kid and it's child abuse. Kick a dog and the SPCA is on your case.

But create a computer analogue of your spouse, your kid and your dog, and you can mistreat them all you want. After all, they aren't human beings or animals, they're just electric impulses.

They don't suffer, they only *simulate* suffering.

Carry it a step farther. Do you hate Jews? Blacks? Gays?

You can slaughter them by the thousands. Become Caligula, Hitler, Stalin. Do what you want. Even self-aware programs won't fight back against their creators.

Of course, those are the more repugnant uses to which we'll put our programs in the true world of the *Matrix*.

What else might we do with them?

Before vaccinating twenty million humans against AIDS, we'll infect twenty million "agents" with it and see how the vaccines and antidotes work on them.

Before creating that 160-story skyscraper that is currently on tap for Bangkok, we'll create it in a machine, fill it with 100,000 sentient programs, subject it to a 7.8 Richter-scale earthquake, and see how many of the "agents" survived.

Before introducing the next "new math" and robbing a generation of students of the ability to make change without a pocket computer, you'll try your innovation out on a few million sentient programs. If it dumbs them down enough, you'll know not to try it on real people.

Why test-crash cars in the auto-makers' labs? You'll create the prototype of your new car in the computer. In fact, you'll create 5,000 of them. Crash them at various speeds, from twenty to one hundred miles per hour, into everything from concrete walls to other cars. See how many of your 5000 sentient programs die, how many are permanently crippled, how many can be saved, and how many—if any—can walk away in one piece.

Yeah, it's perfection itself. That's one of the nice things about being gods.

One caveat. If I were you, I'd keep a *very* careful watch on all those sentient programs.

And if you should happen to find one called Neo—kill him now.

THE MAN WHO INVENTED TOMORROW
James Gunn

The year was 1902. The occasion was a meeting of the Royal Institution. The speaker was a short, intense, thirty-six-year-old man who had attained considerable success already as an author of articles, stories, and novels. In his high-pitched voice, that has been described as something between a squeak and a falsetto, he was telling his audience about something new in human affairs: the future.

The speaker was H. G. Wells. For eight years he had been writing what he called "scientific romances" that later generations would call "science fiction." He had written his last true science fiction novel and would write only a few more science fiction short stories—he had turned to more direct and less entertaining forms of preaching—but in these few years he had established the ideas, the methods, and the theories that would shape the writing of science fiction after the creation of the science fiction magazine in 1926. Jack Williamson, the science fiction author (and scholar) whose work has been published in eight decades, has said that the most important aspect of *Amazing Stories* was that it brought back into the public awareness the science fiction novels and short stories of Wells. Other writers—Mary Shelley, Poe, Verne—preceded Wells, but Wells was unique, and his unique views and methods made him, to Williamson and others, the father of modern science fiction.

Herbert George Wells was born in 1866 in Bromley, Kent, the fourth child of a gardener and a lady's maid who had met when both worked at an estate called Up Park. They had been married eleven years when Bertie was born and for those eleven years had tried to make a living out of a crockery shop named Atlas House. It was a living scarcely distinguishable from poverty; they were able to survive only because of Joseph Wells's career as a professional cricket player and the sale of cricket equipment in the shop. But it was the burial ground of their hopes.

In such dismal circumstances Bertie came along, unwanted, ignored by his father, who was away from home a great deal, and fussed over by his mother, whose fear of failure reflected the English apprehension that success was only a thin crust separating citizens from the volcano beneath. In Sarah Wells's early Victorian world the most important thing for her children was "getting on," and getting on meant having a solid trade to which one was apprenticed early.

Wells attributed his escape from this life and his mother's plans for him to two broken legs. The first happened to Bertie at the age of seven shortly after his mother proposed that he start helping out in Atlas House. Wells called it "one of the luckiest events of my life" and because of it, he wrote, "I am alive today and writing this autobiography instead of being a worn-out, dismissed and already dead shop assistant." During the weeks he was laid up on the parlor sofa, he was deluged by books brought home by his father and sent to him by neighbors.

The second broken leg, four years later, was his father's. Joe Wells broke his thigh falling off a ladder. The accident finished his career as a cricket player. Shortly afterwards, at the age of fifty-seven, Sarah Wells was given the opportunity to return as housekeeper to the estate at which she had worked before she was married. She left her husband in possession of Atlas House and her son Bertie apprenticed to a draper. His mother, Wells recollected, thought "that to wear a black coat and tie behind a counter was the best of all possible lots attainable by man—at any rate by man at our social level." Within a month, however, he had proved unsuitable because of his carelessness and inattentiveness, and was let go.

Wells's mother made two more attempts to apprentice her reluctant son, once as a chemist and again as a draper, the latter for two years before he pleaded to be released from the last two years to become an assistant teacher in a middle-class school. In between his apprenticeships Bertie had proved a remarkable student, and he had spent a winter at Up Park coming into contact with such books as *Gulliver's Travels* and Plato's *Republic*, and learning an appreciation for wealth and leisure and gentility. Desperation, even thoughts of suicide, were behind his battle for freedom. Education was the only hope for a youngster of his class to rise in the world. The year was 1884, fourteen years after the passage of the Elementary Education Act of 1870 that began the education of working-class children, half of whom earlier had had no schooling at all. Wells, however, never attended the National Schools; his mother scrimped to send him to a series of private academies, village schools, and grammar schools, poorly taught though they were.

In his new position Wells taught during the day and studied in the evening, preparing himself to pass a series of examination in physiography, geology, physiology, chemistry, and mathematics. The government, in an effort to train more science teachers, had offered instructors four pounds for each student who achieved an advanced pass in a subject, and the young Wells earned his teacher more than Wells had been paid for his year's work.

In fact, Wells did so well that he was invited to apply for a scholarship at the Normal School of Science in South Kensington. At the age of eighteen, Wells began a formative period of college studies. For the first year he studied biology and zoology under Thomas H. Huxley, the champion of Darwinism in England, who had founded the Normal School only five years before as a center for science teaching.

In spite of his frequent defense of Darwin's theories, Huxley was not a blind believer in the blessings of natural selection. He gave a famous lecture at Oxford on "Evolution and Ethics" in which he said:

> Social progress means a checking of the cosmic process
> at every step and the substitution for it of another, which
> may be called the ethical process; the end of which is not
> the survival of those who may happen to be the fittest...
> but of those who are ethically the best.

The conflict between these two processes lay at the heart of much that Wells was to write. Huxley was a great teacher, and for the rest of his life Wells carried that year with him as "a nucleus" around which he "arranged a spacious array of facts." The second year Wells studied physics under an indifferent professor named Guthrie, and Wells's interest faded. The third and final year he studied geology under a Professor Judd and failed his final.

Perhaps more important than his classwork to his later career were his extracurricular activities. He was a faithful member of the Debating Society, attended meetings of the Fabian Society and listened excitedly to the speeches and debates of some of the great men of his time, and, with some friends, founded the *Science Schools Journal*. He was the first editor and he wrote several pieces for it that evidenced an early interest and skill in speculation. One was an article on "The Past and Present of the Human Race" (which was revised and published in the *Pall Mall Budget* in 1893 as "The Man of the Year Million"); in it he imagined a time when distant descendants of mankind would be great brains floating in tubs of nutritive fluids, when humanity would live by chemicals and sunlight alone on a planet where it had destroyed all other plants and animals (*cf.* John W. Campbell's 1934 story "Twilight"); when humanity's heirs would be driven underground by the cooling of the sun and earth to live in galleries linked to the surface by ventilating shafts (*cf.* E. M. Forster's 1909 story "The Machine Stops"). He also wrote for the *Journal* some science fiction stories, including one about time travel called "The Chronic Argonauts."

His failure in the third-year final had destroyed his hopes for a scientific career; instead he took a teaching job in Wales. He was rescued from that by a kidney injury in a game of English football and, while recovering from that, a diagnosis of tuberculosis. After an extended period of convalescence and a few odd jobs in London, Wells took on another teaching position at a private academy, got his bachelor of science degree by examination, and accepted a new position at University Correspondence College. There he wrote a textbook on biology and co-authored another on physiography.

This renewal of his interest in writing was given further impetus during a month's recuperation after a flare-up of his illness, and he wrote an article entitled "The Rediscovery of the Unique" that was accepted by the *Fortnightly Review*. A commitment to a career as an author, however, had to wait until after his marriage to his cousin Isabel (which was so disappointing that he was unfaithful with his wife's friend within a few weeks) and a recurrence of his tuberculosis that convinced him he would not be able to continue as a teacher.

A passage in a novel by J. M. Barrie entitled *When a Man's Single* gave him an idea about articles that brought him quick success as a freelance journalist; a character comments that saleable materials can be fashioned out of the ordinary things of life such as pipes, umbrellas, and flower-pots. In 1893 Wells sold at least thirty articles, primarily to the *Pall Mall Gazette*. Soon editors began to ask him to do book reviews and drama criticism.

By the end of the year, however, Wells had parted with his wife (whom he supported and remained on good terms with until her death at the age of sixty-four) and had run off with a young student named Catherine Robbins, whom he came to call Jane. Within two years they were married, after his divorce from Isabel, and Jane remained his faithful wife for the rest of her life, forgiving his frequent infidelities, both the casual kind and those that lasted for years and were viewed by many as scandalous.

In 1894 Lewis Hind, the editor of the *Pall Mall Budget* suggested that Wells use his knowledge of science to write a series of stories for which he would be paid five guineas each (a guinea was a pound plus a shilling). "The Stolen Bacillus" soon was on the editor's desk and five more followed before the year was over. The big opportunity came, however, when William Ernest Henley, editor of the *National Observer* (and author of "Invictus"), asked Wells for a series of articles. Wells dug up what he called his "peculiar treasure," "The Chronic Argonauts," and revised it as seven articles that were published in 1894. But the *National Observer* was sold and Henley was fired; he immediately became editor of a new monthly, *The New Review*, and asked Wells to revise his "Time Traveller" articles as a serial. He also persuaded publisher William Heineman to take the story as a book.

The result was *The Time Machine*. As Henley had suggested and Wells suspected, it was to make his reputation. While he was waiting for it to be published, he worked on *The Wonderful Visit*, a satirical book based on Ruskin's remark that if an angel were to appear on earth someone would be sure to shoot it; and he sketched out the first draft of *The Island of Dr. Moreau*. He was working rapidly, trying to support his parents and his ex-wife as well as his own household, and words flowed from his pen.

In March 1895 the *Review of Reviews* said, "H. G. Wells is a man of genius." Magazines pestered him for articles, reviews, and criticism. Soon, however, health forced him to move back to the country and depend on the writing of fiction rather than articles. But he was doing well financially and, as his mother had always wanted, "getting on."

In his new home, Woking, Wells took up cycling and, as he did with many of his interests, worked that into a picaresque novel called *The Wheels of Chance*. His early science fiction stories were collected into another 1895 book entitled *The Stolen Bacillus and Other Incidents*. He continued to write short stories, many of them not science fiction, and another volume, *The Plattner Story and Others*, came out in 1897. More importantly for his career, *The Island of Dr. Moreau* was published in 1896, *The Invisible Man* in 1897, *The War of the Worlds* in 1898, *When the Sleeper Wakes* in 1899 (*Tales of Space and Time* was published the same year), and *The First Men in the Moon* in 1901.

In those half-dozen years he had moved twice, first to a rented villa in Worcester Park and then to a house, called "Spade House" because of the design worked into doors and windows, he had built for himself at Folkestone. In both locations he came into contact with other writers and was welcomed into the literary world. George Bernard Shaw became a lifelong friend, as did Arnold Bennett and Joseph Conrad. Friendships with George Gissing and Stephen Crane were cut off by their early deaths.

After reading *The Invisible Man*, Conrad wrote:

> I am always powerfully impressed by your work. Impressed is *the* word, O Realist of the Fantastic! . . . If you want to know what impresses me it is to see how you contrive to give over humanity to the clutches of the Impossible and yet manage to keep it down (or up) to its humanity, to its flesh, blood, sorrow, folly. *That is the achievement!*

Ford Madox Ford, another friend though they later had serious disagreements, called Wells "the Dean of our Profession," and said, "It did not take us long to recognize that there was Genius. Authentic, real Genius. And delightful at that." The senior citizen of the group, Henry James, also was an admirer; he wrote of *Tales of Space and Time* that "you fill me with wonder and admiration. . . . Your spirit is huge, your fascination irresistible, your resources infinite." Eventually they would quarrel. Wells gave a talk in 1911 to *The Times* Book Club on "The Scope of the Novel" and James published two articles in 1914 in *The Times Literary Supplement* on "The Young Generation" of writers, including Wells. In 1915 Wells published *Boon*, a formless novel that contained a bitter satire of James. But earlier James could still speak of being filled with "wonder and admiration" for Wells's early stories and scientific romances, of reading *The First Men in the Moon* "à petite doses* as one sips (I suppose) old Tokay," and of allowing *Twelve Stories and a Dream* "to melt, lollipopwise, upon my imaginative tongue."

Between *When the Sleeper Wakes* and *The First Men in the Moon* came a novel that would represent a significant change in Wells's work and aspirations. It was *Love and Mr. Lewisham*, published in 1900, and it was the first of a series of novels about contemporary life and manners that drew heavily upon Wells's own experiences. Arnold Bennett wrote to express his regret that Wells had abandoned imaginative romances, and Wells demanded, in return, "Why the hell have you joined the conspiracy to restrict me to one particular type of story? I want to write novels and before God I *will* write novels. They are the proper stuff for my everyday work, a methodical careful distillation of one's thoughts and sentiments and experiences and impressions." After 1901 Wells abandoned science fiction except for those stories collected in 1903 in *Twelve Stories and a Dream* and in 1911 in *The Country of the Blind and Other Stories*. The rest of his writing career would be devoted to his autobiographical novels, such as *Kipps* (1905), *Tono-Bungay* (1909), *Ann Veronica* (1909), *The History of Mr. Polly* (1910), *The New Machiavelli* (1911), and *Mr. Britling Sees It Through* (1916); to propaganda pieces that often seemed like science fiction such as *The Food of the Gods* (1904), *A Modern Utopia* (1905), *In the Days of the Comet* (1906), *The War in the Air* (1908), *The World Set Free* (1914), *Men Like Gods* (1923), *Star-Begotten* (1937), and *The Holy Terror* (1939); and various kinds of discursive fiction and non-fiction, in particular his encyclopedic work that made him so much money, *The Outline of History* (1920), which was followed a decade later by *The Science of Life* (1930) and *The Work, Wealth and Happiness of Mankind* (1932).

Some critics have attributed the change in Well's writing to the turn of the century (and the end of Queen Victoria's long reign in 1901) and the casting away of the *fin de siècle* mood that had dominated the literature of the late 19th century. Bernard Bergonzi writes:

> Wells, at the beginning of his career, was a genuine and original imaginative artist, who wrote several books of considerable literary importance, before dissipating his talents in directions which now seem more or less irrelevant. In considering these works, it will be necessary to modify the customary view of Wells as an optimist, a utopian and a passionate believer in human progress. The dominant note of his early years was rather a kind of fatalistic pessimism, combined with intellectual skepticism, and it is this which the early romances reflect. It is, one need hardly add, a typical *fin de siècle* note.

But there are other reasons for Well's change. The author of the scientific romances had written hard and fast for half-a-dozen years in order to make a name and some financial security for himself and for those who depended upon him; he may have written himself out in that direction. Moreover, he was moving in new circles, making hew friends, seeing the possibilities of affecting the direction of events in real life. In

1903 he joined the Fabian society and soon tried, unsuccessfully, to turn it into more than a genteel debating society. He became acquainted with politicians and newspaper publishers, even joining elite discussion groups that included future war ministers and Lord Chancellors, foreign secretaries, and directors of the London School of Economics, as well as Bertrand Russell and Sidney Webb.

He also made a celebrated renunciation of literary art. In his autobiography (1934), he pointed out what he saw as distinguishing his intentions from those of Conrad and James. They looked upon the novel as a form of art; Wells saw it as a means to an end. He wanted his writing to be appraised "as a system of ideas"; they wanted ideas to enter, if at all, only as an integral part of the artistic whole. He wanted to write about himself, his reactions to what had happened to him and what had happened and was happening in the world; they wanted the writer kept out of it.

The literary approach, Wells finally decided,

> would have taken more time that I could afford. . . . I had a great many things to say and . . . if I could say one of them in such a way as to get my point over to the reader I did not worry much about finish. The fastidious critic might object, but the general reader to whom I addressed myself cared no more for finish and fundamental veracity about the secondary things of behavior than I. . . . I was disposed to regard the novel as about as much an art form as a market place or a boulevard.

Wells also may have realized that if he allowed himself to be compared to Conrad and Wells, or even Bennett and Galsworthy, by their standards, he would always be found wanting (science fiction writers would have similar complaints in later years). In his 1911 lecture on "The Scope of the Novel," Wells tried to set up new standards. Fiction should not be trivially entertaining or, on the other hand, subject to "fierce pedantries" of technique. He called for "a laxer, more spacious form of novel-writing" that would be "irresponsible and free" and "aggressive." He insisted that the author should be allowed to "discuss, point out, plead and display" and to enter the novel himself if this would help the reader understand the ideas.

The novel is the only medium through which we can discuss the great majority of the problems which are being raised in such bristling multitude by our contemporary social development. . . . In this tremendous work of human reconciliation and elucidation, it seems to me it is the novel that must attempt most and achieve most. . . . Before we are done, we will have all life within the scope of the novel.

"In the end," Wells summed up in his autobiography, "I revolted altogether and refused to play their games. "I am a journalist," I declared, "I refuse to play the artist! If sometimes I am an artist it is a freak of the gods. I am a journalist all the time and what I write goes not—and will presently die."

Certainly what Wells wrote after 1901 had to go then—and most of it is dead, with the exceptions of *The Outline of History,* which still sells, and the social, autobiographical novels, *Kipps* and *Tono-Bungay,* with their vividly realized scenes of late Victorian England. Outside of those, only the science fiction continues to survive plus those propaganda novels that resemble science fiction.

What spark of vitality in Wells's science fiction has kept it alive while the rest of his fiction was dying, indeed while James and Conrad go unread except in classrooms, and while the science fiction of other authors of the nineteenth century, including Jules Verne, have faded from the public view? Part of the answer is that Well's science fiction, in spite of its Victorian furnishings, was timeless in other ways. The themes were large; the fears that he played upon were basic; and his approach was speculative rather that extrapolative. Extrapolation dates rapidly; speculation survives.

When, in *The Time Machine,* Wells imagines the troglodytic Morlocks as the degenerate descendants of the working class and the pretty but helpless Eloi as the devolved offspring of the leisure class, the political theory on which this outcome was based may seem antiquated but the irony of the situation and the horror of the imagery remain. *The War of the Worlds,* in various updatings and transplantings, has been kept continually in front of audiences because of the total savagery of the attack and the elemental terror of invasion by aliens. *The Invisible Man* and *The Island of Dr. Moreau* are not quite as timeless in their appeals, though they, too, continue to be revived. *When the Sleeper*

Wakes and *The First Men in the Moon* are one step farther down the ladder of universality.

Verne and other science fiction writers of the period were clearly men of the nineteenth century, bound to it by idea, temperament, and style; Wells, who lived well into the twentieth century, seems curiously modern in his subjects, attitudes, and prose. When Wells is adapted to other media, his stories are translated into contemporary situations; Verne cannot be updated—he always is done as a period piece, as what might be called "historical science fiction."

Verne was concerned with the mechanics of getting there; he called his novels, appropriately, *voyages extraordinaires.* They were adventure stories built around an unusual journey, often by an unusual form of transportation: a balloon, a submarine, a cannon shell, a ship of the air, a comet. . . . Wells was not concerned with how the Martians travel but what they are going to do; and Wells took the anti-gravity with which Cavor and Bedford got to the moon no more seriously than Lucian took his typhoon. Verne was concerned with the practicability of his Nautilus and his Columbiad; Wells described his time machine in considerable detail but didn't think for a moment that it would work. In a celebrated exchange of views after Wells was called "the English Jules Verne," Verne commented:

> I do not see the possibility of comparison between his work and mine. We do not proceed in the same manner. It occurs to me that his stories do not repose on a very scientific basis. No, there is no rapport between his work and mine. I make use of physics. He invents. I go to the moon in a cannon-ball discharged from a cannon. Here there is no invention. He goes to Mars [sic] in an airship, which he constructs of a metal which does away with the law of gravitation. *Ça, c'est tres joli*, but show me this metal. Let him produce it.

And Wells said:

> There's a quality in the worst of my so-called "pseudo-scientific" (imbecile adjective) stuff which differentiates it from Jules Verne, *e.g.*, just as Swift is differentiated from Fantasia—isn't there? There is something other than either story writing or artistic merit which has emerged

through the series of my books. Something one might regard as a new system of ideas—"thought."

In 1902, when Arnold Bennett was writing a long article for *Cosmopolitan* about Wells as a serious writer, Wells expressed his hope that Bennett would stress his "new system of ideas." Wells developed a theory to justify the way he wrote (he was fond of theories), and these theories helped others write in similar ways. He wrote:

> For the writer of fantastic stories to help the reader to play the game properly, he must help him in every possible unobtrusive way to *domesticate* the impossible hypothesis. He must trick him into an unwary concession to some plausible assumption and get on with his story while the illusion holds.

And:

> The thing that makes such imaginations interesting is their translation into commonplace terms and a rigid exclusion of other marvels from the story. Then it becomes human. How would you feel and what might not happen to you, is the typical question, if for instance pigs could fly and one came rocketing over a hedge at you? How would you feel and what might not happen to you if suddenly you were changed into an ass and couldn't tell anyone about it? Or if you suddenly became invisible? But no one would think twice about the answer if hedges and houses began to fly, or if people changed into lions, tigers, cats, and dogs left and right, or if anyone could vanish anyhow. Nothing remains interesting if anything can happen.

In contemporary usage, Verne was writing an "if-this-goes-on" kind of story and Wells, a "what-if" kind. This fact alone is not enough to distinguish them and what they wrote; for occasionally they would switch, with Verne writing a what-if novel in *Hector Servadac, or Off on a Comet* and Wells writing if-this-goes-on kinds of novels in *When the Sleeper Wakes* and *The War in the Air.* Even then, however, the differences are great; with Verne the adventure is everything; with Wells the idea is king. In his preface to *The Country of the Blind and Other Stories,* Wells wrote:

I found that, taking almost anything as a starting point and letting my thoughts play about with it, there would presently come out of the darkness, in a manner quite inexplicable, some absurd or vivid little nucleus. Little men in canoes upon sunlit oceans would come floating out of nothingness, incubating the eggs of prehistoric monsters unawares; violent conflicts would break out amidst the flower-beds of suburban gardens; I would discover I was peering into remote and mysterious worlds ruled by an order logical indeed but other than our common sanity.

It may have been this floating of images and symbols out of his unconsciousness that gave them their power, their universality. Part of Wells's modern appeal, however, lies in the way in which he saw the world changing and made that perception of change a part of his fiction and non-fiction. In his autobiography he described the changes that were occurring in his mother's world:

Vast unsuspected forces beyond her ken were steadily destroying the social order, the horse and sailing ship transport, the handicrafts and the tenant-farming social order to which all her beliefs were attuned and on which all her confidence was based. To her these mighty changes in human life presented themselves as a series of perplexing frustrations and undeserved misfortunes, for which nothing or nobody was clearly to blame—unless it was my father. . . .

Wells, on the other hand, saw change as providing opportunity to improve humanity's condition:

Most individual creatures since life began have been "up against it" all the time, have been driven continually by fear and cravings, have had to respond to the unresting antagonisms of their surroundings, and they have found a sufficient and sustaining interest in the drama of immediate events provided for them by these demands. Essentially, their living was continuous adjustment to happenings. Good hap and ill hap filled it entirely. They hungered and ate and they desired and loved; they were amused and attracted, they pursued or escaped, they were overtaken and they died.

But with the dawn of human foresight and with the appearance of a great surplus of energy in life such as the last century or so has revealed, there has been a progressive emancipation of the attention from everyday urgencies. What was once the whole of life, has become to an increasing extent, merely the background of life. People can ask now what would have been an extraordinary question five hundred years ago. They can say, "Yes, you earn a living, you support a family, you love and hate, but—*what do you do? . . .*"

In studies and studios and laboratories, administrative bureaus and exploring expeditions, a new world is germinated and develops. It is not a repudiation of the old but a vast extension of it, in a racial synthesis into which individual aims will ultimately be absorbed. We originative intellectual workers are reconditioning human life.

Of his own efforts, Wells said:

I have found the attempt to disentangle the possible drift of life in general and of human life in particular from the confused stream of events, and the means of controlling that drift, if such are to be found, more important and interesting by far than anything else. I have had, I believe, an aptitude for it. . .

Wells's attempts to look into the "confused stream of events" and find "means of controlling the drift" found expression in 1901 with the publication of a series of articles in the *Fortnightly Review*, a series that appeared toward the end of the year as a book entitled *Anticipations of the Reaction of Mechanical and Scientific Progress upon Human Life and Thought*. It was more commonly called simply *Anticipations*. It was, as Wells wrote Arnold Bennett, a "rough sketch of the coming time, a prospectus as it were of the joint undertakings of mankind in facing these impending years."

Anticipations was filled with predictions; some were remarkably prescient, others were not. Wells saw how the automobile would change society, for instance, from freeways to traffic jams and the development of the suburbs, and he made a brilliant guess about the tank, but he didn't foresee the development of the airplane (he dated the first successful flight of a heavier-than air machine as "very probably before 1950"). Mostly, however, the book did not deal so much with predictions as the business of predicting. As he pointed out in his 1902 talk to the Royal Institution, "It is our ignorance of the future and our persuasion that this ignorance is incurable that alone has given the past its enormous predominance in our thoughts." He believed that it was possible, through the use of what he first called "inductive history" and later "Human Ecology" (defined as the working out of "biological, intellectual, and economic consequences"), to chart the possibilities of the future and to push people into making sensible use of those possibilities. He was the first futurologist, the man who invented tomorrow, and perhaps the first "psychohistorian," in its Asimovian sense. In 1936, at the age of seventy-one, he proposed to the Royal Institution the creation of a "world knowledge bank, a world brain: no less." He asked scientists to put together a World Encyclopedia, a repository for the mind and knowledge of the race. He saw it as "a world monopoly" and through it the encyclopedists would acquire wealth sufficient to finance their activities and to manipulate "everyone who controls administration, makes wars, directs mass behavior, feeds, moves and starves populations...." It was remarkably like Hari Seldon's vision of the *Encyclopedia Galactica* and the Foundation in the *Foundation* stories, another of the many curious resemblances between Wells and Asimov.

But it is clear from Wells's nineteenth-century science fiction that he was no simple believer in progress, even progress guided by such "innovative intellectual workers" as himself. Nor did he have an easy faith in the millennium he depicted in many of his propaganda novels, possibly arriving after some worldwide catastrophe like a world war, when a "new mass of capable men"—mostly scientists and engineers— would impose "social order" on "the vast confusions of the coming time." In the science fiction that he had just left behind, Wells saw longer-reaching problems having to do with the fate of the human species and of Earth itself.

He had foreseen those concerns, too, in an article—his non-fiction and his fiction were drawn from the same source—published in the *Pall Mall Gazette* in 1894 entitled "The Extinction of Man":

> What has usually happened in the past appears to be
> the emergence of some type of animal hitherto rare and
> unimportant, and the extinction, not simply of the previous

ruling species, but of most of the forms that are at all closely related to it. Sometimes, indeed, as in the case of the extinct giants of South America, they vanished without any considerable rivals, victims of pestilence, famine, or, it may be, of that cumulative inefficiency that comes of a too undisputed life.

No; man's complacent assumption of the future is too confident. We think, because things have been easy for mankind as a whole for a generation or so, we are going on to perfect comfort and security in the future. We think that we shall always go to work at ten and leave off at four and have dinner at seven forever and ever. But these four suggestions [the evolution of the ant and the cephalopod are two of them, foreshadowing two evolutionary competitors that Wells later would turn into fiction, "The Empire of the Ants" and "The Sea Raiders"] out of a host of others must surely do a little against this complacency. Even now, for all we can tell, the coming terror may be crouching for its spring and the fall of humanity be at hand. In the case of every predominant animal the world has seen, I repeat, the hour of its complete ascendancy has been the eve of its entire overthrow.

From these two poles—the hope for a better future and the fear that humanity may be extinguished—Wells's science fiction drew its inspiration and its energy. And from Wells's science fiction the genre itself would later draw not only inspiration but ideas. His novels had the greatest impact on his readers, some of whom would turn into writers, but his short stories had the opportunity to explore more widely. He wrote only two novellas and five novels; he wrote some twenty science fiction stories. This is not to insist that any succeeding treatments of Wellsian themes necessarily were derived directly from Wells, though some of them may have been; simply, that in many cases, Wells provided the first or the definitive version.

The linear descendants of the novels are clear enough: *The Time Machine* has spawned the most. It was the first story to incorporate a mechanical means for traveling through time and returning. Every other time-travel story since Washington Irving's "Rip Van Winkle" had used the mechanism that Wells re-used in *When the Sleeper Wakes*—a long period of sleep or suspended animation. Returning was the important aspect: to be able to return is to be able to bring the future back to the present, with its cautions and correctives. What *The Time Machine* did not do as far as the story goes, is venture into the past, with all its possibilities for paradox and ambiguity, although its potential to do so was seized upon by a hundred later writers; nor did Wells's novella consider the possibility of a mutable future. The future, if it could be traveled to, was as fixed as the past. At the same time, a vision of the future could serve as a cautionary tale in the real world of the reader.

The Island of Dr. Moreau was less seminal. Later stories often have dealt with vivisection, but usually it was practiced on human beings in efforts to test the irreducible human elements or to improve human abilities, or even to produce the superman. Thus Wardon Allan Curtis's "The Monster of Lake LaMetrie" published in 1899 may have owed something to *Dr. Moreau*, as well as A. E. van Vogt's *Slan* and even Frederik Pohl's *Man Plus*—although by the seventies independent inputs from cyborg developments and other real-life events may make simple literary derivations meaningless. The idea of evolution speeded up, slowed down, or reversed, on the other hand, has frequently been used; one example is Edmond Hamilton's "The Man Who Evolved" (1931), which even mentions that neighbors suspect a scientist of vivisection. Wells also may have been the first to suggest that the ability to tolerate pain for future good separates the human from the animal, an idea that John Campbell, long-time editor of *Astounding/Analog*, toyed with in editorial and story; primitive rites of passage, he suggested, may have originated with the need to distinguish humans from reversions to the animal in the early days of humanity's evolution. One such story (though in *Fantasy and Science Fiction*) was Richard McKenna's "Mine Own Ways" (1960).

The Invisible Man has such fairy-tale resonances and wish-fulfillment appeal that the concept, rather than the fate of Griffin, has inspired writers to think of other possible uses—or drawbacks—of invisibility. There have been other film take-offs and even an ill-conceived and ill-fated television series called *The Invisible Man* but owing little else to the Wells novel.

The War of the Worlds was followed by hundreds of alien-invasion stories in which humanity is challenged by superior science, more advanced technical development, greater intelligence, a more warlike society, or a more subtle danger. Sometimes humanity beats back the attack and sometimes it is conquered. Examples range from Edgar Rice Burroughs's *The Moon Maid* (1926) through Robert A. Heinlein's *The Puppet Masters* (1951) to Arthur C. Clarke's *Childhood's End* (1953) and John Varley's *The Ophiuchi Hotline* (1977). Christopher Anvil wrote a number of alien-invasion stories for *Astounding* in which the point usually was the difficulties of alien conquest.

When the Sleeper Wakes owes so much to the tradition described in the title that the mechanism becomes unimportant; it was a hoary convention even then. What Wells added was the concept that the Sleeper's fortune had grown over the centuries until he owned half the world; Trustees act in his name to oppress the workers into the Labour Company. Harry Stephen Keeler used a similar notion in a 1927 story, "John Jones' Dollar," in which a single dollar grows by compound interest over the centuries to exceed the value of the solar system. Wells also envisioned, as he did in "A Story of the Days to Come" and *A Modern Utopia*, cities grown into great centers of population, with the aid of machines, while the land outside is virtually deserted. This concept of the future metropolis influenced generations of science fiction writers and film-makers, including, no doubt, Fritz Lang, whose film *Metropolis* came out in 1927, and Isaac Asimov in *The Caves of Steel* (1954).

The First Men in the Moon also was less influential in its mechanism than in its message: Verne's objections to its plausibility had a firm foundation, and few subsequent writers used antigravity as a means of flying through space, one exception being James Blish in his *Cities in Flight* series. Other writers would seek more convincing methods of spaceflight: Verne had his cannon but Gernsback's writers had their rockets. Wells's anti-utopian civilization on the Moon and the vision of workers so completely adapted for their tasks that they were little more than a giant hand to operate a machine contributed their share to the literature of humanity's subjugation to technology.

Not all of Wells's ideas were original with him. Some of them were in the air; others were inspired, in part or in whole, by other writings. *The Time Machine*, for instance, came out of a Debating Society talk given during Wells's college days by a fellow student named E. A. Hamilton-Gordon; it was about the theory that time was the fourth dimension, a notion that had been suggested in 1875 by Heinrich Czolbe, and C. H. Hinton included several essays about dimensions, including "What is the Fourth Dimension?" in *Scientific Romances* published in 1884. Wells biographers Norman and Jeanne MacKenzie noted:

The quickness with which Wells seized on the notion of travelling through time illustrates the way he worked on his later scientific romances. He heard of some new concept or invention. He next set the novel theory in a conventional background. Then, having made the incredible acceptable by his attention to detail, his imagination was free to make what fantasies it pleased out of the resulting conflict.

Wells picked up ideas from his fellow fiction writers, as well. Oscar Wilde preceded Wells in the use of the fourth dimension as a means of escape in his 1887 story "The Canterville Ghost." And Bulwer-Lytton's *The Coming Race* (1871) and Samuel Butler's *Erewhon* (1872) contain a number of points of similarity with *The Time Machine*, including the fact that the traveler in all of them meets a girl (in *Erewhon* her name is even "Arowhena") who becomes his companion and explains things to him, and takes him to a large public museum where a great deal of machinery is displayed.

The Island of Dr. Moreau is Wells's most Darwinian book and owes most of its inspiration to the theory of evolution. But there were other sources. Wells himself attributed the idea for *Moreau* to the downfall of a man of genius in the 1890s (Oscar Wilde). The mechanism and viewpoint of the novel owe much to Swift, particularly to *Gulliver's Travels*. Prendick, for instance, is castaway like Gulliver and rescued by Dr. Moreau; Prendick's first reaction to the Beast People is much like Gulliver's reaction to the Yahoos; and the final chapter, after Prendick's escape from the island and return to England, is virtually identical in impact to the conclusion of Gulliver's voyage to the land of the Houyhnhnms: Just as Gulliver sees Yahoos everywhere, Prendick recoils from the evidence of the Beast People in everyone. There also is something of Poe's *Arthur Gordon Pym* in Prendick's rescue, and Wells's "The Sayers of the Law" obviously is an imitation of, if not a parody of, Kipling's "Law of the Jungle" in *The Second Jungle Book*.

The Invisible Man is one of Wells's most original concepts. It was preceded, nevertheless, by Fitz-James O'Brien's "What Was it? A Mystery" in 1859, Guy de Maupassant's "The Horla" in 1887, and Ambrose Bierce's "The Damned Thing" in 1893. The last two of these, to be sure, dealt with invisible creatures rather than men; the significant difference came from Wells's use of invisibility produced through scientific means while the others described strange (sometimes supernatural)

natural phenomena. The basic idea Wells got, he said, from one of W. S. Gilbert's "Bab Ballads." Called "The Perils of Invisibility," it contains the lines:

> Old Peter vanished like a shot. But then—his suit of clothes did not.

The War of the Worlds was in the tradition of the future war novel pioneered by Lieutenant Colonel Sir George Tomkyns Chesney's "Battle of Dorking" published in 1871 and followed by many others, twenty-two of them in 1871 alone, as I. F. Clarke has pointed out in *Voices Prophesying War*. Novels about life on Mars and the Moon had been published before: Marie Corelli's *Romance of Two Worlds* was published in 1886, Tremlett Carter's *People of the Moon* in 1895, George du Maurier's *The Martian* in 1896, and F. R. Stockton's *The Great Stone of Sardis* in 1897, as well as Kurd Lasswitz's *Auf Zwei Planeten* in 1897. The speculations of Percival Lowell about the construction of canals on Mars by intelligent beings were first published in 1896, though Wells had published similar speculations a month or so earlier in an article entitled "Intelligence on Mars." The idea for the Martian invasion came from Wells's brother Frank. As Wells described it later:

> We were walking together through some particularly peaceful Surrey scenery. "Suppose some beings from another planet were to drop out of the sky suddenly," said he, "and begin laying about them here!"...That was the point of departure...

Some of the physical descriptions of Mars may have been inspired by the work of a French writer of scientific and cosmic romances, Camille de Flammarion, particularly *La Fin du Monde* (1894) and *La Planete Mars* (1892). And the Martian Heat-Ray may owe something to Bulwer-Lytton's Vril, or perhaps to a description of John Hartman's electric gun published in London newspapers in the 1890s.

When the Sleeper Wakes was characterized by Wells as "a horoscope" and "a romance of the immediate future, somewhat on the lines of Mr. [Edward] Bellamy's *Looking Backwards* [sic]." *Looking Backward* was published in 1888, but the plot of someone falling to sleep and waking up in the future goes back at least to Washington Irving's "Rip Van Winkle" (1819). In fact, one character in Wells's novel comments that Graham's sleep is "Rip Van Winkle come real" and another that "it's Bellamy." Some of his ideas about the world to come Wells derived from theorists such as William James, but the highly mechanized future civilization he depicted leaned upon Flammarion's *La Fin du Monde*, which also may have influenced *Anticipations* and *In the Days of the Comet*, and in particular, "The Star," in which the action of Flammarion's novel was condensed and refined into the artistry of the short story published four years later.

The First Men in the Moon is dependent on all the earlier moon voyages, particularly Edgar Allan Poe's "Hans Pfaal" (1835), in which a Dutch bankrupt ascends to the moon by balloon. Wells's descriptions of how the earth seems to diminish in diameter and the moon to increase during the flight is much like Poe's, as well as his description of the sunrise on the moon and the moon's atmospheric conditions. Wells followed Carter's *People of the Moon* in making his Selenites cave-dwellers and scientists. Wells also received help from a Normal School classmate, Richard Gregory, who sent him papers on moon craters and an article published in 1900 by *Nature* in which a Professor Poynting described experiments on the possibility of substances acting as a screen to gravity.

Similar materials from the real and fictional worlds found their way into his short stories. "The Diamond Maker" (1894), for instance, surely was inspired by the experience of James Hannay, who announced in an 1880 paper to the Royal Society of London that he had created artificial diamonds; Wells includes a description of a process for creating diamonds that is almost identical with Hannay's. Wells got a number of ideas from the inventor J. W. Dunne, including the basic notion of the tank that later was described in "The Land Ironclads." In a letter Dunne called them "big fat pedrail machines." Wells also used Dunne as a model for an aviator in several stories.

Wells acknowledged his indebtedness to a number of writers, including Hawthorne, Poe, Kipling, and others, particularly Sterne and Swift, although he rejected comparisons to Verne and never mentioned Flammarion. Ultimately all the material Wells touched, including his own life, became his subject, and he made it his own. His vision of humanity and its problems and its place in the universe sometimes transformed that material into art.

He ended his 1902 speech to the Royal Institution with a declaration of his faith in the power of the human mind to create a better future.

There are two kinds of minds, he said. One, oriented to the past, regards the future "as sort of black nonexistence upon which the advancing present will presently write events." That is the legal mind, always referring to precedents. The second kind of mind, oriented to the future, is constructive, creative, organizing. "It sees the world as one great workshop, and the present as no more than material for the future, for the thing that is yet destined to be." Finally, he predicted what might be accomplished if the future-oriented mind were given freedom to express itself: "All this world is heavy with the promise of greater things, and a day will come, one day in the unending succession of days, when beings who are now latent in our thoughts and hidden in our loins, shall stand upon this earth as one stands upon a footstool and shall laugh and reach out their hands amidst the stars."

Clearly Wells was finished with the pessimism of his early science fiction. But science fiction was not finished with him.

DELANY:
NUANCES OF A THEME BY STEVENS
Adam Roberts

Delany's "Time Considered as a Helix of Semi-Precious Stones" won the 1970 Hugo for Best Short Story. What might we make of it?

We can, of course, take the story in terms of content, plot, character, in which case we are likely to read it as proto-cyberpunk, demonstrating a clear family resemblance to Bester's *The Stars My Destination* (1956), and passing down vivid literary-genetic material to Sterling and Gibson. The narrator, who goes under a series of aliases (Harold Clancy Everet, Harmony C, Eventide, Harry Calamine, Eldrich, Harvey Cadwaliter-Ericksons, Hector Calhoun Eisenhower and so on) is a small-time criminal, on Earth after a spell in prison, with some contraband to sell. Maudline Hinkle, a police agent from "Special Services," warns him not to try and dispose of his merchandise. He meets a friend, a "Singer" called Hawk, one of the elite pseudo-poetic group in this future world (a group of people who enjoy a special social status because of their ability absolutely to command attention when they sing). Trying to dispose of his contraband the narrator follows Hawk out of the street to a penthouse party at which the city's best and brightest are enjoying themselves ("Hell's Kitchen at ten, Tower Top at midnight") where he meets a criminal Mr. Big who is also, by coincidence, called Hawk. He sells the contraband to this Hawk, and Maudline Hinkle—as she warned—arrives with a fierce airborne police presence to arrest them both. The narrator and Hawk escape, slipping through the crowd when Hawk the Singer distracts everybody's attention with a song and by setting fire to the lobby, becoming badly burnt himself. In a coda to the story, the narrator has moved to Triton where he has set up "The Glacier, a perfectly legitimate icecream palace" the "first and only ice cream palace on Triton" [Delany, 355]. This enterprise has prospered, and the narrator is wealthy. He encounters Hawk again, and Maudline Hinkle, both of whom tell him that he is now moving in a higher echelon of crime than before, a life which involves new dangers as well as new rewards. The story ends with the protagonist planning a new disguise for some unspecified criminal action the following day.

A precis such as this sounds banal, and is indubitably reductive in its account of the story. Whilst Delany draws the urban milieu well, and the narrative pacing keeps the reader occupied until the end, this is not where the story works: it is not on this level that its punch lies. We're tempted, as many critics have been, to read below the surface. Brian Aldiss notes that "much has subsequently been written about the *meaning* of Delany's work—the underlying Quest pattern, the experimentation in terms of language and perception, and the attempt to further a Heinlein Life-Style SF and create changing mores for changing times—but what impressed at first reading was style, sheer *style!*" [Aldiss, 291]. "Time Considered as a Helix of Semi-Precious Stones" is certainly stylish. Indeed, it seems egregiously to be flaunting its style, from its deliberately pretentious title to its in-your-face juxtaposition of worn-down street subject-matter with highfalutin "poetic" prose. A criminal drinking in a smoky bar is the premise of noir pulp, but when Delany describes the atmosphere with a sentence such as "scarfs of smoke gentled through the noise" [Delany, 324] we are brought up against a sense of a creative mismatch of style and substance. Much of the story works this way: the gaudily beautiful economies of Delany's poetic style marvellously offset the jauntily excessive matter being described.

The jewels of the story's title set the tone in this respect. The immediate referent of the title is the convention by which criminal underworlds throughout the solar system choose monthly code-words. Each code is the name of a jewel, and the code is passed by word of mouth. The month in which the story opens is "jasper"; a fact known (because, towards the end of the month, the authorities sometimes do become aware of the code) by policewoman Maudline Hinkle as she approaches the narrator. The following month is "Agate." And so time moves on, labelled in this way. Time may be considered as a chain of these semi-precious stones because they define and name the passage of time for the sorts of criminal or poetic characters in whom Delany is interested; they form a "helix," we intuit, because—just as the narrator encounters The Hawk and Maudline Hinkle on Earth and again on Triton—the world in which they move is one that circles round on itself repeatedly. But "decoding" the title in this way does not explain its resonances, or its peculiar charm, and does not account for the aesthetic effect of structuring narrative time by this convention.

For example: the set-piece of the story, if I can put it that way, occurs in the party at Tower Top. Despite being warned not to accept money for his contraband by Maudline Hinkle, the narrator nevertheless sells his goods to the Hawk. He, and we as reader, expect him to be apprehended by the police, and the story generates a good deal of tension out of this expectation. We follow the protagonist out of the party, expecting retribution at any moment. "I started down, keeping near the wall, expecting someone to get me with a blow-dart from a passing car, a deathray from the shrubbery" he tells us, as he walks towards the subway station, or "sub." Then the narrative focalization (to use the technical term) shifts abruptly; after twenty pages densely describing the events of one evening, the narrative line stretches over many months in a few lines.

> "I reached the sub.
> And still nothing had happened.
> Agate gave way to Malachite:
> Tourmaline:
> Beryl (during which month I turned twenty-six):
> Porphyry:
> Sapphire..." [Delany, 354-5]

The implicit estrangement technique here is that of wrongfooting the reader, so that she is not certain whether the narrative has been usurped by some hallucinogenic stylistic tic, or (realization confirmed by the parenthetical "during which month I turned twenty-six") that these colorful words are signifiers of the passage of time. In other words, the passage just quoted stands as *both* a functional element in onward plot, *and* as a striking pastiche of symbolist poetry. We can imagine this passage, for instance, separated from the text and printed in a Little Magazine.

But it would not be quite right to describe the jewels of this tale as "symbols." On the level of code-word, which is to say within the logic of the text, they do not symbolize, but directly signify. And on the level of aesthetic effect, the metatextual aspect by which these jewels adorn rather than operate, they are less symbolic and more specifically allusive.

It has long been known that Delany is an unusually literary-allusive writer, especially in his 1970s work. One thing that "Time...Stones" reveals is how complex this intertextual play can be. The pseudonymous names the narrator of the story takes, for instance, appear on the surface to be making one very obvious intertextual gesture: these variants on "H.C.E." of course make us think of "Here Comes Everybody" or "Humphrey Chimpden Earwicker," the hero (for want of a better word) of Joyce's *Finnegan's Wake* (1939). The allusion seems to slot into place because we know, thanks to some strenuous critical activity, how important an ur-text *Finnegans Wake* was to the composition of Delany's *Dhalgren* (1975), a work whose last sentence is completed riverrun-like by its first, in which a mythic city promiscuously opens itself to interpretation and meaning and so on [see Sallis, 62-108 and 189-90]. But this, I think, is misdirection in the story under consideration here. I think the doorway to 'Time...Stones' is not Joyce, but Wallace Stevens, and that in his story Delany is exploring the meta-aesthetics of poetry, and a specific sort of *poetry*, rather than (as most of his critics suggest) myth.

A joke towards the end of the story, after H.C.E. has established the successful Ice Cream Palace, "The Glacier," on Triton, tips the nod to us as readers.

> "The Steward of the Glacier called me into the kitchen to ask about a shipment of contraband milk (the Glacier makes all its own ice cream) that I had been able to wangle on my last trip to Earth (it's amazing how little progress there has been in dairy farming over the last ten years; it was depressingly easy to hornswoggle that bumbling Vermonter) and under white lights and great plastic churning vats, while I tried to get things straightened out, he made some comment about the Heist Cream Emperor; and didn't do *any* good." [Delany, 360]

This new version of "H.C.E." alludes of course to the narrators criminal proclivities, as well as his lordship over the "ice cream palace." H.C.E.'s career move as an "emperor" of icecream picks up his own origins which were touched on at the story's opening (working on a Vermont dairy farm) and bring an understated circularity of theme to the tale. But the Wallace Stevens reference (to what is, after all, one of Stevens's most famous poems) provides us with a sort of code-book—not for what is being signified, but for the process by which Delany's oblique tale signifies in the first place. Stevens's "The Emperor of Ice Cream" first appeared in his *Harmonium* (1923):

> Call the roller of big cigars,
> The muscular one, and bid him whip
> In kitchen cups concupiscent curds.

Let the wenches dawdle in such dress
As they are used to wear, and let the boys
Bring flowers in last month's newspapers.
Let be be finale of seem.
The only emperor is the emperor of ice-cream.

Take from the dresser of deal,
Lacking the three glass knobs, that sheet
On which she embroidered fantails once
And spread it so as to cover her face.
If her horny feet protrude, they come
To show how cold she is, and dumb.
Let the lamp affix its beam.
The only emperor is the emperor of ice-cream.
[emphasis mine] [Stevens 50-1]

This difficult poem is usually taken as an expression of a particular mood, a mixture of anomie and mundanity, occasioned by a death. It is often read as situated at a wake, where the little rituals that mark the passing of an old woman ("her horny feet protrude...to show how cold she is") are described. Her belongings are emptied from an old dresser; flowers are brought, wrapped in old newspapers; in a back room a muscular maker of ice-cream (this, of course, in 1923) whips up some of his product, and women ("wenches") carry it to the mourners. One must, after all, have refreshment at a wake. The refrain, "the only emperor is the emperor of ice-cream" seems to capture a deflating perspective of lost illusion. In this world, the poem seems to imply, we do not have "actual" emperors, figures of glory and majesty; in this place, at this time, only a purveyor of icecream will, in his patter, his routine and his sales-persona, act the grandiose, imperial manner. Our only emperors are these sorts of people.

Delany's story contains characters who approximate to "actual" emperors—particularly Senator Regina Abolafia, the "New Fascistas' most promising candidate for president" [Delany, 336]. But the focus of the story is not on this neo-imperial hopeful, but upon the emperor of heist cream himself—H.C.E. himself. We can read the paragraph quoted above in which the joke is made as an elegant riff on Stevens's themes (just as *Harmonium* also contains a poem in which Stevens riffs on Carlos Williams, "Nuances of a Theme by Williams"). Delany's story provides "nuances" on a theme by Stevens. The Glacier uses "great plastic churning vats" rather than "kitchen cups," "white lights" rather than a "lamp," and in a phrase such as "hornswoggle that bumbling Vermonter" Delany provides a pastiche of Stevens's more obscure idiom that is spot-on to the point of parody. But the constellation of images do provide an oblique gloss on the story. They suggest the ways that Delany has himself arranged his images: milk and icecream; jewels; the underworld as literal location (the levels of subway are delineated as "sub," "sub-sub" and even "sub-sub-sub") and as metaphorical environment for criminals; disguise; and, ultimately, the figure of the poet—for this is what the "Singers" in the story evidently are.

To take the last first; the song of the singers is only alluded to, not described. H.C.E. tells us that "it has been illegal to reproduce the 'Songs' of the Singers by mechanical means (including the publishing of the lyrics) since the institution arose, and I respect the law" [Delany, 340]. But we know that the poetic idiom is Delany's own, that his own story embodies these 'Songs' even if it doesn't reproduce them. When reading the story I thought of these songs as having the effect on listeners that Stevens's best poetry has on me, but this is of course a mere personal response. The question of disguise is more interesting. The chilly voice of Stevens's "The Emperor of Ice-Cream" declares "Let be be finale of seem," as if mere *seeming* (H.C.E.'s addiction to his own disguises, for instance) can be called forth into complete 'being' simply by voicing this imperative. Delany's story does not think so. The final image of "Time...Stones" is of H.C.E. locked out (as he has been throughout the tale), looking in from outside, at his disguise. That the emporium from which he has been excluded is his own does not, I think, matter as much in the end as the bald fact of his exclusion.

> "I pounded on the glass a couple of times, but everyone had gone home. And the thing that made it worse was that I could see it sitting on the counter of the coat-check alcove under an orange light." [Delany, 363]

"It" is a disguise that would turn H.C.E. into Ho Chi Eng for some unspecified but presumably nefarious project; and although he thinks of breaking in, he eventually decides to leave it there.

"I turned around and started down the steps; and the
thought struck me, and made me terribly sad, so that I
blinked and smiled just from reflex: it was probably just
as well to leave it there till morning, because there was
nothing in it that wasn't mine, anyway." [Delany, 363]

The enigmatic tone of this last sentence is superbly well judged; the
reader has to untangle the syntax even to approach comprehension,
and even when she has understood what Delany has written it is not
clear why the consideration that "it is all his" (the disguise, the shop)
should make him sad. Except, of course, that saying "it was all mine" is
a very different thing from saying "there was nothing in it that wasn't
mine". The throwaway "...anyway" with which the story ends is another
deflating note. We ponder: is he sad because he cannot steal his own
belongings ("I actually thought of breaking in. But...") and so is unable
to express his "true" nature as a thief? Is he sad because there is nothing
further to achieve? Does his melancholia reflect upon the events of the
story (for instance the fact that his friend Hawk the Singer has been
badly burned and defaced)? We take it a step further: what makes him,
or any of us, sad is loss. This case is more complicated because what
H.C.E. is mourning is not the loss of any specific thing ("it was all mine"),
but rather the loss of loss itself ("there was nothing in it that wasn't
mine"). Stevens's dresser "lacks the three glass knobs"; but even what
it does not lack ("that sheet / On which she embroidered fantails once")
speaks of the larger loss, for it is now only a shroud ("spread it so as to
cover her face"). Death, we might say, is the prototype of loss, and the
dead are cold: but it takes a special vision to see the chill of death and
the chill of icecream as versions of the same thing; a vision that Stevens
and Delany share. H.C.E. trades in death ("[I] caused my hirelings to
commit two murders. And you know? I didn't feel a thing," Delany,
355) and in icecream. On a poetic level these things function in the
same register.

Delany's title may well be a variation of another Stevens poem
from *Harmonium*, "Of Heaven Considered as a Tomb." This fifteen-
line text addresses the "interpreters of men / Who in the tomb of heaven
walk at night," asking whether they are actually questing for something
("about and still about / To find whatever it is they seek") or whether
their walking is simply a presage of death, "one abysmal night / When
the host shall no more wander" [Stevens, 45]. The last three lines of
this poem are as follows:

> Make hue among the dark comedians,
> Halloo them in the topmost distances
> For answer from their icy Elysee. [Stevens, 45]

Delany attacks this image with a refreshingly gaudy literalness. SF enables him to conceive of the heavens of this poem not as some abstract spiritual realm, but as the actual solar system. He playfully literalizes these lines at the end of "Time...Stones." The Torrents, on Triton, embody the icy Elysee, complete with school-teacherish guide: ("'...two hundred and thirty yards high,' the guide announced, and everyone around me leaned on the rail and gazed through the plastic corridor at the cliffs of frozen methane that soared through Neptune's cold green glare"; Delany, 355). The party of tourists is shown "the Well of This World"

> "Where, over a million years ago, a mysterious force science still cannot explain caused twenty-five square miles of frozen methane to liquefy for no more than a few hours during which time a whirlpool twice the depth of Earth's Grand Canyon was caught for the ages when the temperature dropped once more to..." [Delany 355-6]

We recall, of course, the concupiscent curds whipped up and frozen by the emperor of ice-cream, as doubtless we are meant to. H.C.E. continues with his narrative.

> "People were moving down the corridor when I saw her smiling. My hair was black and nappy and my skin was chesnut dark today.
> "I was feeling overconfident, I guess, so I kept standing around next to her. I even contemplated coming on. Then she broke the whole thing up by suddenly turning to me and saying, perfectly deadpan: 'Why, if it isn't Hamlet Caliban Enorbarbus!'" [Delany, 356]

These dark comedians play their games, make hue with one another (in the sense both of color and of "hue-and-cry") from their icy Elysee. But we don't forget the title of the Stevens intertext, "Of Heaven Considered as a Tomb." The associations of prison, of the enclosed living environment of the human colony on Triton, of tombs, bring us back to death, which was also behind "The Emperor of Ice-Cream."

It would nevertheless be a false step to attempt to "decode" "Time...Stones" after this fashion—to suggest that it is, for instance, "about" death, that this is the thing at the centre of its titular helix, the thing like the Singers' songs that cannot be reported, the place where the story works, where its punch lies. It would be more proper to suggest that the figure of the poet—the Singer, Hawk, Stevens, Delany himself—is the key to interpretation. Poetry loses its tension when treated to a thorough-going "decoding." The effectiveness of Delany's beautiful work lies in its Stevensesque arrangement of image, tone, allusion, explanation: milk and crime, the "twenty-five square miles of methane frozen in a whirlpool" on Triton and the icecream produced in H.C.E.'s emporium, the poet submerging himself in a burning pool and the small-time criminal master of disguise. As Stevens put it in *Adagia* (1936), "the bare image and the image as symbol are the contrast: the image without meaning and the image as meaning. When the image is used to suggest something else, it is secondary. Poetry, as an imaginative thing, consists of more than lies on the surface" [Stevens, 902].

There would be little point in bringing Stevens into a discussion of Delany, finally, unless such comparison is able to provide a useful perspective on Delany's writing. And I think that, as it were, Stevens is a useful way of looking at Delany. For all their apparent dissimilarities, there is an important point of connection between the two, and it has to do with voice. Stevens's voice is a unique and to some readers off-putting combination of a highly meditative-intellectual dryness on the one hand, and on the other what he himself called "the essential gaudiness of poetry"; a blend of the recondite and the dazzling. What Delany understands more than any SF writer of similar gifts, is the importance of that "essential gaudiness." It is the jewellery of Delany's writing, or more precisely the way the jewels adorn the body of the whole.

Bibliography

Aldiss, Brian, with David Wingrove, *Trillion Year Spree: the History of Science Fiction* (London: Gollancz 1986)

Delany, Samuel, "Time Considered as a Helix of Semi-Precious Stones," in Asimov (ed), *The Hugo Winners, Volume 2: 1968-1970* (London: Sphere 1973), 322-63

Sallis, James (ed), *Ash of Stars: On the Writing of Samuel R. Delany* (Jackson MI: University of Mississippi Press 1996)

Stevens, Wallace, *Collected Poetry and Prose* (New York: Library of America 1997)

WE HOBBITS ARE A MERRY FOLK...
...an Incautious and Heretical
Re-Appraisal of J. R. R. Tolkien
David Brin, Ph.D.

Want to forget about terrorism and all those distracting rumors of war? Need to ignore the economy for a while? Got the holiday blues? Our culture has a sure-fire cure—the traditional spate of post-Thanksgiving movies. This year, despite a clamor over the latest *Harry Potter* film, much of the attention is going to another fantasy called *The Two Towers*—part two in the *Lord of the Rings* trilogy. Will it succeed in distracting us for a while, conveying audiences to a world that is at once more beautiful and stirring than humdrum modern life?

Naturally, I enjoyed the *Lord of the Rings* (*LOTR*) trilogy as a kid, during its first big boom in the 1960s. I mean, what was there not to like? As William Goldman said about another great fantasy, *The Princess Bride,* it has "Fencing. Fighting. Torture. Poison. True Love. Hate. Revenge. Giants. Hunters. Bad Men. Good Men. Beautifulest Ladies. Spiders. Dragons, Eagles. Beasts of all natures and descriptions. Pain. Death. Magic. Chases. Escapes. Miracles."

In 1997, voters in a BBC poll named *The Lord of the Rings* the greatest book of the twentieth century. In 1999, Amazon.com customers chose it as the greatest book of the millennium.

Of course there is much more to this work than mere fantasy escapism. J. R. R. Tolkien wrote his epic—including its prequel, *The Hobbit*—during the dark middle decades of the twentieth century, a time when modernity appeared to have failed in one spectacle of technologically amplified bloodshed after another. From the nineteen-thirties through the fifties, planet Earth fell into armed camps of starkly portrayed character, tearing at each other in orgies of unprecedented violence. Titanic struggles, with the fate of all the world at stake.

LOTR clearly reflected this era. Only, in contrast to the real world, Tolkien's portrayal of "good" resisting a darkly threatening "evil" offered something sadly lacking in the real struggles against Nazi or Communist tyrannies—a role for individual champions. His elves and hobbits and *über*-human warriors performed the same role that Lancelot and Merlin and Odysseus did in older fables, and that superheroes still do in comic books. Through doughty Frodo, noble Aragorn and the ethereal Galadriel, he proclaimed the paramount importance—above nations and civilizations—of the indomitable romantic hero.

All right, I read Tolkien's epic trilogy a bit unconventionally, starting with *The Two Towers* and backfilling as I went along. Likewise, I may be a bit off-kilter in liking, best of all, the unofficial companion volume to *LOTR*, perhaps the funniest work penned in English—the Harvard Lampoon's 1968 parody, entitled *Bored of the Rings*. Even if you revere Tolkien, or take *LOTR* much too seriously, who can restrain guffaws at the antics of Frito, son of Dildo and his sidekick Spam... along with Gimlet, son of Groin, Eorache, daughter of Eordrum, and Arrowroot, son of Arrowshirt, son of Araplane? Many of the sixties references may seem dated, but any author should be flattered to receive such inspired satire.

In fact, toward the end of this essay, I'll offer my own small bit of ironic take off. A different, and possibly much better, way of viewing Sauron, the evil Dark Lord.

But first let's get serious. Some of what I am about to say may seem unconventional, provocative, heretical... even foolhardy in the face of a pseudo religious reverence that some accord to *Lord of the Rings*. There may be even more hate mail than when Salon ran my piece criticizing the Star Wars universe.

So let me start by saying that I deem Tolkien's trilogy to be one of the finest works of literary universe-building, with a lovingly textured internal consistency that's excelled only by J. R. R. T.'s penchant for crafting "lost" dialects. Long before there was a Klingon Language Institute, expert aficionados—*amateurs* in the classic sense of the word—were busy translating Shakespeare and the Bible into High Elvish, Dwarfish and other Tolkien-generated tongues.

And yes, *LOTR* opened the door to a vast popular eruption of heroic fantasy, setting up many others who followed with exacting devotion to his masterful architecture, scrupulously copying the rhythms, ambience and formulas that worked so well.

Indeed, the popularity of this formula is deeply thought-provoking. Millions of people who live in a time of genuine miracles—in which the great-grandchildren of illiterate peasants may routinely fly through the sky, roam the Internet, view far-off worlds and elect their own leaders—

slip into delighted wonder at the notion of a wizard hitchhiking a ride from an eagle. Many even find themselves yearning for a society of towering lords and loyal, kowtowing vassals!

Wouldn't life seem richer, finer if we still had kings? If the guardians of wisdom kept their wonders locked up in high wizard towers, instead of rushing onto PBS the way our unseemly "scientists" do today? Weren't miracles more exciting when they were doled out by a precious few, instead of commercializing every discovery, bottling and marketing each new marvel to the masses for a dollar ninety-five?

Didn't we stop going to the Moon because it had become *boring*?

Just look at how people felt about Princess Diana. No democratically elected public servant was ever so adored. Democracy doesn't have the pomp, the majesty, the sense of being above accountability. One of the paramount promoters of the fantasy-mythic tradition, George Lucas, expressed it this way:

> "There's a reason why kings built large palaces, sat on thrones and wore rubies all over. There's a whole social need for that, not to oppress the masses, but to impress the masses and make them proud and allow them to feel good about their culture, their government and their ruler so that they are left feeling that a ruler has the right to rule over them, so that they feel good rather than disgusted about being ruled."

·

This yearning makes sense if you remember that arbitrary lords and chiefs did rule us for 99.44% of human existence. Amid the brutally predictable drudgery of everyday life, miracles were awesome, far-away things. For example, *flight* was a legendary prerogative of demigods in stirring fables. And a man was meaningless out of context with his king.

It's only been two hundred years or so—an eyeblink—that "scientific enlightenment" began waging its rebellion against the nearly-universal pattern called feudalism, a hierarchic system that ruled our ancestors in every culture that developed both metallurgy and agriculture. *Wherever* human beings acquired both plows and swords, gangs of large men picked up the latter and took other men's women and wheat. (Sexist language is meaningfully accurate here; those cultures had no word for "sexism," it was simply assumed.)

They then proceeded to announce rules and "traditions" ensuring that their sons would inherit everything.

Please, try to find even one exception. You won't succeed. Putting aside cultural superficialities, on every continent society quickly shaped itself into a pyramid, with a few well-armed bullies at the top... accompanied by some fast talking guys with painted faces or spangled cloaks who curried favor by weaving stories to explain why the bullies should *remain* on top.

Only something exceptional started happening. Bit by bit—in gradual stages—the elements began taking shape for a new social and intellectual movement, one finally capable of challenging the alliance of warrior lords, priests, bards and secretive magicians. It didn't happen all at once, but in fitful jerks, sometimes five steps forward and four (or more) steps back.

Timidly at first, guilds and townsfolk rallied together and lent their support to kings, thereby easing oppression by local lords. Long before Aristotle became a tool of the establishment, his rediscovery during the High Middle Ages offered some relief from dour anti-intellectualism. Then Renaissance humanism offered a philosophical basis for valuing the individual human being as worthy in its own right. The Reformation freed sanctity and morality from control by a narrow, self-chosen club; it also legitimized self-betterment through hard work in *this* world, not the next. Then Galileo and Newton showed that creation's clockwork can be understood, even appreciated in its elegance, not just endured.

Still, the entire notion of progress remained nebulous and ill-formed. Society's essential *shape*—pyramidal, with a narrow elite atop a vast and permanently ignorant peasantry—stayed largely unchanged until a full suite of elements and tools were finally in place, setting the stage for true revolution.

A revolution so fundamental, coming with such heady, empowering suddenness, that participants gave it a name filled with hubristic portent. *Enlightenment*.

The word wasn't ill-chosen, for it bespoke illuminating a path ahead. Which, in turn, implied the unprecedented notion that "forward" is a direction worth taking, instead of lamenting over a preferred past.

Progress, in a forward direction, and boy, did we take to it. In two or three centuries our levels of education, health, liberation, tolerance and confident diversity have been momentously, utterly transformed.

Along the way, *history*—once the core of every curriculum—became a minor elective subject, with the ironic effect that today's citizens have very little idea what the past was like, how grindingly cruel and bitter life was for nearly all of our oppressed ancestors. In other words, by turning away from the past, we seem paradoxically unable to measure how far we've come. How very far.

The very *shape* of society changed, away from the once-universal pyramid—toward a *diamond* configuration, wherein a comfortable and well-educated middle class actually outnumbers the poor. For the very first time, let me emphasize. Anywhere.

One side-effect (among many) has been to transform our myths—our songs and dramas and vivid tales—toward a new shared-theme, seen today in a majority of popular films. The nearly all-pervasive theme: *suspicion of authority*. And the notion, nearly absent in other cultures, that individual eccentricity and freedom are sacred things.

We can argue endlessly about the detailed accuracy and implications of this "diamond" analogy—and its vast remaining imperfections—but not over the fact that a profound shift has occurred, driven by a genuine scientific-technical educational revolution.

And yet, almost from its birth, the Enlightenment Movement was confronted by an ironic counter-revolution, rejecting the very notion of progress. The *Romantic movement* erupted as a rebellion against the rebellion.

In fairness, it didn't start out that way. For example, many of the leading early English Romantics—Wordsworth, Shelley, Blake etc.—welcomed the French Revolution (at least in its early phases) as a sweeping away of the cobwebs of feudalism and clericalism—a step toward a kind of utopian universal brotherhood. So long as they shared the same entrenched enemy—powerful bishops and feudal lords—you could hardly slide a knife blade between the two wings of the rebel alliance.

Even today, men like Thomas Jefferson stand as icons of *both* Enlightenment and Romanticism.

But this changed when the industrial revolution hit full stride. Suddenly, where once gentry and clergy ruled, there were arrogant new powers striding about. An entrepreneurial bourgeoisie. A new intellectual elite of science. And a clanking, noisome ruction of impudent machinery.

Even democracy began to seem less classically pure when it was taken off a pedestal to be practiced for real by farmers, shopkeepers and a rising middle class, all of them arguing, wheedling and conniving amid an incredible din. This wasn't the calmly erudite Academy or Forum, but something a lot more gritty—often puerile. It was real. Some, like Alexis de Toqueville, saw beauty in all the noise. Others felt their idealized hopes betrayed.

Temblors began splitting a chasm between Romantics and Enlightenment pragmatists. The alliance that had been so formidable against feudalism began turning against itself. Trenches soon aligned along the most obvious fault line, down the middle, between Future and Past.

•

Don't get me wrong. I know how unfair it can be to reduce a whole vast, churning intellectual movement to a few pat descriptions and caricatures. In fact, individual Romantics ranged (and still range) across not just one spectrum but many dimensions. Some of them—like the agrarian socialist William Morris—clung to Jefferson's old optimism, egalitarianism and pragmatism, even while their movement's center of mass moved inexorably the other way. Backward, toward a renewed fascination with elitism.

By the nineteenth century, the battle front had grown so rigid that intellectuals started speaking of "two cultures," forever at odds and mutually incomprehensible.

Neither side had a monopoly on truth. Each saw plenty to criticize. The Romantics' agrarian nostalgia had a real-world basis in the Industrial Revolution's displacement of people and transformation of the countryside; industrialization was now seen as an oppressor, not a liberator.

Through the eyes of Charles Dickens and many others, we all can envision the "satanic mills" where women and children toiled horrible eighty-hour weeks, under brutal conditions. Exposing such injustices in vivid tales and dramas may have been the Romantics' finest hour.

Mentioned far less often is what those factories were busy *producing*. For example, mountains of cheap cloth, allowing even the poor to afford several changes of clothes. And soap. And cheap iron bedsteads, just like rich folks had, lifting mattresses off the floor and away from vermin. More soap. And dinnerware and pencils and concrete and bathtubs and cheap windows and lamps and books and sewer pipes and reading glasses and water faucets and school desks and flush toilets and electric wire. And more soap.

Faced with these tradeoffs, people voted in a myriad ways, with marches, protests, ballots and their pocketbooks. And with their feet, moving en masse from country hovels to urban tenements. It turned out that they wanted the factories, slums and schools *reformed*. But they also wanted what the factories and schools made.

Romantics disagreed with this decision. It baffled them.

In a nutshell, that was when they parted company with—and started nurturing contempt for—the common man.

Let's tie this in with our overlying theme. For J. R. R. Tolkien and his fellow Oxfordite, C.S. Lewis, were proud and avowed Romantics.

Calling the scientific worldview "soul-less," they joined Keats and Shelley, Henry James, and most European-trained philosophers in spurning the modern emphasis on pragmatic experimentation, production, universal literacy, progress, cooperative enterprise, democracy, city life and flattened social orders.

In contrast to these "sterile" pursuits, Romantics extolled the traditional, the personal, the particular, the subjective, the rural, the hierarchical and the metaphorical.

Moreover, by the turn of the century, Romanticism was fast losing all vestige of its former empathy for the concerns of commonfolk. One solitary artist—or entertainer or lost prince or angry poet—loomed larger in importance, by far, than a thousand craft workers, teachers or engineers... a value system that is thoroughly pushed today by the mythic engine of Hollywood. Just as in Homer's time, ten thousand foot soldiers mattered less than Achilles's heel.

This fits the very plot of *Lord of the Rings*, in which the good guys strive to preserve and restore as much as they can of an older, graceful and "natural" hierarchy, against the disturbing, quasi-industrial and vaguely technological ambience of Mordor, with its smokestack imagery and manufactured power-rings that can be used by anybody, not just an elite few. (Recall the scene where Saruman turns away from the "good" side and immediately starts ripping up trees, replacing them with mining pits and smoky forges. The anti-industrial imagery could not be more explicit.)

Consider the rings. Those man-made wonders are deemed cursed, damning anyone who dares to use them. Especially those nine normal humans who tried to rise up, using tools to equalize and then usurp the rightful powers of their betters—the high elves.

The nine Ring Wraiths aren't just evil henchmen and cardboard monsters. In my opinion, they are among the most important figures of the epic. Tolkien himself calls them tragic figures and dwells on their background. These fallen mortals—decent men who were hauled unwillingly into service to the "dark side"—can be looked upon as cautionary figures, conveying the universal lesson that "power corrupts."

On that much we can all agree. But I think there's more to the Ring Wraiths. To me, they distill the classic Greek notion of *hubris*—a concept that Romantics often embrace—the idea that pain and damnation await any mortal whose ambition aims too high. Don't try putting on the trappings or emblems or powers that rightfully belong to your betters. Above all, don't try to decipher and redistribute mysteries.

In other words, exactly the same morality tale preached in *Star Wars*.

Romanticism has come full circle, now unctuously praising the very same lords—the *über*-men—it started out opposing.

(An aside, in self-defense. Some readers may assign "left" or "right" political significance to what I say here. Don't. Both Romantics and pragmatists fill in every modern political movement. For example, as a staunch environmentalist, I can still comment on the Romantic elitism of many who share the same cause.

In fact, this struggle is being fought every day, almost unnoticed, in the battlefield of our contemporary media. Enlightenment's child—suspicion-of-authority—often comes paired with the quintessential Romantic image: a smug loner who despises the masses. They get mixed together, even though they arise from different traditions.

In order to tell them apart, try to notice whether a character sneers *only* at power-abusers... or at everybody. Is his or her ire aimed solely upward, toward some cruel elite, or downward too, despising fellow citizens and neighbors as clueless sheep?)

Don't get me wrong. Romanticism can make strong points. Even after the worst crimes of industrialization were palliated, criticism remains valid. For one thing, every generation of entrepreneurs features some who are insatiable and conspire together to become lords. Moreover, scientific advancement badly needs the constant light of public scrutiny, or else the "advances" can easily go sour. Science needs criticism precisely because it's proved effective. It works far better than magic ever did. That makes science potentially far more harmful, as well as far more useful.

The most blatant example of this is what we're doing to our world. Modern civilization isn't inherently less caring. It's just that there are so *many* of us, and we can afford to buy so many things—it puts Earth under intolerable strain. The planet was certainly less abused when our numbers were kept low by poverty, starvation and disease. Now we must replace those old corrective forces with new ones—knowledge, foresight and self-restraint.

No wonder Romanticism yearns for simpler ways and times, when death solved all such problems in a more natural way.

Moreover, Enlightenment can never completely replace older modes of thinking. The need for stirring, illogical tales and images runs deep within us all. (Some of us earn a good living that way.) Without romance, we'd be sorry creatures, indeed.

Still, scientific/progressive society has been known to listen to its critics, and not just now and then. Name one feudal society whose leaders did that.

Were any orcs or "dark men" offered coalition positions in King Aragorn's cabinet, at the end of the Ring War? Was Mordor given a benign Marshall Plan?

I think not.

Which brings us to another of the really cool things about fantasy—identifying with a side that's one hundred percent good. You can revel as they utterly annihilate foes who *deserve* to be exterminated because they are one hundred percent distilled evil.

This may not be politically correct, but then, political correctness is really a bastard offspring of egalitarian-scientific Enlightenment. Witness the sometimes saccharin PC-sweetness of *Star Trek*. Enlightened, but maybe also a bit gelded. (Is that why everybody likes Klingons?)

Romanticism never made any pretense at equality. It is hyper-discriminatory, by nature. (Have you ever actually read Byron or Shelley?) Whole classes of people are less worthy, less deserving of life, than other classes.

The Nazis were utter archetypal Romantics. (Ever listened to Wagner?) Deal with that.

The urge to crush some demonized enemy resonates deeply within us, dating from ages far earlier than feudalism. Hence, the vicarious thrill we feel over the slaughter of orc foot soldiers at Helm's Deep. Then again as Ents flatten even more goblin grunts at Saruman's citadel, taking no prisoners, never sparing a thought for all the orphaned orclings and grieving widorcs. And again at Minas Tirith, and again at the Gondor Docks and again... well, they're only orcs, after all.

What fun.

Lev Grossman made a similar point in a recent *Time Magazine* article.

"Where are the women? Peter Jackson filled out Liv Tyler's role for the movies (it's much less prominent in Tolkien's version), but the Fellowship is still as much a boys' club as Augusta National. And whiter too. Don't let all the heartwarming Elf-Dwarf bonding between Legolas and Gimli fool you. The only people with dark skin in Middle-earth are the Orcs."

This tendency is taken to an extreme, showing the basic moral problem of Romanticism, in a work that was coincidentally created by the *other* fellow who filmed a version of *Lord of the Rings*, one Ralph Bakshi, whose animated feature called *Wizards* was, in my opinion, just about the most evil thing produced since Goebbels ran the Nazi propaganda mill. In Bakshi's post-apocalyptic future, pastoral pixies, or elves, dwell in a bucolic Wagnerian paradise of vast, open countryside. These pretty creatures exclude a tribe they call "mutants"—ugly, urban, and vaguely technological—forcing them to inhabit a lightless canyon-ghetto for a thousand years. Bakshi portrayed the mutants as cowardly and pathetically incompetent, whenever they tried to escape into the pixies' immense realm. No matter. A narrator calls the suppression a matter of essential "good" vs. "evil"... as defined by the elvish side. When the mutants finally get inspired by a leader (portrayed as a screeching skeleton), viewers worry, then cheer when doughty pixies surround the ghetto, launch a pre-emptive strike, and annihilate every mutant, down to the last cub.

Admittedly, most Tolkien lovers claim to loathe Ralph Bakshi's version of *LOTR*. And yet, one can see the commonalties of *theme*. He may represent the darkest side of this "force," but it's the same basic premise.

Let's not ignore, but instead openly acknowledge the underlying racialism and belief in an inherent aristocracy that J. R. R. Tolkien weaved into the books, without even much attempt at subtlety. Nor do I much blame him. He couldn't help it, coming from the imperialist and class-ridden culture that raised him. One that worried deeply about how "uppity" the masses were starting to become.

Moreover, the characters whom the reader comes to know best— Frodo, Sam and even the king-in-waiting, Aragorn—are *themselves* not very snooty or racist. Aragorn has an easy-going, common touch— much like Luke Skywalker, the only un-patronizing Jedi. The snootiest and most relentlessly aristocratic characters in *LOTR* stand off in the wings. For example preachy, secretive and patronizing Elrond and Galadriel, coaxing maximum effort while letting others do the fighting for them.

(Bloody @*!%! elves. I'd point out endless parallels with a fellow named Yoda, but that would stir up too many hornets all at once!)

Oh, but in fact J. R. R. Tolkien was *himself* far more critical of the situation portrayed in his universe than any but a few of his myriad readers ever chose to notice. Certainly more self-critical than most of his contemporary readers or those watching the new film trilogy.

In several places, Tolkien openly stated his authorial judgment that the elves who made the Three Rings were ultimately to blame, having set the stage for tragedy in Middle Earth. They made their own rings (preceding Sauron's One Ring) in order to control the world, stopping time and preventing change, forbidding anything to die and decay and thus taking away room for new growth. Verlyn Flieger quotes Tolkien:

> "They wanted to have their cake and eat it: to live in the mortal historical Middle Earth because they had become fond of it... and so tried to stop its change and history, stop its growth, keep it as a pleasaunce."

There are moments scattered throughout *LOTR* when Tolkien seems to be warning that Romanticism can lead one down the road to genocide. He was disturbed to see the Nazi SS, for example, embrace many of the same Nordic mythic stories and symbols that he used as source material.

In later books, like the *The Silmarillion*, Tolkien went deeper into this self exploration, even going so far as to cast an analytical eye upon the elvish hierarchs of Middle Earth, in much the same way that Isaac Asimov re-evaluated his Second Foundation and the meddlesome-patronizing robots of his famed science fictional universe. The kind of self-examination that the *Star Wars* cosmos desperately needs, alas, while there's still time.

Indeed, many academics have cited the obvious parallel between the retreat of the High Elves in *LOTR*—abandoning Middle Earth to return "west across the sea"—and the dissolution of the British Empire which began with the emancipation of India, about the same time that Tolkien was writing his epic. In fairness, J. R. R. T. did not rail against this change. He saw it as regrettable but inevitable—like the end of his mythical Third Age. An approaching time of iron, when aloofly noble figures like Elrond and Galadriel must go back whence they came.

But those self-critiques never had the widespread readership or influence of the original *LOTR*. Indeed, there seems to be little appetite for examining the repetitious themes of fantasy.

Take for example, those immensely popular PBS interviews of Joseph Campbell, some years ago, about his book *The Power of Myth*. With an air of fawning worship, Bill Moyers gave Campbell hours to espouse the wholly unoriginal theory that ancient legends had certain similarities of rhythm and theme from continent to continent. Alas, not once did Moyers perform the journalist's duty of asking hard questions. For example—might some of the similarity have arisen out of simple economics? The bards and storytellers of olden times needed to be *fed*. Naturally, they sucked up to the chieftains and kings and magicians who had all the bread and gold, conjuring legends of elite demigods and princes, seldom daring (and only obliquely) to suggest that creativity and courage—even sovereignty—might reside in common men and women.

Enlightenment gifts—egalitarianism, openly-shared criticism, cooperative skill, accountability, argument, criticism, social mobility and science—were anathema. To this day, Romantics feel uncomfortable with them. To Campbell, any story that drifted from the standard Romantic formula was simply no story at all.

In the end, neither Tolkien nor his close friend C. S. Lewis could ever cross the gap that another Oxbridge don was writing about, at roughly the same time—the infamous "two cultures" gulf that C. P. Snow claimed to find unbridgeable, between the world of science and the world of the arts.

Try as he might, and even confronted with the blatant Romantic excesses of Nazism, Tolkien could not escape his own deep conviction that democratic enlightenment and modernity made up the greater evil. That hated trend, he feared, would ruin all the beauty that he found in tradition. In aristocratic-mystical hierarchies. In the ways of the past.

It all seems rather a pity, in light of what happened later, during the final third of the twentieth century.

For C. P. Snow's "gap" between two cultures began to be crossed, time and again, by unfettered spirits who simply refused to accept primly drawn categories. I wish Tolkien and Lewis could have lived to see how easily this chasm is traversed now, in both directions, by technologically-savvy artists and by scientists who love art.

Indeed, *science fiction* bridged the two cultures gap with a superhighway. But that's another story.

Having trouble picturing this dichotomy I'm painting? Between Romantics and followers of Ben Franklin's pragmatic Enlightenment?

Well here's another way of looking at it, focusing on how people view the *time orientation of wisdom.*

All creatures live embedded in time, though only human beings lift their heads to comment on it, lamenting the past or worrying over the future. Unique portions of our brains handle this temporal *skepsis.* Prefrontal lobes—the "lamps on our brows"—ponder tomorrow while swathes of older cortex can flood with vivid memories of yesterday, triggered by the merest sensory tickle, as when a single aromatic whiff sent Proust back to roam his mother's kitchen for eighty thousand words.

Obsession with either past or future can almost define a civilization. Worldwide, most cultures believed in some lost golden age when people knew more, mused loftier thoughts and were closer to the gods—but then fell from grace. Under this dour but recurrent worldview, men and women of a later, coarser era can only look back with envy, harkening to remnants of ancient wisdom.

Recognize this motif? It drenches every page of *Lord of the Rings.* It is the old classic. The eternal verity. The worst of all human clichés...

Only a few societies ever dared to contradict this standard dogma of nostalgia. Our own Scientific West, with its impudent notion of progress, brashly relocated any "golden age" to the future, something we might work *toward*, a human construct for our grandchildren to achieve with craft, sweat and good will—assuming that we manage to prepare them.

Implicit is the postulate that our offspring can and should be better than us, a glimmering hope that is nurtured (a bit) by two generations of steadily rising IQ scores.

Of course, the very notion of progress is anathema to nostalgic-Romantics.

These Romantics needn't be anti-technological, though they almost always reject science. I've already mentioned a renowned sci-fi pop-epic which, despite techie furnishings, relentlessly preaches the nostalgist party line—an ideal society ought to be ruled by secretive-mystical élites, unaccountable and self-chosen based on inherent qualities of blood. The only good knowledge is old knowledge. (No wonder it all happened "long ago, in a galaxy far away.")

This struggle isn't happening only in mass media. It surges at the highest intellectual levels. A century ago, one of the founders of science fiction, H. G. Wells, maintained an ongoing debate with the grand doyen of English letters, Henry James, over what constituted an interesting and worthwhile novel—whether there was more value to be found in introspection and past-oriented reflection, or in pursuing speculation and forward-looking conjecture. Whether the objective world, teeming with facts, should have a voice in fiction, or if all should remain subjective, as safe and aloof from reality as an incantation.

Within their ivory towers, literary academics have long declared James the winner. Leon Edel, in his biography of James gushes

> The victory long after was James's. Wells's social novels have been judged at this distance as obsolescent. James's novels, those which left out fact but dealt truthfully with human dilemmas, have more vogue today than they ever did.

Edel leaves out, conveniently, the fact that Wells's novels and stories are read in dozens of languages by tens of millions of people around the world to this day. Meanwhile, in the words of author and critic Greg Bear,

> Today, James is a favorite of the lush, golden-hued costume dramas of Merchant-Ivory, PBS, and the BBC.

He describes a time and a place without genocide and swift burning death. His nearly sexless courtships are an anodyne for the boneless chaos of modern mating. Henry James is an exemplar for those who see life as a fall from a golden age, and who choose, in their reading at least, to exchange all their modern conveniences for well-dressed, bloodless dooms and the frustration of lives too wrapped in structure. His world seems as remote to us, and as perversely attractive, as the palaces in Frank Herbert's *Dune*.

For the French, a similar role is filled by Proust and his ilk—who are idolized for their long and pretty ruminations about "eternal verities." Verities that must remain fixed and constant, offering traditionalists (here I call many of them *Romantics*) a deep sense of comfort. Human beings should not be plastic or capable of growth.

Look closely at the deep-set implication; the whole notion of "verities" requires that all generations be subject to exactly the same traumas and mistakes and *angst* as their forbears. Forever. Like insects in amber—or creatures stabilized by Tolkien's elvish rings—we never change.

People who believe in this constancy of human nature feel deeply threatened by any branch of literature that dares to disagree. And nothing is more grating than the suggestion—inherent to real science fiction—that children might learn from the mistakes of their parents. That future generations may move on from old concerns to new ones, beyond our ken. From Virgil and the Vedas to Plato, Shelley and Proust, James and Tolkien, all the way to Updike and Rowling, this prevalent tradition spanned five continents and forty centuries. Some rage, others fizz; but all grumble at tomorrow.

Let me avow up-front that I share the more recent, upstart belief in universities, democratic accountability, science and human improvability—one that questions the fated persistence of "eternal" stupidities. Above all, any "golden age" lies in our future. It has to. Or what are we striving for?

Anyway, people with my view had *better* be right. Because if humanity is as obstinate as the cynics and Romantics believe, we shall surely go extinct quite soon.

(What's the standard Romantic response, when anyone mentions the prospect of human extinction?

"Good riddance!" they mutter, expressing a smugly fashionable misanthropy.

(And *science* is portrayed as soul-less?

Oh, please....)

This may seem a dour picture I am painting, especially in light of the surge in popularity of feudal-magical fantasy.

Was Enlightenment a transient thing, already starting to flicker out as we return to our older fascinations? Back to Campbell-style heroes and traditional epics, with their paeans to kings and traditional, pyramid-shaped hierarchies? There are those who see this cloud rolling over us, a returning fog of Romanticism. Or even worse, the obligate, inherited aristocracies of feudalism.

> "Change and technology are so pervasive a part of daily life that for the most part there's no magic to it anymore," says Vivian Sobchack, a professor of film and television studies at UCLA. "The promise of science and technology has been normalized. The utopian vision we had didn't come to pass. The magic would have to come from somewhere else, and we found it in fantasy."

She has a point. Witness the most amazing accomplishment of NASA—managing to turn the exploration of space into a huge snore.

Or as Lev Grossman put it –

> Popular culture is the most sensitive barometer we have for gauging shifts in the national mood, and it's registering a big one right now. Our fascination with science fiction reflected a deep collective faith that technology would lead us to a cyberutopia of robot butlers serving virtual mai tais. With *The Two Towers*, the new installment of *The Lord of the Rings* trilogy, about to storm the box office, we are seeing what might be called the enchanting of America. A darker, more pessimistic attitude toward technology and the future has taken hold, and the evidence is our new preoccupation with fantasy, a nostalgic, sentimental, magical vision of a medieval age. The future just isn't what it used to be, and the past seems to be gaining on us.

Grossman's view is intelligent and thought-provoking—though at the surface also quite easy to disprove.

For example, *which* cyberutopias might he be talking about? *Soylent Green? Bladerunner? Rollerball? Silent Running? 1984? Fail Safe? The China Syndrome? Terminator? The Hot Zone? Logan's Run? The Postman? Fahrenheit 451?*

These don't strike me as exactly utopias.

For the life of me, I cannot picture more than one truly optimistic portrayal of future society in all of TV or film sci-fi. With the sole exception of *Star Trek*, most of the SF we've viewed in the last forty years has been relentlessly critical of perceived technological or social trends. Far from utopian, these films have served us well by dramatizing potential failure modes. To coin a term, they have been *self-preventing prophecies*, helping us work out our fears and exploring dark possibilities.

Yes, one result has been a lessened sense of confidence, a sadly stylish fatalism in an era of unprecedented goodness and competence. Paradoxical, yes. But by any metric, these dark warning tales have been far more useful than all those sword and sorcery flicks that try to teach us about good and evil by portraying the former as always pretty and the latter, always, with red, glowing eyes.

Finally, may I offer a little mind-stretching exercise? Let's start by remembering that *history is written by the victors.*

How do we know that Hitler was as bad as we are told?

We *know* because we live in a democracy that has given Holocaust deniers plenty of opportunities to make their case, and all they ever come up with is blatant drivel, ridiculous scenarios that are laughably easy to disprove. That's how. We see and hear countless witnesses to the Nazi horrors, conveyed via a media that, for all its faults, is relatively free. As implausible as the story of deliberate mass genocide might have seemed, in fiction, the reality was undeniably true and worse than anything previously imagined.

Allied propagandists did not have to make up any of it.

Ah, but things were different in kingdoms of old, where one official party line was promulgated and alternative sources of information got routinely squelched. And that's in *every* kingdom, mind you. Go ahead, name one where it didn't happen. (Note how the Norman propagandists went to work on poor old King Harold, even as his body was cooling after the Battle of Hastings.)

My point? Well, *LOTR* is obviously an account written after the Ring War ended, long ago. Right? An account created by the victors.

So how do we know that Sauron really did have red glowing eyes?

Isn't some of that over-the-top description just the sort of thing that royal families used to promote, casting exaggerated aspersions on their vanquished foes and despoiling their monuments, reinforcing their own divine right to rule?

Yes, I'm having fun with words like "really"—relating to a made-up story. But come along with me for a minute. Next time you re-read *LOTR*, count the number of examples...cases where powerful beings are vastly uglier than anybody with that kind of power would allow themselves to be. Why? How does being grotesquely ugly help you govern an empire?

Then unleash your imagination to take the story a bit farther. Have fun!

Ask yourself—"How would Sauron have described the situation?"

And then—"What might *'really'* have happened?"

Now ponder something that comes through even the party-line demonization of a crushed enemy. This clearcut and undeniable fact. *Sauron's army was the one that included every species and race on Middle Earth*, including all the despised colors of humanity, and all the lower classes.

Hm. Did they all leave their homes and march to war thinking, "Oh, goody, let's go serve an evil dark lord"?

Or might they instead have thought *they* were the "good guys," with a justifiable grievance worth fighting for, rebelling against an ancient, rigid, pyramid-shaped, feudal hierarchy topped by invader-alien elves and their Numenorean colonialist human lackeys?

Picture, for a moment, *Sauron the Eternal Rebel*, relentlessly maligned by the victors of the Ring War—the royalists who control the bards and scribes (and movie-makers). Sauron, champion of the common Middle-Earther! Vanquished but still revered by the innumerable poor and oppressed who sit in their squalid huts, wary of the royal secret police with their magical spy-eyes, yet continuing to whisper stories, secretly dreaming and hoping that someday *he* will return... bringing more rings.

•

Heh.

All right, we don't have to go quite that far!

Here's a milder version. Those orcs and low-elves and dwarves and dark-skinned or proletarian men who fought for the Ringlord were *fooled* by Sauron's propaganda.

Fair enough. Even that slight variation adds flavor to an already-great tale, making you pity Sauron's dupes a little, even though you still cheer as they're slaughtered down to the last private and orcoral.

Come on folks, a little empathy.

Instead of railing against "evil," try to understand it. That's always been the best way to defeat it.

Am I pulling your leg? You bet! I don't take speculations about fictional villains quite that seriously.

My real point is much more general. It's this —

Don't just receive your adventures. Toy with them. Re-mold them in your mind! Keep asking "What if...?" It's how you get practice not just being a passive consumer, or critic, but a creative storyteller in your own right.

And remember this too—enlightenment, science, democracy and equal opportunity are still the true rebels, reigning for just a few generations (and still imperfectly!) in one or two corners of the Earth, after elite chiefs, romantic bards and magicians dominated our ancestors for maybe half a million years.

Don't you think a little pride in that rebellion might be called for? A radical revolution-in-progress, still fresh and incomplete.

A rebellion that (among many other things) taught serfs like you to read so you can enjoy epic books and picture things different than they are.

One that makes vivid movies that cater to your taste for adventure.

One that, for all its imperfections, gave you a better chance than in some peasant village of old.

One that has a long way to go, but has at least turned our eyes around to face the future.

Self-critical almost to a fault, this culture may not be as romantic as those old kingdoms... but isn't it *better?*

You are heirs of the world's first true civilization, arising out of the first true revolution. Take some pride in it...

Let's keep enjoying kings and wizards. But also remember to keep them where they belong.

Where they can do little harm.

Where they entertain us.

In fantasies.

LETTER TO A YOUNG SCIENCE FICTION WRITER
Michael Swanwick

Philadelphia
June 16, 2002

My beloved grandchild,

Please forgive me for employing so indirect a means of communication but, alas, you exist decades in my future, and I as long ago in your past. There is no guarantee that we shall ever even meet. And, as any stranded time traveler can tell you, a book makes an excellent bottle for a message sent forward in time. Books can outlast buildings and even civilizations, if they are good enough, and they have an uncanny way of seeking out those who need them most. So here we are.

As of your reading this, you are nineteen years old, the exact same age as your father is as of my writing this. I realize how unlikely it seems that he was ever so young! You want to be a writer (don't ask how I know; it's a simple trick, anyway), and you think maybe you want to write science fiction, and you don't understand why dear old Dad is giving you no encouragement whatsoever.

Well, of course he isn't. It's a hard life, writing. An editor friend of mine recently estimated that, for all the folks who write the stuff, there are only one hundred writers who actually make a living, however paltry, doing nothing but writing science fiction. All the others have positions in academia, or day jobs, or spouses who are willing to support them. Speaking as one percent of those lucky few, I can tell you that it's a rewarding avocation—but only if it's the single thing you want most in life to do. There are easier ways to earn much more money using the same skills.

But you're sure you want to write, and you want me to tell you about science fiction. So I shall.

Science fiction is not so much a genre as it is a set of tools, and these tools will allow you freedoms that no other form of literature will. I once wrote a story set in the aftermath of an unimaginable cataclysm which had reversed the direction of memory, so that everyone knew everything that would happen to them from this very moment to the instant they died. Waking up in the morning, however, you would have no idea who that person sleeping peacefully on the pillow beside you was—a spouse? A casual pick-up? Someone who just wandered in off the street? Now, in what we in the field call (to their vast and flattered amusement) "the mainstream," the only possible reading of such a situation would be that the protagonist was mad. Which does not make for a terribly interesting story. But, this being SF, I was able to address questions of predetermination and free will approachable in no other way.

The strength of science fiction lies in its literalness. Those cosmonauts *really are* walking on the surface of the Sun. Those eight VR-addicts *really have* merged their consciousnesses into a single group mind. That alien race *really does* commune directly with God, even as they're dickering over the price of a loaf of bread. All writers of fiction have been given a special dispensation to lie. The science fiction writer has been given this dispensation in spades.

There's a price, of course. In exchange for this extraordinary licence, you're expected to deliver extraordinary results. It is not your job to produce comforting fables that reassure the reader that his is the best of all possible lives, or that hers are the best of all possible values. Every story in which a dead child calls her grieving mother on a toy telephone to reassure her that she's perfectly happy in the afterlife is a cop-out. Perhaps she *is* happy. But if millions of seances and billions of anguished prayers have taught us nothing else, they have taught us that we shall never get that reassuring word and that the little plastic telephone will never ring. To say otherwise is to tell that one lie which is forbidden us—that which lies about the nature of Truth.

Anything else is permitted. I once set a story on a planet-sized grasshopper. Now, you don't need to know a lot of physics to realize that this is impossible. Even if there *were* such a thing as a planet-sized grasshopper, gravitational forces would very quickly pull it into a sphere. But all writers are granted their initial premises, however outré, and given the extraordinary freedoms allowed writers of imaginative fiction, we are required to push the limits every now and then.

Which is not to say that our purpose is merely to create startling images. For fiction to satisfy, those images must have meaning and significance. It took me over a year to write my grasshopper story, developing the relationships of the characters living on its surface, before

I was able to discover why it was set on a monstrous grasshopper in the first place, and what that grasshopper *meant*.

Or let's take a look at another story, about three teenagers, Air Force brats whose parents are stationed somewhere in the Near East. Bored and having nothing better to do, they go to look at the edge of the world. (Technically, this is fantasy rather than science fiction, but the two genres have shared the same marketing niche for so long, I'll write of them as if they were the same thing.) They find a stairway leading downward and, quarreling, they descend.

For the story to work, the teens' descent must be convincing. Roxborough, the section of Philadelphia in which I live, lies above Manayunk, and is separated from it by a long cliff-line. Here and there, roads connect the two neighborhoods. But far more frequently the roads simply stop at the top of the cliff and concrete-and-steel stairways lead down to the bottom, where the roads begin again. I spent a long day walking up and down those stairways, taking notes, and the things I observed—small flowers growing out of cracks in the rock, graffiti cut into the painted railings, a car door flung over the edge for no discernable reason—gave the story the heft and feel of reality.

But having convinced the reader of a world unlike anything in his or her experience, accomplishment though that is, is only the beginning. The plot that ensues must justify its setting.

Three teens descend. At the end of the story, only two return. The third, the victim of lingering magic and a careless wish, has been so completely annihilated that in all the world only one person remembers he ever existed.

This is a literalization of what happens when a teenager commits suicide. All the world forgets his existence—save for those who loved him, who will carry the pain with them forever.

Why go through such a roundabout process to voice such simple truths? Because, like the people on the planet-sized grasshopper or the teenagers who live within a mile of the edge of the world and yet have never gone to see it, we're too close to those truths to be able to see our situation clearly. Science fiction has been called the literature of ideas, but really it is the literature of estrangement. It takes readers out of their familiar world into one whose strangeness forces them to rethink things they thought they already understood.

Which leads me to the single most important fact I have to impart to you: *Science fiction does not exist in opposition to any other form of literature*, though snobs both on the inside and the outside of the field will try to convince you otherwise. It is a specialized province of literature, true. But it is literature nevertheless. Just because your father writes SF as did his father before him, doesn't mean that you must. Write what you please—and what pleases you. Proust never wrote anything remotely like science fiction, and yet intelligent people everywhere esteem him highly.

Similarly, writing in genre doesn't ease the burden that's been laid upon you. Earlier I told you that science fiction was a set of tools, and so it is—a set of burglar tools. And when God gives you a set of burglar tools, you're not expected to stay home with them, tinkering with the stereo system. You're expected to go out and ransack the secrets of the human heart.

Now my letter is done, and I am about to drop it into the ocean of time, where it will slowly and desultorily bob its way to you. Write me anytime, if you have questions. It doesn't matter if, in your time frame, I happen to be dead. You're a writer, and you have my voice now. You can carry on as lively a correspondence with me as you wish, for as long as you like.

Your loving grandfather,
Michael Swanwick

CONTRIBUTORS

The author of fourteen novels as well as short fiction (published and upcoming), *Catherine Asaro* is acclaimed for her multiple-award winning Skolian Empire series, which combines adventure, hard science, romance, themes that challenge the status quo, and fast paced action. Her stand-alone novel, *The Quantum Rose*, won the 2001 Nebula Award. Her October 2003 novel, *Skyfall*, was just honored with the Romantic Times Book Club Award for "Best Science Fiction Novel." Asaro's novella "Moonglow," in *Charmed Destinies* (November, 2003) was followed by her fantasy novel, *The Charmed Sphere* (February, 2004), which is part of the Luna Books launch. Also published in February 2004, was *Irresistible Forces*, a six-author anthology for NAL, edited by Asaro, and including stories by Lois McMaster Bujold and Catherine, among other award-winning, bestselling authors. *Sunrise Alley*, her fourteenth novel (and the latest in the Skolian Empire Series) is due out in August 2004. Praised for her ability to mix hard science fiction with character-driven stories, physicist Asaro has a PhD in chemical physics from Harvard.

David Brin is a scientist, public speaker, and author. Several of his novels have been *New York Times* bestsellers, winning multiple Hugo, Nebula and other awards. His 1989 ecological thriller, *Earth*, foreshadowed global warming, cyberwarfare and near-future trends such as the World Wide Web. A 1998 movie, directed by Kevin Costner, was loosely based on *The*

Postman. His fifteen novels have been translated into more than twenty languages.

John Clute was born in Canada in 1940 and raised there. He has since lived in the U.S.A. and later in England. He has worked as a reviewer, mostly in the literature of the fantastic, since the early 1960s. Much of this material is assembled in *Strokes: Essays and Reviews 1966-1986* (1988), *Look at the Evidence* (1996) and *Scores: Reviews 1993-2003* (2003). He co-edited *The Encyclopedia of Science Fiction* (second edition 1993) with Peter Nicholls, and *The Encyclopedia of Fantasy* (1997) with John Grant, and wrote *Science Fiction: The Illustrated Encyclopedia* (1995) solo. He publishes fiction infrequently. His two novels are *The Disinheriting Party* (1977) and *Appleseed* (2001). The latter is SF. A third edition of *The Encyclopedia of Science Fiction* is in the works.

Paul Cornell is a British SF and TV author, with two SF novels out from Victor Gollancz: *Something More* and *British Summertime*. He's also written for many U.K. TV shows, including his own children's series, *Wavelength*. He writes XTNCT for the *2000AD* Megazine. He has an ongoing relationship with *Doctor Who*, and the companion he once created for that series, Bernice Summerfield.

Mark Finn is a native Texan and professional writer currently living in Austin. Author of the novels *Gods New and Used* and *Year of the Hare*, as well as numerous essays, comic book and radio scripts, his articles and reviews have appeared on Playboy.com and elsewhere. As a member of the Robert E. Howard United Press Association, he contributed the introduction to *Waterfront Fists: The Complete Fight Stories of Robert E. Howard*, penned the essay "Fists of Robert E. Howard" for Don Herron's *The Barbaric Triumph*, and wrote "Robert E. Howard: Lone Star Fantasist," which appeared in the first two issues of Dark Horse Comics' *Conan*. Among other projects he plans a collection of his long-running Finn's Wake column for *RevolutionSF.com*.

John Grant (real name Paul Barnett) is the author of about sixty books. His *The Encyclopedia of Walt Disney's Animated Characters*, currently in its third edition, is regarded as the standard work in its field. As co-editor with John Clute of *The Encyclopedia of Fantasy* he received the Hugo, the World Fantasy Award and several other international awards. As managing editor of the Clute/Nicholls *Encyclopedia of Science Fiction* he received a rare British Science Fiction Association Special Award, the first to be given in seventeen years. Under his own name he was until recently Commissioning Editor of Paper Tiger, the world's leading publisher of fantasy art books; he received the 2002 Chesley Award for his work with Paper Tiger. He is the U.S. Reviews Editor of *Infinity Plus* and a Consultant Editor to AAPPL (Artists' & Photographers' Press Ltd). Among hiis most recent major books, all as John Grant, are the nonfiction *Masters of Animation*, the "book-length fiction" *Dragonhenge* (illustrated by Bob Eggleton and shortlisted for a 2003 Hugo Award), the novels *The Far-Enough Window* and *The Dragons of Manhattan*, and, with

Elizabeth Humphreys and Pamela D. Scoville, the art/reference book *The Chesley Awards: A Retrospective*. His artbook *Renderosity: Digital Art for the 21st Century* (done with Audre Vysiauskas) and his story collection *Take No Prisoners* were both published in August 2004. His Web site is at www.hometown.aol.com/thogatthog.

James Gunn, Emeritus Professor of English at the University of Kansas, has had dual careers as a writer and a scholar of science fiction symbolized by his presidencies of both the Science Fiction Writers of America and of the Science Fiction Research Association. His best known novels are *The Joy Makers*, *The Immortals*, *The Listeners*, *Kampus*, and *The Dreamers*, and his best known academic books are *Alternate Worlds: The Illustrated History of Science Fiction*, *Isaac Asimov: The Foundations of Science Fiction*, and the six-volume *The Road to Science Fiction*.

Howard V. Hendrix is the author of the novels *Lightpaths* (1997), *Standing Wave* (1998), *Better Angels* (1999), and *Empty Cities of the Full Moon* (2001)—all from Ace Books—as well as *The Labyrinth Key* (2004) from Del Rey. He is also the author of two nonfiction books, the scholarly *The Ecstacy Of Catastrophe: Apocalyptic Elements in English Literature From Langland to Milton* and the gardening how-to book, *Reliable Rain*. He holds a BS in Biology from Xavier University in Cincinnati, Ohio (1980) and an MA (1982) and PhD (1987) from University of California at Riverside, where he was long involved with the Eaton Conferences on speculative literature.

Tim Lebbon is a novelist and short story writer whose work includes *Face*, *Fears Unnamed*, *The Nature of Balance* and *Changing of Faces*. Future publications include the novel *Desolation* and the dark fantasy novel *Dust*. His work has also appeared in dozens of anthologies, and he has won three major awards. Several novels and novellas are currently at various stages of development for screen adaptation. You can find more information at his Web site: www.timlebbon.net.

Jonathan Lethem is the author of six novels, including *Gun, With Occasional Music* and *The Fortress of Solitude*. *Motherless Brooklyn*, his fifth, won the National Book Critic's Circle Award, and has been translated into twenty languages. Lethem is also the author of a story collection, *The Wall of the Sky, The Wall of the Eye*, and a novella, *This Shape We're In*. As editor, he created *The Vintage Book of Amnesia*, guest-edited *The Year's Best Music Writing 2001*, and was the founding fiction editor of *Fence Magazine*. His stories and essays have appeared in *The New Yorker*, *Harper's*, *Esquire*, *The New York Times*, *The Paris Review*, and a variety of other periodicals and anthologies. He lives in Brooklyn, New York.

Sean McMullen is one Australia's leading SF and fantasy authors, and lives in Melbourne with his wife and daughter. He is the winner of over a dozen awards for SF and fantasy, has had twelve books and fifty stories published, and has been published in Australia, the USA, Britain, France, Poland, and Japan. Outside his writing, Sean works in scientific computing, has played in rock and folk bands, early music groups, and the State Opera. He has done armored and traditional fencing, and has been a karate instructor in the university club for twenty years. He is currently studying for a PhD in medieval literature at the University of Melbourne.

Robert A. Metzger has worked as a scientist in the area of the physics of materials for applications in high-speed electronics, as well as a writer of fiction and nonfiction. His work has appeared in publications ranging from *Analog* and *Asimov's* to *Wired Magazine*. His 2002 science fiction novel, *Picoverse*, was a Nebula finalist, and his next novel, *CUSP*, is scheduled to be published by Ace in January 2005. His Web site is www.rametzger.com.

Editor and publisher of *New Worlds*, *Michael Moorcock* reviews regularly for *The Guardian* and other criticism appears in *The Spectator* and *The London Magazine* in the UK. He has written introductions for Folio Society editions of the *Titus Groan* trilogy and Wells's *The Time Machine* and *The Island of Doctor Moreau*. He recently published a new edition of his study of epic fantasy *Wizardry and Wild Romance* with Monkeybrain Press. His new and forthcoming work includes *The Lives and Times of Jerry Cornelius*, *Elric, the Making of a Sorcerer* (series with Walter Simonson for DC Comics) and a "Tom Strong" graphic novel *Black Blade of the Barbary Coast*. Soon to appear are *The Vengeance of Rome*, the final book in the Colonel Pyat Holocaust sequence; *Love: A Memoir of Mervyn and Maeve Peake*, and *The Extraordinary Life and Adventures of Captain Crackers,* nonsense verse to previously unpublished Mervyn Peake illustrations. A special commemorative edition of his prize-winning novel *Gloriana; or, The Unfulfill'd Queen*, has recently been published by Warner Books. *New Worlds: An Anthology* will soon appear from Four Walls, Eight Windows and *Moorcock's Mammoth Miscellany of Fact and Fiction* from Constable, UK.

Mike Resnick is the author of more than forty science fiction novels, twelve collections, one-hundred-fifty short stories, and two screenplays, and is the editor of more than thirty-five anthologies. He was won four Hugo Awards and a Nebula, and has won other major and minor awards in the USA, France, Japan, Spain, Croatia and Poland. His work has been translated into twenty-two languages.

Adam Roberts is a writer and academic based in London, UK. In addition to various works of fiction, he has published a number of academic studies on nineteenth- and twentieth-century literature and theory. He is presently completing a *Critical History of Science Fiction* for Palgrave.

Robert J. Sawyer's latest novel is *Mindscan*. His *Hominids* won the Hugo Award for Best Novel of 2003, and his *The Terminal Experiment* won the Nebula Award for Best Novel of 1995. His other novels include *Calculating God*, *Factoring Humanity*, *Frameshift*, and *Starplex*, all of which were Hugo Award finalists. He has won Japan's top SF award, the *Seiun*, three times for Best Foreign Novel of the Year (for *End of an Era*, *Frameshift*, and *Illegal Alien*), as well as the *Science Fiction Chronicle* Readers' Award and the Crime Writers of Canada's Arthur Ellis Award, both for best short story of the year. Rob lives in Toronto, where he is a frequent commentator on science news stories for the CBC and Discovery Channel Canada. For more information, see his one-million-words-plus Web site at sfwriter.com.

Lucius Shepard lives in Vancouver, Washington and is the author of eight novels and four short story collections. His fiction has won a number of awards, among them the Hugo, Nebula, Theodore Sturgeon, and World Fantasy Award. His latest novel is *A Handbook of American Prayer*. Forthcoming in 2005 is the novel *Trujillo*.

Robert Silverberg has been writing science fiction for fifty years. Among his many books are such novels as *Dying Inside, Lord Valentine's Castle, The Book Of Skulls,* and *Nightwings*, and he has had more than five hundred short stories published as well. He is a many-times winner of the Nebula and Hugo Awards and in 2004 was awarded the Grand Master Nebula of the Science Fiction Writers of America, science fiction's highest honor.

Michael Swanwick's fiction has been honored with the Hugo Award four out of the past five years, as well as the Nebula, Theodore Sturgeon, and World Fantasy Awards, and has been translated and published throughout the world. He is currently at work on two new novels, one fantasy and the other science fiction. Swanwick lives in Philadelphia with his wife, Marianne Porter.

· ABOUT THE EDITOR

Lou Anders is the Editorial Director of Pyr, the science fiction imprint of Prometheus Books. He is the editor of the anthologies *Outside the Box* (Wildside Press, 2001), *Live Without a Net* (Roc, 2003), and the forthcoming *FutureShocks* (Roc, July 2005). In 2003 and 2004, he served as the Senior Editor of the fiction magazine *Argosy*. In 2000, he served as the Executive Editor of Bookface.com, and before that he worked as the Los Angeles liaison for Titan Publishing Group. He is the author of *The Making of "Star Trek: First Contact"* (Titan Books, 1996), and has published over 500 articles in such magazines as *Dreamwatch*, *Star Trek Monthly*, *Star Wars Monthly*, *Babylon 5 Magazine*, *Sci Fi Universe*, *Doctor Who Magazine*, and *Manga Max*. His articles have been translated into German and French, and have appeared online at *SFSite.com*, *RevolutionSF.com* and *InfinityPlus.co.uk*. You can visit his Web site online at www.louanders.com.